PENGUIN BOOKS

Sword of God

Chris Kuzneski is the international bestselling author of *Sign of the Cross*, an acclaimed thriller that has been translated into more than a dozen languages. His first novel, *The Plantation*, introduced the characters of Payne and Jones, and received rave reviews. Although he grew up in Indiana, PA, he currently lives on the Gulf Coast of Florida. To learn more, please visit his website: www.chriskuzneski.com.

Praise for *Sword of God*

'A non-stop locomotive of a thriller. Combines labyrinthine plot twists, global terrorism and the darkest depths of psychological warfare in a thriller that had me burning the midnight oil till breakfast . . . Kuzneski is a master in the making.'
Vince Flynn, author of *Consent to Kill*

'*Sword of God* is as convincing as it is terrifying. Riveting and relentlessly paced, here is a novel that will be consumed in one sitting. Chris Kuzneski proves again that he is a thriller writer for the new millennium.' James Rollins, author of *The Judas Strain*

'Reading *Sword of God* is like jumping on a runaway freight train hurtling towards disaster, with the fate of the world in the balance . . . A fabulous premise, great characters, rich settings and Mach-five pacing. Explosive!' Douglas Preston, author of *The Codex*

'Action-packed and full of taut suspense, *Sword of God* crosses continents in a world-class adventure that will keep you guessing, chuckling, terrified and utterly riveted. Go into lock-down mode. You won't want to leave your favorite chair until you've finished this terrific tale.' Gayle Lynds, author of *The Last Spymaster*

By the same author

The Plantation
Sign of the Cross

Sword of God

CHRIS KUZNESKI

PENGUIN BOOKS

PENGUIN BOOKS

Published by the Penguin Group
Penguin Books Ltd, 80 Strand, London WC2R ORL, England
Penguin Group (USA) Inc., 375 Hudson Street, New York, New York 10014, USA
Penguin Group (Canada), 90 Eglinton Avenue East, Suite 700, Toronto, Ontario, Canada M4P 2Y3
(a division of Pearson Penguin Canada Inc.)
Penguin Ireland, 25 St Stephen's Green, Dublin 2, Ireland (a division of Penguin Books Ltd)
Penguin Group (Australia), 250 Camberwell Road,
Camberwell, Victoria 3124, Australia (a division of Pearson Australia Group Pty)
Penguin Books India Pvt Ltd, 11 Community Centre,
Panchsheel Park, New Delhi – 110 017, India
Penguin Group (NZ), 67 Apollo Drive, Rosedale, North Shore 0632, New Zealand
(a division of Pearson New Zealand Ltd)
Penguin Books (South Africa) (Pty) Ltd, 24 Sturdee Avenue, Rosebank,
Johannesburg 2196, South Africa

Penguin Books Ltd, Registered Offices: 80 Strand, London WC2R ORL, England

www.penguin.com

Published in Penguin Books 2007
This edition published in Penguin Books 2009
1

Copyright © Chris Kuzneski Inc., 2007
All rights reserved

The moral right of the author has been asserted

Printed in England by Clays Ltd, St Ives plc

ISBN: 978-0-141-04890-1

www.greenpenguin.co.uk

Penguin Books is committed to a sustainable future
for our business, our readers and our planet.
The book in your hands is made from paper
certified by the Forest Stewardship Council.

Acknowledgements

As always, I would like to start off by thanking my parents, Andrew and Joyce Kuzneski. They have been with me from the very beginning – literally – and their love and support have never faltered. I feel truly blessed to be their son.

Professionally, I'd like to thank Scott Miller, my remarkable agent. Before we teamed up, I couldn't find a publisher. Now my books are available in multiple languages around the world. While I'm at it, I have to mention Claire Roberts, my foreign agent at Trident Media, who landed my British deal. To say that I've been thrilled with Penguin UK would be an understatement. In particular, I'd like to single out my editor, Alex Clarke. He is simply amazing. I swear, every time I hear from him, he has more good news.

Next, I want to thank my friend Ian Harper for living in Los Angeles. When I'm writing, I tend to call him in the middle of the night with all kinds of strange research questions, and that three-hour time difference means he is actually awake. Thanks for being there and thanks for all your help!

Finally, a big round of applause to all the readers, booksellers, and librarians who have read my books or recommended them. Obviously, at this stage of my career, I need all the help I can get, so I truly appreciate your support.

He who leads a holy war wields the sword of God.

Paccius, Roman general
(*c.* AD27)

I

Saturday, 23 December
Jeju Island, South Korea
(60 miles south of the Korean Peninsula)

The boy could smell the blood from fifty yards away.
It was a strong, pungent odour that made him gag
yet piqued his curiosity. Common sense told him to
turn around and get some help. His father. His
mother. One of his neighbours. Anyone who could
protect him from what he was about to discover.
But common sense rarely mattered to an eight-year-
old.

Especially when he was somewhere he didn't
belong.

The valley to his right was lined with camphor
trees, many seventy-five feet tall and a hundred feet
wide. The path in front of him was rugged, made of
black volcanic rock that dominated the subtropical
island and formed its very core. The temperature was
cold, in the low forties, but would climb steadily as
the day wore on, a by-product of the nearby Kuroshio
and Tsushima currents. The sun was still rising over
the eastern sea when he made his choice. He zipped

his jacket over his nose and inched forward, following the stench of death.

For years his family had warned him about this place, claiming it was built for evil. It was a story that wasn't difficult to believe. Sometimes, late at night, he could hear the screams – bloodcurdling shrieks that ripped through the hillside and jostled him from his sleep. The first time he heard them he assumed he was having a nightmare, but the sounds didn't stop when he sat up in bed. In fact, they got louder. This went on for days, weeks, until he could take no more.

He had to know the truth.

Ignoring his family's wishes, he sneaked into town and asked one of the village elders about the sounds from the hill. The old man laughed at the boy's audacity. He, too, had been a curious child and felt this trait should be rewarded – but only if the boy could understand the truth.

'Look at me,' the old man ordered in Korean. 'Let me see your eyes.'

The boy knew he was being tested. He stared at the old man, refusing to blink, hoping to prove his courage even though his palms were sweating and his knees were trembling.

Tension filled the hut for several seconds. The entire time the boy could barely breathe.

Finally, the old man nodded. The boy was ready for the truth, if for no other reason than to keep him afraid of the place on the hill, to keep him alive. Sometimes fear was a blessing.

With a grave face and a gravelly voice, the old man whispered a single name that was known throughout Jeju, a place that sent shivers down the boy's spine and woke the hairs on his neck.

Pe-Ui Je Dan.

The boy gasped at its mention. The place was so infamous, so ominous, that other details weren't necessary. He had heard the stories, just like everyone else on the island. Yet until that moment he had thought they were just a myth, an urban legend that had made it across the Sea of Japan for the sake of scaring children into doing their chores. But the old man assured him that wasn't the case. Not only was it real, it was close. Just up the path.

At that moment, the boy promised that he'd never venture up there. And he meant it, too. It was a vow he intended to keep. Not only for his safety, but also for the safety of his village.

Unfortunately, all of that changed on the morning he smelled the blood.

As strange as it seemed, there was something about the scent that attracted him. Something magnetic. Animalistic. One minute he was walking to the store, the next he was tracking the scent like a wolf. Crunching up the rocky path, looking for its source as if nothing else mattered. Sadly, this happened all the time in the world of children –

courage and curiosity taking them places where they didn't belong – yet rarely did it lead them into so much danger.

The boy didn't know it as he trudged up the hill, but he was about to kill his village.

2

The Payne Industries Building sat atop Mount Washington, high above the city of Pittsburgh. It was a vantage point that showcased one of the best skylines in the country. From his office, Jonathon Payne could see the confluence of three rivers (the Monongahela and Allegheny flowing together to form the Ohio), two pro sports stadiums (PNC Park and Heinz Field), and a Second World War submarine (the USS *Requin*).

Yet on this day, the thing that captured his attention was the helicopter.

He heard it roar down the river valley, nearly brushing the Gateway Clipper and the top of the Smithfield Street Bridge. It soared over the twinkling lights of Station Square and flew parallel to the 635-foot track of the Monongahela Incline, a landmark built in 1870. The old-fashioned cable car chugged up the hill at six miles per hour, a slow pace compared to the chopper, which banked sharply and aimed right towards Payne's building.

The glass and steel structure had been built by his grandfather, a self-made millionaire who went from mill worker to mill owner in less than thirty years. Payne revered the man, yet bypassed the family business for a career in the military. There he'd led a Special Forces unit called the MANIACs, an elite counter-insurgency team comprised of the top soldiers that the Marines, Army, Navy, Air Force, and Coast Guard could find. Whether it was personnel recovery, unconventional warfare, or counter-guerrilla sabotage, the MANIACs were the best of the best.

Payne reflected on those days as he listened to the roar of the chopper while it hovered outside his window. It transported him to another time and place, back when he carried a gun for protection and a knife for fun. When he risked his life and killed for his country without giving it a second thought. Back before his grandfather died and left him a corporation to run. That was the main reason he had left the military – to honour his grandfather's dying wish.

The shrill of the desk phone cut Payne's memories short. Annoyed, he let it ring a few more times before he answered, finally turning to face the window to see who was calling. He stared at the chopper, eye to eye, more than a thousand feet above the city. The only thing separating them was three inches of bullet-proof glass and Payne's reluctance to get back in the game.

'This is Payne.'

'This is Colonel Harrington. Sorry to drop in like this, but we've got a situation.'

Payne had heard those words hundreds of times before, and it always meant trouble. Once in his lifetime, he wanted to hear the term *situation* followed by a dose of good news.

'Colonel, I'm guessing you didn't get my memo, but I'm retired.'

Harrington growled. 'I'm guessing you didn't get *my* memo. I don't give a fuck.'

The chopper landed on the building's helipad, where it was greeted by four armed security guards who questioned the pilot and searched the aircraft before escorting the colonel inside. Unarmed, he wore the clothes of a civilian – khaki trousers, white dress shirt, black overcoat – an outfit that would have blended in with the business world, if not for his dramatic arrival. Normally Payne's visitors parked in the garage under the building instead of on the roof.

Then again, his entrance wasn't the only thing that stood out. There was something about Harrington, a quality that one noticed but couldn't put a finger on. Maybe it was his board-straight posture or his striking white hair, shorn tight on the sides. Whatever it was, he had a presence. An air. One felt it when he walked into a room. The man commanded attention.

Payne waited for him in the conference room, a

chestnut-lined chamber equipped with the latest audio-visual gadgets – computers, plasma screens, high-speed connections. Plus it was windowless, which was the best safeguard against laser-guided listening devices. Or getting *lased*, as the military called it. A single video camera, mounted in the far corner, tracked Harrington as he strode towards Payne, who stood at the head of the conference table.

Instead of saluting, Harrington simply nodded. 'Colonel Joshua Harrington, US Army.'

Payne looked him straight in the eye. 'Jonathon Payne, US Navy. Retired.'

'Yes, Payne, you've made that quite clear. Still, I think you'll want to hear me out on this.'

'Oh, yeah? Why's that?'

'Because it involves you.'

Payne was not surprised. 'That's a shocker.'

Harrington sneered and sat in one of the leather chairs. He waited there, poker-faced, until Payne took a seat as well. 'This also involves that buddy of yours, David Jones. Is he here?'

Payne nodded. 'Yeah, I think he's still around. Do you want me to get him?'

'No need. I'll get him myself.' Harrington pointed towards the video camera in the corner of the ceiling, then pointed to the chair next to Payne. 'Don't worry. He'll be here shortly.'

Payne grinned, duly impressed. The colonel had been in the room less than thirty seconds yet had properly assessed the situation. Jones was watching

8

them from an adjacent room, running a background check on Harrington while Payne handled the small talk. The fact that the colonel was able to sort things out so quickly said a lot about the man. Somehow it proved his worth.

So did the credentials that appeared on Jones's computer screen. Harrington was a graduate of West Point and had earned his silver eagle the old-fashioned way: by going to war and being a hero. In fact, the more Jones read, the more surprised he was that he'd never met him before. His résumé read like a Tom Clancy novel. Only 600 pages shorter.

A moment later, Jones entered the room with the look of a busted schoolboy, a combination of shame and embarrassment that would have been much more apparent if his flushed cheeks showed through his black skin. He was tempted to offer an apology but realized it wasn't necessary. He was simply running security on an officer he had never met. It was protocol.

'So, did I check out? Did I pass your little test?' Harrington pulled his bifocals from the inner pocket of his overcoat and slipped them on. 'Or do you want my fingerprints, too?'

Jones was tempted to flip him off and say, *Yeah, let's start with the middle finger.*

But Payne didn't give him a chance. 'So, Colonel, what can we help you with?'

'Who said anything about *helping* me? Do I look like I need your help?'

Payne and Jones exchanged glances. They were confused by Harrington's tone.

'Correct me if I'm wrong,' Payne said, 'but you just buzzed my building with your chopper and demanded to speak with me ASAP. My guess is you're either here for help or you're out delivering Christmas cookies. And if that's the case, you're three days late.'

Jones stared at Harrington. 'You have cookies? Do you have any with green sprinkles?'

The colonel ignored their banter – he had been warned about Payne and Jones's antics – and flipped through his folder instead. It was filled with maps, photographs, and reports. All of them stamped CLASSIFIED in red letters. 'Gentlemen, let me be blunt. I don't want to be here, talking to non-army personnel. I think it's a total waste of time, both mine and yours. However, the Pentagon felt you might offer something to my investigation, although I can't figure out what.' With a disapproving eye, he glanced around the room. 'It's obvious you've gone soft.'

'Soft?' Payne echoed.

'Yes, *soft*. You and your fancy-ass leather chairs and your Radio Shack surveillance equipment. How long have you been out of the service? Four years? The entire infrastructure of the military has changed in that time. How in the hell can you possibly help me?'

Somehow Payne managed to keep a straight face. He pondered things for a moment, trying to read between the lines of the colonel's rant. No one in his right mind would show up with this much attitude unless he was trying to pick a fight. And the only purpose that would serve is if Harrington wanted to end this conversation before it got started. And that didn't make sense. If Harrington wanted to have a fifteen-second chat, he could've done that by phone. The fact that he flew here from Washington meant something else was going on. Something less obvious.

Suddenly, Payne figured it out. At least he hoped he had.

'Colonel, I have to admit I was *this* close to throwing you out of my fancy-ass chair. Then it dawned on me, there's no way the Pentagon would've sent a total prick like you without giving me some kind of warning. Therefore, I'm going to assume that you're acting like an ass in order to test us, maybe trying to see if we've lost any discipline during the past few years. If that's the case, I gotta commend you. Because you've got that asshole thing down pat.'

Payne hoped he had guessed right, but if not, so what? He was retired and had enough money to live on for the rest of his life. What did it matter if he told off some jackass from DC?

Still, the room grew uncomfortable while Payne waited for a reaction.

Finally, he got the one he was hoping for: Colonel Harrington broke into a smile.

*

'Forgive my rudeness,' Harrington explained, 'but I had to know what I was dealing with. There's no way I was going to entrust you with this information if I didn't think you could handle some heat. Because, trust me, there's going to be some major heat on this one.'

'What kind?' Jones asked.

'International, domestic, political. We've got the potential for a world-class shitstorm, and right now we're missing our weatherman.'

Payne deciphered the statement. 'Does this weatherman have a name?'

'One you're familiar with: Captain Trevor Schmidt. I believe you trained him with the MANIACs.'

Payne and Jones both nodded. They had run the unit for several years, and Schmidt was one of their favourites. A black-haired kid from Columbus, Ohio, who had a passion for war and a taste for revenge. Then again, that could have described anyone in the MANIACs. They were a special group with a unique assignment. Do anything necessary, but don't get caught.

'When was Schmidt last seen?' Jones asked.

'We aren't really sure.'

'How about where?'

'We don't know that, either.'

'Okay, Colonel, let's approach this from a different angle. What *do* you know?'

Harrington shrugged. 'We know that he's missing.

Him and his entire squad. Gone, like fucking ghosts.'

Payne grimaced. 'I don't believe in ghosts.'

'Neither did I. At least not until recently. Now I'm not so sure.'

Somehow the Department of Defense had managed to lose an entire squad, which was pretty tough to do with modern Combat Survivor/Evader Locator (CSEL) radios, technology that provided precise geoposition and navigation data to rescue parties. That meant Schmidt was running a classified black op, a covert operation that the Pentagon didn't want anyone – not even Combat Search and Rescue (CSAR) – to know about.

'Tell me, how black was the mission?'

'Black as you can get,' Harrington answered. 'And it's my job to keep it that way.'

'If that's the case, why bring us into it? Why go out of house?'

'Is it because *I'm* black?' Jones asked.

Harrington ignored him. 'The reality is you trained Schmidt so you might be able to give us some insight into the way he thinks – where he'll go, what he'll do, who he'll rely on. The truth is you MANIACs are an interesting breed, one with a unique sense of warfare that no one fully under-stands but yourselves. Furthermore, two generals and an admiral assured me I'd be a fool if I didn't use you as a resource.'

'Just a resource? Nothing more than that?'

'Actually, I'd welcome you aboard in any capacity. Whether that's here or in the field.'

Payne glanced at Jones, who was nodding eagerly. That wasn't a surprise, because Jones was always up for another mission. Upon his retirement from the military, he became a private detective, setting up shop in Payne's office building, a way for the best friends to grab lunch whenever possible. Unfortunately, the life of a Pittsburgh PI was not nearly as glamorous as Jones had imagined, especially compared to the missions he had run for the MANIACs. How could taking pictures of cheating spouses ever compare with killing terrorists or blowing up bridges?

Payne, on the other hand, was more reluctant. He wasn't fully comfortable in the corporate world, opting to donate most of his time to local charities instead of living at the office the way his grandfather had. But that didn't mean Payne was willing to risk it all. If he was killed without an heir, he knew Payne Industries would be dismantled, piece by piece, and sold to the highest bidder. And that was something he couldn't let happen. He loved his grandfather way too much to dishonour his life's work by doing something reckless.

Still, Payne felt a similar obligation to his military career, an unwavering devotion to his country and the men he had trained. If one of them was in trouble, he knew it was his duty to help – whether that was as a behind-the-scenes resource or as an expert in the field. Hell, he couldn't live with himself if he opted to sit on the sidelines while one of his men needed him. In his mind, that would be far more irresponsible than risking his own life to help.

'Okay, Colonel. We're willing to lend you a hand. What do you need us to do?'

'I need you to come with me. We'll have plenty of time to talk en route.'

'En route?' Jones asked. 'To where?'

Harrington stood from his chair. 'Korea.'

Payne winced. He wasn't expecting such a long trip. 'North or South?'

'Does it matter?'

'Of course it matters. I need to know how much ammo to pack.'

Harrington smiled an all-knowing smile. 'Don't worry, Payne. Packing *won't* be an issue. I already sent some men to your homes. Your clothes are waiting at the airport.'

3

Mecca, Saudi Arabia

Shari Shasmeen was a lot of things, many of which caused her problems in this part of the world. For one, she was an American. Born and raised in Florida, she was the child of a Muslim father and a Christian mother – neither of whom was overly religious. Each of them had their own beliefs and raised their daughter in an environment where she was allowed to believe whatever felt comfortable. Naturally curious, Shari read the holy texts of several religions and compared their major attributes. After much consideration she came to a conclusion that pleased both of her parents. Instead of choosing a faith, she chose a career. She opted to become a religious archaeologist, hoping to answer all the questions that plagued her.

Yet her job was problematic. Women were second-class citizens in the Middle East, one of the main areas in which she conducted her research. Whether natives or tourists, women were expected to follow the rules and customs of the land – laws that restricted their dress, travel, and ability to socialize. Things were especially strict in Saudi Arabia, where the Commission for the Promotion of Virtue and Prevention of Vice (CPVPV) employed religious police called *mutaween*, who patrolled the streets like Nazis, looking for even the slightest violations of Islamic law. They arrested unrelated males and females caught speaking, enforced Islamic dress codes and prayer schedules, prevented the consumption of non-Muslim food such as pork or alcohol, and seized inappropriate products such as American books, magazines, CDs, and movies. Sometimes punishment for these violations was a public flogging; at other times it was a prison sentence. Occasionally it was much worse.

On 11 March 2002, the Saudi mutaween stopped hundreds of schoolgirls from leaving their burning school in Mecca because the girls were not wearing the *abayas* (long robes) and headscarves that were required in public by Islamic law. Some mutaween were seen beating scorched teenagers as punishment, while others locked the school gates from the outside, preventing the students from fleeing the fire. Fifteen girls were killed and several dozen were injured – many of whom were crushed against the barricades while trying to escape the flames. In addition, many of the schoolgirls' parents witnessed the carnage from across the street and were punished when they tried to intervene and save their daughters.

Shari knew about the mutaween and their violent ways before she ventured to Saudi Arabia for her current project, but fear wasn't going to stop her from her work. In America she was a respected academic known for her fierce determination and dedication, so there was no way in hell she was going to let anything stand in her way. Even if it meant risking her life.

Of course, she wasn't reckless about it.

At least not in public.

Shari was an attractive woman in her late thirties. Not flashy or glamorous, more like an exotic soccer mom who lived down the street. In most parts of the world, she went to work in casual clothes, staying as comfortable as possible while she slaved away in the hot sun. But in Mecca, she played it safe and followed the local dress code, hiding her tanned and lithe body under an abaya, which scraped the ground every time she moved. A veil covered her shoulder-length black hair. She wore no make-up or jewellery. She even travelled with a chaperone.

In private, it was a completely different story. The instant she got inside the tunnel that had been carved underneath the old city, she started taking off her clothes, stripping down to the T-shirt and cargo shorts that she wore under her robe. It was her way of flipping off the mutaween and everything they stood for. Her way of showing independence and great legs at the same time. Her co-workers, an American crew of two scholars and three security guards, thought it was amusing. Not only because Shari was so dramatic about it, but because all of them knew her behaviour wouldn't make a damn bit of difference if the Saudi government figured out what they were doing down there.

If that happened, her lack of clothes would be the least of their worries.

'Shari!' called Dr Drew Hennessy, an energetic professor from an Ivy League school. His salt-and-pepper hair and boyish features were covered with a thin layer of caramel-coloured stone that had fallen from the tunnel wall while he chiselled away its surface. Unsure if she had heard him, he pulled the dust mask from his face and shouted even louder. 'Shari!'

'Good heavens,' she said, laughing at his enthusiasm. 'I'm standing right behind you.'

'Oh, sorry. Didn't see you back there.'

'Did you need something? Or were you just stretching your lungs?'

'We did it!' he exclaimed, his voice filled with pride. 'We made it through.'

'We're through the wall?'

Hennessy nodded as he pointed to the tiny hole that he had punched through the stone almost five feet above the tunnel floor. No more than six inches in diameter, it traversed the chamber wall, revealing a dark expanse on the other side.

'Did you take a look?'

He shook his head. 'I decided to wait for you.'

Shari smiled underneath her dust mask. 'Thanks, Drew, that's awfully sweet.'

'Not really. You have the torch.'

'Oops! I guess I do. That's one of the perks of being team leader.'

She walked a few steps closer, praying this wasn't a false alarm. Their dig had taken much longer than expected, and the man who had hired her was pressuring her for results. If she didn't have something to report soon, she knew he was going to send in a replacement crew. And considering all the Arabian laws that her team had broken, there wouldn't be a damn thing she could do about it. It wasn't like she could call the mutaween to file a grievance.

'Then again,' she said, feeling guilty, 'I also have the authority to delegate responsibility whenever I see fit. And in this case, I think it's only fair that you look first. You made the hole, so you get the torch.'

He shook his head. 'Not a chance. Ladies first.'

She smiled again. 'I was hoping you'd say that.'

Taking a deep breath to steady her nerves, Shari approached the hole and flicked on the torch. In actuality, it wasn't a normal torch – they had plenty of those on the dig. This was a compact, high-intensity, light-emitting diode (LED) that was three times as bright as a store-bought model. Often used for tactical purposes to temporarily blind an attacker, its lens guaranteed a focused beam of white light that came in handy while exploring fissures.

She leaned forward, placing her forehead on the dusty stone while tilting the light back and forth. It was a tight fit, with barely enough room for her eye and the tiny light, yet the beam was so focused that it cut through the darkness like a laser.

'What do you see? Tell me everything.'

'It's a large room, probably fifteen feet deep and ten feet wide. Nothing elaborate. No artwork or carvings. Very old. Very plain.'

'Any damage to the ceiling?'

'None that I can see. From here it looks structurally sound.'

Hennessy nodded, relieved. 'Anything else?'

'In the back of the chamber, there's a large stone altar that was assembled by hand. Stone stacked upon stone, nearly five feet high. It almost looks like a pizza oven.'

'A pizza oven?'

'Don't worry, Drew. It's *definitely* not a pizza oven. It just looks like one.'

'So,' he said, 'what do you think?'

'About what?'

'The site! What do you think about the site?'

Shari handed him the torch and grinned. 'I think we found it.'

4

The plane departed from a cargo hangar at the Pittsburgh International Airport, far away from the main terminal. It was a non-stop flight to Los Angeles, followed by trips to Hawaii, the Marshall Islands, and Japan. Harrington would accompany them to California, briefing them on the way. After that, Payne and Jones would travel overseas on their own, which was the Pentagon's way of ensuring deniability.

Payne got comfortable for the long trip, changing into a grey Naval Academy sweatsuit that accommodated his 6´4˝, 240-pound frame. He had played two sports (football and basketball) at Annapolis, yet made his name in a different arena: kicking ass. It didn't matter if he was facing ninjas or Nazis, Payne had the innate ability to isolate his opponent's weakness and exploit it, using a combination of strength, quickness, and leverage. He had refined his skills over the years, training at Fort Bragg, Naval Base Coronado, and several dojos around the world. Yet none of them could take full credit for turning Payne into a warrior. That particular gift was a blessing from God. A part of his DNA, just like his brown hair or hazel eyes.

He made his way to the back of the plane, where

a conference area had been assembled. Four first-class chairs surrounded a wooden table, cluttered with three laptop computers, several manila folders, and a thermos full of coffee. Harrington sat on the left, growling into his cell phone, telling someone to do something ASAP or he was going to kill the guy's mother. Meanwhile, Jones sat on the right, staring at his computer screen.

'Anything interesting?' Payne asked as he buckled himself into his seat.

'Not really. The colonel blocked every porn site on the Internet.'

Harrington hung up at the mention of his name. 'What was that, Jones?'

'I told Jon that you've been keeping important details to yourself.'

He knew Jones was lying but wasn't going to press it. 'So, Payne, now that you're in your jammies, are you ready to begin?'

Payne gave him a mock salute. 'I'm comfy and accounted for.'

'Oh, goody.' Harrington opened the top folder and removed a single photograph. 'Captain Trevor Schmidt, 35, served as a MANIAC until three years ago. Based on your recommendation, he was selected to lead his own crew, one that did special projects in the Persian Gulf.'

'Meaning what?' Jones asked.

'Meaning they're none of your goddamned business.'

'Great! Thanks for clearing that up.'

Harrington stared at him, unaccustomed to backtalk. 'As I was saying, Schmidt kicked a lot of ass during his first year. No matter what we asked – and we asked a lot – he got it done. We were thrilled with his results and quickly increased his workload. That is, until the incident.'

Payne arched an eyebrow. 'The incident?'

'You know how it goes. We got some piss-poor intel and dropped his crew into a zone that was much hotter than we expected. Of course, he kept his composure and handled himself brilliantly. I don't know how he did it, but the bastard managed to fight his way out. Several injuries to his crew but no deaths.'

Jones beamed. 'That doesn't sound like an incident. That sounds like a MANIAC.'

'Actually, that *wasn't* the incident. The incident came later.' Harrington opened one of his folders and slid it across the table. Neither Payne nor Jones looked at it. They knew that what Harrington was about to say was far more important than what was written in the report.

Reports were written in black and white. They were more interested in colour.

'As you know, our military has a strong presence in the Persian Gulf. Iraq, Iran, Kuwait. Every Arab nation in that godforsaken desert. We've been there for years and we'll be there for years – even places the President doesn't know about. Unfortunately, when you're talking about thousands of soldiers, you can't keep everything a secret. Bases are sitting targets. Troop movements are constantly monitored. So are our warships in the Gulf and the Red Sea. We do our best to protect our men, but let's face it: war is war. There are going to be casualties.'

Harrington tapped his folder for emphasis. 'Your boy Schmidt did everything right. He protected his wounded, secured transportation, and got the hell out without announcing his position. He avoided the hostiles for several hours, waiting until he was far from the hot zone before calling in air support. Eventually, his crew was picked up, patched up, and taken to Taif.'

Taif Air Base was in the foothills of Saudi Arabia, approximately an hour's drive to Mecca and a two-hour drive to Jeddah, a historic Muslim city near the Red Sea. Taif was home to the US Military Training Mission (USMTM), a joint training programme between the Kingdom of Saudi Arabia and US Central Command from MacDill Air Force Base in Tampa, Florida. The goal was to provide military advisers to the Royal Saudi Air and Land Forces while providing protection to US Department of Defense personnel who were stationed in Taif. More than 300 Westerners, working for companies such as McDonnell Douglas and Pratt & Whitney, lived in the Al-Gaim Compound, a modern community with an American feel. Al-Hada Hospital, a Saudi facility staffed mostly by Westerners, provided basic medical and dental care. But in emergencies, USAF flight surgeon support was available from Prince Sultan Hospital and other neighbouring bases.

'Obviously, we didn't admit our fuck-up. We rarely do. But we knew we couldn't send Schmidt's crew right back into action. Half his men were hospitalized; the other half were pissed. So we decided to give them some extended downtime in the plush confines of Al-Gaim.'

Jones smirked. 'Not exactly a trip to the Ritz. Yet better than Baghdad.'

Payne ignored his partner, focusing on the missing details of Harrington's explanation. 'Unless I'm mistaken, you still haven't mentioned the incident.'

Harrington nodded. 'Schmidt and his men were valuable assets, and we tried to smooth things over by flying in the families of the wounded. Some of them were in intensive care, so we figured it was the least we could do for morale purposes . . . Turns out it made things worse.'

'How so?'

'Just look at the report. Everything's in there.'

Payne shook his head. 'I'd rather hear it from you.'

Harrington stared at Payne, still trying to figure him out. Payne's credentials were impeccable, yet Harrington still didn't have a feel for the man. Who was he? The decorated soldier who captained one of the finest fighting units in modern warfare, or a burned-out officer who retired from the military in his mid-thirties for a cushy desk job in a penthouse office? Until he figured that out, Harrington was going to analyse Payne's every move and second-guess his every action.

But for the time being, he decided to play along and answer his questions.

'As I mentioned, we brought in their families. I'm talking parents, wives, kids, girlfriends. We even flew in a dog. We had extra housing at Al-Gaim, so we figured what the fuck.' Harrington paused, gathering his thoughts. 'The third morning we bussed them over to the hospital for visiting hours, just like we'd done the previous two days. Schmidt actually drove them himself, making sure his wounded men and their families were as comfortable as possible before he left for a briefing back at Taif Air Base.'

Jones smiled. 'That sounds like Trevor. He was a top-notch soldier but a better person.'

'Maybe back then. But after the incident, the Schmidt you knew ceased to exist.'

5

Friday, 29 December
Taif, Saudi Arabia
(41 miles east of Mecca)

A cloud of sand followed the car as it turned off the main highway and bounced across the rough road that led to the compound. Fred Nasir was a tanned middle-aged man wearing a baseball cap, sunglasses, and casual clothes. He grinned as he parked his Toyota Camry, the most popular car in Saudi Arabia, near the front gate. He was thrilled to finally be there.

A team of American soldiers, wearing desert camouflage and carrying assault rifles, swarmed around the car before Nasir had a chance to open his door. Some looked under his vehicle with mirrors attached to long poles, while others probed his trunk for explosives. The men moved in unison, like a NASCAR pit crew, doing their designated task without getting in each other's way. Finally, after thirty seconds, an *all clear* was given.

But instead of returning to their posts, the soldiers took five steps back and aimed their weapons at the car. Suddenly Nasir was in their crosshairs, a split second away from death. Certainly not the greeting he was expecting.

His heart leaped into his throat.

The lead guard moved forward, raised his handgun, and aimed it at Nasir's face. He held it there. Silent. Poised and ready to shoot. He did not smile. He did not blink. He simply waited for Nasir to do something stupid. A flinch. A twitch. Even a sneeze would have resulted in a nasty scene. But Nasir remained frozen. Calm. At least on the outside. Internally, he was having a far different reaction. His heart was racing, his stomach was churning, adrenaline was surging like a tsunami. Yet what could he do? At this moment he had to play by their rules.

Seconds ticked like minutes while the tension continued to mount. Finally the guard tilted the angle of his gun upward and used its muzzle to tap on the glass. The *click, click, click* was a welcome sound to the driver, who took a deep breath and slowly lowered his window. A rush of hot desert air surged into the car, returning the colour to Nasir's cheeks.

'Papers?' the guard asked. It was more of an order than a question.

Nasir obliged, careful not to move too quickly. Still conscious of the crosshairs.

'Nationality?'

'I'm an American.'

'Really? You look foreign to me.'

'Yet I'm an American. Look at my passport.'

The guard sneered and leaned closer. 'Are you telling me what to do?'

'No! Of course not. I would never do that . . . I'm just –'

'You're just *what*?'

Nasir took a deep breath. He couldn't believe he had been talked into this. It was going all wrong. 'I'm just an American. That's all I'm saying.'

The guard stared at Nasir's face, then glanced at his passport. It looked valid. So did his travel visa and the rest of his paperwork. He lowered his weapon and signalled to the on-duty officer in the security booth. 'State your business.'

'I'm here to meet a friend in the main dining hall.'

He glanced at a list of visitors and noticed Nasir's name. His visit had been pre-approved. 'Good choice. The delivery truck just rolled in from our commissary over in Riyadh. Those guys hook us up whenever they can. Rumour has it they brought in a case of Oreos today.'

Another security guard, who heard the tail end of the conversation, approached with Nasir's parking pass. '*Double-stuff* Oreos. That means twice the cream.'

Nasir tried to look enthused but had more important things to worry about than cookies.

'Put this on your dash and park your car in the guest lot.' The guard pointed to a row of cars just inside the compound walls. Flashing his gun, he added, 'And don't worry about it being stolen. It's the safest parking lot in the world.'

If not for the snipers and the barbed-wire fence, Al-Gaim would have felt like Main Street, USA. Nasir was surrounded by dozens of American-style homes of all shapes and sizes, each of them furnished with televisions, dishwashers, microwaves, washers, and dryers. An Olympic-size swimming pool graced the community, as did racquetball, tennis, and basketball courts. Farther down, there was a movie theatre and a four-lane bowling alley.

All in all, it wasn't a bad place to live – as long as the first axiom of real estate was ignored. The one that stressed the importance of location, location, location. Despite having all the charms of suburbia, Al-Gaim was nestled in the volatile foothills of Saudi Arabia, deep in the heart of Islam. Where the average daytime temperature was pretty close to hell's.

Thankfully, Nasir's walk to the rendezvous point was a short one. He strolled quickly, trying to ignore all the snipers who were watching him. His only concern was getting to the dining hall, where he had to follow the strict orders he'd been given over the phone.

Take a seat. Pour a glass of water. Try to remain calm.

But the truth was, Nasir was petrified. If he was caught, he was going to be killed. It was as simple as that. There wouldn't be a trial. There wouldn't be a jury. There would simply be an execution, one where his body wouldn't be found and his family wouldn't be notified. He would simply disappear into the desert, a mystery that would never be solved.

Today's number-one goal was to prevent that from happening.

His contact walked across the dining hall like he had worked there for years. He certainly looked the part, wearing the same greasy white apron as the kitchen staff while doing all the things that a good worker should. He pushed in chairs. He rearranged condiments. He stacked dirty dishes in a plastic bin. All of this seemed ordinary – even to Nasir, who was looking for him. Yet none of his actions seemed out of place. Even his approach to his table was normal.

He pointed to the glass of water. 'You done with that, or will you be eating something?'

It took a moment for the question to register. When it did, Nasir's heart skipped a beat. It was the code they had agreed upon. *This* was his contact. For a moment, he forgot how he was supposed to respond. Then it came to him. 'I don't know. Is it safe eating here?'

'I eat here every day and I'm still breathing.' A huge smile filled his face. 'Our food ain't fancy, but it's better than eating camel.'

The man reached into his apron's pouch and pulled out a take-out menu, which he casually handed to Nasir. At least that's how it appeared to the guards who were monitoring the dining hall via security cameras. This was the twelfth menu he had handed out during his shift, so his action appeared innocuous. No reason for any alarm or concern.

Of course what the guards couldn't see was what was hidden inside. It was the reason Nasir had risked his life to visit Al-Gaim. The reason why all that money had been given to him and why this hand-off was taking place in the middle of a US military compound.

As amazing as it seemed, the menu was the key to everything.

6

US Army Base Kwajalein,
Republic of the Marshall Islands
(2,136 miles south-west of Hawaii)

After being briefed by Colonel Harrington, Payne and Jones slept for an entire day – at least according to the calendar. In reality, they took a four-hour nap during their flight from Hawaii to the Marshall Islands but crossed the International Date Line (longitude 180°) in the middle of the Pacific Ocean, a spot halfway around the world from Greenwich, England.

So far their mission had gone as planned, flying from Pittsburgh to LA to Honolulu without any delays. They might have been a few years removed from the military, yet Payne and Jones were seasoned veterans when it came to long trips. They knew when to eat, when to sleep, and when to piss – all in order to hit the ground running. Most travellers would have bitched and moaned about spending so much time in the air, but not them. They were so accustomed to jumping out of planes in the dead of night, not knowing if they were ever going to see the sunrise again, that they viewed this trip as luxurious.

No parachutes or drop zones. Just pillows and playing cards.

Technically, the Marshall Islands was a sovereign nation that signed a Compact of Free Association with the United States in 1986. But that was just fancy political talk. In simple terms, the US had full authority and responsibility to protect the Marshall Islands. In return, the US Department of Defense was given use of the Kwajalein Atoll, which consists of ninety islets and has one of the largest lagoons in the world, and allowed to lease eleven nearby islands for the Ronald Reagan Ballistic Missile Defense Test Site – also known as the Reagan Test Site, or RTS. This Pacific weapons site was a vital cog in America's defence system, not only because of its strategic location but also because of its sophisticated research technology.

Once the plane touched down, Jones grabbed one of his bags and headed for the front hatch. 'How long do we have to kill?'

Payne shrugged, trailing his partner. 'A few hours. They're making final arrangements.'

The duo stepped into the warm night and glanced around the semi-deserted airfield. Bright lights shone in the distance, highlighting the periphery of the fence line. A tropical wind blew across the tarmac, kicking up the scent of jet fuel and burned tyre. It was a smell they remembered well. Not quite as sexy as napalm in the morning, but memorable nonetheless.

A young woman with Asian features and dark hair stood at the bottom of the plane stairs. She wore a khaki skirt and an open-collared white blouse that danced around her petite frame in the gentle breeze. It was the middle of the night, yet she had a smile on her face and a gleam in her eyes that said she was honoured to be there. 'Welcome to the Marshall Islands.'

To Jones, this was a pleasant surprise. He wasn't expecting a welcoming committee.

'Aloha!' he said as he kissed her on both cheeks, a common greeting in Hawaiian airports. 'Or however you say hello in Marshallese.'

The woman's cheeks flushed, an equal mixture of anger and embarrassment. The smile that had been present a moment before was replaced with an angry growl. This was not the delicate lotus blossom that Jones had first perceived. She was a typhoon to be reckoned with.

'Why in the world did you kiss me?' she demanded while poking Jones in the chest. 'Just because I have an island complexion you automatically assume I'm some kind of air tramp ready to give you a lei. Do you see any flowers in my hand? Do you hear any Don Ho music?'

'Ah, crap,' Payne mumbled, trying not to laugh.

'You're in the middle of a US Army base, not on some island tour. What is wrong with you?' It was a rhetorical question. 'While you're in my presence, I expect to be treated with the respect I deserve or else we will stop dealing with each other and I will file sanctions with the base commander. Have I made myself clear?'

Jones nodded, completely mortified. 'Yes, ma'am.'

'I'm a soldier, not a tart.'

'Sorry, ma'am, I didn't mean to imply . . .' He stopped in the middle of his sentence. 'You're right. I'm sorry. I was *completely* out of line.'

She glared at him for a moment longer before nodding her head. 'Fine. Apology accepted.'

Without delay, she brushed past Jones and stopped in front of Payne, giving him a quick salute. 'Captain Payne, it is an honour to work with you. I know you weren't used to working with women in the Special Forces, but I swear I'll be of great assistance to you.'

A look of confusion filled Payne's face. 'In what way?'

'Wait,' she said. 'You mean, you don't know? I'll be joining you on your mission.'

'Excuse me?'

'I'll be joining –'

Payne signalled her to stop. 'Yeah, I heard you the first time.'

Puzzled by the news, Payne glanced at Jones, who gave him a shrug from a very safe distance. No way was he going to re-enter the conversation. Besides, it was obvious he had no idea who she was either, or he wouldn't have kissed her. At this point the only thing Jones knew was that she was a soldier, not a tart. And since Payne already possessed that intel,

Jones did the smart thing and retreated to the safety of the hangar.

Payne growled to himself. 'What did you say your name was?'

'Choi. Sergeant Kia Choi. US Army.'

'And who assigned you to my team?'

'Colonel Harrington, sir.'

'Really? In what capacity?'

'Full capacity, sir.'

He shook his head. 'That's not what I meant. What's your skill set? Your speciality?'

'Oh,' she said, embarrassed. 'It's linguistics. I'll be serving as your translator.'

'My translator? Damn, Sergeant, why didn't you say so?' He handed her one of his bags, letting her know that she was going to be treated like any other member of his squad. 'I hope to hell you know a lot of swear words, because we cuss a lot.'

'Don't worry, sir. I know them all.'

Payne dumped his gear inside the hangar, then followed Kia to an army jeep that had been built for the Second World War. No key was required. Just a touch of the ignition button and the engine roared to life. 'I hope our plane is newer than this.'

Kia laughed, a smile once again brightening her face. 'Don't worry, sir. RTS is equipped with the best technology in the world. We keep relics like this for personal use only. Most of the major roads on Kwajalein are paved, but when you hit the smaller atolls, you're forced to deal with coral-lined tracks. And jeeps tend to thrive in that terrain.'

Payne nodded while shifting his attention to the night-time sky. The alabaster moon, tucked behind a bank of clouds, occasionally showed itself, lighting the coconut palms that dominated the tropical land-scape. The temperature was in the mid eighties, a pleasant change from the harsh Pittsburgh winter that Payne was used to facing in December.

As if reading his mind, Kia said, 'The temperature here is remarkably consistent, averaging roughly eighty-two every month. Strangely, the night-time temperature is three to five degrees *warmer* than the afternoon temperature. Mostly because of all the daytime rain.'

'A translator *and* a weather girl. It looks like the colonel found me a winner.'

'Actually, sir, I found Colonel Harrington.' The jeep squeaked to a halt as she stopped outside the airport command centre. 'I was born on a US Army base near Seoul, so I know the language and people of South Korea better than most. I realized an old-school soldier like the colonel wouldn't consider a woman for this job unless he was talked into it. So I called in every favour I possibly could for the oppor-tunity to join your team.'

'You did *what*?'

'I called in several favours –'

'Hold up! Let me get this straight. You're saying you're *not* used to fieldwork.'

'No, sir. But –'

'Tell me, Choi, what *are* you used to doing?'

'Translating.'

'I know, but where?'

'Behind a desk.'

Payne groaned as he climbed out of the jeep and walked towards the building. It was bad enough that he was asked to run a mission with no prep time, but to assign him a rookie in such a critical role? What the hell was Harrington thinking? Her inexperience was going to cause a whole new set of problems.

'Sir,' she pleaded as she hustled after him, 'I know this isn't what you were expecting, but I promise I won't let you down.'

'Glad to hear it, Choi. Because if you do, there's a good chance we'll all end up dead.'

7

Saturday, 30 December
Jeju Island, South Korea

The seventy-mile boat ride across Jeju Strait was eerily silent, partially due to the trio's jetlag and partially from a lack of camaraderie. Their flight to Japan had gone smoothly, as did their trip to the southern tip of the Korean Peninsula. Good weather, no red tape, few delays. Kia showed off her translating skills at the Tokyo airport, easily switching from Japanese to Korean. According to her file, she was able to speak seven languages and read three more, which was a remarkable feat – especially since Payne and Jones had worked with some Americans who could barely speak English. Still, one issue gnawed at them: how would Kia react under pressure? It was one thing to ask a stewardess for more honey-roasted nuts in a foreign language; it was quite another to lie to an armed guard who was one flick of his finger away from blowing off your head.

In the field, *that* was the skill that made a good translator.

Normally, Payne and Jones, who had reputations

for cracking jokes and encouraging levity in their squad, would be in the midst of playful banter, but neither of them was in a talkative mood. Payne occupied his time studying the approaching coast through binoculars, while Jones sat upright in the rear of the boat's cabin, catching a nap. His body swayed to the rhythm of the pounding waves. Left and right, back and forth, up and down. Never opening his eyes and never appearing unsteady. It was a skill he had developed in the MANIACs – sleeping whenever and wherever he could.

Kia, on the other hand, was anxious. She had taken some seasickness pills before they shoved out to sea, and so far her stomach had cooperated. At least in terms of seasickness. Unfortunately, the medication did little to quell the anxiety that was raging in her gut. So much was riding on this mission, much more than she was willing to admit. If she screwed up . . . Hell, she didn't even want to think about it. Dwelling on the possibilities would only make her more nauseous.

The trio's silence continued until their boat approached the northern end of the island. Jones sensed their change in speed and opened his eyes. 'Are we there yet?'

'Looks that way,' Payne said as he secured one of the ropes to the back of the boat. 'My guess is that's our welcoming party.'

An Asian-American soldier, wearing blue jeans and a thick sweater, met them at the dock with a midsize

SUV. He didn't salute and warned them about displaying any military behaviour outside the cave. Don't use ranks. Don't use names. And don't tell anyone, including the soldiers who were guarding the site, why they were actually there. Only a select few – those inside the cave – knew what was going on, and it was imperative that things stayed that way.

The weather was crisp, somewhere in the low forties, but it felt much colder because of the icy breeze that surged off the water. The people of Jeju often referred to their home as Samdado: the island of three abundances – wind (Pungda), rocks (Seokda), and women (Yeoda). Jagged cliffs of black stone lined the northern face and made up the island's core, formed by a volcanic eruption during the Quaternary Period of the Cenozoic Era. No historical records exist before the life of Christ, but local folklore insists that three leather-clad gods rose from the earth and used Tamnaguk (now called Jeju) for hunting. This continued until the gods stumbled upon a wooden chest that contained three princesses from the East Sea. The three gods married the three ladies and spent the rest of their lives raising five different grains, cows, and horses.

'You guys ever been here?' asked the soldier as he pulled their SUV on to the highway that led to Mount Halla, the highest mountain in South Korea. Its white peak rose 6,000 feet above sea level, spreading east to west across the centre of the 712-square-mile island. 'The coastal areas are swarming with tourists, particularly newlyweds. Asians view Jeju as the ultimate destination for honeymooners. Some people call it the Korean Hawaii.'

Payne studied the distant landscape – thick groves of alpine trees covered the black basalt – and disagreed with the comparison. 'Doesn't look like Hawaii.'

'Doesn't feel like it, either,' Jones declared from the back seat. 'Turn on the damn heater.'

The soldier smiled and cranked up the temperature. 'Koreans actually embrace the variety of climates on Jeju. It's one of the only places in the world where you can find both polar and tropical animals living on the same island.'

Payne nodded. 'That's kind of unique.'

'That's *nothing*. This mountain we're driving up right now, the one with all the snow on the top? It's actually a volcano. When was the last time you saw snow on a volcano?'

'It's been a while. We don't have volcanoes in Pittsburgh.'

'Obviously it's dormant now, but Mount Halla's eruption formed this island millions of years ago. Everything you see – the hotels, the lakes, the trees – is sitting on volcanic rock. But the most remarkable part is what you can't see. The core of this entire island is surging with lava tubes, massive wormholes snaking through the earth like giant veins. And I'm not talking small caves. I'm talking *huge*. The largest is more than eight miles long.'

Running throughout the north-eastern corner of the island, Manjanggul was one of the longest lava tube systems in the world. The width of the main cave varied between six and seventy feet, while the height soared to over ninety feet in certain spots. Tourists flocked to three main entrances, where they were able to explore the naturally formed lava pillars and stalactites, including a landmark called Turtle Rock, which looks like an ancient turtle crawling out of the depths of the Earth. Public tours were stopped six-tenths of a mile deep, leaving seven and a half miles to the scientists, who observed bats and other underground creatures in their natural habitat. They also studied the tubes themselves, trying to ascertain why rivers of lava that once flowed deep underground burst to the surface, leaving massive chasms behind.

Experts believed there were more than a hundred lava tubes on Jeju, but only 60 per cent had been documented in public records. The others were either undiscovered or being used for alternative purposes, such as the cave that the US military was studying. It was being protected by the top soldiers in the Pacific fleet.

A thick rope hung between two camphor trees at the bottom of the rocky trail, blocking all unauthorized personnel. Two soldiers dressed in casual clothes sat on folding chairs, checking IDs. If they were trying to look inconspicuous, they were unsuccessful. Their size and skin colour gave them away. Thankfully, other soldiers fared much better. Their painted faces and camouflage uniforms blended in with the nearby woods, making them virtually invisible. They scanned the terrain with their sniper scopes, poised to eliminate any trespassers who tried to approach the cave. Although this island was South Korean, this hillside temporarily belonged to the United States of America.

Members of Payne's team flashed their credentials and were given immediate access to the site. Led by the soldier from the SUV, the trio climbed the path behind him, careful where they stepped. First Jones, then Kia, then Payne, his eyes darting back and forth, noticing everything. Azalea bushes, no longer in bloom, dotted the lower landscape, as did fields of long brown grass that rustled like dead leaves every time the wind blew. Up ahead, larger trees lined the basalt trail, roots and trunks squeezing out of narrow fissures in the stone. Fingerlike branches waved overhead, swaying against the breeze, as if urging them to stop. Under their footsteps, rocks crunched like broken bones, the sound mixing with the stale stench that wafted down the hillside. The entire place felt macabre, like nothing Payne had ever experienced before. In his mind, he likened it to the setting of an Edgar Allan Poe story.

'Good Lord,' Payne said. 'What in the world is that smell?'

The driver answered coyly. 'It's the reason you're here.'

8

Despite its depiction in movies, archaeology was more science than adventure. Most digs resulted in shards of pottery or crumbled architecture, not lost cities of gold. In fact, this was the first time in Shari Shasmeen's career that she was in charge of a project with modern-day significance. It was an opportunity to shatter myths or reaffirm religious history, but she wouldn't know which until they got inside and examined the vault.

Their first order of business was cutting an entryway into the chamber, one that was large enough to walk through yet did as little damage as possible – not only to preserve the site but to guarantee the structural integrity of the tunnel. A few stones were removed with loving care, making sure that they weren't chipped or cracked before they were wrapped and labelled and hauled outside to a large van where the artefacts would be stored. The security guards did most of the heavy lifting while Shari and her colleagues documented everything.

A tedious process but crucial nonetheless.

As that was being finished, Shari set up a telescopic video camera to inspect the interior of the room. Attached to a long pole, the camera and spotlight weighed less than two pounds and was capable of rotating in every direction via a handheld remote control. A military-grade umbilical cord ran down the shaft, feeding the cables into a nine-inch LCD screen that would allow them to view everything inside, including the back of the wall they were slicing into.

One of Shari's worst nightmares as an archaeologist was breaching a site only to discover that she had cut through the most important part – like busting through the ceiling of the Sistine Chapel in order to investigate the floor.

Thankfully, modern-day technology made mistakes like that less likely.

A wireless monitor was set up twenty feet down the tunnel near a locked gate, allowing the entire team to watch the visual sweep of the interior without getting in the way. The only people near the wall were Shari, who manoeuvred the remote control, and Drew Hennessy, who helped feed the pole through the opening, making sure he didn't smash the lens on the rock.

'Tell me when we're in,' he said.

She watched the image as the camera passed through the hole and entered the chamber. Suddenly her picture turned from a close-up of the caramel-coloured stone to a wide chasm of darkness. 'We're through.'

He nodded, then rushed behind her to watch her screen. 'This is so cool.'

Shari agreed, but kept her focus on the task at hand. With a flick of her thumb, she tilted the camera downwards, trying to get a view of the wall that they had punctured. She twisted a dial on the unit and the power of the spotlight increased, illuminating several feet of surface space. Dust particles floated upwards like air bubbles from a sunken ship, as if they were exploring a watery grave at the bottom of the Pacific, not the contents of the room in front of them.

The angle of the camera was almost parallel with the wall, so she pushed the pole forward, hoping to get a wider view. After adjusting the focus, the outline of a large rectangle appeared in the stone. Its dimensions were approximately six feet high and three feet wide. Its top was slightly curved, like an arch.

'I'll be damned,' she muttered to herself. 'This is so strange.'

'What is?'

She tapped the image on her screen. 'There's a door in the wall.'

'A door? I don't see a door.'

'It's right here,' she said, tracing the shape with her finger.

'That's a door?'

'Here,' she offered, 'let me zoom closer.'

As she did, details of the door emerged. It was made of ancient timber and held in place by hinges near the top and bottom that were attached to the frame. Simple in design, it was coated with so much dust and dirt that it had taken on the colour of the rest of the room, blending in like a chameleon crawling up the side of a tree.

Shari turned towards Hennessy. 'This is good news.'

'How do you figure?'

'Hold this for a moment and I'll show you.'

Hennessy took the remote control and held it steady, keeping the camera focused on the back of the door while Shari walked over to the tunnel wall and tapped on it a few times. It sounded distinctly hollow.

'Did you hear that?' she asked as she placed her ear against the surface. 'Ninety per cent of this wall is made out of solid stone. Built like a fortress. But this middle space is nothing but dried mud over wood. Someone concealed this door before this chamber was buried.'

'But why? That seems kind of redundant. I mean, if you were going to bury this place underground, why worry about camouflaging the door?'

She shrugged. 'To be honest, I have no idea. But the fact that someone went to so much trouble tells me something valuable was hidden inside.'

'And that's the good news?'

'Nope,' she said coyly.

Grabbing a chisel off the floor, she carefully tapped it against the wall. The point sunk into the dried mud with a thump, forming a crack that spread across the surface like a brick hitting a windshield. She rocked the chisel back and forth until the tool was free, then repeated the process again and again until large chunks of debris crumbled to the ground. In a shower of dust, the wooden door slowly emerged right before their eyes, as if it had grown out of the wall.

'*This* is the good news. Getting into that room just got a whole lot easier.'

After examining the frame, Shari realized that the door was on the verge of falling off the wall, which wasn't surprising since the site had been buried underground for 1,400 years. Shari talked with her colleagues at length and all of them agreed: the door needed to be removed before they entered the chamber. Working carefully, she chiselled around the bottom hinge while Hennessy focused on the top. Less than five minutes later, the ancient door was being carried to the truck by the security guards, who, despite their job titles, were really glorified labourers. Shari had worked with each of them on previous digs, so she was able to vouch for their honesty and work ethic, two crucial factors when assembling a team.

Once the entryway was clear, Shari flicked on her torch and stepped inside the room, making sure that the floor was sturdy before anyone followed. Hennessy walked in next, trailed by Dr Milton Wheeler, a retired professor from the University of Chicago, who specialized in ancient texts and languages. He took one look at the unadorned walls and ceiling – no paintings, carvings, or pageantry – and remarked, 'It's not exactly the Taj Mahal.'

'Which is a *good* thing,' said Shari as she continued to inspect the interior for structural damage. 'If this place was filled with gold and treasures, we'd be shit out of luck.'

Wheeler smiled. 'That's not something you hear an archaeologist say every day.'

'You know what I mean.'

'Guys,' Hennessy said. 'You need to take a look at this.'

'At what?' Shari asked, swinging the light towards him. He was crouching in the back of the room, partially hidden by a large stone altar that held the relic they were looking for. At least, she hoped it did. If it wasn't inside then all of their time and effort had been wasted, and she'd be forced to break the news to the Arab who had hired her for the excavation.

'Unfortunately,' he said, 'we weren't the first ones here.'

Shari took a deep breath, trying to calm her racing heart. A minute ago, she had been on top of the world, thrilled with the prospects of their discovery. Now she felt disappointment coursing through her veins, worried that the site had been robbed. 'Are you positive?'

'Definitely. Because one of them never left.'

The skeleton was fully dressed, still wearing the simple clothes of his era – although the clothes had practically disintegrated. Nothing fancy or excessive. Much like the decor of the room. Extravagance had been looked down upon in his culture, a tradition that still existed today.

The lone exception to the rule was his sword, a magnificent weapon that he continued to grasp, even in death. The blade was forty inches long and two inches wide, inscribed with ancient Arabic verse that was too faint to read in the darkness of the chamber. The handle was gold in colour and curved under his bony grip, a position he'd held for fourteen centuries. A dedicated soldier who refused to leave his post. Or wasn't allowed to.

'Why would they seal him in?' Hennessy asked as he examined the body for clues. 'As far as I can tell, this guy wasn't stabbed or killed. He died when the air ran out.'

Shari shuddered at the thought. Although she wasn't the least bit claustrophobic, the thought of being sealed in a stone room without hope of escape gave her the shivers.

'To him,' Wheeler suggested, 'it was probably viewed as an honour. He was the last line of defence. Here to protect the treasure for eternity.'

'Is it eternity already?' Hennessy joked. 'Because that treasure is coming with us.'

Wheeler ignored his comment. 'As both of you know, the Islamic mindset is very different from the Christian one. In his culture, dying for your god is the noblest sacrifice that one can make, one that is rewarded with a free pass to paradise.'

Shari sighed, remembering a famous Muslim expression that was often quoted by terrorists. 'Surely, the gates of paradise are under the shadows of the swords.'

Wheeler nodded solemnly. 'And because of that belief, this warrior was willing to die.'

9

Fifteen feet from the cave entrance, each member of Payne's team was given three things: a surgical mask, surgical gloves, and crime-scene booties to be slipped over their shoes. Yet no instructions or details were provided.

Jones eyed the driver. 'Are you worried we'll contaminate the scene?'

'Just the opposite. We're worried about the scene getting on you.'

'What does that mean?'

The driver inched backwards. 'You'll find out soon enough.'

Kia frowned. 'You're not coming with us?'

'Not a chance. I saw it once and that was enough for me.'

Confused, she turned towards Payne. 'Sir, what's going on here? What is this place?'

He shrugged while sliding his mask over his nose and mouth. 'We're about to find out.'

In the summertime the six-foot crack in the stone mountain would have been covered by leaves and vines that dangled from the overhead cliff. Now the only thing protecting it was the team of snipers who hid in the trees. Payne studied the natural opening, looking for clues as to what might lie ahead. The only thing that stood out was the stench that seeped through his mask. It was a smell he recognized, one that foreshadowed a change in their assignment.

This wasn't going to be a rescue mission. It was something far worse.

Turning on his torch, Payne took a few steps inside and let his eyes adjust to the gloom. Jones and Kia followed closely. The breeze that had been prevalent on the outside had relented, replaced by a dampness in the air that made the stone floor slick and the walls seep. The year-round temperature in the caves on Jeju was roughly fifty degrees, but the high humidity made it feel colder. Moisture clung to their clothes, their hair, their skin. So did the ghastly stench. It was far worse than a sewer. It was like walking into an autopsy.

Payne focused on Kia. 'Are you squeamish? If so, I need to know right now.'

'No, sir. I'm not squeamish. Why?'

'Because this is going to be bad. Worse than anything you've seen before.'

Kia grimaced. 'How do you know?'

'Experience.'

'You used to investigate crime scenes?'

Jones answered for him. 'No, we used to cause them.'

Payne said nothing as he turned from Kia. He knew she was aware of their background with the MANIACs and the types of missions they used to run. Still, for a split second, he was embarrassed. Not for his actions – he was quite proud of his military record – but the way his past had been framed. Kia was a new member of his team, and he didn't want her to get the wrong impression. He wasn't a killer or a criminal. He was a soldier. Nothing more, nothing less.

Up ahead a shadow danced on the cave wall. Payne spotted it and headed towards the source of the light. It was a faint glow deep within the bowels of the mountain, yet he knew its intensity would increase tenfold when he reached the scene. Each step brought new sensations that he noted. The rumble of a portable generator. The artificial heat from overhead lights. The echoing drip of seeping liquid. And a stagnant cloud of that god-awful stench. It was inescapable. Unforgettable.

'Don't touch anything,' he stressed to Kia. 'And if you feel nauseous –'

'I *won't* feel nauseous.'

Payne stopped and put his hand on her shoulder. 'But *if* you feel nauseous, just leave the scene. Don't ask for permission. Just go. Get some fresh air, collect your thoughts, whatever you need to do. Just don't get sick at the scene. That's very important.'

'I'll be fine, sir.'

'Thankfully,' Jones joked, 'if she does vomit, this place will smell better.'

'I'm *not* going to vomit,' Kia insisted. 'I'm not the least bit squeamish.'

Payne nodded, hoping she was right. 'Well, we'll find out soon enough.'

Kia lasted less than ten seconds before she bolted towards the entrance. But Payne and Jones didn't stop her. Or blame her. During their time in the military, they had never witnessed anything like the scene inside the cave. It was beyond gruesome. It was barbaric.

Blood covered everything. The ceiling. The walls. The floors. Crevices in the stone were filled with sticky red puddles. Cracks looked like surging rivers, the liquid flowing from one point to the next, as if the cave had been drenched with a crimson rain, the downpour searching for a way to escape. Only there was nowhere for it to go because the entire chamber was saturated with fluid. Like a giant heart had exploded and coated everything in its wake.

A table and a chair sat in the middle of it all. Both were bolted to the floor. Both were splattered with arterial spray. So was the light that hung overhead. It looked ancient. No fancy fixture. Not even a pull string. Just a solitary bulb that was caked with dried blood. A single wire ran from its base, snaking across the ceiling, held in place by mining staples that were old and rusty. Obviously from another generation. In fact, the whole chamber had that feel, a giant time capsule that had been cracked open, revealing the way things used to be done when no one was watching. Payne closed his eyes and tried to imagine the screams.

Four floodlights were set up along the periphery, but only one was currently on. Jones glanced at its base and noted a lack of blood. No way it was there when the violence occurred. Same with all the others. They were spotless. Obviously brought there to light the scene.

'Can we go in?' Jones whispered.

Payne shrugged, unsure if all the evidence had been processed. He was ready to call out when a man wearing a surgical mask peeked his head out of a passage at the back.

'I *thought* I heard someone.' He wore a butcher's apron that was streaked with blood. It matched the stains on his surgical outfit and booties. 'Please come in.'

Payne didn't move. 'Are you sure? We don't want to disturb —'

'Yes, yes! I'm positive. Everything has been collected.'

Jones glanced around at all the gore. *'Everything?* I think you missed a spot.'

The man walked across the bloody cave, barely leaving footprints in the residue. Until then Payne and Jones had been under the impression that the chamber was wet. But the dampness was an optical illusion, a combination of the bright light and the crimson stains that made the surface glimmer, a red version of the Amber Room in St Petersburg, Russia.

Only the tint in this room was biological.

Payne extended his gloved hand and introduced

himself, using the opportunity to study the masked man before shifting his focus to the crime scene. Dr Ernie Sheldon was short and frail, with little hair other than the grey fuzz that covered his temples and the back of his head. The corners of his eyes creased with wrinkles whenever he smiled. It was one of the few things that Payne could see behind his mask.

'You're sure we can come in?'

Sheldon nodded. 'Of course! How can you help me if you can't come in?'

'Good question. Better yet, why are we here? It's obvious this isn't a missing-person case.'

'Why do you say that?'

Jones motioned towards the floor. 'There's less blood at the Red Cross.'

'True, there's a lot of blood in here. But how do you know who the blood belongs to?'

'We don't,' Payne admitted. 'In fact, there are a lot of things we don't know. People have been pretty tight-lipped about why we're here. And to be honest, it's starting to piss us off.'

'Then allow me to apologize, because that's all my fault. I'm the one who wanted you kept in the dark. Me and no one else. I'm completely to blame.'

Payne glanced at Jones, who shrugged as he studied the cave. 'Go on.'

'Actually,' Sheldon said, 'there's not much to explain. I want you to form your own opinion based on your observations, not mine or anyone else's.'

'That's understandable. But to do that, we need a

starting place. Some basics that'll let us form a rational conclusion. Otherwise, DJ is liable to guess that this place is nothing more than a Korean slaughter-house.'

Jones grinned. 'Moooooooooooooooooo.'

'Fair enough. What would you like to know?'

'What's your job description?'

Sheldon shook his head. 'That's something I'd prefer not to reveal at this time. Concentrate on the scene, not me.'

'Fine. What is this place?'

'It's a lava tube, formed when molten rock burst forth from –'

Payne interrupted. 'I know what a lava tube is.'

'Then why'd you ask?' Sheldon's voice was playful, not demeaning. Like a mentor forcing his pupil to ask the right question.

'I meant this facility. It's obvious this place wasn't used for public tours.'

'What's your best guess? Take a look around and hypothesize. If you guys are as good as –'

'Some sort of prison. Fairly old.' Jones knocked on the table, listening to the metal thump as it echoed throughout the chamber. 'Possibly Second World War, maybe later. It's been around for a very long time.' He crouched to examine the floor bolts which held the table and the chair in place. 'If I scraped away the blood, I could probably find a manufacturer. That would tell us if it was Korean, Japanese, or American . . . My guess is American.'

Sheldon smiled. 'Why do you say that?'

Jones shrugged. 'Because *we're* American. Why else would we be called in?'

'Touché.'

Jones shifted his focus to the lightbulb that dangled above his head. It wasn't on, so he was able to stare at it, searching it for clues. 'Jon, come over here.'

Payne strode across the cave, his eyes focused on the bulb. 'See something?'

'Maybe. I'm not sure if this table will hold me. Can you give me a hand?'

Holding Payne's shoulder, Jones stepped on to the chair, then the table itself. The surface was remarkably solid, refusing to sag under his body weight. He flipped on his torch and studied the light socket. To his eye, there was a tiny piece that didn't belong. It was circular and curved. Definitely modern. 'Just what I thought. It's a camera, embedded in the base. I bet if I took it apart, I'd find a microphone inside, too.'

Sheldon clasped his hands together, clearly amused by Jones's discovery, yet not the least bit surprised. 'And what was its purpose?'

Payne answered as Jones hopped off the table. 'To record interrogations.'

'Heavens! You two *are* good.'

Jones ignored the flattery and studied the black cable that ran along the ceiling to the rear of the cave. It stretched into the passage where Sheldon had originally emerged, which meant this facility continued beyond the current chamber. Possibly much deeper. What had the SUV driver told them? *The longest lava tube on the island is more than eight miles long.*

'That camera is next-generation American technology. Definitely military. Expertly placed. And since these walls are way too thick to transmit to an outside source, that means the recording device has to be . . .'

His words hung in the air as he followed the wire into the next chamber.

Unprepared for what he was about to see.

10

Halfway down the path, Kia sat on a tree stump, her head perched between her knees. Breathing was still difficult, but no longer from the bile that had risen in her throat. Now it had more to do with her behaviour than with anything she had just seen.

Good Lord, she thought. *Did I really just run out of the cave?*

In all her life she had never been more embarrassed by her actions. Sure, she'd talked a good game, bragging that she wasn't squeamish, pretending she could handle anything, but all it took was one look at the crime scene and she started running. Of course, the good news was that she had followed through on one promise to Payne. At least she didn't vomit on any evidence.

Kia untied the surgical mask that hung around her neck and tossed it down the rocky path. Her booties came off second, followed by her surgical gloves. With a rubber snap, she flicked them into the air. Even if she was ordered back to the cave, there was no way she was going in. Not with all that blood. Deep down inside, she knew her stomach wouldn't allow it.

'Nasty scene,' said a voice from behind.

Kia whirled around so fast she almost fell off the

tree stump. Her lack of grace caused the driver of the SUV to laugh as he emerged from the trees.

She apologized. 'Sorry about that. I didn't mean to disturb you.'

'Don't worry about it. You weren't the scene I was talking about.' The driver wore thick gloves and carried a bag labelled Medical Waste. He used it to collect her garments. 'Remember what I said when I gave you these? I'd been inside the cave, and once was enough for me.'

She nodded, no longer quite as mortified.

'All of us have our limits. And all of us have a speciality. My guess is you *weren't* selected for forensic work or combat. You were brought in for another purpose.'

'Is it *that* obvious?'

'Then why'd you go in the cave in the first place?'

She shrugged, not really sure of her answer.

'Let me guess. You were trying to fit in, weren't you? Trying to impress your squad leader. Trying to show him how tough you were.' He laughed, the sound of someone who had been in her position and had made the same mistake. 'Listen, I know this is going to sound pretty simplistic, but I'll let you in on a little secret I learned long ago. The *best* way to impress your boss is to do your job. That's it. That's the key to getting ahead in this world. Do what you're supposed to do and you'll get noticed.'

'Too late. I think I already got noticed.'

He grinned. 'Yeah, sprinting out of the cave probably wasn't your best choice.'

'Probably not.'

'In that case, may I suggest Plan B?'

'Which is?'

'Do something that will make everyone forget about Plan A.'

'Such as?'

The driver glanced into the trees. He knew they were being watched by several snipers, all of them ready to pull their triggers over the slightest indiscretion. Still, he wanted to assist Kia. Lowering his voice to a whisper, he said, 'There's a village nearby, filled with several people who probably aren't very good with English. As far as I'm concerned, their statements might come in handy as this investigation broadens. Heaven knows what they heard or saw.'

'You mean no one's talked to them?'

'No one's even been over there. We've been waiting for a translator.'

Shame motivated people to commit desperate acts. Some large. Some small. Some completely foolish. As Kia walked towards the village through the camphor trees, she pondered these categories and wondered how she would classify her decision at the end of the day.

The daughter of an American soldier and a Korean mother, she was born on a US Army base near Seoul, 275 miles north of her current location. Foreign marriages rarely worked in the military – they were often based on loneliness and little else – but her parents were the exception. Kia lived in South Korea until she was seven, learning the language, land, and customs from her mum. Then, when her father was transferred to a Stateside base, she learned all about America from him. Ironically, when she was old enough to choose her home, she split the distance between the countries, opting for a job on the Marshall Islands, in the middle of the Pacific.

Near the end of the rocky path, Kia spotted a *harubang*, also known as a stone grandfather, a ubiquitous grey figure found everywhere in Jeju. It marked the beginning of the village. Made of porous basalt, the six-foot sculpture had two hands – one resting slightly higher on its belly than the other – but no feet. A curved hat sat atop its friendly face. Bulging eyes. A big nose. A gentle mouth. Island elders once believed they drove away evil spirits. Nowadays they were simply a symbol of Jeju, the only place in the world where the original figures were located.

Kia touched it as she walked past, her eyes no longer focused on the relic but on the tiny village that lay ahead. She felt foolish for her thoughts but hoped the statue had done its job, protecting these people from the violence of the cave.

Little did she know that the villagers had played a major role in the bloodshed.

Both past and present.

11

Mecca, Saudi Arabia

On the outskirts of the sacred city, there was a massive blue sign. Its message was written in Arabic and English, an equal dose of welcome and warning. For true believers of Islam, it marked the gateway to their holy land, the one place on Earth they were supposed to visit before they died. But to others, the sign was more ominous. A threat that shouldn't be ignored.

STOP FOR INSPECTION

ENTRY PROHIBITED TO NON-MUSLIMS

Fred Nasir stared at the sign and realized this was the point of no return. There was an exit road to the right of the checkpoint, a final chance to turn around and drive back to Taif. Or Riyadh. Or anywhere else he wanted to go. But if he stayed in this line of traffic, which he'd been sitting in for the longest thirty minutes of his life, there was a chance he was going to be pulled from his Toyota Camry and taught the kind of lesson he would rather not learn.

For a culture that preached peace, many Muslims were skilled at violence.

Guards were standing up ahead, armed with rifles. He knew that additional men, carrying more significant firepower, were stationed in the nearby security building. Video cameras recorded everything: faces, cars, licence plates. A sophisticated system whose sole purpose was to weed out the unwanted. Non-believers, who didn't belong.

'Relax,' he said to himself. 'You'll be fine.'

After taking a deep breath, Nasir eased his car under the blue warning sign and waited for the inevitable. The part he feared the most. Two soldiers came out of the booth, neither of them smiling. The first asked for his travel visa and passport; the other glanced inside the car, searching for things that didn't belong. Mecca was a strict city with strict rules. No exceptions. This wasn't like Tijuana, Mexico, where a tourist could slip a couple of bucks to a guard and smuggle Pepe the Dancing Mule across the border for a bachelor party. This was far more serious. The type of place where bribe attempts were greeted with gunfire.

As requested, Nasir placed his papers in a tiny basket and handed it to the guard, who quickly disappeared into the booth, where he would inspect everything, putting extra emphasis on the paperwork that granted travellers access to Mecca. To get clearance, Muslims had to file the proper certificates (vaccinations, marriage, birth, etc.) weeks in advance, pay the proper entry fees, and include a notarized letter from the director of their mosque that certified their faith. Passports were required as well, but unlike some cities that frowned on visitors from certain nations, Mecca was the ultimate melting pot, a city whose sole existence was to greet visitors from all countries, as long as the visitors believed in Islam.

This time of year – the last month of the Islamic calendar – the city was particularly busy, hosting more than two million guests who were there for the hajj, the pilgrimage that all able-bodied Muslims were required to make at least once in their lifetime. To accommodate the influx of travellers, the Saudi government built a special airport in Jeddah, the largest in the world in overall area, consisting of a dozen terminals. Traffic flow was so specialized that it was open only for the hajj season. The rest of the year it sat dormant, unable to handle normal operations.

Unfortunately, the airport sat fifty miles to the west of Mecca, meaning everyone who flew in for the hajj still had to pass through the same security checkpoints as those who drove. This clogged the roadways with cars, vans, and tour buses, plus the occasional hearty soul who walked the entire way through the desert heat. Nasir had heard stories of men passing through security on the hump of a camel, but thus far he hadn't seen any.

Three minutes later, the guard returned with his approved paperwork. Everything had checked out;

Nasir was free to enter the city. Lifting the metal gate, the guard welcomed him with a common Islamic greeting. '*Salaam aleikoum.*'

Nasir replied, '*Aleikoum salaam.*'

Peace be upon you.

And on you, peace.

Nestled in bleak mountains that were barren from the desert heat, Mecca (spelled Makkah in Saudi Arabia) is a bustling city of more than 1.2 million people. Founded in about AD400 as a nomadic trading post, it had expanded through the centuries, becoming the holy centre for one of the world's biggest religions. Five times a day, more than a billion Muslims turn towards Mecca and pray. This direction of prayer is known as the *kiblah*. All mosques around the world were built to face the Kaaba, a holy shrine that stood in the centre of the Great Mosque in Mecca.

The Kaaba is located at 21° 25´ 21.70″ N, 39° 49´ 33.64″ E.

The city itself has no railroads or airports, and its drinking water has to be pumped in from surrounding areas due to a lack of underground wells, yet it is still a modern metropolis, filled with restaurants, malls, museums, and skyscrapers. Nasir was expecting none of those things as he drove through Mecca for the first time. He was anticipating something more ancient, more hallowed – a collection of mosaics and domes that showcased the beauty of Islamic art and architecture – not a steady flow of tourists looking for clearance items at an outdoor bazaar.

His biggest shock came when he spotted a Kentucky Fried Chicken, not far from the Kaaba. He was tempted to stop, just to see if Colonel Sanders was wearing his southern white suit and tie or if they'd dressed him up in a robe and sandals. The possibility made him laugh, a welcome tension-breaker before he completed the last part of his mission.

Nasir drove to the designated area, not far from the Great Mosque, and parked his car. This part of town, known as the old city, was once crammed with houses and apartments that had been there for generations. But most of them were bulldozed to widen the streets for the millions of pilgrims who flooded this area during the hajj, and to erect a colossal new building project known as the Abraj Al Bait Towers Complex.

Ironically, it was during the razing process that an important discovery had been made.

While clearing the way for something new, an ancient relic had been found.

If Nasir hadn't known where to look, he never would have seen the tunnel entrance. Accessed by a wooden shack and protected by a chainlink fence, it was hidden behind several piles of debris and an assortment of construction materials. On the surface, it appeared that another building was going up. But the opposite was true. They were going *down*, excavating deep into the ground underneath Mecca.

Wearing jeans and a short-sleeved shirt, Nasir stepped around the rubble and peeked inside. Lights had been strung along the ceiling, giving him a glimpse of the thin wooden boards that lined the interior. It looked like an abandoned mine shaft, the kind found in an Arizona ghost town. Dusty and unstable. Creaking all the time. Like it was liable to collapse at any moment.

Suddenly, he regretted their meeting place. They wanted him to go in *there*?

No wonder they paid him all that money. He had risked his life several times in two days.

And for what? A take-out menu?

None of it made any sense.

But who was he to argue with fortune? If he kept his cool, he'd be done in five minutes. Just make the drop and leave. No sense hanging around. After that, he'd drive to the airport and disappear for a long time. Maybe take a long vacation. Or buy a new house.

With all that cash, he could do whatever he wanted.

Nasir glanced at his watch and smiled.

It was time to get this over with.

I 2

A generator purred in the gloom while Jones tried to grasp what he saw. The first image that leaped to mind was the interior of an anaconda. Recognized as the largest snake in the world, it often bit its prey with its sharp teeth before squeezing it to death with its muscular coils. Afterwards it swallowed its meal whole, sometimes unhinging its own jaw in order to engulf the entire carcass. Larger victims, such as sheep or deer, could often be seen through the snake's flesh, slowly dissolving inside.

In Jones's mind, he had just walked through the mouth, a gruesome cavity filled with blood and gore. Now he was staring at the belly, the place where the bodies were disposed.

The cave stretched farther than his eyes could see, fading to black somewhere in the depths of the mountain. Thick metal bars were anchored at irregular intervals on each side of the expanse, makeshift cages that were part man-made, part geology. Computer lights blinked in the distance, the glow of technology in an otherwise archaic world.

To him, none of it made any sense.

Like pieces from several jigsaw puzzles all mixed together.

Payne noticed the confusion on Jones's face and came forward to investigate. Seconds later, he was just as bewildered. 'What is this place?'

'I have no idea.'

Dr Sheldon heard the comment and asked, 'Have either of you heard of Roh Tae-woo, the former president of South Korea? In the early nineties, a large cave was discovered on Jeju that housed the remains of several islanders slaughtered just after the Second World War. Instead of announcing the discovery to the world, Roh sealed the cave, hoping to keep it quiet. Eventually word of his cover-up was unearthed and he was imprisoned for his actions.'

Jones considered the information. 'And this is his cave?'

'No. *That* cave is on Mount Halla. This cave is still a secret.'

'*Whose* secret?'

'Ahhh, now we're getting somewhere. Whose secret indeed?!'

Sheldon squeezed past the duo and walked towards the small table that sat in a natural nook along the right-hand wall. He clicked on a desk lamp and rummaged through a large stack of folders. Each of them classified. Each of them critical. Yet in his mind there was no need for a locked safe since the front door was being guarded by snipers.

'Here you go,' Sheldon said. 'Who wants to read it first?'

Jones took the file while Payne held the torch. No

arguing. No bickering. No ego of any kind. Both men knew that Jones was better at analysing information. It was his speciality. He had an innate ability to spot important facts and incongruities faster than anyone Payne had ever met. So Payne did the smart thing and let Jones decipher the data.

According to the folder, they were standing in a lava tube that was discovered by locals in 1824. It measured 1.2 miles in length. Parts of it were narrow, less than four feet wide at times, while other sections were spacious. One gallery soared to more than twenty-two feet in height and was originally used as storage space for smugglers, who valued the constant cool temperature and natural protection of the black stone. Decades ago smuggling was the main source of income on the island, so the exact location of the cave was a fiercely guarded secret. Villagers protected it with their lives and were rewarded for their efforts.

Unfortunately, their loyalty was used against them in the aftermath of the Second World War.

In an attempt to establish control on Jeju, the South Korean government labelled everyone who was associated with smuggling as Communists and demanded their capture. This set off a chain of events that led to the bloodiest event in the island's history: the Jeju Massacre.

On 3 April 1948 rebels from Jeju's 'people's army' attacked police stations and government offices on Jeju, causing the deaths of an estimated fifty people while freeing many islanders who they felt had been wrongly accused. They kept control of the island until 25 June, when the South Korean government invaded from the mainland and overwhelmed Jeju forces. Thousands of islanders were detained and sorted into four groups (labelled A, B, C, and D), based on their supposed security risk. Unfortunately, the South Korean Navy realized they didn't have the manpower to guard that many people in captivity. So they did the unthinkable. Instead of letting people go, they ordered the local police to execute everyone in groups C and D.

No trials. No appeals. Just bloodshed.

Thousands of innocents were slaughtered. Bodies were stacked in the streets.

Yet this brutality didn't stop the rebellion. Over the next six years, a reported 80,000 islanders were killed – nearly a quarter of Jeju's population.

Jones glanced up from the file. 'How accurate are these numbers?'

'Very,' Sheldon answered. 'They're based on first-hand accounts of American troops.'

Payne interrupted. 'You mean we watched the executions?'

Sheldon nodded. 'We were summoned to South Korea after the Second World War to help set up a provisional government. Unfortunately, we had no authority to intervene in an internal conflict. All we could do was keep meticulous records and pray the violence stopped on its own.'

Payne scowled because he knew that was bullshit. The US military had a long-standing tradition of butting into battles where they didn't belong. Not that he had a problem with that. Sometimes the biggest kid on the block needed to flex his muscles to protect the weakest. Yet for some reason that wasn't the case on Jeju. The only question was, *why*?

Jones wondered the same thing. 'What was our *real* reason for doing nothing?'

Sheldon smiled under his mask. 'Take a wild guess.'

'Because we had more to gain by staying out of it.'

'Such as?'

'Damning information against the new government.'

'And why was *that* important?'

Jones gave it some thought. 'Because Jeju is an island in the Korea Strait. The perfect place for Americans to spy on Japan, Russia, China, and North Korea.'

Sheldon nodded, then signalled for them to follow him deeper into the cave. 'Smugglers used this facility until 1951. That's three years *after* the revolt started, which goes to show how secret this place actually was. Outside of locals, no one knew about it. Not the police. Not the government. Not even us. At least until much later.'

He stopped in front of the first cell and admired its simplicity. Iron bars were anchored in the volcanic rock, creating a series of jail cells that stretched deep into the darkness. 'Local villagers were held here by the South Korean government. Young, old, men, women. It didn't matter. Everyone was locked in this cave for weeks. Then, one by one, they were tortured for information about the rebel army that most of them knew nothing about. To this day, the unlucky ones are still buried in the deepest sections of this cave. Hidden behind piles of rock.'

Payne hated stories like this — especially ones that happened so long ago — because no matter how good a soldier he was, there was nothing he could do about tragedies from the 1950s. Of course, there *was* something he could do about the present. That is, if he was given all the facts. Yet for some reason he sensed that Sheldon was hiding something important from them. He wasn't sure what it was, but his patience was wearing thin.

'Not to be rude, but can we fast-forward to recent history?'

Sheldon glanced at Payne. 'Of course we can. What would you like to know?'

'Everything you're keeping from us.'

The smile faded under his mask, the crinkles disappearing from the corners of his eyes. 'Nothing like cutting to the chase.'

'Actually, the chase started two days ago, when we first got on a plane. Yet for one reason or another, you've been stonewalling ever since. First by proxy, now in person.'

'What do you mean?'

Payne pointed at him. 'There you go! A *perfect* example. Most people respond to questions with answers, not other questions.'

'Jon,' Jones whispered, trying to calm him down.

But Payne brushed him aside. 'Seriously, Doc, it's time for some straight facts. No more history lessons. No more bullshit. Why the hell are we here?'

'To find a missing person. Actually, several missing people.'

Payne rolled his hand in front of him, urging Sheldon to go on. 'Some names would help.'

'Before I continue, I need to give you some more background info on –'

'Holy hell! Give me a fuckin' break!'

'Seriously. This is important information.'

Payne shook his head, unwilling to listen further. 'DJ, I swear to God, if he starts talking about the Korean War, I'm going to kick him in the balls.'

'Jon!' Jones shouted, thankful his mask covered his smile. 'Let the guy talk.'

'Talk? All he does is talk. Ten minutes ago I asked him about this facility, and he started blabbing about the effects of molten lava . . . Seriously, who the hell does that?' He pointed at Sheldon. 'Why would you do that? Do I look like I give a damn about molten anything?'

Jones stepped between the two, knowing full well that Payne wasn't really mad or the least bit out of control. But when it came to acquiring information, they realized fear often went a long way towards lessening someone's reluctance to speak – especially someone like Dr Sheldon, who was holding his cards much tighter than he should have been. Thankfully, when someone as large as Payne started to roar, people usually did whatever they could to calm him down.

This was their version of good cop/bad cop.

They called it *Payne in the ass*.

'Jon,' Jones said, 'calm down. Let me talk to him for a minute. Alone.'

'Fine! Maybe you two can discuss the history of molten liquor.'

Jones rolled his eyes. 'It's called *malt* liquor. And my guess is he doesn't drink Colt 45.'

'Okay, Billy D. Discuss whatever you want. But I'm going outside to make a call.' He pulled out his cell phone and fiddled with the buttons. 'If you learn any news about this century, you know where to find me.'

Payne stormed off, the sound of his footsteps echoing in the cave like rolling thunder. Jones waited for the rumble to pass, then apologized for his friend's behaviour, blaming it on jet lag and his close connection to Trevor Schmidt.

'You have to understand,' Jones said, 'Jon is very protective of his protégés. Two days ago Colonel Harrington told us that Trevor was missing and asked for our help, but that's the last we've heard about it. No updates. No progress reports. No nothing. That's tough for us to take.'

Sheldon nodded. 'Trust me, I'm empathetic to your situation. I truly am. But there's a reason why I've been rambling on and on about this cave's background and answering all of your questions with questions of my own. I know you think I'm playing games with you, but I swear that's not the case.'

'Then what *is* the case?'

Sheldon fidgeted with his gloves, trying to delay his answer. 'Honestly, we've been on Jeju for several days now, and in all that time we've only learned one thing.'

'Which is?'

'None of us have any idea what happened here.'

13

Payne smiled as he walked outside. The smell of blood still lingered in the air, yet compared to the interior of the cave, he felt like he was standing in a daisy-fresh meadow. His mood brightened further when he scrolled through the picture gallery in his cell phone and saw the clarity of his latest image: Dr Ernie Sheldon, the unwitting star of a sneak attack.

Laughing to himself, Payne typed an encrypted text message to Randy Raskin, one of his best contacts at the Pentagon, asking him for basic intel on the man in the photo. He gave him Sheldon's name but stressed it might be an alias. At this point it was too early to tell.

After hitting *send*, he returned his attention to his current surroundings. With a quick glance he scanned the rocky path that sliced through the trees towards the road. No sign of Kia. She'd fled the scene several minutes earlier, but he had fully expected to see her sitting there. Her head between her knees. Cheeks flushed with embarrassment. Several excuses ready to spring from her lips to explain her actions. But none of them was necessary, since it wasn't her fault.

If anyone was to blame, Payne knew it was

himself, for he was the one who had let her enter the cave. The one who knew she was a translator, nothing more. Certainly not trained for that type of gore. Yet for some reason he had urged her to tag along, even though she served no purpose inside. Even though he knew they were about to stumble into something much worse than a rescue mission. Not with that smell. Not with all those soldiers carrying all that firepower outside the scene. Obviously this wasn't about a missing person. This was something different. Something more significant. But for the life of him, he didn't know what it was. That's the main reason he had wanted to step outside and get some fresh air. He needed time to think. To figure out why they'd brought him in. What role they wanted him to play.

Now all of that would have to wait. His focus was no longer on the cave. It was on Kia. She was his number one priority. Not because she was a woman or defenceless, but because she was part of his team. And that's what leaders were supposed to do. Protect their squads at all costs.

Payne knew snipers were nestled in the camphor trees and buried on the hillside, tracking his every move through mounted scopes. He couldn't see them, but he knew they were there. Watching. Waiting. Hoping someone did something aggressive so they could pull their triggers. The key was not to give them an excuse. Slowly he turned and studied the rock face behind him, trying to determine where he would have positioned his men if he'd been in charge of security.

One up top. A couple over there. A few more down the path.

No way Kia had gone anywhere without being watched. Without them telling her where she could puke and where she couldn't. This was their land. Their terrain. They were the spiders and this was their web. They could tell him her exact location. No problem at all.

But first he had to get one of them to talk.

Payne crunched down the trail, focusing on a thick grove of trees. It looked dark and impenetrable. The perfect place to take residence. With a grin on his lips, Payne pointed towards the dense brush and signalled for the sniper to come out. Then Payne just stood there, staring and smiling, until he heard some movement. A snap was all Payne needed to know that he was right.

A few curse words later, the guard emerged from the thicket. Mud on his young face. Twigs on his helmet. A rifle in his hands. 'Dammit, sir. How'd you see me in there?'

Payne shrugged. 'Who said I did?'

The sniper cursed again, this time even louder. Angry at himself for giving up his position to someone who hadn't even seen him.

'Wow. When you were a kid, you must've sucked at hide-and-seek.'

'Actually, sir, I *never* lost.'

Payne smiled. 'Actually, son, you just did.'

The sniper was tempted to argue, but what could he say? Instead, he quickly changed the subject. 'Was there something you needed?'

'I'm looking for my translator. Female. Asian features. Probably covered in vomit.'

'You mean the hottie? She headed towards the village.'

'There's a village?'

The sniper pointed down a side path that cut through the woods. 'Can't tell you much about it. Haven't been there yet.'

'Is it secure?'

'Don't know. Don't care.'

Payne nodded, not surprised by the answer. In the military, most information was compartmental-ized – especially on secured projects such as this one. A guard over here didn't need to know what was going on over there unless it posed an immediate threat. And even then, he sure as hell wasn't going to talk about it with someone he didn't know or trust.

'We done here?' asked the sniper, who waited to be dismissed before he slipped back into the woods to find a better place to hide. Payne watched him for a while, then turned his attention to the village path. It was dark and foreboding, like everything else in the area. Protocol told him that he should let Jones know where he was going, but something in his gut told him that time was of the essence. That Kia was in a lot more danger in the village than Jones was in the cave.

And as usual, Payne's gut was right.

Kia walked through the centre of town, staggered by the silence. It was the middle of the day, yet there were no dogs barking, no kids playing, no errands being run. No movement or activities of any kind. Tiny stone huts sat back from the rocky road, separated by stone walls and guarded by dozens of *harubang* – their friendly stone faces no longer quite so inviting. In fact, in the stillness of the village, their presence was somehow disconcerting, as if the people themselves had been consumed by these ancient stone figures. As if *they* were suddenly the only residents.

A gust of wind added to the chill that Kia felt surge through her body. She was accustomed to the warm tropical breezes of the Marshall Islands, not to the whipping wind of this volcanic ghost town. Or was the chill from something else? Perhaps more to do with her fear and apprehension than the temperature itself. The thought was an unpleasant one, especially after her recent behaviour in the cave. No way was she going to turn and run again.

Once was bad enough. Twice would be unbearable.

The strength of the wind increased, this time bringing the faint scent of burning wood. Not maple. Not oak. Maybe pine. The musk filled her nose, quickly erasing the memory of the bloody cave and replacing it with the promise of survivors. She turned towards the smell, staring into the face of the breeze, looking for a sign of life. Any sign. And then she saw one. A tiny wisp of smoke rising from a stone chimney at the far end of the village. It wasn't much, but its presence gave her hope. A rope to cling to as she journeyed forwards, searching for answers.

Kia passed house after house, yard after yard, all of them seemingly deserted. Each adding to the mystery of this vacant town; each filling her head with more questions. Were the villagers dead? Or were they hiding? If so, from whom? Or what? She prayed the blood in the cave didn't belong to them, but every empty home, every abandoned car, made that seem less likely.

Obviously there was a connection between the two mysteries.

She hoped it wasn't a tragic one.

Payne heard the scream from the far end of the village and reacted instinctively.

In a single motion, he pulled his Sig Sauer P226 from his waistband and broke into a full sprint. His eyes scanned the horizon, searching for danger. The only movement he saw was the bouncing of tree limbs as they swayed in the breeze. Payne leaped a log gate in a stone wall that lined one of the nearby yards and checked his weapon. His magazine was full.

At least until he found a target.

Because of the wind and the echoing effect of the rock, Payne couldn't gauge where the scream had come from. He knew it was somewhere up ahead, but that's all he knew. Maybe from a house. Maybe in a yard. Maybe in the woods beyond town. To him, it was like tracking gunfire in an open canyon. The first shot announced trouble; the second shot gave its location.

Thankfully, the scream was followed by the murmur of voices. Close enough to be heard, but too far away to be understood. Yet Payne didn't care about diction. He cared about location. Every second of sound gave him a better chance to find the threat and stop it.

Moving silently, Payne skirted the stone wall and crept forward, his weapon raised in an offensive position. His eyes focused. His breathing controlled. Just like he'd been taught to do. In fact, this whole scene felt like a training exercise. Like he'd stumbled into Hogan's Alley – the mock city at the FBI Academy in Quantico, Virginia – and was being tested for speed and marksmanship. Only this was the Asian version. And it was real. No fake terrorists armed with paint guns. No spring-loaded wooden targets. And absolutely no do-overs.

He was up against an unknown enemy with unknown numbers.

And he was facing them alone.

14

Jones stared at Dr Sheldon, unsure if he was telling the truth. How could several days of fieldwork turn up nothing? 'Doc, I'm not calling you a liar, but –'

'You find my lack of answers hard to fathom.' Sheldon smiled, not the least bit offended. 'And if I were you, I'd feel the exact same way. All this blood, all this evidence, I have to know what happened. Unfortunately, there's one thing preventing me from drawing any conclusions.'

'Which is?'

'I don't have a lab. My entire investigation relies on forensic evidence, yet I can't test anything myself. As it stands, every single sample has to be smuggled off this island so it can be examined at some classified facility. That tends to slow things down.'

'I guess it would.'

'Right now I'm still waiting for test results I should've received days ago.'

Jones nodded, sympathetic to the situation. Early in his career, he had worked for the military police, so he knew all about forensic delays and what they did to a case. 'Then let's concentrate on other things. Like Trevor Schmidt. How do you know he was here?'

'How? Because this was *his* facility. He was running the show.'

'What do you mean?'

'They brought him in several months ago. First as a guard, later in a more significant role. My guess is they wanted to see if he could handle this place, and he ended up thriving.'

'Doing what?'

'Doing everything we're not supposed to do.'

The voices came from a house at the far end of the village. One male, one female. Both of them shouting in Korean. Or Chinese. Or some other language that Payne didn't speak. He tried to get as close as possible, hoping to get a view of the argument, but the stone wall that surrounded the yard was much taller than the others he had passed. It was ten feet high and was made of thick volcanic rocks that were held in place by some kind of natural paste.

The only entrance was a carved wooden gate that depicted all four seasons on Jeju. Royal azaleas blooming in spring. Waves crashing in summer. Leaves dancing in autumn. And snow falling on Mount Halla in winter. A stone grandfather stood on both sides of the gate; each was rough and weathered, as if they'd been there longer than the home they were protecting. A stone chimney anchored the right side of the house, exhaling wisps of brown smoke that soared above the thatched roof and filled the air with a piney aroma.

Gun in hand, Payne crept closer until he was able to lean his body weight against the right gate. It groaned ever so slightly as it swung open, just enough space for him to slip inside.

Kia stood at the far side of the yard, her back against the wall, tension etched on her face. She was arguing with an old man, who wore a *jeogori* robe and *baji* pants. Pleading with him. Begging for something in Korean. None of this made any sense to Payne until he saw the weapon in the guy's grasp. It was long and sharp and pointed at Kia's midsection. Maybe a pitchfork. Maybe a trident. Whatever it was, it was fully capable of ruining her day.

Payne inched forward, approaching his target from behind. His hair was long and white and pulled into an elaborate ponytail that was bound tight with a fancy clip. Every time the old man talked, it swayed back and forth, up and down, as if punctuating his words with extra emphasis. His voice was guttural, his phrases choppy. Fear was evident despite the language barrier.

Kia spotted Payne about twenty yards away. Much to her credit, she didn't smile or point or call out to him. Instead, she kept arguing with the old man. Kept his focus straight ahead so Payne could ease into position and do whatever he needed to do.

Ten yards out, Payne lifted his gun and aimed it at the back of his target's head. One simple squeeze and the old man would have been dead. Brains splattered everywhere. Game over. But Payne sensed that was the wrong move. This guy wasn't a killer. He was scared. Probably more so than Kia. He was wearing a robe and slippers in his backyard. Simply defending his property. No way did he deserve to die. Then again, neither did she.

Five yards later, Payne made a choice. No gun was necessary. He tucked his P226 in his belt and slipped behind the old man. In a fluid motion, Payne grabbed his ponytail with one hand and flicked away the pitchfork with the other. It fell harmlessly to the ground. The old man was next. Payne eased him backwards, supporting his body weight with his own, making sure he didn't bang the man's head or break a hip or anything else.

It was his good deed for the day. No sense hurting the guy if he didn't have to.

'You okay?' Payne asked Kia, refusing to take his eyes off his target.

She nodded as she grabbed the rusty pitchfork. 'I'm fine.'

'Glad to hear it.' Payne patted down the old man, who seemed stunned by the sneak attack, then took a few steps back. Just enough space to feel comfortable. He felt even safer once his gun was back in his hand. 'What the hell happened?'

'He *attacked* me.'

'Yeah, I kind of figured that. But why?'

'I don't know,' she blurted, punctuating the words with the pitchfork. 'I saw the smoke and came here to ask where everyone was, because the entire village is empty and I thought maybe he could tell me what was going on, but before I could even ask, he *attacked* me.'

Payne smiled, recognizing the symptoms of adrenaline. The rambling. The exaggerated hand movements. The white knuckles as she clenched the handle. Common traits for a soldier who was new in the field. 'Kia, sweetie. Remember to breathe.'

'What?'

'*Breathe.*'

She nodded, sucking in a deep breath that returned some colour to her cheeks. She repeated the process, and everything about her calmed down. At least a little bit.

'Now, what else can you tell me?'

'About what?'

Payne pointed to the old guy. 'Him.'

'I heard someone working out back. So I walked around the side of the house to investigate. I got halfway there when he came charging at me with *this*.' She held up the pitchfork. 'I'm not armed, so I did what my father always taught me to do when attacked. I screamed.'

'And I heard you. You did it very well.'

Kia smiled, the stress of the moment melting away. 'Thanks.'

'What were you two arguing about?'

'Everything! I said I wasn't going to hurt him, but he disagreed. I told him I was Korean, but he didn't believe me. No matter what I said, he claimed I was lying.'

Payne nodded, starting to grasp the situation. Either the old guy was completely delusional, or he'd suffered a recent trauma. Something so significant that he'd developed some major trust issues. Why else would he be deathly afraid of Kia?

'Does he speak English?' Payne wondered.

She asked him in Korean but the old guy ignored her, refusing to say anything.

'Fine,' Payne said, 'then he can't help us. We're just gonna have to kill him.'

The old man flinched on the ground, reacting to what Payne had said. Obviously a big mistake. Right then and there, Payne knew he spoke English. Or at least understood it.

In a calm voice, Payne said, 'Don't worry, sir. I'm not going to hurt you. I just wanted to see if you could understand me. And clearly you can.' He stepped forward and offered the guy his hand, but it was rejected. The old man wanted to stand on his own. 'My apologies, sir. I figured since I pulled you down, the least I could do was help you up.'

'Just like an American,' the old man muttered in a thick Korean accent. He took a moment to dust himself off – first his robe, then his trousers – before finishing his thought. 'Why do *your* people always assume that an act of kindness will make up for one of violence?'

95

Payne shrugged. 'Probably the same reason that *your* people always sound like a fortune cookie when you're talking to *my* people.'

The old man frowned. 'What's a fortune cookie?'

'It's not important. What is important is why you attacked my friend.'

'She came into my yard where she didn't belong. I was defending myself.'

Kia objected. 'I came into your yard because I was worried about you and your neighbours. And according to *sammu*, I'm allowed to enter your yard when I know you're home.'

Now it was Payne's turn to be confused. 'What's *sammu*?'

'It's a tradition on Jeju. The people here are direct descendants of those who founded the Kingdom of Tamna, islanders who always prided themselves on honour and independence. The concept of sammu guarantees that this island is free of thieves, beggars, and gates. When you walked through town, did you notice the three logs that blocked the thresholds on all the walls? Those logs are known as *jeongnang*. They aren't used as protection but rather to inform visitors if the master of the house is home or when he is coming back. If one log is there, he'll be back shortly. Two means around dinnertime. Three means he is far away from home. On the other hand, if the logs are missing, you are welcome to pay him a visit.'

Payne glanced at the old man. 'No log means she wasn't trespassing.'

'Not only that,' Kia added, 'but he doesn't *have* a log. He has a huge wooden gate. I'm surprised his neighbours let him get away with that. It's disrespectful to the entire village.'

The old man bristled, unwilling to be insulted by two strangers. 'One shouldn't mock what one doesn't understand.'

Payne frowned. 'Meaning?'

'If you had my past, you'd have a gate, too.'

15

Because of its proximity to the altar, the skeleton had to be moved out of the way, a delicate process considering the age of the victim. Shari eased the sword from its grasp, careful not to break its fingers, and handed it to Wheeler, who tried to read the Arabic text that was inscribed on the weapon. The poor lighting coupled with the dusty conditions made it difficult.

Using a fine cloth that wouldn't scratch the metal, Wheeler caressed the blade's surface, trying to remove the grime that had accumulated over the centuries. Hennessy stood behind him, shining his torch on the ancient sword.

'Any better?' Hennessy wondered.

'A little,' Wheeler admitted. 'I can make out some of the lettering now. Of course, I don't want to rub it too hard for fear of permanent damage.'

'What does it say?'

Wheeler tilted the blade back and forth, trying to use the lights and shadows to his advantage. 'I can see the word *noble*. It's fairly distinct. And over here, I see what looks like . . .'

'What?' Shari asked, noticing the puzzled expression on his face.

Wheeler glanced at the skeleton, then back at the blade, not wanting to mistranslate something so important. But to his eye, there was no doubt about the inscription. 'It says *Muhammad*.'

In the world of Islam, the prophet Muhammad is such a revered figure that all Muslims were required to say *sallallahu alayhi wasallam* after speaking his name, which means *may the peace and blessings of Allah be upon him*. English-speaking Muslims often use a shortened phrase, *peace be upon him*, to show their respect. This is done every single time his name is mentioned. The same reverence is expected with the written word, although it is considered appropriate to use an abbreviation (*s.a.w.* or *p.b.u.h.*) instead of the whole expression.

'What else does it say?' Hennessy wondered.

Wheeler tried to read more but was unable to. 'That's all I can make out for now. Like I mentioned, I don't want to damage the artefact with over-scrubbing. Once I get it back to the hotel, I'm sure I'll be able to clean it up using the appropriate equipment.'

'Fair enough.'

'In the meantime, I'd love an explanation. What does this inscription mean to us?'

Shari looked at Wheeler and smiled. 'It means we're on the right track.'

Of all the security guards, Shari was fondest of Ivan Klimkiewicz, a massive man who had more hair on his chest than most guys had on their head. Because of this condition and the constant butchering of his last name, he encouraged people to call him Ape.

It was a nickname that made her laugh.

Despite his size and intimidating presence, Ape was one of the nicest guys that Shari had ever met, which was only one of the reasons she had hired him. Hard-working and quick-witted, he watched over her like a big brother, a job he had trained for most of his life since he had helped raise five younger sisters after his mother died at an early age.

Ape was working outside the chamber door, shovelling debris into a wheelbarrow, when he heard a noise coming from the tunnel entrance. He paused for a minute, just to make sure he wasn't imagining things, then rushed inside to tell Shari.

'We have company.'

She glanced at her watch and nodded. Her boss, Omar Abdul-Khaliq, had informed her that someone would be visiting the site today to drop off a package. She wasn't sure why – the exposure seemed kind of risky – but she had learned long ago never to question his decisions.

'Crap. I'm going to need some time to get cleaned up. Do you think you can stall him?'

Ape nodded. 'With pleasure.'

Boards creaked as Fred Nasir walked down the steep slope of the tunnel. When the path levelled off, it turned gently to the east. Lightbulbs hung above him, barely lighting the way. He walked fifty feet further, at which point he was greeted by a locked metal gate. It wasn't what he was expecting to find so deep underground.

'Hello?' he called, his voice echoing through the shaft. 'Is anyone home?'

Ape emerged from the darkness, carrying a torch in one hand and a pickaxe in the other. Sweat dripped from his brow, mixing with the dirt that covered his face. To Nasir, it looked like the guard was leaking mud. Like a mole man who lived in the Earth's core.

'What do you want?' Ape asked in a deep voice.

'I have a delivery.'

'Stay there.'

Nasir nodded. What choice did he have? The gate was locked, and the person he needed to meet was on the other side. At least he hoped he was. The truth was he didn't know anything about him. Much like it had been at Al-Gaim. He was given a time and a place but wasn't quite sure who was going to be there when he showed up. He was told it was done for security. The less he knew, the better. Obviously it made perfect sense, but it was still unsettling.

He glanced at his watch again. Five more minutes had passed.

Finally, Nasir heard movement up ahead. He stared through the metal gate, hoping to get a glimpse of his contact before he had to talk to him. Praying it wasn't another mole man.

One glimpse and he realized that wasn't the case. In fact, it wasn't a *him* at all.

It was a woman. A sexy woman. Striding confidently through the darkness. Her hair was covered and she wore a robe, but there was something about her that was captivating.

Suddenly he wasn't in such a hurry to leave.

'May I help you?' asked Shari, who had put on appropriate clothes for her visitor.

'Yes. I have a delivery.'

'Great. I've been expecting you. Please slip it through the gate.'

He looked at the fence and frowned. 'You mean I can't come in?'

'Why would you want to come in?'

'I don't know. Just to look around. I'm kind of curious.'

Before Shari could respond, Ape emerged behind her. He still held the pickaxe in his grasp. 'You know what they say about curiosity.'

Nasir gulped. 'It killed the cat.'

'It's gonna kill the deliveryman, too, unless you get your ass out of here.'

Shari fought the urge to smile. 'You heard the man. Give me the package, then you'd better get going. I'm not big enough to protect you if Ape gets angry.'

Nasir nodded and slipped a sealed envelope through the gate. Inside the envelope was the take-out menu he had picked up at Al-Gaim. Inside the menu was a tiny computer disk.

Shari glanced at it and frowned. 'Is that every-thing?'

'Yes. That's everything.'

'Okay, then. Thanks for coming.' She turned to get back to work but realized he was still standing there, just watching her. 'Can you find your way out? Or do you need some help?'

'I'll gladly help you out,' Ape growled.

'No thanks. I'm fine.' Nasir backed away from the gate. 'No problem at all.'

'Great,' Shari said with a laugh. 'Take care now. Stay safe.'

Nasir turned and hustled up the ramp, dying to get out of the tunnel. Dying to see the sunlight.

Ironically, it was one of the things that led to his death.

There's a split second when people first leave the darkness when their eyes are unable to adjust. The sun's rays are just too bright; pupils are unable to compensate. To a trained killer, it's something that can be taken advantage of. A moment when his target is temporarily blind. And a blind target is an easy mark.

The man calmly waited until Nasir stepped outside the tunnel. Then, before Nasir could focus, the man took his *jambiya*, a curved Arabic dagger, and slid it across Nasir's throat. One quick slash and it was over. His scream emerged as a bloody gurgle, a short burst of spray followed by a quick loss of life. No resist-ance. No struggle of any kind.

One minute the target was alive, the next he was dead.

Just like the man had been taught to do.

After that, he simply dragged Nasir back into the tunnel and dumped him on the ground, blood pouring from him like a gutted pig. No need to hide the body. No need to clean up the scene. That would defeat the purpose of this violent act.

This murder was a message.

One he wanted them to see.

16

Payne spotted a wooden bench in a small flower garden. Always cautious, he checked it for hidden weapons before letting the old man take a seat.

Payne had been raised by his grandfather, so he had a special place in his heart for the elderly. He believed in respecting them. And listening to them. Always soaking in as much wisdom as he possibly could while they were alive. Of course, he also knew that some senior citizens were total assholes. Therefore, he planned on taking every precaution until he knew more about this guy and his past.

'So,' Payne said, 'tell us about the gate.'

The old man stared at him, sizing him up. Several seconds passed before he was willing to speak. And when he did, there was a bitter tone in his voice. Filled with anger and acrimony. 'This isn't the first time Americans have come to Jeju. You've been visiting for decades. And I don't mean tourists. I mean soldiers like *you*. Threatening our island.'

On the inside, Payne felt like a total ass. Embarrassed for being there. Ashamed for holding this guy at gunpoint. Mortified by the lack of US military support during the Jeju Massacre. Yet what could he do? It was crucial for him to stay in control of the situation, so he revealed nothing. No emotions. No response. No reaction of any kind.

'I was one of the men who was arrested back in 1948. My entire family was pulled out of my home, *this* home, at gunpoint. The women were carried away first, their screams echoing through the night. Then we were blindfolded and dragged into a nearby cave, where we were beaten, starved, and tortured for the next three years. During that time, my father, uncles, and brothers were killed. Out of nine of us, I was the only one who survived.' The old man rubbed his eyes, wiping away the tears that streamed down his face. 'You want to know why I have a gate? *That's* why I have a gate.'

Kia sat next to him and whispered something in Korean. Something soft and comforting. The tone of her voice revealed that much. Payne had no idea what was being said and realized it would be inappropriate to ask. The old man needed a moment, and Payne was willing to give it to him. That was the least he could do. So he took the pitchfork from Kia and let them talk.

Eventually, after a few minutes of dialogue, Kia turned her attention to Payne. 'Do you have any questions?'

Payne nodded. He had several. Yet he realized things would go smoother if someone else did the asking. Someone the old man could trust. Someone who hadn't grabbed his ponytail and pulled him to the ground.

'Actually, why don't you interview him? I figure, you found the guy.'

Kia smiled, thrilled with the opportunity. And her excitement seemed to brighten the old man's mood. Five minutes earlier, he was holding her at bay with a rusty pitchfork. Now the two of them were bonding.

She started simple. 'Can you tell us more about the Americans?'

'They've been coming here since the fifties. Mostly in the dead of night when they didn't think we were watching. But we saw them. We noticed what they were doing. Bringing in others, sneaking them through the woods.' He turned towards Kia, lowering his voice to a whisper. 'Things died down a few years ago. All of us hoped they'd finally moved on, that they'd found somewhere new. But all of that changed a few months ago when the screams returned to the island. Pe-Ui Je Dan had been reborn.'

'Pe-Ui Je Dan?'

The old man nodded. 'The Altar of Blood.'

Jones stared at Dr Sheldon, still trying to figure him out. So far, their conversations were like a game of poker. A lot of bluffing, a lot of gamesmanship, yet no obvious winner. Every once in a while Sheldon toyed with him – dropping a hint, raising the stakes – but he refused to lay his cards on the table. And until he did, the game would continue whether Jones wanted it to or not.

Unfortunately, Sheldon's last comment was his most puzzling yet. He had claimed Trevor Schmidt was in charge of this facility. But how could that be? It didn't make any sense. Schmidt was a highly decorated Special Forces soldier, hand-picked for the MANIACs and trained in their specialized form of warfare. Those skills could not be used in a cave. Not as a guard, nor as a facility supervisor. To achieve full impact, he needed to be in the field.

Then again, Colonel Harrington stressed that Schmidt was no longer the same man he had been. That he had *ceased to exist* after the incident at Taif. Those were Harrington's exact words. Schmidt *ceased to exist*. Like Schmidt had died with everyone else in the incident. As if he was unable to shoulder the pain and loss of the tragedy and had simply given up. Jones had seen many soldiers who could no longer handle the pressures of war, who could no longer bounce back from their emotional scars and remain on active duty. But he had never heard it described in Harrington's terms. His friend *ceased to exist*.

A loud ding echoed throughout the cave, a sound that snapped Jones back to reality. He glanced at Sheldon, who told him not to worry. The sound meant that Sheldon had received a classified e-mail. Probably the test results he'd been waiting for. Jones wasn't sure if he was allowed to see them, but there was no way he was going to miss this opportunity. He followed Sheldon into the next room, hovering over his shoulder, hoping to catch a glimpse of the e-mail. But his persistence wasn't necessary. After Sheldon had scanned the report, checking and double-checking the information, he passed it to Jones. No fanfare. No explanation. No games of any kind. He knew Jones was smart enough to figure things out, so he simply handed it to him.

Unfortunately, the news was worse than Jones had expected. A lot worse.

Payne made sure he heard the term correctly. 'The Altar of Blood?'

The old man nodded, refusing to look at him, focusing on Kia instead. 'No matter who was taken there, they always screamed to their gods, begging to be saved from the pain they endured. Sometimes this went on for days. Sometimes weeks. But their prayers were *never* answered. Their blood was *always* spilled.'

The old man trembled, remembering the time he had spent in the cave and all the family he'd lost. Kia tried to soothe him, touching his shoulder, whispering words of encouragement in Korean before she asked him another question. 'And the Altar was recently reborn?'

'Our village was quiet for many years. But a few months ago the spirits were reawakened. The screams started again at night, in a language I've never heard. An ancient language. Something barbaric. Like the Devil speaking in tongues.' He glanced towards Payne, still refusing to look him in the eye but making sure he heard every angry word. 'But the Devil didn't come here alone. *Your* people brought him here. *Your* people lost control. Yet *my* people were the ones who suffered . . . Why does my village *always* suffer?'

Payne wanted to tell him that he had nothing to do with this, that he'd come to this island to help his people and his village, but the old man wouldn't have listened. There was too much anger, too much history for Payne to overcome. At least with words. The only way to make a real difference was to find out what had happened and close the cave for ever.

Thankfully, Kia continued to ask the right questions, proving to be a valuable asset. 'Speaking of your village, where is everyone?'

'They're out back.'

Without saying another word, the old man stood and walked out of his side garden, stepping carefully on flat stones that had been laid in the ground. Kia followed closely behind, while Payne brought up the rear. He walked with his weapon drawn, eyes scanning the terrain, ready for the unexpected. Pruned trees and shrubs filled the landscape, everything perfectly manicured, as if the old man spent all his time doing nothing else. During the summer months, the flowers would have been in bloom, a rainbow of colours bursting in every corner of the yard. But this time of year everything looked dreary, as if a curtain of gloom had been dropped on the entire village. The sky was grey. The mood was dark.

Originally Payne had assumed the stench of burning pine had come from the old man's chimney, which continued to belch a steady stream of smoke, but as they rounded the corner of the house, he noticed the actual source. A giant fire pit had been constructed in the middle of the backyard. Volcanic rocks lined the exterior, stacked three feet high and fifteen feet across. Wooden embers smouldered on the inside, casting no flames but burning intensely like a furnace. No sparks. No light. Just a lot of heat. The type of fire that was used to cook meat.

An ancient wheelbarrow, covered in rust, sat abandoned in the yard, next to an axe, a pick, and a variety of cutting tools. All of them splattered with the same hue. The same rust colour as the wheelbarrow. In a flash, Payne sensed what had happened. What the old man had done.

'Where are your neighbours?' Kia wondered. 'I thought they were back here.'

The old man nodded, his eyes filling with tears as he stared into the fire. 'They are.'

17

In ancient times, bodies of the dead were often burned en masse to prevent the spread of disease, a common act during times of war when blood-soaked battlefields were sometimes littered with thousands of victims, soldiers so brutalized that identification was next to impossible. The clean-up process was so essential that some generals actually called a truce with their enemies after a major battle, giving both sides enough time to properly dispose of the corpses before their war reignited and more soldiers were slain.

While a student at the Naval Academy, Payne had read grisly accounts of the disposal process perfected by the empires of yesteryear, and prayed he would never see it in person. Yet here he was on Jeju, a tiny island in the middle of nowhere, and he was forced to stare at the ashes. Maybe forced to sift through them to figure out why this crazy old bastard had loaded the bodies of his neighbours on to a wheelbarrow and burned them in his backyard.

For all Payne knew, he might have done the same thing with the victims from the cave. That would certainly explain where everyone went. Why they suddenly disappeared.

Of course, that wouldn't explain who killed them

or why. But one thing at a time. He would worry about those details later. For now, he had to get this guy talking.

Payne's thoughts were interrupted by the vibration of his cell phone. He glanced at the caller ID and saw *David Jones*. Their phones had been designed with a special encryption chip, so they could talk without concern. No hijacked signals. No security leaks. As safe as whispering.

Payne clicked *send*. 'We need to meet.'

Jones agreed, his voice sombre. 'Where are you?'

'In the village.'

'There's a *village*?'

Payne laughed. He'd said the exact same thing to the sniper who'd led him here. He gave Jones directions, then added, 'When you come, bring some back-up. I've got a major situation.'

He nodded. 'That makes two of us.'

Twenty minutes passed before Jones arrived at the old man's gate. He led a split squad – both security and forensics – in a convoy of SUVs. Payne didn't recognize any of the men, which led him to believe that there was a full platoon stationed nearby, hiding somewhere in the woods. Waiting for something to happen. For a mission that was supposedly black, there were a lot of potential leaks. Too many, as far as he was concerned.

Jones climbed out of the lead SUV, leaving the rest of the soldiers behind. None of them moved.

They just sat there. Patiently. Awaiting further instructions.

'Who are your friends?' Payne asked. 'They're very well behaved.'

Jones didn't answer. Instead, he grabbed Payne by the elbow and turned his back to the men. Just in case one of them could read lips. 'Things have changed.'

'No shit . . . How bad is it?'

'Very. But you go first. How should we deploy?'

Payne explained the basic layout of the village and where he needed troops. Mostly on the periphery. Far from the evidence in the backyard. At least until he got a better handle on things. As for forensics, they'd have to wait until the area was secure.

Jones jogged to the lead SUV and gave them instructions. In an instant, the team sprang to life. Men hustled from the vehicles, scattering to the four corners of the town. Seconds later, they couldn't be seen. Blending perfectly with the landscape. Payne watched their movements from a distance, impressed by their efficiency. Either they were elite soldiers, who adapted on the run, or they'd been here before and knew exactly where to go. Both possibilities raised intriguing questions. Things he'd discuss with Jones at a later time.

But first there were other issues to resolve.

'Your turn,' he said to Jones. 'What's changed?'

'The parameters of our mission. I just got word from forensics. About Trevor.'

Payne nodded, realizing what that meant. Deep down inside, he'd hoped Schmidt was still alive, but he sensed that wasn't the case the moment he saw all the blood. There was simply too much of it. But now things were official. His former student was dead. Killed by unknown forces for unknown reasons. Which meant this was no longer a rescue mission. It was something far worse. A homicide investigation.

Jones continued. 'Schmidt's team, including himself, consisted of four men whose DNA was on file with Colonel Harrington. Forensic testing proved it was their blood. And they found so much of it, there's no way any of them could've survived.'

'Anything else?'

'They found three additional samples. Strike that. Three *recent* ones but no names. And not in the main cave but in one of the back chambers. That's where the prisoners were kept.'

'So Sheldon admitted it was a prison?'

Jones nodded. 'If you think about it, it makes sense. It's far from America but close to North Korea, which is our biggest nuclear threat. This location gave us deniability *and* a lot of freedom when it comes to persuasion. No one was looking over their shoulders.'

'And what was Schmidt's role?'

'Sheldon claims he was running it.'

'The mission or the torture?'

He shrugged. 'Maybe both.'

Payne winced at the news, instantly thinking back

to the years he'd spent with Schmidt, all the training, all the missions, and wondering where he'd gone wrong. *If* he'd gone wrong. The life of a Special Forces soldier was a complex one, an equal mix of aggression and discipline, humanity and brutality, always searching for a peaceful solution in an ultra-violent world. Balance was difficult to maintain, nearly impossible, which was one of the reasons why Payne was glad he had got out when he did. While he still had a sense of honour. While he still had control.

But some soldiers weren't nearly as fortunate. Sometimes tragedies occurred that pushed them too far over the edge, causing them to lose track of their humanity. Their morality. Their ability to tell the difference between right and wrong. And when that happened, the military usually did one of two things. Either they counselled them on their behaviour, hoping to cure it. Or they gave them a change of duty, hoping to exploit it.

And *that's* what happened to Trevor Schmidt.

The incident changed his life. And the military took full advantage.

According to Colonel Harrington, Schmidt had acted heroically during a mission gone wrong. Bad intel caused his squad to be dropped in the middle of occupied ground, surrounded by the enemy, yet Schmidt led his men to safety without any fatalities. Many injured, but none dead. A modern-day miracle. They were airlifted to Taif Air Base in Saudi Arabia, where they were treated at Al-Hada Hospital, a Saudi facility that catered to Westerners. To boost morale, families were flown in from the States to the Al-Gaim Compound, where they were allowed to stay while their loved ones recovered. Anything, Schmidt had argued, to help his men get better.

On the day of the incident, he had loaded up a shuttle bus with all the family members – wives, parents, girlfriends, even a couple of kids – and driven them to the hospital. His men were quartered in a separate wing, one that offered privacy from the regular patients, allowing them to talk freely about their missions without being overheard. Security was posted outside their doors, and every time the shift changed, the new guards swept the wing for listening devices. Far from perfect, but it would have to do until his men were healthy enough to be transported home.

Schmidt parked in a secured lot and herded everyone towards the front entrance, where they were greeted by another member of his squad, one of the uninjured ones, who led them into the building, through metal detectors, and past security. Schmidt made sure each of his men was doing well before he got back on the shuttle bus and drove to Taif, where he had a meeting to discuss what the hell went wrong with his last mission and whose head was going to roll. Someone had to pay for the fuck-up that nearly killed his squad. He'd make sure of it.

Unfortunately, the meeting lasted less than three

minutes. Schmidt barely had time to open his mouth when the conference room started to rumble. The floor began to shake. The walls began to quiver. Thunder ripped across the sunny sky. Everyone in the room was a seasoned veteran, so all of them knew what had happened. There had been an explosion. An attack of some kind. The only questions were where and why.

The amazing thing about war is that there can be silence in the middle of so much noise. Phones started ringing and people started shouting, a cacophony of sounds that rose above the distant rumble of a building collapsing to the ground, but Schmidt heard none of it. Not a single sound after the initial blast. As if his brain had hit the mute button.

Just like that, something inside him clicked.

Chaos swirled around him as he walked down the corridor. Alarms going off. Soldiers running everywhere. The anger from a moment before had been replaced with a temporary numbness, a stark realization that his current life would be over the instant he walked outside and saw what had been destroyed by the blast. How many squad members had been killed.

He paused at the door, his hand resting on the latch, trying to soak in his last few seconds of hope before he was overwhelmed by a thirst for revenge that wouldn't be quenched until he had punished every last person who was responsible for this tragedy.

Until he squeezed the life out of all of them.

Finally, as if accepting his own fate, Schmidt took one last breath, then stepped into the brutal heat of the Saudi sun, where he stared at the hospital burning in the distance.

The flames igniting his rage within.

18

Kia sat next to the old man, no longer fearing him. His name was Dong-Min Kim. After she explained who she was and why she was there, he apologized several times for attacking her with a pitchfork. She brushed it off like it was the type of thing that happened every day, but Kim knew better. He wasn't the least bit delusional, as she had first feared. He was actually clear-headed and caring. The stereotypical village elder.

The two of them talked in Korean, keeping the subject matter light. Nothing about the fire pit, the cave, or what had happened during the past week. Those were topics she wanted to save for Payne and Jones. Instead, she talked about her childhood on the army base near Seoul, explaining how blessed she was to have been exposed to so many cultures at such an early age and how it gave her a head start in her current career. By the age of ten, she could speak four languages.

Kim was impressed by her accomplishments, especially her world travels. In all his life, he had never left the island of Jeju. Not even to go fishing. As a young boy he had nearly drowned while learning to swim, and after that he had an intense fear of the sea, which prevented him from going anywhere. No boats. No planes. No travelling of any kind. Instead he pored over books, learning the ways of the world from the comfort of his own home. Unfortunately, that was the main reason why he was so outraged by the presence of the cave. He rarely strayed from his village, yet the dangers of the world kept finding him there.

With a wave of his hand, Payne caught Kia's attention. She excused herself from Kim and walked into the backyard, where Payne and Jones were waiting by the fire pit, the smell of smoke still filling the air.

'Is he lucid?' Payne asked.

Kia nodded. 'Very. He knows exactly what's going on.'

'Good. We're hoping he can tell us what happened. Any advice on how to approach him?'

'Sir?'

'Will he be receptive to *my* questions, or should *you* continue to conduct the interview?'

'Honestly, sir, I think it would be best if I handled it. He doesn't trust Americans. And I think he'd be more comfortable speaking in Korean.'

Payne nodded, agreeing with everything she'd said. Unfortunately, he didn't have time to fill her in on the latest news about Trevor Schmidt, so he gave her a short list of questions that he and Jones had composed and asked her to look them over. Thirty seconds later she had them committed to memory. It was one of her strengths.

'Try to keep things conversational,' he suggested as he tossed the list into the fire and watched it burn. 'Use your rapport to open him up. Then, and only then, ask him the important stuff. We need some honest answers from him. No time for bullshit. Remember, the longer he thinks about a response, the less likely he'll tell the truth.'

Kia nodded, then returned to Kim, who gave her a warm smile as she approached. Except for his long ponytail, he looked like her maternal grandfather, a man who'd died long before she was born. Otherwise, Kia's mother wouldn't have been allowed to marry an American.

'Sorry about that,' she said in Korean. 'My bosses were asking about you.'

'And what did you tell them?'

'I told them you weren't a flight risk.'

Kim laughed. 'That much is true. If I didn't leave for this . . .' His voice trailed off.

'About that,' she said, ignoring Payne's advice to take it slow. 'Can you tell me what happened here? None of it makes any sense to me. The cave. The empty village. The fire.'

'In the past we always left the soldiers alone and they left us alone. It was a mutual understanding, one that has gone on for decades. But this time, fate intervened.'

She said nothing, hoping he would fill in the blanks.

'A few weeks ago, a village boy named Yong-Su

came to me and asked about the screams from the cave. I told him about its past, hoping to scare the curiosity out of him. But my efforts failed. Last weekend he went to the cave on his own.'

'What did he see?'

'I'm not sure,' he admitted. 'But when he returned, he was covered in blood.'

'*His* blood?'

'Someone else's.'

Kia paused, memories of the cave flooding through her mind. Ten seconds were more than enough to make her nauseous. She couldn't imagine what Yong-Su must have felt when he walked into the cave, completely alone, no one there to protect him. It had to be traumatic.

Kim seemed to read her mind. 'The boy came back unable to speak. His mother was crying, simply terrified, unsure of what to do. She cleaned him off and searched for injuries, but found none. Meanwhile the boy's father, an honourable man named Chung-Ho Park, ran from house to house, asking if anyone had seen what had happened. It didn't take long to figure it out. The boy had left a trail of blood every-where he walked. We were able to follow it to the edge of the village and into the woods. Drip . . . drip . . . drip.'

The sound of his voice and the look on his face told Kia that his emotions were starting to resurface. To keep him calm, she put her hand on his shoulder and rubbed it gently. Trying to comfort him. Hoping to keep him focused. Still, several seconds passed before he spoke again.

'I'm an old man with a long memory. I know what kind of evil goes on in that cave, so I told Chung-Ho that the village was no longer safe for him and his son. Much to my relief, he didn't question me. He just put his boy in their car and left. His wife and the rest of his family planned on following, but they never had a chance.'

'Why not?'

'The soldiers came into town in waves, dressed in black and wearing masks. Some of them followed the blood to the boy's home, while others spread throughout the village. I heard angry voices punctuated by screams, but that's all I could distinguish. I was too worried about finding a place to hide to make out their words.'

Kia sat quietly, waiting for him to continue.

'The first shot was the loudest. It sounded like a cannon, echoing through the town. Others soon followed, one after the other, coming in sporadic bursts like firecrackers. My house is the last one in the village, which gave me all the time I needed. After the first massacre, I'd built a small shelter under the floor of my house, just in case history repeated itself. I stayed down there for more than four days, barely eating or sleeping. Going to the bathroom in my own trousers. When I could take it no more, I slipped into my backyard and listened. There were no sounds. I glanced out my front gate, but there were no movements. That's when I knew they were gone.'

'Did you call the police?'

He waved his hands in disgust. 'The police? Why would I call the police? They were in charge of the first massacre! To this day, half of my family is still somewhere in that cave, their bodies crammed behind a pile of rocks and left there to rot. It is such a disgrace to my family name, but there's nothing I can do about it. Believe me, I've tried.'

He took a deep breath before continuing. 'Did you know the size of a grave plot in this country is larger than the average amount of living space that our citizens have? That's right. The dead take up more room than the living. And the cost of all their burials? It would have been more than I could afford.'

She nodded, finally beginning to understand his perspective.

'So I took matters into my own hands. First I went into the boy's house, but everyone was dead. His mother, his brother and sister, his aunt, his cousins. Everyone. Same with the rest of the village. Every single person had been shot and killed. Bodies just lying there in puddles of their own blood, the smell starting to build. So I walked back to my yard and built a fire. I threw in some pine needles and incense to cover the odour. Then one by one I loaded them into my wheelbarrow and did the proper thing. I freed their souls to the sky.'

19

Ape found Fred Nasir's body near the tunnel entrance. His throat was slashed and he'd been left to die. Blood covered the wooden planks that lined the floor, dried by the desert heat that seeped in from the outside world.

From the looks of things, he'd been dead at least an hour.

Panicked, Ape sprinted down the steep slope, unlocked the metal gate that protected their site, and told Shari what had happened. Her face went pale when she heard the news. As project leader, it was her job to make all of the important decisions – what they did, where they worked, and so on – and to take responsibility when things went wrong. And until then, she had accomplished it with remarkable ease. She had fifteen years' experience in the field and was recruited for her expertise. She was so gifted at her job that the project financier, the Arab who had hired her, was willing to overlook the fact that she was a woman – a remarkable concession in this part of the world.

But murder? That was *way* beyond anything she was prepared to handle.

She was an archaeologist, not a detective.

Obviously this was a situation she couldn't handle on her own, not with all the politics involved. So she did the one thing she was told to do if there was ever a major problem. She called her boss, Omar Abdul-Khaliq.

He answered the phone on the third ring, his voice as composed as ever. 'What is wrong?' he asked.

She explained everything – the delivery, the murder, her concerns. The entire time he said nothing. He just listened, occasionally taking notes.

'This is troubling indeed.' He paused for a moment. 'But it can be handled.'

'Handled how?'

'You must listen to me and do exactly what I say.'

She knew not to question him. So far he had proven his worth at every turn. Not only did he finance the project with his deep pockets, money his family had earned in the oil business, but he had done a remarkable job of getting work permits from the Saudi government, a minor miracle since they were digging right down the street from the Great Mosque, and keeping the police away. Several times she had wanted to ask him how that was possible, but she realized it was one of those questions better left unasked.

'Have you touched the body?'

'No! We checked to see if he was dead, but other than that we haven't touched anything.'

'Good. This is good. You must not touch the body. Leave it as it is.'

She grimaced. 'For how long?'

'It will be removed today.'

'But –'

His voice grew stern. 'Please allow me to finish.'

She nodded, regretting her mistake.

'I will send a new team of guards, men more equipped to handle this crisis. They will remain at the site, night and day. You shall brief them when they arrive. They'll need to see everything.'

'Of course.'

'Activity around the mosque will only increase as pilgrims arrive. The old city will be crowded, filled with millions of witnesses.' Abdul-Khaliq paused, thinking things through. 'Until the hajj is over, all work should be stopped at the site. No workers, no digging, no attention. No one but the guards to protect our work . . . Do you not agree?'

She answered carefully, realizing it was a loaded question. 'Whatever you think is best.'

'Besides, you and your team deserve some time off – a reward for all your efforts. It will help you forget this tragedy . . . Mecca is a historic city, one you've barely seen. Use your time wisely. Roam the streets, observe the celebration. It is one to behold.'

Shari was quite familiar with the hajj and its customs. While preparing for her dig, she had read several first-hand accounts, tales of tragedy and triumph, loss and salvation, written by men and women whose lives were changed by their journey. Deep inside she knew she would never participate as a pilgrim – she was a non-practising half-Muslim – but as an academic, she realized her observations would be invaluable.

Maybe he was right. Maybe this was the best thing to do.

Considering the circumstances, it was certainly the safest.

'Before we conclude,' he said, 'there is one more item to be discussed.'

'Which is?'

'The delivery of my package. Did it arrive safely?'

She held the sealed envelope in her hand. 'Yes. I have it right here.'

'Good. That is good.' He paused briefly. 'Is it unopened?'

'It seems to be.'

'Excellent!'

She was dying to find out what was inside, especially since the man who'd delivered it was dead in her tunnel. Still, she knew not to ask too much. 'What should I do with it?'

'Hold it at all times. One of these days, it will come in handy. You shall see.'

The guards showed up sooner than expected, less than an hour after she'd called Abdul-Khaliq. They were highly trained and highly unsociable. Only one of them spoke to Shari, and even then it was to tell her to stay out of their way.

Their first order of business was the body. One of the men went through Nasir's pockets, finding the keys to the Toyota Camry, while another man backed a van as close to the tunnel entrance as possible, until his rear bumper nearly hit the chain-link fence that protected it. They unloaded an Arabic rug that had been purchased at a nearby bazaar and unrolled it next to Nasir. Two of the men moved him to the edge of the rug, then rolled him up inside like a burrito.

Seconds later, the body was in the back of the van.

The bloodstain was even less of a challenge. Since most of the blood had dried on the wooden planks that lined the floor, they simply lifted the boards and replaced them with fresh ones from the building supplies that filled the vacant lot outside. Two men tossed the stained wood on to the rolled-up rug, closed the van door, and sped away.

The whole process took less than five minutes.

'Anything else I should know?' asked the lead guard.

Shari shook her head, stunned at their efficiency.

'In that case, please take me below.'

She led him underground, giving him a brief tour along the way. 'Most of this digging was done before I even arrived at the site. They were laying water pipes for the Abraj Al Bait Towers Complex up the street when the discovery was made. That complex is so humongous they had to build their own pumping station just to handle the demand.'

She pointed out where the tunnel branched. 'The water pipes go that way towards the Complex, but our site is back here. We only had to dig this small stretch. It was rather simple.'

He listened to every word, studying the layout. Searching for weaknesses.

'Just about the only water in the old city is the spring that feeds the Zamzam Well in the Great Mosque. Have you heard of it?'

According to Islamic tradition, Hagar, the wife of Abraham and the mother of Ishmael, was desperately seeking water for her son in the scorching heat of the valley. She ran back and forth seven times between the hills of Safa and Marwah, searching for water. God sent the angel Gabriel, who scraped the ground with his heel, causing a spring to bubble forth from the sand. When she found it, she collected the water in a tiny pool reinforced by small stones.

Pilgrims still honoured her during the hajj, walking between Safa and Marwah seven times. They also drank from the Zamzam Well, water that many Muslims believe to be blessed.

'Some people actually bottle that water during their pilgrimage and sell it on the Internet. You wouldn't believe how much money it costs.'

Her keys jingled in the tunnel like a bell as she unlocked the gate that protected their discovery. She started putting them away when he grabbed her hand.

'You'd better leave those with me.'

Angry, she yanked her arm away. 'You'll get a copy when I leave. Not a moment before.'

He stared at her with unblinking eyes. Annoyance filled his face. A look that said he was accustomed to getting his way, especially with women.

Suddenly, Shari realized she was alone with this guy. Several metres underground. With nowhere to run or hide. The thought was unnerving, even to a courageous woman like herself. An old Middle Eastern proverb flashed through her mind, one that explained her status in their society. *Women belong in the house or the grave.*

She gripped her keys a little tighter, just in case she had to use them as a weapon.

'What's up ahead?' he asked, not showing any remorse.

'The main site.'

'You'd better show me. After all, that's what I'm here to protect.'

20

From a distance Payne and Jones watched the conversation between Kia and Kim. Far enough to give them space but close enough to intervene. Violently, if necessary.

'You're sure she can handle this?' Jones wondered.

'She was doing great *before* you showed up. Let's hope your lips don't distract her.'

Jones ignored the joke about his initial encounter with Kia. 'Good. Then let's talk about our mission. We were brought in to rescue Schmidt, even though one glance in that cave proved he was dead several days ago. Colonel Harrington must've known that long before he talked to us in Pittsburgh. So the question remains. Why were we brought in?'

'My guess is revenge. Cold-blooded revenge.'

'You think?'

'Why else was this village unsecured? The moment that cave was discovered they should've sent men here to look for hostiles. And within minutes he would've known about the slaughter. But guess what? He wanted *us* to find it. Otherwise this place would've been swarming with forensic teams long ago. But he assumed our discovery would fuel our rage, making us even more motivated. First Schmidt, then this. He wants us to do his dirty work.'

Jones considered the facts, trying to decide if Payne was right.

'And all that bullshit at the cave? Making us tour the scene but refusing to tell us anything? Nothing but theatrics. And Dr Sheldon? Not only did he lead us on, but he was smiling the entire time. Like he was having fun.'

'So you don't trust him?'

'I don't trust him at all. In fact, I snapped his picture before I left the cave and sent it to Randy Raskin. No telling what we'll get on him.'

Jones nodded, glad to see that Payne was thinking clearly. 'Have you heard back from him?'

'Not yet. But when I do, I've got several questions.'

'Such as?'

'Who were Schmidt's prisoners? They might have something to do with why we're here. Maybe they're people we've dealt with before. Who knows? Maybe Harrington didn't give a rat's ass about Schmidt. Maybe he cares about the prisoners.'

'You know, that's a possibility.'

Payne smiled. 'Just because you're smarter than I am doesn't mean that I'm dumb.'

'Well, let's talk about *that* some other time. In the meantime, let me ask you something. How do you want to proceed?'

'In regard to what?'

Jones lowered his voice. 'In regard to Harrington. I say we keep digging but don't tell him anything until we get some answers of our own.'

Kia finished her conversation with Kim, and then watched as he was escorted inside, where an armed guard watched over him. Even though she trusted Kim, Payne and Jones did not. And it would stay that way until they found out what had happened in the village.

She filled them in on everything – from the appearance of the young boy to the burning of the bodies in the fire pit – before they started asking questions.

Jones began. 'Did he take anyone from the cave?'

'No way. He's scared to death of that place. Too many bad memories. Plus, I don't think he's strong enough to push a wheelbarrow up that hill. And even if he could, there's no way he would've risked it. For all he knew, the soldiers were still up there. Besides, he was concerned about his neighbours, no one else.'

'Speaking of which,' Payne asked, 'any theories on the boy and his father?'

'He thinks they left the village but probably not the island.'

'Why's that?'

'First of all, he warned them about being spotted at the airport or any of the major docks. Kim is highly paranoid about all authority, so he stressed how important it was to avoid departure points. Second, he feels confident that Chung-Ho wouldn't abandon his family. Odds are they were going to rendezvous somewhere close so they could decide what to do next. The only reason he took his boy was because Kim told him to, but he wasn't going to leave the rest of his family behind.'

'So Kim talked to them?' Jones asked.

'The father, yes. The boy, no. Yong-Su was pretty incoherent, just mumbling something over and over about the black stone. In fact, that's all he said the entire time.'

Payne frowned. 'The black stone? What the hell is that?'

Jones glanced at him and shrugged. He was unfamiliar with the term. 'Maybe he was talking about the interior of the cave? There's nothing but volcanic rock in there.'

Payne nodded, no other theories in mind. 'Did the father say anything to Kim?'

'Not really. He went to Kim for advice, not the other way around.'

'And what was the advice? To leave ASAP?'

'Yes,' she said. 'And considering what happened next, it proved to be wise.'

The vibration of Payne's phone broke his concentration. The caller ID said *Randy Raskin*, so he stepped away to answer it while Jones continued to debrief Kia.

'Randy,' he said, 'how you been?'

'Overworked. People like you are *always* calling in favours.'

'Those selfish bastards. Do you want me to take care of them?'

Raskin laughed. As a computer researcher at the Pentagon, he was privy to many of the government's top secrets, a mountain of classified data that was just there for the taking if the right person knew how to access it. His job was to make sure the latest information got into the best hands at the most appropriate time. Over the years, Jones had used his services on many occasions. Eventually Raskin fostered a friendship with Payne, too, and realized he probably could eliminate anyone he wanted. Of course, that made Payne's comment even funnier.

'Is suicide out of the question? Because *you* seem to bother me more than anyone.'

'Sorry, pal, it ain't gonna happen. I know I'm going to hell someday. No need to buy an early ticket.'

'In that case, let's talk about your message.' Raskin stared at the photo on his computer screen, toying with the brightness and contrast of the image until he saw a man wearing a surgical mask standing in some sort of underground lair. 'What do you want to know?'

'Anything you can tell me. Background, speciality, whatever. My guess is he isn't who he says he is.'

Raskin hit a few keys and pulled up the personnel records on Dr Ernie Sheldon. No photo was included with the file, but it didn't take a computer genius to tell there was a discrepancy. 'Score one for you, big guy. I just spotted a critical fact that's pretty important.'

'What's that?'

'Dr Sheldon is dead. Has been for three years.'

Payne nodded, all kinds of theories floating through his head. 'Yep, I'd say that's important.'

'That's why they pay me the big bucks. I point out the obvious.'

'What about the non-obvious?'

'Such as?'

'Prisoners in black-op facilities.'

Raskin grunted. '*That* might take me a while. I'll have to check your clearance on that one.'

'You're not serious.'

'I'm dead serious. That's one of our extra-special secrets. So you might not qualify. Unless, of course, you have a permission slip signed by the right person.'

Now it was Payne's turn to grunt. Mentioning Colonel Harrington's name was bound to get him the answer he needed. Unfortunately, it would also tip off Harrington to their current line of pursuit, which was something he wanted to avoid. 'Let me get back to you on that.'

Raskin nodded, reading between the lines. 'Anything else? Or are you done using me?'

'Just one more thing, then I'll let you go. Do you have any information on something called the black stone?'

He punched in the term and scanned the results. Hundreds of possibilities. 'What part of the world are you calling from? Or is that classified?'

'South Korea.'

More typing, followed by a pronounced sigh. 'Dude, you didn't tell me you were on vacation. Why didn't you invite me? You never take me anywhere.'

'What are you talking about?'

'You're in Jeju, right?'

Payne raised his eyebrows, intrigued by the question. 'How did you know that?'

'Don't play dumb with me.'

'I swear, Randy, I'm not. I have no idea what you're talking about.'

Raskin sighed again. 'If you're lying to me, you know I'll find out. I can check your credit card statements with a touch of a button. I can cancel them, too. I don't care *how* rich you are, I can mess with your credit. You won't even be able to buy a Twinkie at Seven-Eleven if —'

'Randy, I *swear* I'm not lying. I'm on company business here. Honest!'

'Fine,' he said with a grunt, still not believing him. He wrote himself a note to make sure. 'On the west coast of Jeju, there's a brand-new world-class golf resort. I hear it's amazing. The PGA even had a tour event there.'

'So? What does that have to do with anything?'

'It's called the Black Stone.'

21

Route 12 is a scenic beltway that encircles Jeju Island. Meandering along the 157 miles of rocky coastline, it provides some of the most breathtaking views in all of Asia. The SUV, borrowed from the military and driven by Jones, hummed along at 40 miles an hour, just under the legal limit. Payne rode shotgun, staring out the window, while Kia sat in the back seat, stressing how important it was to drive slowly because of all the surveillance cameras on Jeju. Tourists and speeding tickets were two ways the local government made its money.

An hour earlier, Payne would have laughed at the mention of tourists. Back then he was standing in the middle of a dreary village, surrounded by grey skies, bare trees, and the omnipresent odour of death, pondering what to do and where to go next. The concept of tourism would have seemed ridiculous to anyone but the most morbid of Stephen King fans.

Suddenly things were different, almost like night and day. Thanks to a tip from Randy Raskin, they were driving towards the Black Stone resort, passing palm trees, tropical beaches, and the type of architecture that can only be found in the Far East. A perfect example was the Jeju World Cup Stadium, which was designed to look like an *oreum* – a parasitic volcanic cone topped by a large crater that was unique to this island. Adding to its grandeur, the stadium was half-covered with a *teu*-shaped roof that symbolized the traditional fishing boats in the region. To Payne, the roof looked like a giant white sail, pulled tight by a strong gust of wind, anchored down by diagonal metal poles and thick white cables that contributed to the visual effect, as if the entire stadium were slowly being pulled across the terrain and into the nearby sea.

Minutes later they were stopping at Cheonjaeyeon Falls. Flanked by a thick forest of trees, three waterfalls cascaded from one pond to the next until the water reached the ocean below. Legend claimed that the falls were named after seven nymphs who descended from the heavens to play in the crystal-clear water. They were still honoured at the site, their images carved into Sonimkyo, a large bridge that arches across the pine-strewn valley, passing near a small pavilion that overlooks the main pond.

After parking the SUV, Jones dropped to his knees and glanced under the dirty frame, checking for tracking devices. He found one near the front left wheel and quickly prised it off. He handed it to Payne, who attached it to a nearby tour bus that was filled with a group of singing Germans, who either didn't notice him or were having too much fun to care. Jones kept searching, eventually finding a second device, stuffed under the base of the dashboard. This one was used for listening, not tracking. The military's way of keeping tabs on their investigation. Payne took it as well, this time pitching it into a nearby ravine.

'For the time being, let's assume we're still not clean,' Jones said as he walked over to the guard rail. 'If we need to talk, we should do it away from the car.'

Kia nodded, realizing the comment was for her benefit. 'Since we're outside, does that mean I can ask a question? Because I'm really curious about something.'

'Go on.'

'What are we hoping to find at Black Stone?'

Both Payne and Jones shrugged, neither of them prepared to answer.

Kia translated their body language. 'In other words, you have no idea.'

'Nope,' Jones said.

'None at all,' said Payne with a laugh.

A cold gust of wind blew through the valley, gently tossing Kia's hair across her face. Although she had grown up in South Korea, she was accustomed to the warm temperatures of the Marshall Islands, not the cold gusts of winter. Shivering slightly, she leaned closer to Payne, trying to absorb his warmth. If he noticed, he said nothing. He just stood there, staring out over the falls, watching the water surge over the rocks and splash into the pond below.

It was a tranquil moment in an otherwise horrendous day.

One they hoped would improve as time went on.

The phone call came from America. Within seconds, the signal was transmitted halfway around the world, where it was received by a hotel employee at the Black Stone resort. She double-checked the client's name and financial status before transferring the call to the appropriate extension. In an instant, the phone started ringing in Mr Lee's office.

He answered the call in English, his voice warm and welcoming, an equal mix of personality and professionalism. He wrote all the details in Hangul, the Korean alphabet. Spaces between words. Western punctuation. Rows from left to right, not columns from top to bottom, as in yesteryear. The traditional style of his language had slowly become Americanized. Not that he was complaining. He always had an affinity for the Western world, which was the main reason he took this job. It gave him a chance to meet the best and the brightest, to network with power brokers, to make contacts for the future.

Technically, this was the off-season at his resort. The winter temperatures made golfing unpleasant, the grounds less scenic. Sailing was downright brutal because of the rough waves and stinging spray. When the flowers were in bloom, honeymooners from all over Asia would descend on his island like locusts.

Horny, lovemaking locusts. They often stopped by his resort for spa treatments or fancy meals, rarely staying overnight because of the expense. This was a place that catered to the wealthy. People who didn't blink when they got their bill.

And on those occasions when the ultra rich were in town, Mr Lee got a call.

The SUV pulled up to the main hotel, which looked more like a Scottish fortress than a Korean resort. Thick pillars supported a large overhang that sheltered arriving guests from inclement weather. Beige stones, cut with laser precision, made up the bulk of the exterior, occasionally giving way to arched windows that soared towards the stone banisters on the second floor.

'Nice place,' Jones said as he parked the car. 'Maybe too nice.'

Payne was about to agree with him. He was about to say there was no way that the father and son from the village could ever afford this place. That this was a waste of their time. That they'd be better off pursuing other leads instead of going inside and looking like fools. But before he could open his mouth, the resort staff, wearing tailored uniforms and crisp white gloves, swarmed around their SUV. Smiles were plastered on their faces, as if the king of Korea had just decided to pay them a visit. Everyone was bowing and paying respect. It was borderline creepy.

The passenger-side door was opened with a flourish, a young man mumbling greetings in Korean while giving a theatrical bow. The same was done with the back door, only this time a gloved hand was proffered to Kia, who grabbed it and stepped out of the car. She smiled, bemused by the pageantry of it all. A third man reached for the driver-side door, but Jones glared at him and opened it himself. Strangely, this made the staff smile even wider, for they interpreted it to mean that Jones was treating them as equals, not as servants.

Payne stepped out last, suddenly cognizant of his casual clothes, which reeked of smoke and blood. Not to mention their dirt-splattered vehicle. None of that would have mattered at an out-of-the-way hotel. But here it was sure to be frowned on.

His concerns disappeared a moment later, when Mr Lee strode out of the hotel. He wore a tailored Italian suit, freshly polished shoes, and a grin the size of his head. Jet-black hair framed his boyish face, although he was probably in his mid-thirties. He stood a foot shorter than Payne, but that didn't prevent him from staring directly into Payne's eyes with a confident gaze, the look of a man who was used to dealing with the rich and famous. Someone who wasn't intimidated by it.

With a slight bow, he handed Payne his business card and welcomed him to the Black Stone resort. Payne smiled at the card's simplicity. It said *Mr Lee* and listed his cell phone number.

'It's a pleasure to meet you, Mr Lee. I'd give you one of my cards, but I'm fresh out.'

Lee nodded at the gesture. 'It's not necessary, Mr Payne. We've been expecting you.'

22

The lobby glistened under the recessed lights; the black and gold pattern of the stone floor appeared three-dimensional due to a fresh coat of wax, giving it the illusion of depth. A circular atrium soared above the centre lobby, interspersed with decorative black railings fifteen feet above the main desk. Several guests waited in line, but Mr Lee ignored them all. The only people he cared about had just arrived. Jonathon Payne, party of three.

'I like the colour scheme,' Payne said, trying to make small talk. Despite his large inheritance, he wasn't comfortable with the trappings of wealth. He was more of a beer and burger guy than wine and caviar.

Mr Lee nodded appreciation. 'Did you know Hines Ward is South Korean? When he won Super Bowl MVP, we redecorated the lobby in Pittsburgh Steelers colours. We were very proud.'

Payne glanced at Jones, who stared back, both of them stunned by the statement.

Eventually Mr Lee started to laugh. 'I am just joking. The colours never changed. They have always been black and gold. I make joke since you are a Pittsburgh fan.'

Payne laughed at his own gullibility. 'How did you know that?'

'Because Mr Lee knows all.'

'Glad to hear it, Mr Lee. Because I have a bunch of questions you could help me with.'

'And I have a bunch of answers. But first, allow me to show you to your room. Perhaps all you need is a hot bath and a gourmet meal to help you discover some solutions on your own.'

Payne's *room* turned out to be a massive suite, three small bedrooms separated by sliding doors from the living area. It was equipped with a plasma TV, multiple couches, a wet bar, and a small kitchen. The parquet floor blended perfectly with the light stone in the only bathroom. A two-person sauna sat underneath a tinted bay window, offering sweeping views of the Yellow Sea, where waves crashed in the distance, barely audible yet somehow comforting.

Kia showered first, dying to wash the smell from her hair. While they waited, Payne and Jones went to the far end of the suite, turning on the TV to drown out their conversation.

Payne spoke first. 'I'm sorry about all the fuss downstairs. Randy must've called the hotel and told them we were coming, just to make a point.'

'In that case, I wouldn't be surprised if a hooker knocks on our door.'

'Yeah, a fat one.'

Jones laughed loudly, glad to have a moment of levity in an otherwise dreadful day. Back when they were with the MANIACs, they often relied on laughter to get them through the tough times. That was one of the reasons the nickname suited their unit. No matter how deep the shit, the humour never quit. So much so that other squads thought they were crazy. Actual maniacs.

'So,' Payne said, changing the subject, 'how do you want to handle this? Should we snoop around the hotel, asking about the father and son? Or is that a waste of time?'

'We can try. But we don't have much to go on. All we have is the picture.'

Jones pulled out a photograph of the Park family that they'd taken from their house before leaving the village. They'd rummaged around a little bit, checking cupboards and drawers, trying not to step in any blood in case the cops were eventually called in, but the place was so small, so cramped, it was obvious that the Parks didn't have much money. As far as they could tell, there were nine people living in a house that was built for four. No way were they staying at the resort.

'What are the other possibilities?'

'There's no guarantee the old man heard correctly,' Jones suggested. 'Or he mistranslated the term. Or the boy was just muttering about black stones he saw inside the cave. There are dozens of explanations that would make more sense than this place.'

Payne rubbed his eyes, half-regretting his seat on the couch. It was soft and plush and made him want to sleep. 'Let's go back to the cave for a sec. Let's focus on that. What do we know about the operation?'

'Schmidt's team consisted of himself and the three squad members who weren't killed at the hospital. That means four of them in total. Dr Sheldon said Trevor was in charge of the facility, doing torture or whatever. Forensics found three samples that weren't in the system, probably from the prisoners or the men who killed Schmidt's crew.'

'In other words, professionals.'

'Definitely. No way they got to Schmidt otherwise.'

Payne sighed, still trying to grasp the situation. 'Professional soldiers mean one of two things: we captured a foreign official that was important enough to be rescued. Or –'

'We snagged a terrorist with a lot of secrets.'

'Exactly. Someone big. Someone worth saving.'

'That makes more sense to me. Terrorists are off-the-grid to begin with. No reason to bring them into the system. Smuggle them to a cave and let Schmidt work them over until he gets them to talk.' Jones paused, thinking things through. 'Let's face it, Schmidt and his men would've been perfect candidates for that type of work. Still angry from the hospital attack.'

'Plus it explains the village.'

'How so?'

'A foreign national wouldn't cover up his escape.

If anything, he'd blow the whistle on the cave, show-casing the evil nature of America. But a terrorist? He'd want everyone dead.'

'Good point.'

'Speaking of which, did I mention that Dr Sheldon is dead?'

Jones arched his eyebrows. 'No.'

'Raskin searched his personnel file, and he was listed as dead. Died three years ago.'

'Wow. He was a little pale, but he didn't look dead.'

'Just because he's *white* doesn't mean he's *pale*.'

Jones smiled, no racial tension at all. 'What else did his file say?'

'Not much. Randy was supposed to see what he could find. Maybe we'll luck out.'

'Maybe we already have.'

'How so?'

'Think back to our meeting with Colonel Harrington. When he talked about Schmidt, he said he *ceased to exist* after the incident. That term's been bugging me ever since. At first I thought he meant Schmidt went nuts. But maybe he was talking in different terms. Maybe that's when they recruited him into black ops. One minute he was in the system, the next he wasn't.'

'And you think the same thing happened with Sheldon? They killed him on paper so he had more freedom overseas . . . That's not a bad theory.'

'I have my moments.' Jones yawned, suddenly

feeling tired. 'What else did Randy mention? Anything about the prisoners?'

'Unfortunately, he was pretty tight-lipped on the topic. He hinted that Harrington could get us clearance, but if you don't mind, I'd prefer to fly solo for a while. I'm still pissed about his lack of disclosure. He should've told us about Schmidt from the very beginning. It would've saved us a lot of legwork.'

'Any thoughts on where we can get the intel?'

Payne nodded. 'Don't worry. I've got someone in mind.'

Nick Dial was known for two things: one professional, one personal. He ran the homicide division at Interpol, the first American ever promoted to such an illustrious position in the French-based agency. But to his friends, he was known for his chin. His world-class chin. The type that movie stars would pay big bucks for. It sat at the bottom of his face like a perfectly sculpted granite masterpiece. A heroic chin. Like Dudley Do-Right's.

Because of his job, Dial kept strange hours, often flying from country to country to cut through red tape or handle border disputes whenever they interfered with a case. Never knowing where he might fly to next. Or when he might get there. Interpol was a worldwide organization, which meant his duties were international. And his knowledge was extensive.

The sound of Dial's phone was followed by a low growl. One of utter frustration. He was sitting at his desk in Lyon, France, trying to catch up on his paper-work. But this was one of those days when his phone wouldn't stop ringing – six times in the past fifteen minutes – and his only recourse was to growl at it, trying to intimidate it. Hoping it would stop. Yet the damn thing kept ringing over and over again. Finally he felt obligated to pick it up.

'What?' he barked.

'Oh, crap, someone's cranky.'

Dial grinned, recognizing the sound of Payne's voice. 'Sorry, Jon. Long day.'

'Me, too. I'm getting too old for this shit.'

'You mean lounging in your corporate penthouse, counting your cash? Yeah, tough life.'

'Not today I'm not. They pulled me back in.'

No further explanation was necessary. Dial knew who *they* were. He'd met Payne and Jones several years ago at Stars & Stripes, a European bar that catered to Americans who worked overseas. They were in the MANIACs at the time, and Dial was still rising through the ranks at Interpol. The three of them hit it off, and they'd kept in touch ever since – occasion-ally bumping into each other in the strangest places. Last time was in Italy. At the airport.

'Anything I can help you with?'

'That depends. How secure is this line?'

'Hold on.' Dial stood from his leather chair and walked over to his office door. He locked it with a loud click. 'Okay. We're good.'

'How good?'

'The phone's encrypted. The office is soundproof. And we sweep daily for bugs.'

'Good enough for me.'

Dial leaned back in his chair, intrigued. 'What's going on?'

'Can't get into specifics. But it looks like we hooked a big fish.'

Fish was a slang term for international fugitive. 'We talking shark?'

'I'm talking whale.'

'That's great news, isn't it?'

'It *was* until he slipped off the hook. Took a lot of fishermen with him.'

Dial knew he wouldn't get any further details, so he didn't bother to ask. 'Sorry to hear that, Jon. How can I help?'

'Pardon the pun, but some things are rather fishy on my end. I'd appreciate it if you could talk to some of your sources and let me know what you find. Facts, rumours, anything.'

'Not a problem. Of course, things would go much smoother if I had a name.'

'Yeah,' Payne agreed. 'That makes two of us.'

23

For the first time since her arrival in Mecca, Shari Shasmeen did not want to be in the tunnel. The murder of Fred Nasir had spooked her. The lack of an explanation from Abdul-Khaliq, who normally had an answer for everything, made things worse. But the final straw was her isolation with this new guard. It was unbearable. There was something about him that creeped her out. Maybe it was the way he grabbed her hand when he tried to take her keys. Or the detached way that his men disposed of the body. Or the way he looked at her.

Whatever it was, he made her squirm.

At first, she figured she'd be allowed to leave as soon as she'd given him a short tour. But he stopped halfway through to make a phone call to one of his men. Followed by another. And another. Any other place and she would have simply left and gone back to her hotel. Her time was valuable, and he was wasting it. On purpose. But in Saudi Arabia, women weren't allowed to walk the streets alone. They had to travel with a close male relative, who could protect their virtue, or several other women, who could protect their reputation. Abdul-Khaliq had provided her with phony paperwork that claimed kinship with the other American scholars – it's what allowed her to work with them in close proximity. But the lead guard had sent her co-workers away when he first arrived, and they wouldn't return until they were summoned.

That meant she was trapped in the tunnel until he said she could leave.

To kill time, she entered the main site and made sure everything was all right. Like a protective mother who was about to go away for the weekend, worried about leaving something so precious in someone else's hands.

Plus, she wanted to see it one last time before she left for the week.

A mental snapshot of her progress.

Right now it didn't look like much, nothing more than the outer shell of a document chamber. Simple in design, it had been assembled out of local stones, carved by Muslim craftsmen, and then placed underground for protection. Just like folklore had said. Her team dug around the vault, exposing four sides that could be measured, photographed, and tested. Preliminary research proved it was built in the seventh century, not ancient by biblical standards but the perfect age for what they were hoping to find.

Staring at it, she remembered the initial phone call from Abdul-Khaliq. His interest in her research. Questions about her training and background. And eventually, an invitation to join the dig. A week later she was flown halfway around the world to run a project in the heart of Islam, right down the road from its most holy shrine. It was the type of opportunity that all archaeologists dreamed of.

The Qur'an is the central religious text of Islam. Muslims believe it is the literal word of God, revealed to Muhammad over the last twenty-three years of his life. Whereas Christians believe Jesus Christ is the Son of God, Muslims do not worship Muhammad as a deity; rather they honour him as their most important prophet, the man responsible for establishing Islam in its purest form.

According to Islamic scholars, Muhammad was born in Mecca in AD 570. He was orphaned by the age of six and eventually lived with his uncle, Abu Talib, who was the leader of the Banu Hashim, one of the clans in the Quraish tribe. At the time, Mecca was a thriving economic centre, partly because of the Kaaba, the great Islamic shrine that Muslims still worship, which attracted throngs of merchants during the pilgrimage season because violence between the various tribes was outlawed. Muhammad eventually became a merchant himself, travelling to Syria and other parts of the world, opening his eyes to many beliefs and cultures.

During his middle years, Muhammad often retreated to the peak of Jabal al-Nour near Mecca to fast and meditate. In AD610, while inside the Cave of Hira, he received his first revelation from God, delivered to him by the Archangel Gabriel. At first, most people were sceptical – including Muhammad himself – but when the revelations continued, he began to preach and eventually attracted a small band of followers that continued to grow until his death.

Despite his privileged upbringing, Muhammad never learned how to read or write; therefore it was incumbent on his companions to record his recitations, often on pieces of loose parchment or whatever materials they could find, including the leafstalks of date palms, and scapula bones. Remarkably, during his lifetime, Muhammad's revelations were never bound into a single volume.

The modern form of the Qur'an is widely attributed to Uthman ibn Affan, the third caliph of Islam, who formed a committee to compile a standard version of the holy book, based on all the teachings they could find. Upon its completion sometime around AD650, Uthman sent a copy to every Muslim city and town and ordered all other versions of the Qur'an to be destroyed, his way of guaranteeing a unified message.

Unfortunately, despite the claims of some, many modern-day historians doubt that any of Uthman's original copies have survived. Some feel the oldest existing Qur'an was written in the eighth century, nearly one hundred years after the Uthman version was distributed. Barely a blip on the radar screen in terms of human evolution, but a wide chasm in religious history. Obviously, many Islamic scholars have wondered what changes might have occurred during that century. Even the slightest alteration of syntax could have profoundly altered Muhammad's original message, thereby affecting an entire religion.

One of those scholars was Shari Shasmeen, who had spent many years searching for one of Uthman's Qur'ans, only to have her dream crushed at every turn. That is, until she received a phone call from Abdul-Khaliq, who implied that he might have found something better.

Something so astounding that it dwarfed what she had been looking for.

The guard made all of the arrangements on an encrypted cell phone. He spoke with his crew. He ordered equipment. He coordinated times and places. If this was going to work, there could be no mistakes. Nothing could be overlooked. Everything had to be perfect.

He glanced at his watch and noted the time.

Right on schedule.

Now all he had to figure out was what to do with that bitch archaeologist. She was going to be a problem – he could tell that already. The way she had fought back when he tried to take her keys. The way she stared at him. Defiant. Unyielding. The exact opposite of what he expected from a Muslim woman. Weren't they supposed to bend to the authority of men?

In a perfect world, he would slit her throat and dump her in the same place they took Nasir. That would make things much easier, giving him all the time he needed to accomplish his mission. But her death would bring too many questions. Questions he didn't have time to answer. At least for now. In the near future that was bound to change, and the moment it did he would teach her a lesson about the power of men.

Until then, he would simply have to work around her.

24

Payne closed his eyes for just a moment. When he woke up, it was two hours later, and Kia was standing in front of him, quietly whispering his name. Her hair was done, her make-up perfect. A light floral scent filled the air. She wore a tight black sweater and even tighter jeans, which showed off her feminine figure, something Payne hadn't noticed until that very instant. Stylish black boots and simple earrings finished her outfit.

'Wow,' he said, searching for adjectives. 'You look great.'

She beamed at the compliment. 'Thanks.'

He stared at her for a few more seconds, temporarily at a loss for words, a combination of grogginess and unexpected thoughts. 'How long was I out?'

'Not as long as DJ. He's still sleeping in the other room.'

'That's because he's old and creaky. Not a world-class athlete like I am.' Payne held out his hands for Kia to grab. 'Now do me a favour and help me up.'

She grunted as she pulled him to his feet, pretending it took all the strength she could muster. Despite her high heels, she was still several inches shorter than he was. 'Are you hungry?'

'I'm starving.'

'In that case, why don't you get cleaned up and take me out to dinner?'

He laughed. 'Wow, you're being kind of forward, aren't you?'

'Not really. You're the one taking me to dinner. So *you're* the one who's out of line.'

Payne smiled. 'I guess I am.'

'But don't worry, I'm not going to report you. I mean, you did save my life today.'

Thirty minutes later they were walking into one of the restaurants at the Black Stone, where they were given a window seat that overlooked the Yellow Sea. Compliments of Mr Lee. Payne was dressed comfortably in jeans and a dress shirt, not as formal as the other diners, but nobody seemed to care. Everyone was too busy eating and drinking, soaking in the atmosphere, to pay much attention to them. The entire dining room was bathed in candlelight and romance.

'Thank God we're alone,' Payne joked as he helped her with her chair. 'If DJ was here, he'd probably get liquored up and try to kiss me.'

'Please don't remind me. Been there, done that.'

'That's right. I almost forgot about the kiss! That was, what? Almost two days ago?'

She did the maths in her head. 'Oh, wow. That *seems* so long ago. Two days doesn't seem possible. Two weeks, maybe. Not two days.'

'Well, that's something you'll learn. Clocks tick at a different rate of speed in the field.'

Kia paused while a waiter filled their glasses with water. 'Speaking of the field, I'd like to officially apologize for my behaviour. I shouldn't have wandered away from the cave without telling you where I was going. I put you in an awkward position, one where you had to swoop in and rescue me. I never should've let that happen.'

'Don't worry about it. In fact, I should be thanking you for your efforts. There's no way we could've gotten Kim to talk without your help. He opened up because of you.'

She smiled, appreciative of his praise.

'Of course, that being said, you *might* want to stay a little bit closer in the future.'

Her smile grew wider. 'Why do you think I'm here?'

It was a rhetorical question but a good question nonetheless. The truth was Payne didn't know why she was there. There had been some innocent flirting during the past hour, but up until then he had viewed Kia as a member of his squad. Nothing more. Now all of a sudden he was sitting across from her, staring at her in candlelight as waves crashed upon the rocky shore, romantic thoughts dancing through his head. He had never been put in this position before, working so closely with a beautiful woman. He wasn't sure where to draw the line.

Hell, he didn't even know if a line was necessary.

In reality, he was no longer in the military, meaning he was no longer bound by their strict rules and codes in regard to social interaction. Still, she viewed him as a superior; there was no doubt about that. However, he wasn't sure if *that* was even important on such a temporary assignment. For all he knew, their official mission – to rescue Schmidt and his men – was already over. So if something happened between them, was there really any harm?

To him, it was a question that needed to be answered before he'd let anything progress.

'You know,' Kia said, breaking the silence, 'this isn't my first trip to Jeju. When I was a young girl, my father brought me here to see the *Haenyo*, the women divers of the island.' She pointed out the window to the Yellow Sea, where three yachts, their lights twinkling against the horizon, floated on the rolling darkness. 'To watch them work was amazing. Most of them were in their forties or fifties, but some were in their sixties or seventies. They'd tie rocks to their belts and jump into the deep water, sometimes sinking more than twenty metres down to the ocean floor, where they'd collect abalone and sea urchins and a variety of other treasures. They'd stay down there for several minutes, longer than I thought was possible to hold one's breath, before they'd untie the rocks and swim back to the surface with baskets full of goods.'

She took a sip of water before continuing. 'For some reason it's taboo on the island for men to do any diving. No one's really sure why. Some say it's because women have more fat on their bodies, which allows them to endure the cold waters of the deep. Others say it's because women are more buoyant, allowing them to swim to the surface faster after filling their baskets. But whatever the reason, they're some of the best divers in the world. Male or female.'

Payne nodded in agreement. He had heard stories about the women divers of Korea but didn't know they were based here. Some Navy SEALs even used their breathing techniques.

'To be honest,' she continued, 'that's one of the reasons I pushed so hard for this assignment. I've been a translator for many years, working for military bases around the world, but I've always wanted to work in the field. It's something I've always wanted to do. Sadly, I never had the guts to pursue any openings until this assignment became available. As soon as I heard *Jeju*, I figured a higher power was telling me something. My father brought me here to learn from these courageous women. Now I have a chance to show some courage of my own.'

He smiled at her story, glad to know something about her background that wasn't found in a personnel file. 'I have to admit I was sceptical at first. But truthfully, things have worked out well. Of course, I'm still not sure how you convinced Harrington to give you a chance. There had to be dozens of other applicants who spoke Korean.'

'There probably were. But unlike most of them, I'm also pretty good with Arabic.'

Payne froze, his warning sensors going off. 'Excuse me?'

'I speak Korean, Arabic, Japanese –'

'Hold up.' Payne glanced around to make sure no one was listening. He lowered his voice just to be safe. 'Arabic was one of your requirements?'

She nodded. 'Korean and Arabic, though I'm not sure why Arabic was so important. It's not very common in this part of the world.'

'Sonofabitch!' Payne mumbled. A major piece of the puzzle had just fallen into his lap, and he needed to act on it immediately. 'Kia, I'm sorry, but we don't have time for dinner.'

'We don't?'

'No,' he said as he stood from the table. 'We have to leave now.'

25

Payne hustled back to his suite, where he roused Jones from his nap. Meanwhile, Kia was dispatched to find Mr Lee, whose local knowledge might come in handy.

Jones said, 'You're telling me Arabic was a requirement of her job posting?'

Payne nodded. 'Which means Harrington was expecting Arab witnesses.'

'Or prisoners.'

'Which supports our terrorist theory. It also explains something Kim said. He mentioned hearing ancient voices, like the Devil speaking in tongues. That's how Arabic might sound to someone who's never heard it before.'

Jones agreed, then went into the bathroom to brush his teeth. He had showered before falling asleep so he was ready to leave whenever necessary. 'Any word from Dial?'

'Not yet. But it's only been a few hours. Nick's good, but not that good.'

'Unfortunately, Arabic doesn't do much to limit our candidates.'

'Sure it does,' Payne joked. 'Only 300 million people speak Arabic as their main language. We've just eliminated several billion suspects in the world.'

Jones gurgled in front of the sink. 'G-g-g-g-g-ooood point.' He spat for emphasis.

'The thing that confuses me the most is Harrington. What's with all his games? He dragged us here under false pretences, then gave us only half the intel we needed to succeed. That doesn't make sense to me. Why bring us in if he wants us to fail?' Payne paused, thinking back to their plane trip with Harrington. 'Do you remember what he said when you asked him about Schmidt's latest missions? He told you it was none of your goddamned business. That should've told us something right there. He's been keeping stuff from us from the very beginning.'

Jones emerged from the bathroom. 'Unless he hasn't been.'

'What does *that* mean?'

'Who knows? Maybe Harrington isn't messing with us. There might be other possibilities.'

'Such as?'

'*Maybe* he's a crappy colonel.'

Payne laughed. 'A crappy colonel?'

'Maybe he's not keeping us in the dark. Maybe he's just clueless.'

'Sorry, but I didn't get that sense in Pittsburgh. He seemed pretty perceptive.'

'Fine. Then maybe it's something else.'

'Like what?'

Jones paused, trying to think of an alternative. 'Maybe he's in the dark, too.'

'In what sense?'

'Well, we used to run black ops. How often did we report to our superiors?'

Payne smiled. 'Not as often as we were supposed to.'

'Exactly! So maybe the same thing happened here. Maybe Schmidt followed our example and failed to tell his boss what was going on. Days go by and Harrington finally sends someone to check up on him. And when he got there, he found the cave covered in blood.'

'You know, that's not half bad.'

Jones nodded, impressed with his own theory. 'Actually, it would explain a lot. Early on I asked Harrington when Schmidt was last seen, and he said he didn't know. Then I asked him where, and he didn't know that either. That sounds like a soldier who didn't report very often. Just like us back in the day.'

'Which might explain Harrington's comment about the MANIACs. He said we were being brought in because we thought differently from normal soldiers. He must've figured we'd be able to piece together Schmidt's final mission, maybe shed some light on what happened here.'

'If that's the case,' Jones added, 'he probably didn't know Schmidt was dead until he got the blood results. For all we know, he might've thought this was actually a rescue mission. Just like he told us in the very beginning.'

'Crap!' Payne said. 'Maybe I pegged the guy wrong.'

Suddenly confused, he walked out of the bedroom and went straight to the small kitchen, where a small basket of tangerines sat in the corner, adorned with a sign that said *Grown Fresh on Jeju*. Payne grabbed two and tossed one to Jones, who caught it like a wide receiver. Whenever Payne got hungry, he found it difficult to think clearly. And right now, he was famished, his stomach grumbling like a bad muffler.

Payne started peeling his fruit. 'So what you're telling me is that Harrington might not be messing with us?'

'Maybe not.' Jones took a bite and quickly regretted it, realizing that toothpaste and tangerine didn't mix. 'He still should've told us about the Arabic. If he felt it was an important skill for our translator, we should've known about it.'

'Agreed.'

Just then the electric lock on the suite started to beep. Someone was entering.

Most likely Kia and Mr Lee.

'Speak of the Devil,' Jones said as he lowered his voice to a whisper. 'If you don't mind, I'll let you handle Mr Lee. He wants to kiss your ass, not mine.'

Payne walked into the kitchen and rinsed the tangerine pulp from his fingers, realizing that nothing ruined a meeting quicker than a sticky handshake.

Kia walked in first, followed by Mr Lee, who glanced around the suite, making sure everything met his high standards. He said a quick hello to Jones before he spotted Payne in the kitchen.

'Good evening, Mr Lee. Would you like a drink? I make a mean glass of water.'

The smile on Mr Lee's face grew wider than normal, honoured that Payne had remembered his name and respected him enough to offer him a beverage. He politely declined, then walked over to the couches, where he stood patiently until everyone was ready to be seated. Payne and Kia sat on one couch, he and Jones on the other.

Payne said, 'I know you're a busy man, so I'd like to thank you for coming here on such short notice. All of us appreciate your time.'

Mr Lee bowed slightly, his way of showing respect.

'The three of us came to Jeju on a personal quest, one that's left us puzzled. We are searching for a boy who lives in a tiny village near the base of Mount Halla. We found his home with little difficulty, yet he wasn't there. One of his neighbours heard the young boy speak of the Black Stone on the day that he disappeared with his father. However, the opulence of your resort leads us to believe that he was mistaken. These are poor people with limited means.'

Jones handed Mr Lee the photograph of Yong-Su Park and his father, Chung-Ho. He studied their faces but recognized neither.

'None of us is an expert on Jeju or its customs. Therefore, we're hesitant to make our search public, afraid that our questions might be perceived as a nuisance. Kia can speak the language – she was actually born in South Korea – but we need some guidance with our journey.'

Mr Lee nodded, grasping the situation. 'I would be honoured to help you with your quest . . . If it's appropriate, may I ask a question?'

'Of course,' Payne said. 'Ask whatever you'd like.'

'I would imagine a man of your stature is here on a fruitful mission, one that would bring no harm to the father or son.'

Payne met his gaze, assuring him of his decency. 'We are here to help, not harm.'

'Yet you're unwilling to involve the authorities?'

'At this point, we think the Parks are hiding from the authorities.'

Mr Lee frowned at the mention of their name. 'Their name is Park?'

Payne nodded. 'Is that a problem?'

'Possibly. Ten per cent of all South Koreans are named Park.'

'Really?' Jones blurted. 'That's a lot of Parks.'

'Still, it could have been worse. Twenty per cent of us are named Kim.'

Payne laughed at the comment, glad that Mr Lee was an optimist. 'If you'd like, we'd be happy to write down everything we have. Names, addresses, and everything else we can think of. Plus you're welcome to make a photocopy of their picture if you think it would help.'

Mr Lee stood and gave him a slight bow. 'I shall do it at once.'

'And if there's any expense to you –'

He held up his hand to cut him off. 'There will be no expense. I am honoured to help.'

'Are you sure? Because –'

'Yes,' he said firmly. 'I am sure.'

Then, before Payne could say another word, Mr Lee took the photograph and hustled out of the suite – the safety of the father and son suddenly in his hands.

26

Sunday, 31 December

Early in Payne's military career, these were the moments that drove him crazy. Not the training or the long hours or the constant threat of dying, but the waiting. The time during missions when all he could do was sit on his ass and stare at his watch. It contradicted everything he believed in.

Payne's grandfather was the hardest-working man he had ever met, someone who used to work double shifts in the steel mills of Pittsburgh, trying to earn enough money to open his own business and give his family the chance of a better life. Then, once his small investment paid off and Payne Industries blossomed into one of the biggest names in the world of manufacturing, he still set his alarm clock for 4 a.m. because there was no way in hell he was ever going to be outworked by anyone. In his mind, laziness was a mortal sin.

Growing up, that's the work ethic that was instilled in Payne. The creed he lived by. It enabled him to become a top student, a better athlete, and one of the best soldiers in the world. Yet the reality of military life was nothing like the movies or the recruiting commercials he saw on TV – especially the one that bragged, *We do more before 6 a.m. than most people do all day*. Payne liked to joke that that was true but only because they spent all night drinking and beating off.

Eventually, once he was given his own command, he started to view things differently. That's when he realized how much time and preparation went into a mission. How long it took to acquire foreign intelligence. To gather supplies. To wait for the enemy to make a mistake. And once that started to sink in, his guilt began to fade and the waiting game became much more tolerable. Within a few months, he transformed himself from an over-eager warrior to a patient one. Someone willing to eat, sleep, and joke while all the pieces fell into place.

But once they did, he became a man possessed.

The room phone rang before sunrise. Payne was already awake, lying in bed, analysing their next move while he waited for additional information – whether it came from Raskin, Dial, or Mr Lee. Surprisingly, the call didn't come from any of them. There was a new voice on the line. One he hadn't heard before. A male. Distinctly Korean. Speaking in hushed tones.

'Is this Mr Payne?'

'Yes,' he said, sitting up in bed. 'Who's this?'

'Are you looking for the father and his boy?'

'Who is this?' he repeated.

'Be downstairs in twenty minutes. You and your friends.'

'Hold up! We're not going anywhere unless –'

Click. The caller hung up. No names. No explanation. No additional instructions. Just be downstairs in twenty minutes. Payne set the phone in its cradle as footsteps filled the hall. Jones reached his room first, followed by Kia. Both of them were wide awake. Ready to roll.

'Who was it?' Jones asked.

'He didn't say.'

'What did he want?'

Payne looked at them, confused. 'Us.'

Twenty minutes wasn't enough time for most people. But these were the type of contingencies that Payne had trained for. When he walked into a room, he searched for exits. Danger zones. Blind spots. Sometimes it wasn't even a conscious act. His mind automatically worked through the possibilities like a computer crunching data. All the details were just sitting there in his brain, ready to be used if he ever thought they were necessary. And today they were.

He walked outside at 7 a.m., still forty minutes before daybreak. The weather was breezy and brisk, colder than it was when he had arrived on Jeju twenty-four hours before. He wore jeans, a thick sweater, and a winter coat. It concealed his gun and body armour. Anonymous phone calls were a rarity in his business. He would take every precaution.

To Payne, the front exit was too obvious. Too predictable. The perfect spot for an ambush. So he left the hotel through one of the employee lots, walking behind trees and bushes until he reached the front of the hotel. He was virtually invisible in the pre-dawn light.

But no cars were waiting for him. No one was standing around. Even the valets were inside, trying to stay warm. Some people would have been spooked by this, but not Payne. He preferred it this way. The fewer distractions, the better. Just him and whoever wanted to meet.

He'd take those odds any day of the week.

He heard the vehicle before he saw it. A rumble, a sputter, and the occasional grinding of gears. The sound echoed through the darkness like a rooster greeting the sun. It finally came into view as it entered the resort grounds, passing the chiselled entrance sign that gleamed in its spotlight. The truck was American, decades old, probably abandoned at the end of the Korean War because it was too old to salvage even back then. How it still worked was a mystery. It coughed and sputtered as it crawled past the mani-cured shrubs, belching smoke as it did.

The man behind the wheel looked older than the truck, his wrinkles bathed in light every time he passed under one of the fancy lamp posts. White hair, gaunt face, his eyes nothing but slits – partially from his

Asian features, but mostly because he had to squint to see.

If ever a man and his truck belonged together, it was these two.

Payne watched him as he drove up the hill and through the parking overhang, stopping on the downslope of the other side, as if he needed momentum to get started again. The back of the truck was filled with a variety of fishing tools. Rods and reels. Several nets. Two ice chests that were big enough for salmon. Nothing new or expensive. Simple tools for an age-old craft.

The motor continued to run as he stepped out of the truck. He wore grimy old clothes that reeked of the sea. His spine was crooked, his posture hunched, his skin splotched from the sun. He just stood there, whistling absently, his eyes straining to see the pocket watch that he held next to his face. Anxious. Waiting. This was a man who was meeting someone.

Cautiously, Payne stepped into the light. Just far enough to be seen. 'Good morning.'

The old man froze until he spotted Payne in the shadows. Moving slowly, he trudged towards him until he was close enough to whisper. The same voice as on the phone. 'Are you Payne?'

'Maybe. Who are you?'

The old man leaned closer. 'A friend of Mr Lee.'

'In that case, I'm Jonathon Payne.'

The old man smiled, glad he had found him so easily. 'Are your friends coming with us?'

'That depends. Where are we going?'

'To find the boy.'

Payne arched an eyebrow. 'Which boy are you talking about?'

The old man pulled out a copy of the photograph. The one Payne had taken from the Parks' house. He pointed to it with gnarled fingers that were covered in calluses. 'Yong-Su.'

'You know where he is?'

'I know where he was. That's the best I can do.'

Payne considered the old man's answer, trying to read between the lines. Trying to figure out how he fitted into all this. Was he a relative of the Parks? A friend? Or was this some kind of trick meant to distract Payne from a danger that waited around the bend? His gut told him he was safe, that there was no real threat, but he realized a second opinion never hurt.

So he casually unzipped his coat – his signal to Jones – and waited for a response.

Three seconds later, his cell phone rang. He grabbed it with one hand and signalled for the old man to wait with the other. Very calm, very natural. Like any other day at the office.

'Hello?' Payne answered.

Jones was positioned on the hotel roof, which offered him views of the grounds, roads, and sea. Visibility was poor due to the lack of sun and a thin layer of fog that had settled over the golf course, but from his vantage point, nothing looked suspicious. 'We're clear.'

'Hello?' he repeated, as if there were a bad connection. It prevented him from faking a conversation. It also allowed Jones to call right back if anything changed. '*Hello?*'

The old man laughed. 'You need a new phone.'

Payne shrugged and smiled. 'And you need a new truck.'

He laughed louder. 'You are probably right.'

'So,' he said, 'how do you know the boy?'

'I don't. I've never met him before. I am just a poor fisherman who lives at sea.'

'Then I don't understand.'

'But my son,' the old man clarified, '*he* helped the boy. *He* knows the father. He helped him in his time of need.'

'Well, I'd love to speak to him.'

'Then let's get going. It's a long drive.'

'Can't we just call him?'

'Not with your phone. It doesn't work.' He cackled softly. 'Besides, my son needs to meet you in person. He needs to look you in the eye. He needs to judge your character.'

Payne nodded, willing to take the risk. 'In that case, I'd be happy to meet him. But I'm going in my own truck. I'd feel safer that way.'

'Suit yourself,' said the old man. 'But my truck is going to outlast us all.'

27

The man who planned the attack had a healthy fear of computers. He respected their place in the world and understood their importance in certain situations, but during the past decade he had seen too many colleagues arrested or killed because of computer issues. No matter how much training his people had, they were no match for the American agencies who spent billions of dollars on the latest technology that had been designed to catch them in the act.

Somehow, someway, his men always screwed up.

Intel was intercepted. Information was deciphered. Evidence was recovered.

In his heart, he knew this mission had to be different from all the others. Its impact would be global, reaching the farthest corners of the world in a way that had never been attempted. To do that, deception was the key. Everyone had to believe one thing – when, in fact, the very opposite was true. But that wasn't possible if he left a trail of binary bread-crumbs for the authorities to follow. Never knowing what they would find. Or when they were going to find it.

So early on, he made a gutsy decision. All informa-tion pertaining to this mission would be delivered by hand, passed from person to person in the most damning places possible, for the sole purpose of documentation. Unlike most criminals, he wanted to record what was going on because it would actually help his cause in the long run.

Then, when the time was right, he'd give the authorities more than just breadcrumbs.

He'd give them the whole loaf of bread.

According to the soldier's sources, the facility would be deserted for the hajj. A few security guards might be roaming around, but his team didn't have to worry about engineers, technicians, or custodians, even though it didn't matter to his men. Their orders were to kill everyone inside, and they'd do so without remorse. One. Ten. Twenty. What difference did it make?

They'd kill many more in the near future.

Scanning the horizon, he drove the van forward, tyres crunching on the gravel driveway that was laid in the arid ground to provide traction for the heavy trucks that would stream in and out of here like worker ants. Surrounded by a barren landscape that stretched all the way back to Mecca, the main building sat ahead, obscured by the cover of darkness. Although construction had been finished three months before, the place wasn't fully operational.

Of course, it would be once his men were done.

They were dressed in black and fully armed when they exited the van. The leader checked his list and entered the security code into the main entrance's keypad. The door buzzed open. One after another, all four soldiers streamed into the lobby, each scattering in a different direction, their footsteps barely audible. Communication would be done through a series of earpieces, each equipped with a transmitting device that allowed speech as well as audio while scrambling their signals to outside receivers.

The team leader was the most experienced soldier, so he had the most important job. He was in charge of the security office that sat at the end of a long corridor on the first floor. Monitors cast an eerie glow on his face as he studied the images that flickered in the dark room. Twenty-four screens in all, each offering a different view of the facility.

He sat in the chair and fiddled with the buttons. Before long, he was able to zoom in and out on different cameras. Able to warn his men if necessary.

As a precaution, each of them was given a code name to be used in the field. Something simple. Some thing easy to remember. In this case, they opted for the names of the four evangelists, the men who wrote the Gospels in the New Testament. It seemed fitting to use Christian names while inflicting damage on the Islamic world.

'Matthew?'

'Check.'

'Mark?'

'Check.'

'Luke?'

'Check.'

John, the team leader, scanned the screens, searching for trouble, eventually spotting a guard in the rear of the plant, strolling down the back walkway. 'Mark, we have a live one. Two rooms to your left. Coming your way.'

'Armed?'

He zoomed in tighter. 'Nothing in his hand. Maybe in his belt.'

'I'll let you know.'

Mark slid behind a large generator and waited patiently for his target to approach. Twenty seconds passed before he made his move. When he did, it was quick and silent. No gun was necessary. Just a hand over his mouth and a brutal snap of his neck, instantly killing the guard. John watched the scene with pride.

'I'm clear.'

'Search the body, then stash it.'

Mark frisked the dead guard, finding a gun in a hidden holster. He held it up to the camera so John could warn the others.

'Be aware, the guard was packing.'

'Check,' said the other two.

Not that they were worried.

Meanwhile, John returned his attention to the video screens. First checking for other guards, then looking at the building itself. Valves and pumps filled half the rooms, mostly in the rear of the structure. Some of the pipes went through the walls, leading to the empty reservoirs out back. They'd get to them eventually, but right now he had other concerns. Foremost was finding the main control room. It was somewhere on the first floor, protected by additional codes.

Matthew spoke. 'I think I see it.'

John punched a few buttons and zoomed in closer on the room that Matthew was pointing to. He spotted another keypad, just to the left of the metal door, but couldn't read the sign, since it was written in Arabic. The walls were reinforced with extra concrete, plus there were no windows. From his perspective, it seemed like the right place. Why add extra protection if this room wasn't important?

'Thoughts?'

Matthew looked back at the camera and shrugged.

'Can you hear anything?'

He put his ear next to the door. Not a sound.

He dropped to the floor and looked under the door. But the room was dark, at least from his limited perspective. From his knees, he shrugged again.

'While you're down there, say a prayer to Allah. Because if we punch in the wrong code, we might sound an alarm.'

Matthew looked at the camera and flipped it off.

'Was that to me or Allah?'

He ignored the question. 'Listen, there's no way this system is one-and-done. There has to be a margin for error. People hit wrong buttons all the time.'

'You're probably right.'

'Then give me the code. I'll try it once. If it doesn't work, we can try something else.'

John nodded and glanced at his list. He read the numbers aloud.

Carefully, Matthew entered them into the keypad, each sounding a tiny beep.

One. *Beep.*

Nine. *Beep.*

Eight. *Beep.*

Seven. *Beep.*

Then, as if by magic, the door popped open with a quiet click.

28

Yesterday, Kia had warned Payne and Jones about the threat of speeding tickets. Traffic cameras and detection units were spread evenly across Route 12. But on this day it wasn't a concern, not as long as they followed the old man and his truck, which smoked and wheezed more often than a fire-breathing dragon with asthma. It was simply unable to speed.

Jones drove, once again, while Payne studied a road map of the island. Kia hovered over his shoulder, answering questions and explaining the significance of certain areas, including the Jungmun Tourist Complex, which sprawled for several miles along the south-western coast of Jeju. It featured several dozen attractions – including Cheonjaeyeon Falls, where they had stopped the day before – with Americanized names that he could barely read let alone pronounce.

Yeomiji Botanical Garden was reputed to be the largest in Asia, growing more than 2,000 varieties of tropical and subtropical plants in 150,000 square yards of indoor and outdoor fields, all of it centred around an observation deck that stood more than 125 feet high. Down the road was Jusangjeolli Cliff, a series of 60-foot stone pillars that formed when lava from Mount Halla poured into the raging sea. Jungmun

Beach lined the nearby shore, filled with white sand that contrasted sharply with the surrounding black hillside, home to Haesikgul Cave, a natural sea cave featured in dozens of movies because of its scenic beauty.

Unfortunately, none of these sites could be seen from the highway, blocked from view by parasitic volcanoes and thick blankets of trees, a surreal mix of pines and palms sprouting up through the black core of the island. Payne followed their progress by watching road signs, tracing their route with his finger, looking for auxiliary routes in case they needed to escape.

They continued their journey along Route 12 until the old man approached the exit for Daeyu Hunting Ground. He eased his truck on to a secondary road and started driving north to the base of Mount Halla, its snowcapped peak rising 6,000 feet above the rocky shore.

Jones stared at the mountain and sighed. 'Bet you ten bucks he doesn't make it.'

Payne laughed, even though it contradicted the anxiety he felt for the first time since they'd left the resort. To him, hunting grounds meant guns. Lots of guns. People legally armed, carrying weapons in full view. And there was nothing he could do about it. No time for advanced scouting. No way to secure the perimeter. It was three of them against an entire lodge of potential threats. Never knowing where a fatal shot might come from.

He turned towards Kia. 'What do you know about this place?'

'Not much. I've never been here before.' She flipped through her tour book, hoping to find something useful. 'It says it's the only official hunting range in all of Asia. There's bird hunting, clay shooting, target ranges for pistols and rifles. You can rent guns. And guides. And even bird dogs. Plus there's a breeding farm with more than 50,000 pheasants.'

'Damn!' Jones said. 'That's a lot of birds.'

'I'm more concerned with the guns.'

'Me too. But still, that's a lot of birds. I'm talking *Hitchcock*.'

Payne ignored him. 'What kind of restrictions?'

She scanned the information. 'None. It's a private resort. Beginners are welcomed.'

'No licences or permits?'

'Not according to this.'

'Good.'

'Why's that good?'

Payne smiled. 'Because we don't have any.'

The main facility was straight ahead, at least according to the road sign. But instead of continuing forward, the old man turned on to a narrow dirt path that curved to the right and disappeared into the surrounding trees. The old truck rumbled and shook as it left the pavement, its bald tyres struggling for traction in the mud and fallen leaves. Yet the damn thing never stopped. Not once. It just kept chugging along.

As Jones made the turn, Payne rolled down his window and listened to the cacophony of gunshots that filled the air. Rifle blasts to the left. Handguns to the right. All of them too close for comfort. Discreetly, he tilted his side-view mirror and made sure no one had turned in behind them, a sure sign of an upcoming ambush. Thankfully, the path remained clear.

A quarter mile later, a large hunting cabin came into view, nestled among a grove of pines that towered above it. A Korean man dressed in khakis and a plaid shirt stood in the doorway. He smiled and waved at his father, who pulled into the driveway, did a three-point turn, then drove back towards Payne and Jones. They slowed to a stop, expecting the old man to pull alongside of them to deliver further instructions, but the old man just waved and kept going. Late for another day of fishing.

Payne shrugged. 'Guess he was busy.'

'When you're *that* old, you don't have time to waste,' Jones joked as he backed into a parking spot. Just in case there was trouble. 'How do you want to play this?'

'I'll talk, you snoop. Kia stays near me.'

The three of them exited the SUV and walked on to the front porch, where they were greeted by Chi-Gon Jung, who was in his mid-forties and spoke perfect English. He was the owner of a hunting and fishing service that worked closely with the resorts on the island, providing tourists with boats, guides, and whatever else they needed. He handled logistics from the cabin, taking advantage of its proximity to Mount Halla and the Daeyu lodge, but mentioned that customers rarely stopped by. This was his personal office, nothing more. Most of his employees were scattered around the island, manning booths in hotel lobbies or guiding tours in the field.

Jung led Payne and Kia inside his spacious cabin, which was decorated with an assortment of mounted animal heads that would have looked at home in any hunting lodge in the States. Meanwhile, Jones opted to stay outdoors, claiming he needed some fresh air after their long drive from the Black Stone. In actuality, he wanted to snoop around and make sure they were alone. To warn them of potential danger. To protect them from interlopers.

'How did you meet Mr Lee?' Payne asked as he took his seat in front of Jung's desk. 'Was it through your business?'

'Yes,' Jung said with a smile. 'Mr Lee is a wonderful man who takes care of his guests. We've been helping each other for years. Referring clients and so on.'

'And he called you about me?'

Jung nodded, his grin quickly fading. 'He called me late last night, asking for my help. Hoping I would fax the photo of the Parks to all of my guides. So we could keep an eye out for them in all our locations.' He paused, measuring what he was going to say next. 'But I told him it wasn't necessary. I already knew where they were.'

'You did? How is that possible?'

'They came to me earlier in the week, looking for a guide.'

'A guide? Why did they want a guide?'

'Honestly,' Jung said, 'they wanted to disappear.'

'And you could help them with that?'

There was a long delay. 'Yes.'

Payne nodded, noticing the stress in Jung's face. The tension in his voice. The indecision in his eyes. In a heartbeat he had gone from a cordial host to a nervous one, a metamorphosis that concerned Payne. If Jung got spooked, there was a chance he would lie and give them bad information about the boy. In the long run, that could prove disastrous.

So Payne did what he was trained to do when dealing with an anxious witness. It was a simple trick, but one that worked quite well. He made him feel comfortable by talking about something less threatening. Something to brighten his mood. And in this case, it was the first innocuous thing that popped into Payne's mind. Something he knew would make Jung laugh.

'Out of curiosity,' Payne asked, 'what's the deal with your father's truck?'

Jung's smile returned. 'He's married to that thing. It's much older than I am.'

'That's what I figured. Honestly, I didn't know what to think when I saw him pull into the Black Stone this morning. Especially after his phone call. *That* made me so jumpy.'

'My father made you nervous?' Jung laughed for several seconds before he could continue. 'How could such a little man make you nervous?'

'He didn't sound little on the phone. He ordered me into the lobby in twenty minutes. Then, when I tried asking him a question, he hung up on me. I thought the guy was crazy.'

Jung laughed louder. 'My father isn't crazy. He hangs up on me, too! The man can barely hear. I doubt he heard a word you said!'

'Oh,' Payne grunted, pretending to be embarrassed. 'That would explain a lot.'

'I'm sorry if I worried you. I would've met you myself, but this is my busy time of year. Not only is it hunting season, but thousands of tourists fly in for our New Year's celebrations. And tourists mean money.'

Payne waved him off. 'Not a problem. I'm just thankful for the lucky break. I didn't know who to turn to until Mr Lee offered to help. He's been a saviour.'

'I will tell him you said so. He will be honoured.'

'It is I who is honoured. Both of you have been so gracious and friendly.'

Jung bowed, showing his appreciation.

'Anyway, I know you're a busy man and I feel guilty for taking up so much of your time.'

'Not a problem, Mr Payne. I am glad I could help.' He paused for a moment, once again struggling for the right words. 'But before I do, there is something

I need to ask. Why are you looking for the boy?'

It was a question Payne had anticipated, one he'd been thinking about all night. In his mind he had two options: he could tell the truth, or make up a story. Obviously, both had risks. The fewer people who knew about the village, the better. Not only for national security but also for international relations. There was a chance the South Korean government knew what was going on in the cave, but if they didn't, he didn't want to be responsible for spilling the secret. On the other hand, if the Parks had told Jung about the violence, then Payne couldn't afford to lie. One misstep and Jung was liable to point him in the wrong direction. Or notify the Parks. Or both.

In the end, it was something the old man had said to Payne that helped him decide. He mentioned his son needed to look him in his eye. He needed to judge his character. That's the reason they couldn't talk on the phone. He needed to trust him before he would speak.

Based on that, Payne made a gut decision and opted to tell the truth.

'Recently a prisoner escaped from American custody and killed several islanders, including some members of the Park family. We believe Yong-Su witnessed much of the violence. Anything he can tell us will be useful, not only to capture the killer but also to protect the Parks and everyone on this island. The sooner he is caught, the safer Jeju will be.'

Jung paused, studying Payne long after he had finished speaking. Several seconds passed – several excruciating seconds – before Jung nodded his approval. He believed what Payne had said. 'Are you familiar with Seongsan? It is a massive peak on the eastern side of Jeju.'

Kia spoke up. 'I know where it is.'

'Tonight there is an important festival honouring the New Year. The entire coast will be jammed with boats from Japan and Korea. That is how the Parks are leaving Jeju. Masked by the large crowds. Under the cover of darkness.'

'And you're sure of this?' Payne asked.

Jung nodded. 'I am positive. They have rented *my* boat.'

29

The hotel was booked to capacity, yet at first glance it appeared to be closed. The lobby was virtually empty, same with the concierge desk, gift shop, news-stand, and café. Occasionally a small group of tourists would pass through, whispering to themselves as if they weren't allowed to be there, but then they would slip out the revolving door at the front of the building and everything would become quiet again. The only sound was the constant hum of the escalators that connected the main foyer with the non-alcoholic lounge.

Dr Drew Hennessy left the business centre, where he had been doing research on the Internet, and walked into an empty lift. A few days earlier, he had stood in line for nearly ten minutes because there were so many people waiting to get to their floor. But not today. Just about everyone who was staying at the hotel was participating in hajj, the annual Islamic pilgrimage, which meant they weren't currently in Mecca. Their rooms were full of clothes and personal items. But the hotel was eerily empty.

Entering the suite on the twelfth floor, Hennessy locked the door behind him. Shari was sitting on a plush purple couch, her feet tucked underneath her as she glanced through a stack of notebooks she had filled during her time in Mecca. Meanwhile Dr Milton Wheeler worked at the breakfast table, cleaning the sword that they had found at the site. He was hoping the Arabic inscription would reveal the identity of the skeleton and why he was sealed in the chamber.

'Good news,' Hennessy said. 'I got some great information.'

Taking a seat next to Shari, he opened the folder that contained all of his research. Wheeler walked across the room to listen, carrying the sword with him. He sat on an adjacent chair, waiting to share some news of his own.

'As both of you know,' Hennessy said, 'Islam is a religion that preaches peace. Yet during the last ten years of Muhammad's life, he was considered a fierce military general, leading his men in raids and sieges that resulted in hundreds of deaths. Most Muslims claim that these were acts of self-defence, completely necessary to preserve their religion. Whereas many non-Muslims feel that he was the aggressor, imposing Islam on non-believers. Whatever the case, one thing is certain. Muhammad was a man of the sword.'

Hennessy flipped through his papers until he found what he was looking for. 'During his lifetime, Muhammad amassed a dazzling collection of swords, many of which were given names. There's al-Ma'thur, the sword he possessed when he received his first revelation from Allah. It had been willed to him by his father. The Hatf, a famous weapon which was once owned by King David. And my personal favourite, al-Battar. Also known as the sword of the prophets.'

'Why did they call it that?' Shari wondered.

'Because it was inscribed with the names of David, Solomon, Moses, Aaron, Joshua, Zechariah, John, Jesus, and Muhammad. In addition, the blade has a rather unique feature. Down near the handle, there's a childlike drawing of David cutting off the head of Goliath. In fact, rumour has it the sword originally belonged to Goliath and was taken from him as booty.'

'That's some rumour.'

'Amazingly, that's not the best one. According to legend, al-Battar is also the sword that Jesus will use when he returns to Earth to slay the anti-Christ, known as al-Dajjal, or the Imposter.'

'Jesus is going to use Muhammad's sword?'

Hennessy joked, 'Personally, I find it hard to picture Jesus as a sword-wielding warrior. Then again, the guy could walk on water so I'm not going to sell him short.'

Shari ignored the comment. 'Did you find anything else?'

He nodded. 'I ran a search for *noble* and *Muhammad* since those words appeared on our sword's inscription, and I got a hit.'

'What kind of hit? Because while you were gone, Milton finished his translation.'

'You did?' Hennessy asked, looking at the grey-haired professor. 'What does it say?'

Wheeler glanced at the blade and smiled. 'This is

the noble sword of the house of Muhammad the prophet, the apostle of God.'

Hennessy sat there, stunned. 'Oh my Lord, you're not going to believe this. But I know that inscription.'

'What do you mean?' Shari demanded.

'I saw that *same* inscription on another sword.' He dug through his folder until he found the document he was searching for. 'The sword is named Qal'i. It's currently on display at the Topkapı Museum in Istanbul. It's one of three surviving swords that Muhammad acquired as booty from the Banu Qaynuqa, a Jewish tribe that was expelled from Medina in the seventh century.'

He flipped the page and stared at a grainy black-and-white photo of Qal'i. Shari glanced over his shoulder to study the picture and smiled at what she saw. The shape of the blade and handle were similar to the weapon that Wheeler held in his hand. Not identical, but close enough to be confused at first glance. Throw in the inscription, and the odds were pretty good that they had found an authentic sword, once owned by Muhammad.

'What does the word *Qal'i* mean?' Shari wondered.

Wheeler answered for him. 'It means white lead.'

'Lead?'

Hennessy nodded, agreeing with Wheeler's translation. 'That's one of the theories. Other experts maintain it was named after a sacred place in Syria. But the truth is no one knows for sure.'

In fact, there was much uncertainty about the Banu Qaynuqa, including the reason that they were expelled from Medina, a city called Yathrib at the time of their expulsion. Many experts claimed the dispute started in AD624 over a Muslim woman who was wronged in a Qaynuqa marketplace. According to historians, a Jewish shopkeeper pinned the woman's clothes in such a fashion that she was stripped naked when she tried to walk away. A Muslim man came to her defence and killed the shopkeeper. In retaliation, the Jews killed the Muslim, which eventually escalated into a series of revenge-based murders. Before long, the entire community was at war.

It was a story that Shari was quite familiar with. Some of her female colleagues even joked that the woman was the Muslim equivalent of Helen of Troy.

'If I remember correctly, didn't the Banu Qaynuqa flee to Syria after their eviction? Maybe that is why there's some discrepancy over the name Qal'i.'

Wheeler nodded. 'It's a possibility. Of course, for our purposes, the only name that truly matters is Muhammad. And since our sword has the same inscription as the Qal'i sword, the odds are pretty good that its owner was one of Muhammad's most trusted warriors.'

'And if that's the case,' Shari said, 'then the odds are pretty good that we found the site we're looking for.'

30

Seongsan Peak is a picturesque land mass on the eastern end of Jeju that was formed more than 100,000 years ago when a volcano erupted under the sea. The resulting peak stands 600 feet above the blue water below, its crater stretching more than 325,000 square feet, adorned with 99 natural peaks along its outer edge, creating the illusion of a majestic crown – an image that is heightened in the early morning when the sun rises above the Korea Strait, bathing the volcanic cone in golden light. The view is so breathtaking it was described nearly 800 years ago in the *Tripitaka Koreana*, the most complete collection of Buddhist texts still in existence.

Every year thousands of revellers flood the local village nestled near the base of the peak to participate in the Seongsan Sunrise Festival, a massive celebration that begins on New Year's Eve with a ritual known as a *gut* – where a shaman offers a sacrifice to the spirits – and continues well beyond sunrise on New Year's Day. In between there is much eating, drinking, gambling, and many fireworks, none of which Payne and Jones would be enjoying. Their sole purpose was to find the Parks as quickly as possible and gather as much information as they could.

Chi-Gon Jung had given them a map of Seongsan Harbour, explaining where his boat was docked and how to get there. The boy and his father were scheduled to arrive at midnight, the most chaotic moment possible, when they hoped to slip on board unnoticed. An hour later, one of Jung's most reliable tour guides would pilot them to the open sea. By morning, they would reach one of the small ports on the southern coast of South Korea, where they hoped to disappear into the countryside. At least that's what Jung had gathered.

Unfortunately, he had no additional information about the Parks. No hotel. No phone number. Not even a back-up plan. They had stumbled into the Daeyu Hunting Lodge looking for a guide and were given Jung's business card. They showed up at his cabin unannounced, told him what they needed, and gave him a small cash deposit. The entire time the boy never spoke. He just stood near his father, clutching his hand or holding his waist. More like an infant than an eight-year-old boy. Jung knew something was wrong, but every time he asked Mr Park, he became angry. Aggressive. Protective. Eventually Jung got the hint and stopped asking.

That was two days ago, and he hadn't heard from them since.

Payne, Jones, and Kia arrived in Seongsan just before dinner. The town was abuzz with tourists, the pulse of the festival just springing to life.

The trio lucked into a parking spot adjacent to the harbour, five minutes from the marina entrance. Jung's boat was just where it was supposed to be, tied off at the end of a long wooden dock. No one on board. Nothing suspicious. Payne glanced at his watch and noted the time. They would check back in a few hours, just in case someone showed up early.

But until then, they had plenty of time to kill.

Dozens of *pojangmachas* – street stalls on wheels where Korean food was cooked and sold – lined the narrow roads. Clouds of steam rose off the metal carts, the smell of spices filling the air. Payne and Jones browsed the selections as Kia translated the menus. There was *gimbap* (rice rolls), *sundae* (Korean sausage in hot sauce), *tteokbokki* (rice cakes in red pepper sauce), and *odeng* (simmered fish cakes on a skewer). Plus an assortment of items they recognized on their own. Egg rolls, dumplings, fritters, and meat on a stick – although no one knew what kind of meat it was. Payne ordered *okdom*, a fish found only off the coast of Jeju and Japan. It was broiled in sesame seed oil and served with a side of spring onion pancakes. Jones bought a combo platter, grilled pheasant and pan-fried *kimchi* (fermented vegetables), plus a seafood egg roll. Meanwhile, Kia fed her sweet tooth, getting a persimmon shake and a small bag of *yugwa* (grain cookies), treats she used to eat when she was a little child growing up near Seoul.

They took their food to a nearby table and ate in relative silence, watching people stroll by as the sunlight began to fade. Every few minutes firecrackers burst in the distance. The *pop! pop! pop!* echoed across the harbour like gunshots in the night. Kia flinched the first few times but eventually filtered out the sound, realizing it posed no threat. The whole time Payne and Jones never budged, years of experience honing their senses.

Suddenly, as if on cue, hundreds of paper lanterns were lit by villagers, who hung them in their windows and trees, while a giant bonfire was ignited at the top of the crater. Sparks and ash erupted into the night like a volcano. In an instant the entire village was bathed in firelight. Everyone's attention soon shifted to the outdoor theatre at the base of the peak. The rumble of a Korean drum, beaten with pulsating precision, heightened the drama, as if the mother ship from *Close Encounters* was about to land in Seongsan, as it did at Devil's Tower. A rainbow of colours exploded from the bank of spotlights as a provincial dance team, dressed in white masks and ancient robes, started their performance, leaping and twirling to the sounds of a Korean orchestra hidden in the wings. Tourists surged forward, jostling for the best view possible, trying to soak in the pageantry of centre stage.

Kia spoke above the clamour. 'This is only the beginning. The festival goes on until tomorrow morning, when we welcome the New Year. In fact, the sunrise is the most important part.'

Jones joked, 'I guess that's why they call it the Sunrise Festival.'

Kia smiled. 'I guess so.'

Payne asked, 'You mean nothing goes on at midnight? Jung said it was going to be crazy.'

'Don't worry. It will be. The whole night will be crazy.'

'Yeah, that's what I'm worried about.'

They made their way through the crowd, casually searching for the Parks, even though it would have taken a small miracle to find them. Too many people. Too much frivolity. Everywhere they looked, Koreans were dancing and singing, their faces shielded from the cold with hats and hoods. Others wore elaborate masks, painted with festive colours that obscured their identities.

Ironically, the two people who drew the most attention were Payne and Jones. Not because of their actions, but because of their genetics. Payne stood 6'4", almost a head taller than most of the Asians he passed. Couple that with Jones – a black man in a non-black world – and people assumed they were American athletes. Kia laughed the first few times someone asked to take their picture, even goading them on, whispering in Korean that they were NBA stars but didn't like to be bothered. Payne played along at first, even signing fake autographs for his 'fans', until the crowds started to grow out of control and he realized it might have an adverse effect on their mission. After that, they excused themselves and found a table that overlooked the harbour.

It was nearly 11 p.m. An hour still to go.

Thirty minutes later, Payne's phone started to vibrate. His caller ID said *Nick Dial*, his buddy from Interpol. He excused himself and answered the call.

'Hey, Nick, Happy New Year!'

'Same to you, Jon ... Sounds like you're out partying.'

'Yeah, I wish. I'm actually on a stake-out.'

'A stake-out, huh? I didn't know soldiers went on stake-outs.'

'Maybe that's why I suck at it. I've been signing autographs all night long.'

'You *what*?'

Payne explained the situation as he walked along the water's edge, looking for somewhere private to sit. Although he doubted anyone was listening, all this open space made him vulnerable to parabolic microphones. 'So, any luck with your search?'

'That depends on your definition of luck. I attribute my recent success to being so damn good.' He laughed to himself. 'Anyway, I talked to multiple sources, who briefed me on the rumours that have been floating around. Over the past few months, several big fish have fallen off our radar screen. Not surprising, since they're terrorists. Of course, we don't know if they were killed, if they're playing bingo in a mosque basement, or if we got sloppy and lost them.'

'That's the problem with terrorists. They never tell us anything.'

'Actually,' Dial said, 'sometimes they do. Two months

ago the French government nabbed a Muslim named Abdul Al-Amin trying to sneak a firearm into an art museum in Paris. Why? I have no idea. I'm guessing it had something to do with *The Da Vinci Code*.'

'Go on.'

'Anyway, Abdul's paperwork seemed clean, so the French decided to give him a slap on the wrist and let him go. But before they could, the idiot started blabbing, claiming he was part of an active terrorist group called the Soldiers of Allah and he'd be willing to give up vital information if they would cut a deal for his release.'

Payne laughed. 'What an idiot.'

'Yeah, a real Einstein. Anyhow, this is where it gets good. Once the French did some legwork, they realized the Soldiers of Allah had committed most of their acts of terror in America. So what did they do? They called Interpol and asked us to get involved. Long story short, I got access to a whole lot of info.'

'Anything useful?'

'That's for you to decide. Abdul was exactly who he said he was: a mid-level asshole for the Soldiers of Allah. He gave us names, dates, locations – the type of intel that only an insider would have. Some of it proved quite useful. We actually busted some of the smaller cells.'

'Good.'

'But not good enough. We told Abdul that we weren't going to let him go unless he gave us some intel on their leader, an Arab named Hakeem Salaam.'

Payne frowned. 'Never heard of him.'

'Me neither. So I called one of my buddies at Homeland Security to get some background info, and he nearly popped a boner when I mentioned his name. I honestly thought he was going to drop the phone and play with himself right there. Turns out Salaam is at the top of one of their special lists. I'm talking *extra*-special. You ready for this? He's what they call a Big Tit.'

'Did you say *tit?*'

'Stands for *Towel-headed Islamic Terrorist.* And no, I'm not making that up. Half those boys at Homeland Security are racist bastards. They claim it helps them do their jobs.'

'Go on.'

'So I make a joke of it. I tell him we should trade information, you know, *tit for tat*, but for some reason he didn't think it was funny.'

Payne stifled his urge to laugh. 'He tell you anything else?'

'Actually, he wanted me to tell him what I knew. Turns out Salaam and his top advisers disappeared a week after the incident at the museum. Poof! Just like that. No one knows why or where, but no one's heard from them since.'

Payne winced. Three days ago Colonel Harrington had used similar terminology to describe Schmidt and his squad. *They had disappeared, but no one knew why or where.* Now the same thing was being said about Salaam and his advisers. The major difference? The terrorists

208

disappeared several weeks ago, back when Schmidt was running a black op for Harrington in the Persian Gulf. Something he was reluctant to talk about when Jones questioned him.

A coincidence? Probably not.

In Payne's mind, the most likely scenario had Schmidt tracking down Salaam and his men, dragging them to the secret cave, and torturing them for information. At least until something went wrong. Now Schmidt and his crew were dead, Salaam was missing, and the only witness was an eight-year-old boy who had managed to disappear.

'Where's Abdul now?'

'Good question,' Dial said. 'Unfortunately, I don't have access to that information.'

'Why not?'

'Because he's no longer in Interpol custody.'

'He was released?'

'Hell, no. We don't release terrorists. Even dumb ones.'

'So what happened?'

'About a week ago, we cut a deal with some country who took possession of Abdul. I'm not sure who because the transfer papers were sealed. But the obvious choice is America.'

Perched on a picnic table, Jones scanned the crowd for fathers and sons. The only memorable pair was across the street at one of the gambling booths. The chubby kid was no more than two years old and wore a bright orange snowsuit that made him look like a pumpkin. Gamblers, possibly confusing the child with Buddha, let him hold their bets for good luck while they wagered on cards being dealt by his father, who seemed proud that his boy was following him into the family business. Every so often the kid would get caught up in the excitement and throw all the money in the air, causing a mad scramble among the participants.

It was a comical scene on an anxious night.

Several minutes passed before Payne strolled back to the table. He briefed Jones and Kia on his phone call from Nick Dial, explaining his theory on Hakeem Salaam. From Payne's perspective, it fitted all the pieces of the puzzle. Schmidt's black op in the Persian Gulf. Kia's need to speak Arabic. And everything else he could think of. He still wasn't sure what had happened in the village, but he hoped Yong-Su Park would fill in all the details.

That is, if he showed up with his father, like he was supposed to.

'May I ask a question?' Kia wondered. 'You mentioned that Salaam and his advisers recently disappeared. Does that mean we knew where they were beforehand? If so, why didn't we pick them up back then?'

'Actually,' Jones grunted, 'I wish it was that easy. That's the most frustrating thing about the war on terror. Sometimes we *know* people are terrorists – because of their associations, their business dealings, their ideologies – but can't prove it in a court of law. And in those cases, our hands are tied, especially if they're living outside of American jurisdiction. All we can do is track their movements and hope they screw up.'

Payne added, 'It's kind of like the Mafia. A lot of times we know who the bad guys are. We even know where they live. But we can't arrest them until we find the smoking gun.'

Jones agreed. 'That's a great analogy, because organized crime has the same basic structure. The goal of a terrorist cell is to protect the larger organization. Team A knows nothing about Team B, and so on. The leaders know what's going on – they're the ones pulling the strings – but the pawns don't know squat about long-term objectives. They keep everything compartmentalized, just in case the group is infiltrated.'

'And some terrorists are protected by so many layers that we can't prove anything. That means they can walk the streets and we can't arrest them. Or even threaten them. And if we do, *we're* the ones who get crucified.'

'By whom?' Kia wondered.

'The UN, the media, his home country. Everyone expects us to be global peacekeepers, but no one wants us to get our hands dirty. And let's face it: that's just not practical. Sometimes, for us to do our job, we have to cross the line.'

'You mean, like the cave?'

Payne frowned. 'Obviously, that's an *extreme* example. But yes –'

'Hold up!' Jones whispered.

He nodded his head to the left, pointing out two people who had just opened the gate to the marina. One tall, one short. Both wearing winter coats and hunting caps that were clasped around their chins. They clung to each other like family. Maybe for warmth. Maybe out of fear. Darkness prevented a positive ID, but this looked like them.

Payne checked his watch. It was nearly midnight.

'Kia,' he ordered, 'you stay here. DJ, come with me.'

As luck would have it, the marina was a dead end. One way in, one way out. A long wooden dock ran straight from the gate into the centre of the cold water. Maybe fifty yards in length. Most of the slips were empty – owners had taken their boats into the harbour for a better view of the celebration – so there was nowhere for the Parks to go. They were trapped. Unless they decided to swim for it. Which was pretty damn unlikely in the middle of winter.

Payne and Jones decided to play it cool. They walked slowly, like tourists, talking to each other while pointing out the sights. Who knew how desperate the father would be? Was he armed? Was he irrational? After all he had been through, the odds were against a peaceful conversation. That meant they needed to get as close as possible before they made their move. And even then, it would probably get messy. Screaming. Shouting. Kicking. And *that* was just from Jones.

No telling what the father might do.

Payne hit the first plank as the clock struck midnight, punctuated by a cheering crowd and a bolt of lightning that streaked across the sky. Then another. And another. But instead of thunder, the sky exploded with a burst of colours – fireworks being launched above Seongsan Peak. The burning embers fell towards the water as every boat in the harbour turned on their lights and sounded their whistles to greet the New Year. A raucous symphony of sights and sounds.

Up ahead, the two suspects stopped on the pier and admired the pageantry. They stood and turned like every other tourist in town. They smiled and clapped and enjoyed the moment. The taller one even pulled out a camera. And that's when Payne realized they had made a mistake.

They were following the wrong people.

He reached for Jones's shoulder, but it wasn't

necessary. He'd spotted the same thing. They quickly turned around, hoping to retreat before the real Parks showed up. But it was too late. One glance was proof of that. The boy and his father were standing there, panicked. Watching them from the other side of the gate.

And the father had a gun.

The first shot was fired without warning. Just a muzzle flash and a splash of water, somewhere near Payne's feet. Common sense said to run in the other direction. But what good would that do? They needed to talk to the boy, and the only way to accomplish that was to subdue his father. So they did the irrational. They ran towards danger.

A second shot rang out, this one much closer. It buzzed between Payne and Jones and buried itself in the dock. Wood splintered in a puff of smoke as the two tourists dived into the harbour.

It was a sane response to an insane situation.

The father fired once again, this time hitting Jones in the upper arm. The bullet tore through his coat and ripped through his skin, casting goosedown and blood spatter in every direction. The impact knocked him sideways, twisting him just enough to ruin his balance. One second he was running forwards, the next he was falling backwards on the slippery wood. His left hip took the brunt of the fall, followed by his injured arm and the left side of his face. Not enough to knock him out, but enough to leave him dazed.

Payne screeched to a halt, more concerned about his friend than the suspect, who suddenly stopped shooting and ran into the crowd. Blood oozed from Jones's left bicep but didn't squirt, a good sign with any injury. Jones would have a scar but would survive. No worries there.

'Get out of here,' he grunted. 'I'm fine.'

'You sure?'

'Yeah.' He blinked a few times, dazed from the fall. 'But I keep seeing flashing lights.'

Payne laughed. 'Those are fireworks.'

'Oh . . . then I'm fine.'

A shrieking gate stopped their conversation. Payne raised his gun before he could decipher the threat. But it was a false alarm. It was Kia.

'Oh my God! Is he okay?'

But Payne ignored her question. 'Where are they?'

'To the right. They ran to the right.'

'Stay with him,' he ordered as he ran past. He leaped the gate, swinging his legs sideways without breaking stride, and sprinted into the surging crowd. The Parks had a head start, but they were no match for Payne's speed. He dodged people when he could, knocked them over when he couldn't, and didn't slow down until he spotted them hustling towards the outdoor theatre.

Fireworks continued to burst and boat whistles continued to sound, all of it masking the drama that was developing in the tiny town. All of that changed when the father used his gun again, this time firing a shot into the night-time sky. People turned and stared, unsure if it was a firecracker or something more dangerous. What they saw caused them to panic. A muscular white man was running down the road, knocking everyone out of his way while waving a large firearm. It didn't matter that he was innocent. That the shot had come from someone else's gun. All they knew was that he needed to be stopped.

Things got much worse when Mr Park started shouting in Korean. He screamed, 'He's trying to kill my boy! He wants to kill my son!'

That was like fuel on a fire. In a flash, it was Payne versus an entire village.

Moments before, a team of six men had been centre stage, displaying their martial arts skills in a performance they called *Tiger-Strike*. All of them were dressed in black and wore permanent scowls. Three of them carried swords. The others held nunchucks. They ran towards him en masse, hoping to overwhelm Payne with their sheer numbers. Assuming their *Tiger-Strike* teamwork would cause him to cower.

But they were wrong.

Payne started with an elbow, throwing it with such power and precision that he shattered the nose and cheekbone of the first ninja before he could even raise his blade. The sword bounced to the ground with a loud clank that echoed through the crowd, soon followed by a louder gasp. Payne's momentum propelled him forwards, helping him throw his leg skywards in a roundhouse kick that caught his next victim under the chin. His head snapped back with the force of a car crash, tumbling into the third attacker, who knocked over several chairs, then scampered away.

The fourth man was far wiser, charging into battle behind the point of his sword. He swung it back and forth, flipping his wrists in fluid circles, a dazzling display of precision and grace. The type of showmanship that could win awards. Yet not very effective in a street fight. Payne pointed his gun and pulled the trigger, blowing the man's kneecap through the back of his leg. A second later, his screams filled the night as he fell to the ground in a puddle of his own blood.

The remaining duo wasted no time, swooping in from behind before Payne could turn around. One landed a solid strike with his nunchuck, hitting him in his ribcage. Thankfully, his jacket and body armour softened the blow. So much so that Payne was able to grab his attacker's weapon and pull him closer. An instant later, Payne thrust his knee upwards, hitting him in his groin. Balls ruptured from the force. As the man bent over in agony, Payne grabbed the back of his head and slammed his knee into the guy's face, knocking him unconscious. But Payne didn't let him fall to the ground. Instead, he pushed him towards his friend, who mistakenly tried to catch him. Before the guy could react, Payne launched himself forward, striking him in the mouth with the butt of his gun.

Teeth cracked and nerves frayed as Payne spun and waited for a counter-assault.

But none was to follow.

Payne stood tall in the middle of six men, all in various states of pain, unwilling to test him further. The same could be said of the crowd, which had scattered in every direction.

He stood there alone, staring at the father and son.

The father stared back, gun still in hand.

Willing to die for his boy.

32

Jeddah, Saudi Arabia
(41 miles west of Mecca)

Hakeem Salaam had been a terrorist since he was a young child growing up in Medina. He had learned the craft from his father, a man who stood up for his beliefs even when they weren't popular in his native Saudi Arabia. Sometimes using violence, sometimes using words. Doing whatever he felt was necessary to make sure his message was heard.

At the age when most boys were taught how to play sports, Salaam learned how to assemble weapons and make explosives out of household chemicals. How to plan a sneak assault in an urban environment. And how to escape afterwards. To him, there was nothing strange about it. This was the only life he knew, and his father was his role model. If anything, he felt pity for the other Arab children who wasted their lives, listening to music and playing silly games instead of making a difference in the world.

Didn't they know that they were being corrupted?

The country he blamed the most was the United

States, a seed his father had planted in him from the very beginning but one that grew more obvious with each passing year. Everything about their culture was immoral. Their drinking. Their depravity. Their lack of religious structure. The way they glamourized sex and drugs in their movies and books. Half-naked women walking around in public. And teenage girls doing the same.

And what did their government do about it? *Nothing.*

They were too busy fighting wars in places they didn't belong.

Ten years ago, Salaam founded the Soldiers of Allah, an organization destined to become one of the most feared terrorist groups in the world. He started small, recruiting a few trusted lieutenants who preached his word while protecting his identity, always maintaining the veil of secrecy that surrounded him.

Unlike some terrorists, he didn't crave personal attention. He craved results.

When he first started out, he had a specific agenda: to protect the religion of Islam. He figured the best way to accomplish that goal was to punish its corruptors, to make them pay for the erosion of his people and their morals. Just like Muhammad had done when he purified the Kaaba by removing all the false idols that were worshipped there.

Salaam's group focused on the United States, labelling it as their biggest threat. Targeting it and its allies every chance he got. He supplied weapons. He blew up embassies. He attacked buses and subways. He did everything he could to hurt his enemy, all in hopes of uniting his people under a common cause. Hoping his passion would be contagious.

Yet his actions were for naught. Islam remained a house divided.

Ultimately, he realized he needed to alter his approach. He had to figure out a way to bridge the gaps that separated his people, gaps that were significant. There were more than 1.2 billion Muslims scattered around the world, making it the second-largest religion behind Christianity. Yet Islam wasn't isolated in the Middle East. In fact, there were more Asian Muslims than Arab ones – more than 150 million in Indonesia alone. Not to mention a large number of Muslims in the United States, nearly twice as many as Jews there.

Still, the variety of cultures and languages was just part of the problem.

The biggest hurdle was the diversity of beliefs.

There were the Sunnis, the largest subgroup, which contained more than 80 per cent of Muslims, who believed one school of Islamic thought. And the Shiites, who followed another. Then there were the Wahhabis, whose influence was spreading quickly. Plus all the minor sects that had so many subtle differences that even he couldn't tell them apart.

How was he going to unite all these people under

one flag when most of them weren't even willing to be in the same room?

He knew it would take a miracle.

Ironically, it was the tragedy in New York City that gave him the idea.

He watched in amazement as the events of 9/11 unfolded on his television screen. The way the planes crashed into the Twin Towers and sent them toppling to the ground in a burst of fire and ash. How people scurried for their lives and mourned those who didn't survive. It was an amazing sight to see in such a diverse nation. The way Americans and their allies joined together and formed a united front. Men and women. Young and old. Rich and poor. Blacks and whites. Democrats and Republicans. It didn't really matter. Everyone was equal.

In their time of tragedy, they became one.

Salaam disappeared into the mountains for days, meditating like Muhammad had done, thinking about his problem from all angles, weighing the positives and the negatives, trying to determine the best way to take advantage of what he had witnessed in America.

In his mind, all he needed to do was find a common thread among all Muslims, and once he did, he would give it a yank. The natural reaction would be to pull together. To unite. Whether it was out of love, sorrow, or fear, it didn't really matter, as long as they were standing as one.

Of course, he needed to find that thread.

And then it dawned on him. There was only one thing that all Muslims – Sunnis, Shiites, and all the sects – agreed upon. One thing they would fight for. One place they cared about.

The birthplace of their greatest prophet.

The site of their most holy mosque.

The centrepiece of Islam.

33

The boy buried his face in his father's hip, unable to look at the blood. He had seen enough in the past week to last him a lifetime.

Trembling, his father held him tight. One hand on Yong-Su's head, the other on his gun. He tried aiming at Payne but was doing a poor job. Adrenaline made him shaky. Emotions made him unstable. Tears flowed from his eyes as he grasped the situation. Four shots fired. One man down. Cornered and unable to run. No other options in sight.

Thankfully, Payne recognized the mindset. The desperation. The feelings of hopelessness. Many of his former enemies had felt the exact same way. So he knew how to deal with it.

'Chung-Ho,' he said. His voice was calm, steady. 'My name is Jonathon Payne, and I'm here to help. I know it doesn't seem that way, but I am.'

He waited for a response, but none was forthcoming.

'Can you understand me? Do you speak English?'

Several seconds passed before he nodded.

'Good. That's good.' Payne lowered his weapon six inches, a gesture of goodwill. 'Your neighbour

Mr Kim told me what happened to you. I'm sorry for your loss. I truly am.'

But Park said nothing.

'He's worried about your safety. Same with Yong-Su's.'

'You no talk about my son! Leave him alone!'

'Of course. I'm sorry. I didn't mean to ...' He bowed his head slightly. 'I'm sorry.'

'How you find me?'

'I talked to Chi-Gon Jung, the man you rented your boat from. He told me where to find you.'

'Why? What you want?'

'I want to help. I simply want to help. I'm not here to hurt you. I swear I'm not.'

'It no look like that! Look what you did to me!'

'I had no choice. *You* shot my partner. *You* started a riot. I had to defend myself.'

'No!' he shouted. 'I defend myself!'

Payne nodded, taking a small step forwards. 'I know you are. That's why I'm not upset. You were scared, so you did what you could to protect yourself. There's nothing wrong with that. In fact, it's instinctual. You felt threatened, so you fought back.'

Park stared at him, his gun still trembling.

'Unfortunately, sometimes a problem can be so big, you can't face it alone. Sometimes you need help to survive. Which is why I'm here. I'm here to help.'

'How you help me?'

Payne stepped closer. 'First of all, I can take you

somewhere safe. That's most important. Wherever you want to go. To the mainland. To Japan. To the States. Anywhere you'd like.'

He paused, letting that sink in. 'Then, once I know you're okay, I'm going to hunt for the men who attacked your village. No matter what, no matter where, I will search for them. And when I find them . . .' His voice trailed off for just a second. 'Let's just say what happened here tonight is *nothing* compared to what I'll do to them. I promise you that.'

The wail of sirens cut through the night, somehow rising above the fireworks, gunshots, and screams from the crowd. Payne heard the sound and realized what it meant: Park had to decide immediately. No way could they risk police involvement. Not with so much on the line. Unfortunately, he wasn't sure if Park felt the same way. For all he knew, Park might view the cops as a better option. Safer than talking to Payne. It was a risk Payne couldn't afford.

'Mr Kim told me horror stories about your village and all the atrocities that have happened in the cave. Through it all, the thing that surprised me the most was his hatred of the local police. The way they killed innocents during the massacre, the way they betrayed their own people. Until that point, I couldn't under-stand why you had decided to run. Then it made perfect sense. This island isn't safe for you. And it isn't safe for your son.'

The sirens grew louder, coupled with the glow of flashing lights.

'I know you don't trust me. And the truth is you probably shouldn't considering all that's happened in the past week. But in my heart I know you trust your neighbour, Mr Kim. That's why you ran to him in your time of crisis. You trusted his wisdom and guidance above your own.'

Payne lowered his gun, going for broke.

'So tell me this. If he was here right now, which would he recommend? The police or me?'

The Korean National Police Agency (KNPA) was the only police organization in South Korea. Based in Seoul, it was divided into fourteen local bureaus, including one on Jeju.

During the Sunrise Festival, most on-duty officers were assigned to crowd control, helping the flow of traffic, arresting drunks, and doing what they could to make the celebration safe. Seongsan was a small village with very little crime, so the last thing they expected was a series of shootings. Not only at the marina, but at the theatre as well.

By the time they were notified, crucial time had been lost, made worse by the hordes of people who blocked the roads. Sirens sounded and lights flashed, but the streets were so narrow that people had nowhere to go. A journey that usually took a minute suddenly took ten. Way too long to make a difference.

The first officers at the scene – proudly wearing the new police insignia, a Steller's sea eagle carrying a Rose of Sharon – checked the theatre for gunmen before rushing to the aid of six victims, all of whom had black ninja outfits and a number of bruises. One was missing a knee, and the others were visibly shaken.

Their *Tiger-Strike* teamwork had been ineffective against a more worthy opponent.

Other witnesses were rounded up. Some Koreans. Some Japanese. Even a few Europeans. When questioned, all of them said the exact same thing. A crazed American had started the brawl. A tall, muscular guy who carried a gun and wiped out half the crowd.

Then again, they said, his violent behaviour should have been expected.

Why? Because he played in the NBA.

Payne knew the main roads would soon be blocked. So they left town to the east, taking Jung's fishing boat to the open sea.

The hardest part of the journey was the first thirty minutes. Sneaking the Parks into the marina. Convincing Jones, who was bleeding from his bicep, to play nice with the guy who'd just shot him. Hot-wiring the boat, since they didn't have time to wait for Jung's guide. And keeping the Parks calm as Payne steered past hundreds of boats that filled the harbour. Kia played a major role in the last one, speaking to the Parks in Korean, doing whatever she could to reassure them of their safety. Still, despite her best efforts, Chung-Ho refused to part with his gun.

He clung to it with one hand, his son with the other.

The waters of the Korea Strait were notoriously tough to handle, especially in the dead of night. The sea was deep, the currents were strong, and all the boat's gauges were in Korean. After some translation help from Kia, Payne called Jones to the wheel.

'How's the arm?'

'It's fine. I found a first-aid kit and patched myself up. I'm sending the bill to Harrington.'

Payne laughed, glad to see Jones's sense of humour still intact. 'Any mobility problems?'

'Jon,' he stressed, 'I'm fine.'

'Good. Glad to hear it. Because we have a decision to make.' He pulled out a map of the East Sea. 'We don't have many choices. Either Japan, mainland Korea, or one of the islands along the way.'

'Forget the islands. We could never blend in.'

'What about Korea? We could make it in a few hours.'

'That depends. How many people did you hurt back there? I hear Korean prisons are kind of brutal on pretty boys like yourself.'

'Good point. In that case, what about Japan?'

Jones studied the major ports along the Korea Strait. There were several options. 'Fukuoka is the closest big city. Roughly two million people. Plenty of places to sneak ashore. That might be our best bet . . . Then again, what are we going to do when we get there?'

Unfortunately, Payne never got the chance to answer.

He was too distracted by the helicopter that hovered up ahead.

34

Monday, 1 January

The roar of Jung's boat masked the chopper's engines until it was too late. Throw in the wind and the choppy seas, and Payne didn't spot it until it was a hundred yards away. Of course, even if he had, what could he have done? The damn thing just hovered there, directly in his path. No movement. No lights. Like an iceberg in the night, just waiting for the *Titanic* to strike.

Payne swore to himself and eased the boat to a stop. He told everyone on board not to panic, that everything would be all right. But deep down inside, he wasn't so sure. Technically, they were in a stolen boat and had just fled a country where he'd shot someone and assaulted five others. Park was carrying a gun and had recently fired it several times in the crowded streets of Seongsan. Jones was bleeding. The boy was traumatized. And Kia was privy to everything.

Yeah, they were screwed.

Things got worse when the chopper turned on its gigantic spotlight and shined it directly on the boat.

Payne shielded his eyes, trying to figure out who he was dealing with. The police? The coastguard? The Korean Navy? Any of those would have ruined his New Year.

Suddenly a booming voice – like the voice of God – filled the night. It was broadcast in English over the chopper's speaker system, echoing louder than the roar of the turbines. 'Do not be alarmed . . . Do not make a move . . . Prepare to be boarded.'

Jones grimaced at the announcement. 'That sounds painful.'

'Let's hope not,' said Payne as he inched his way towards Mr Park, who sat in the back of the boat. When he got there, he spoke firmly into his ear. 'If you want to help your son, drop your gun overboard. If they see it in your hand, you will be arrested. Or worse.'

Park nodded in understanding.

Five seconds later it was sinking to the bottom of the sea.

The next few minutes were a whirlwind of surprises. The chopper rose several feet above the water, then crept forward until it hovered directly above the cramped deck of the boat. Payne heard the rumble of a large winch as two men were lowered on board.

Both of them were dressed in black, their faces covered with visors.

No patches. No badges. No insignias.

Neither man carried a weapon.

Confused, Payne stood there, assessing the situation. He knew they were in Korean waters, yet no one on the chopper had identified whom he worked for. The orders to halt had been given in English, not Korean. And the men standing across from him were tall and muscular, closer to Payne's size than Park's.

Something about this didn't seem right.

Things got stranger when one of them whipped out a cell phone and waited for it to ring. A few seconds later, it did. But instead of answering the call, which would have required him to take off his helmet and show his face, he walked forward and handed it to Payne.

The man said, 'It's for you.'

'It is?' Payne took the phone and answered the call. 'Hello?'

The voice on the other end was American. Masculine. All business. He said, 'We've been sent to evacuate you and your friends.'

'Who is this?'

But his question was dismissed. Simply ignored. 'We'll hoist you up one at a time. Jones first, then the others, then you. Later tonight you'll be briefed in *private*. Am I clear?'

'Crystal.'

'Good. My men will remain on board. Tell them where to dump the boat and it will be done.'

The United States and the Republic of Korea signed a Status of Forces Agreement (SOFA) in 1966, guaranteeing the presence of US military personnel to protect against external threats. Currently, there were more than 30,000 American soldiers stationed in Korea, scattered around the country on several official bases. And several more that were *unofficial*.

Payne and his crew were taken to one of those, tucked in the rolling hills of Jeollanam-do Province, near the south-western tip of the peninsula. On paper, the base had been decommissioned a decade ago, yet it still housed enough soldiers to start a small war. From the outside, the facility looked abandoned – a series of dilapidated hangars and warehouses that should have been razed – but the inside was a different story.

It was buzzing with activity.

From the moment they got into the chopper until they were escorted to a small room on the northern end of the compound, the Parks were blindfolded. Kia sat next to them the entire time, whispering in Korean, assuring them that everything was being done for their safety. Her dedication continued once they reached the base. She refused to leave their side, even after their blindfolds were removed and they were locked in their holding cell, which had the feel of a cheap hotel room – equipped with a bed, desk, TV, and bathroom. A video camera was mounted in the far corner of the ceiling, allowing a team of guards to monitor them at all times.

Meanwhile, Payne and Jones were taken to a different building, this one in the centre of the camp, where they met the senior enlisted adviser in a tiny office with cement walls and an American flag as its lone decoration. His name was Crawford, and his rank was command sergeant major. He wore a beige T-shirt and camouflage cargo trousers that had been recently ironed. His hair looked brown but was shaved so close its colour hardly mattered. The type of guy who smiled so infrequently it looked like he had wind when he actually tried.

Payne recognized Crawford's voice the moment he spoke – he was the man who'd called him on Jung's boat. 'I hope you realize the position you put us in, having to save your ass in the middle of the night. We didn't appreciate the exposure.'

'Excuse me?'

'You heard me. This is supposed to be a low-key operation.'

'Yeah,' Payne snapped. 'I gathered that from your office decor. I meant the *saving my ass* part. I never asked to be saved.'

'That's not what we heard from the Pentagon.' He opened the lone folder that sat on his desk. 'At 0002 hrs, we were notified of a possible medical evac on Jeju Island. Details to follow. At 0011 hrs, medical evac was changed to personnel evac. Three soldiers, two civilians. Aerial resources were diverted from a training mission in the Korea Strait, course south-southwest towards Seongsan. At 0017 hrs, our rendez-vous point was updated when your boat was tagged by satellite.' He glanced up from the folder and stared at them. 'Shall I go on?'

Jones spoke first. 'Can you repeat the part about medical evac? *That* was *so* exciting!'

'You think this is a joke?'

'No,' Payne said, 'we don't. But unless you have transcripts of an unauthorized broadcast on our part, I think it would be best if you dropped your attitude. Last time I checked, sergeant majors were several notches below captain in the chain of command.'

Crawford stood from his chair. 'Maybe so. But last time *I* checked, you were retired.'

He walked towards his office door, then stopped. 'Stay put. I'm calling Washington.'

Payne and Jones waited for Crawford to close his door before they spoke. And even then, they did it in hushed tones, trying not to be overheard.

Jones asked, 'Did you call for evac when I was shot?'

'Are you crazy? I was running down the street, chasing a gunman. When could I call?'

'What about Kia?'

'What about her? She was taking care of *you*. Did she use your phone?'

Jones shook his head. She was busy, too. 'Well, *someone* called.'

Payne nodded, confused. 'Yeah, but the question is who.'

35

Twenty minutes passed before Crawford returned. When he did, he said nothing until he had punched a series of buttons on his desk phone. Its speaker crackled to life.

He muttered, 'Washington is on the line. Hang up when you're done.'

Then he turned and left the room. No explanation. No name or hint of what was to follow. Payne couldn't tell if Crawford was angry, embarrassed, or pleased with himself, because the bastard had no facial expressions. Like the ultimate poker player. Or someone with Botox.

Payne pulled the speaker closer. 'This is Jonathon Payne. Who am I speaking to?'

There was a lengthy delay before a gruff voice filled the line. 'Randy Raskin. Pentagon.'

Jones started laughing, happy to hear from his friend. 'Damn, Randy, you scared the hell out of us. We thought you were someone important.'

'Thanks, man. I appreciate it. I love you, too.'

Payne said, 'You know what he means.'

'I know, I know.' The ever-present clicking of Raskin's keyboard could be heard in the background.

He was the quintessential multitasker. 'I'm guessing your host is out of the room.'

'Yeah. We're clear.'

'Thank God! That guy is an idiot. I've been forced to sound official for the past three hours. No matter what I did or said, he kept quoting rules and regulations. Blah, blah, blah. Even when DJ was shot, he gave me flak about evac.'

Jones leaned forward. 'I'm fine, by the way. Thanks for asking.'

'Oh, now I get it,' Raskin teased. 'You don't consider me *important*, yet you want me to care about your health? Sorry, fellas. You can't have it both ways . . . Besides, I already knew you were fine. I've been monitoring your progress all night.'

Payne frowned. 'How so?'

'The amazing thing about Korea is their technology. They're *way* ahead of us when it comes to implementation. It's actually kind of creepy. Sorta like Big Brother.'

'Meaning?'

'Did you know Jeju has more than 6,000 traffic cameras? With a touch of a button, I tapped into their mainframe and followed your movement all over the island. I'm telling you, it was great. Just like a movie! When you got attacked by ninjas? Man, that was awesome! You were like, kick, punch, shoot! And that guy was like *aaaaaaaagh*! Only I couldn't hear him scream because there's no sound on their cameras.'

'Are you done?'

'Not yet. If you want, I can burn you a copy on DVD. You know, like a home movie.'

'I'd like one,' Jones said. 'Please send it to –'

But Payne cut him off. 'Actually, I'd prefer it if you deleted all traces of us from their system. If Korea sees that footage –'

'I know, I know. Don't worry. I already took care of it. I wiped out the entire feed from Seongsan. Their computers will interpret it as a power surge, but we know the truth.'

'Thanks,' Payne said. 'You're the best.'

'I know that, too.'

'So,' Jones said, 'was there a reason you called? Or were you just calling to brag?'

'Damn! The guy gets shot one time, and now he's all business.' Raskin pounded away on his keyboard until the correct file filled his screen. 'You asked me to do more research on Dr Ernie Sheldon, and I found some interesting nuggets. Is there somewhere I can send them, or will I have to go through Crawford?'

'Fill us in now,' Payne said. 'You can send it through him later.'

Raskin scanned the data. 'Don't crucify me on this one, but I gave you some misleading intel the last time we talked. Turns out Dr Sheldon might not be dead. In fact, I'm pretty sure of it. His main file lists him as *deceased*. Yet I tracked him through some back doors and found a fairly recent posting. For the past three years he's been working as a special projects coordinator at Fort Huachuca.'

Fort Huachuca was a major military installation in Arizona that became home to the US Army Intelligence Center and School in 1971. Since then, its post had changed several times, yet in the past three decades one thing had remained constant. If a soldier wanted to be certified as an interrogator, he went to Fort Huachuca – where they taught all the necessary skills to become a 97E (pronounced 97 echo), everything from the art of interrogation to the rules of deception.

Payne and Jones were quite familiar with the installation, a place both of them endured while prepping for the MANIACs. At times their training was horrific, bordering on inhumane.

But it prepared them for what they'd face in the Special Forces. And how to handle it.

Payne said, 'Define special projects.'

'Everything from the latest torture techniques to mind-control experiments. Plus I hear there's been progress with gamma-aminobutyric acid. Combining GABA drugs and physical exhaustion to extract confessions.' Raskin cleared his throat, as if catching himself before he revealed too much. 'Of course, that's *probably* just hearsay. I have no specific knowledge as to what Sheldon was working on.'

'And these projects,' Payne wondered. 'Are they being used in the field?'

'Honestly, Jon, I really don't know. I sit behind a desk all day, fiddling with my keyboard. You're the one in the real world. You tell me. Are these techniques being used?'

Payne knew the answer was yes. Torture had been around for as long as there had been pain, and it wouldn't stop anytime soon. The problem was that torture had proved to be unreliable because *all* prisoners eventually talked, although what they said was often fabricated, a way for the brain to protect the body from further abuse.

That's why men like Dr Sheldon conducted their research.

They were looking for better ways to obtain information.

Recent studies had shown that some of the simplest techniques – exhaustion, sleep deprivation, prolonged exposure to heat or cold – were the most effective. Yet in recent years, the one technique that had been in the news the most was *waterboarding*. It was even mentioned by Vice President Dick Cheney in a White House interview, who called it a 'very important tool'.

Prisoners were immobilized with ropes or cords. Feet slightly inclined. Head below legs. Cellophane was wrapped around the subject's face and water was poured over him. Almost instantly, the gag reflex kicked in and the subject panicked, terrified of drowning and certain death. Rumour had it that several CIA officials volunteered to go through the ordeal to understand its physiological devastation. Their average endurance time was fourteen seconds.

Payne was familiar with all this information. What he didn't know was Dr Sheldon's role in what was going on. Had he been called in as an expert to assess the crime scene? Or was the cave one of his experiments gone wrong? And if so, who was the intended victim?

'Bear with me,' Payne said as he changed the direction of their conversation. 'Last time we spoke, I asked for the names of prisoners in black-op facilities. Unfortunately, you were unable to help. So let me approach this from a different angle. One of my sources recently gave me the name of a known terrorist who we think might be part of this. If I mention his name, would you be able to confirm or deny his capture?'

Raskin chose his words carefully. 'Technically, I couldn't confirm anyone's capture without proper clearance. But I'd be happy to deny any rumours that I felt could hurt your mission.'

'Fine. The name we heard is Hakeem Salaam.'

Raskin said nothing for the next fifteen seconds.

'Thank you,' Payne said, reading between the lines. 'That's a big help.'

'My pleasure. Now unless you have something else, please put the sergeant major back on the phone. I want to mess with him some before I get back to work.'

Whatever Raskin said to Crawford was effective, because from that moment on he was on his best behaviour. He led Payne and Jones to a private computer terminal, where they were able to download Dr Sheldon's file and print several photographs they had requested.

Armed with this new information, they were escorted across the facility grounds to where the Parks were being detained. Kia was called out of the room for a quick briefing, and filled them in on the past few hours, describing what was said on the boat, in the helicopter, and in the holding cell. Amazingly, just like Mr Kim in the village, the Parks had warmed to her in a short time – incredible, considering the circumstances.

'Is the boy talking?' Payne wondered.

'Not about the cave, but he *is* talking about other things. He's a great kid who's been through a whole lot. I'm stunned he's even coherent.'

'What about the dad?'

'Scared. Angry. Anxious. Emotional. Everything you'd expect from a guy who's lost his family and doesn't know why.'

'What do you recommend?'

'About what?'

'About talking to them. We need to know what they know. ASAP.'

'But Jon –'

'I *know*,' he said, not letting her get started with an emotional plea. This was one of those situations where he wouldn't be dissuaded. 'Trust me, I realize they aren't ready to talk and won't be ready for some time. Unfortunately, this interview can't wait. We've got some new intel that we need to act on immediately, and the only way to do that is by talking to them. So whether it's you, me, or all three of us combined, this conversation needs to take place right now.'

36

Kia led the Parks into an interview room and prepared them for what was about to happen. She assured them that Payne was a decent man who would do them no harm, that he'd lost a good friend during the violence at the cave, and needed their statements to find the people responsible. When put in those terms, Chung-Ho was more than willing to help – even though he knew it would be painful for him and his son – because it was the honourable thing to do.

Payne came in next. Polite. Respectful. Empathetic. None of it an act of any kind. He'd lost his parents at an early age, killed by a drunk driver when he was in junior high, so he was all too familiar with sudden loss. His years as a soldier, surrounded by death and destruction, hadn't dulled any of those feelings, and they never would.

They'd be a part of him for ever.

'I know some of these questions are going to be difficult, probably the last thing in the world that you want to answer, but I wouldn't be asking them if they weren't so important.' Payne paused, trying to ease into the interview. 'Obviously, if you'd feel more comfortable speaking in Korean, we can use Kia as an interpreter.'

Chung-Ho shook his head. 'My English is good. So is my son's. We speak good.'

'Yes, you do. Much better than I speak Korean.' He smiled, hoping to keep the conversation friendly. 'To make things easier, I'd like to start with you. I figure the more you can tell me, the less I'll have to ask your son. In the long run, I think that would be best. Don't you?'

He nodded in appreciation, thankful for Payne's kindness.

Meanwhile, Yong-Su sat in a chair in the back corner, staring at the floor in a semi-daze. Kia sat next to him, telling him about her childhood in Korea, occasionally brushing the black hair from his eyes, like a mother might do. More worried about his well-being than the interview that was taking place ten feet away.

'If we can,' Payne said, 'I'd like to talk about last Saturday.'

Chung-Ho described what he could remember. Yong-Su had stumbled home from the cave, covered in blood. After checking him for injuries, Chung-Ho went from neighbour to neighbour, asking if they had seen anything, but no one had. Soon they discovered a trail of blood leading towards the cave. Panicked, he rushed to Kim and asked him what he should do. His advice was to take his son and leave town immediately. So he did, just like that. His wife and family were supposed to follow and meet them an hour later. But the people from the cave prevented it.

'Have you been to the village since?'

'No. It is not safe.' He looked back at his son, choosing his next words carefully. 'When my wife not arrive, I call Mr Kim from pay phone. He tell me what happen to village. He tell me never come back and not call police. He handle everything.'

Kim hadn't mentioned the phone call, but it explained why Chung-Ho had never returned to check on his wife and the rest of his family. He already knew what had happened to them.

'Did you see anyone from the cave that day?'

'No.'

'What about beforehand? Maybe a stranger walking in the woods?'

'I see nothing. We stay in village. They stay in cave. No strangers.'

'But your son,' he said delicately. 'He saw some people, didn't he?'

Chung-Ho turned and looked at his boy.

'Did he tell you what he saw?'

He took a deep breath, then nodded. 'He see blood. People in cave with blood.'

'You mean dead people?'

He shook his head. 'No. People still alive. They were talking.'

Payne paused, confused. Until that moment, he had assumed that Yong-Su had stumbled into the scene *after* everyone was dead, possibly overhearing the killers talk about the black stone as they left the cave. But now his father was telling him the exact opposite. Yong-Su was in there while people were still alive.

In a heartbeat, the direction of the interview had to be changed.

Payne thought back to the cave, recalling the layout of the initial chamber. A desk and a chair were bolted to the middle of the floor. A single lightbulb, equipped with a tiny camera, hung from the volcanic rock. Everything was bathed in blood – the floor, the ceiling, the walls. On the bright side, if there was one, the blood was primarily contained in that one room, the place where interrogations occurred. And since Yong-Su was covered in blood, he'd obviously been in there. Maybe during a torture session. If so, who knew what he could answer?

The possibilities were endless.

Payne sorted through all the questions in his head – who was being tortured, what was being said, who killed Schmidt and his crew – trying to figure out which was most important. In the end, he realized the most pressing question was one that Chung-Ho couldn't answer.

They needed to speak to the boy himself.

Payne asked Kia to join him in the hall, where they were met by Jones, who'd been watching the interview in an adjacent room. He had wanted to take a more active role but realized the bullet hole in his arm might be disconcerting to Chung-Ho, since he had pulled the trigger.

Jones spoke first. 'We need to talk to the kid.'

'I know,' Payne replied. 'But it shouldn't be me.'

They both looked at Kia, who appeared less than thrilled with the concept.

'Fine.' She groaned. 'What do you want me to ask?'

Jones handed her a manila envelope filled with pictures that had been e-mailed by Randy Raskin. 'We need to know who the kid saw. Who was alive, who was dead, who was being tortured, and so on. After that, we'll have a much better grasp of things.'

'Right now the timeline is pretty fuzzy,' Payne admitted. 'The kid walks into the cave and sees people covered in blood but claims they were alive. If so, how did he get so much blood on him? Maybe he saw the killers after the fact. Or maybe he walked in during an interrogation. Either way, we need to know who he saw so we can figure out what happened.'

Kia grimaced. 'You know, this *isn't* going to be easy. I can barely get the kid to talk, and when I do, it's about silly things. What he likes to eat. What he does for fun. Now you want me to ask him about the cave?' She took a deep breath. 'Any recommendations?'

Payne nodded. 'Yeah. Make a game of it.'

'A game?'

'The kid's eight and scared out of his mind. The lighter you make it, the better.'

'Easier said than done.'

'I realize that, but you've been doing great with him. I have the utmost confidence in you.'

'I do, too,' echoed Jones. 'I've been watching you in there, and the kid really likes you. You're a natural at this.'

'Thanks. But I'm still nervous.'

'Don't worry about it. You'll do fine . . . Of course, if you think it would help, I'd be happy to give you a kiss for good luck.'

Kia laughed, thankful for the levity.

'Yeah. Didn't think so.' Jones started to back down the hall. 'But if you change your mind, let me know. Just wink at the camera and I'll come running.'

Payne and Kia sat on one side of the table, the Parks on the other. Kia spread twenty pictures in front of Yong-Su and told him they were going to play a game. The rules were simple. Some of the men in the photos had been to Jeju, while many others hadn't. For every one he got right, he would be given a sweet – his favourite food in the whole world. However, for every one he got wrong, a piece would be taken away.

'Do you understand?' Kia asked. 'If you aren't *sure* about someone, you shouldn't guess. Only choose the ones that you're absolutely positive about. Okay?'

Yong-Su glanced at the pictures and nodded.

He could taste the sweets already.

37

Before the incident, Yong-Su was a typical eight-year-old boy. He was adventurous, active, and loved getting dirty. His hair was black and grew way too fast, falling into his eyes if he didn't get it trimmed every other week. Three of his front teeth were missing – two on top, one on the bottom – giving him a jack-o'-lantern smile that was common among his age group.

Of course, during the past nine days there had been little to smile about. From the moment he stumbled out of the bloody cave, he was a changed person. Partly in shock. Partly in grief. Dealing with things that would devastate most adults.

And yet there he was. Staring at all the pictures, playing Kia's game.

Looking forward to all the sweets he was going to win.

In a complex world, sometimes it was the simple pleasures that got us through.

He studied the images for several seconds, choosing all the people he saw in the cave. Selecting them in his head before he made his choices. Finally, without saying a word, he picked up a photo. Then another. And another. Two over here, three over there. Gathering them in his hands like a deck of cards. Tapping them against the table to make sure they were nice and straight. Sixteen photos in all. Some Americans. Some Arabs. A wide variety of ages.

When he was done, he handed the stack to Kia. It was much larger than she was expecting.

She said, 'You saw all of these people?'

Yong-Su shook his head and pointed to the desk. 'No, *those* people.'

Four photos were spread across the surface. Payne recognized them at once.

It was Trevor Schmidt and his crew.

'Can you tell us where you saw them?' she asked.

He nodded, then explained what had happened that day.

Yong-Su had been playing in the woods when he smelled the blood. A strong, pungent odour that piqued his curiosity and gave him the courage to investigate the one spot he was forbidden to go. He knew he should have turned around and run in the opposite direction, but he couldn't help himself. He was drawn to the place. He had to see it for himself.

So he crept up the hill, carefully. Listening for the screams he sometimes heard at night. But on this morning, everything was silent. It gave him the nerve to continue.

The tunnel opening was dark. Almost black. The

only hint of light was somewhere up ahead, cast by a single bulb that hung from the ceiling. He listened for voices but heard none. The cave was quiet, peaceful. The only sound was the occasional crunch of stone under his feet – and even that was just a whisper. The one thing that stood out to him was the smell. The air was thick with it, filled with the putrid odour that reminded him of a hunting trip he once took with his dad.

The first chamber was unlike anything he had ever seen. Much of the floor and some of the walls were dripping with blood. Not smeared with it, but actually leaking it. Like the earth had been gashed and was starting to bleed. He walked over to the closest wall and touched it. Ran his fingers through it. The light was faint, yet bright enough to prove he wasn't imagining it.

His hand was now crimson. His face was now pale.

That's the moment he heard the voice. Initially, he thought he was just spooked by the liquid that covered his hand. Then he heard a second one. And a third. Voices emerging from the depths of the cave. Panicked, he turned to run outside but slipped on the slick floor. Soon, his skin and clothes were covered in red – a colour that saved his life.

He scampered to the far corner of the cave and curled into a tiny ball, partially hidden by a crevice in the rock, partially camouflaged by the blood. In the faint light, he was nearly invisible to the naked eye, especially since no one was looking for him. If they had been, they would have found him immediately. No doubt about it. The chamber was small and they were trained soldiers, but at that moment they assumed they were alone. It wasn't until much later when they saw his footsteps that they realized their facility had been breached and their secret had been spilled. That's when they were forced to invade the nearby village and kill everyone they found.

To them, their mission was too important to be derailed by sympathy.

From the back corner, Yong-Su saw four men as they approached the table and chair that were anchored to the middle of the floor. Each of them carried a small box. Each box was filled with three plastic bags. Each bag was filled with blood. The men laughed and joked as they punctured the bags with their knives and squirted the blood everywhere for the second time that day. On the floor. On the ceiling. On the walls. Bag after bag, squeeze after squeeze, until the cave glistened like a ruby in the faint light of the bulb.

There was no violence or torture on that final morning. Just a bunch of clever men who faked their own murders with bags of their own blood, liquid that had been collected over several days and stored in the cave.

DNA evidence that would prove their deaths while actually giving them life.

*

254

Payne excused himself from the interview and met Jones in private, both of them stunned by what they'd just heard. For the past two days, they had been under the impression that Trevor Schmidt and his crew had been murdered inside the cave. Butchered and brutalized by some unknown group that was trying to rescue a terrorist. But now, thanks to the testimony of an eight-year-old boy, they knew the truth about the cave. Not only was Schmidt alive, but his team was probably responsible for the massacre in the village.

One minute Payne wanted to avenge his friend's death. Now he wanted to kill him.

'Schmidt was already running a black op,' he said. 'No one knew where he was or what he was doing. So why in the hell would he fake his own death?'

'If I had to guess, I'd say to hide from the man he was working for.'

'Colonel Harrington?'

Jones nodded. 'Think back to our time with the MANIACs. We were given a lot of latitude when it came to our missions. If we didn't report on time, no big deal. They came to expect that from us to a certain extent. But deep down inside, we knew there was a line we couldn't cross. And if we did, they'd send someone after us – whether we wanted them to or not.'

'And Schmidt's death erased that line.'

'No more Harrington. No more checking in. He's a free man to do whatever he wants.'

'Which ain't a good thing.'

'No, it's not. One of my instructors at the Academy told me, "Soldiers should fight for freedom but they shouldn't have it." I never knew what he meant until I went overseas and saw what happened when no one was watching.' He paused, gathering his thoughts. 'Structure is in place for a reason. Commanding officers are there for a reason. Without them, a soldier like Schmidt is capable of doing a lot of damage.'

'I'm assuming he already has.'

'You mean the village?'

Payne nodded. 'Less than an hour after he faked his death, he killed how many innocents? And for what reason? To make sure no one knew he was alive?' He paused. 'Unless –'

'Unless what?'

'Maybe he didn't kill them to protect his death. Maybe he killed them to protect his mission. Obviously he saw Yong-Su's bloody footsteps outside the cave. That's probably what led him to the village. And if Schmidt was discussing the mission while the boy was in there? You know damn well he would've been forced to plug the leak before anyone could talk about it.'

'The black stone,' Jones suggested. 'The boy kept muttering something about the black stone. Maybe that has more significance than we think.'

Ten minutes later, they'd realize how much more.

38

Payne walked into the interview room with a bagful of sweets, the first time in his career that he'd ever resorted to a confectionery bribe. Yong-Su's eyes lit up when he saw the wide assortment that Payne had borrowed from Crawford's desk.

'Now, don't get too excited. You earned only four.'

Yong-Su nodded and smiled, practically knocking over the table as he reached for the bag.

'Wow! You *really* like sweets, don't you?'

He nodded again, grinning.

'In that case, how would you like to make a deal?' Payne glanced at Chung-Ho, seeking his permission. 'If it's okay with your dad, I'd like to ask you a few more questions. If you get them right, we can double your reward.'

'Do you know how many sweets that is?' Kia asked.

Yong-Su held up both hands, spreading his fingers wide.

'That's right! Eight!'

'Sir,' Payne asked, 'is that all right with you?'

Chung-Ho nodded, thrilled that Yong-Su was happy about anything.

'Great!' said Payne as he shook the bag for emphasis. The boy stared at it like a pit-bull eyeing a pork chop. 'Then let's get started.'

The photographs of Schmidt and his crew were still on the table. Payne pushed them closer to the boy so he could get a better look. 'When I was talking to your neighbour Mr Kim, he told me that you heard the men speaking in the cave. Do you remember what they said?'

Yong-Su nodded.

'Do you remember who was talking the most?'

Yong-Su nodded again, this time pointing to one of the photos. It was Trevor Schmidt.

'That's good, real good. That's what I figured.'

Payne collected the other three photos and moved them out of the way so Yong-Su could focus on the only person that mattered. 'Okay, now here's the fun part, the part that's going to double all your sweets. I'd like you to tell me what this man was talking about.'

Yong-Su glanced at his dad, who whispered something to him in Korean. Whether it was fatherly advice or a reminder of what Yong-Su had told him earlier in the week, Payne wasn't sure. But whatever he said, it was effective, because Yong-Su started to talk.

'Man say black stone.'

'Black stone?'

'He say black stone come from heaven.'

'It came from heaven?'

'But he send it to hell.'

Payne grimaced. 'He wanted to send the black stone to hell?'

Yong-Su nodded. 'Me get sweets now.'

'In a minute,' Kia said, giving Payne a chance to think. 'As soon as he's done asking you questions, you'll get your sweets.'

'Okay. Me wait.'

The problem was Payne didn't know what to ask next. He didn't know what the black stone was or why Schmidt wanted to send it to hell. Obviously he wasn't talking about the hotel on Jeju, but it could have been anything else – maybe even a code that only Schmidt and his crew understood. For all he knew, *Black Stone* could have been the name of Schmidt's mission.

But if that was the case, what did heaven and hell have to do with anything?

Payne paused for a minute, glancing through his small notebook. He had jotted different phrases in his personal shorthand, his way of guaranteeing secrecy, although with this mission, it wouldn't have mattered who read it. There were too many holes to make sense of anything. Thankfully, just as his frustration was starting to build, he was saved by a knock on the door.

Handing the bag to Kia, he told her to give Yong-Su one sweet for good behaviour. Otherwise he knew the kid might start gnawing on the table. Never in his life had he seen a kid who liked sweets *that* much. He figured it was probably the reason he was missing three teeth.

Payne opened the door and was surprised to see Jones standing there, smiling wider than Yong-Su with a Tootsie Roll. A grin that told him something good had happened.

'You gotta see this.'

'See what?'

Jones led him next door, where he'd been watching the interview on one of the monitors. 'While you were glancing at your notes, I cross-referenced "black stone" and the word "heaven". And guess what? I got a hit. Something that makes a lot of sense.'

He pointed to the image on his computer screen, an ancient stone building surrounded by a sea of people, all of them dressed in white robes. 'What do you know about Islam?'

Payne shrugged and took a seat in front of the computer.

Jones said, 'That's the interior of the Great Mosque in Mecca. To put it simply, it's the centre of the Islamic world. When Muslims pray, that's what they face. Not the mosque itself, but the ancient stone building in the middle. It's called the Kaaba. It's their most sacred shrine.'

Payne stared at the picture, focusing on the massive granite cube that towered above the thousands of people who filled the courtyard. It stood close to fifty feet high and was covered by a black silk cloth, decorated by gold calligraphy embroidered in Arabic.

'Go on.'

Jones tapped a few keys, zooming in on one of the cornerstones. 'According to Islamic tradition, the Kaaba was built by Abraham and his son Ishmael, the same prophets from the Old Testament. While searching for rocks in the hills of Mecca, they came across a pure white stone and immediately recognized its worth. To them, its greatness was so obvious they used it to anchor their building.'

He zoomed in closer, focusing on a black stone that was embedded five feet above the ground in the east corner of the Kaaba. The stone was roughly twelve inches in diameter and framed by a silver band that was fastened to it with silver nails.

'Remarkably, the stone has changed colour through the centuries. What used to be pure white is now pure black. Some true believers attribute it to all the sins it has absorbed over the years. Of course, most scientists have a more pragmatic view.'

'Which is?'

Jones leaned back in his chair. 'It's a meteorite.'

'They *worship* a meteorite?'

'They don't actually worship it. But it is sacred to them.'

'An actual meteorite?'

'That's the theory. Then again, there's no way to know without testing it – something the guardians of the mosque won't allow. Still, it fits all the facts.

Over time, a lot of meteorites change from white to black because of oxidation. Plus there's a major impact crater at Wabar, which is close to Mecca. When it hit the desert, it blasted molten sand high into the air, where it cooled, then fell back to the earth as chunks of glass. It was *literally* raining glass.'

'Glass?'

'Some scientists think the Black Stone is that substance, known as impact glass. Others think it's part of the meteorite itself. Either way, the Black Stone fell from heaven.'

'Just like Schmidt said.'

Jones nodded. 'Unfortunately, that's not everything he said. He also mentioned that he wanted to send it to hell. And *that's* the part I'm worried about.'

'How so?'

'This stone is in the middle of a massive mosque in the centre of a protected city. It's constantly surrounded by armed guards and thousands of devout Muslims who would fight to the death to defend it. No way he's going to get into a gunfight.'

'True.'

'Therefore, in my mind, that leaves Schmidt with only one viable option.'

'Which is?'

'He's gonna blow it up.'

39

In Saudi Arabia, where oil is the lifeblood of the economy, tanker trucks are a common sight, rolling throughout the region both day and night, a constant reminder of the nation's wealth and its place in the global market. The trucks are so commonplace that they blend into the scenery like desert wildlife, barely registering when they stream past in large convoys.

Even when they are driving somewhere they don't belong.

Trevor Schmidt and his crew had counted on this when they took over the Abraj Al Bait water facility the night before. Their assault had been remarkably easy. One armed guard during the takeover. Another guard during the shift change. No other workers were present due to the hajj celebration and because the facility was not scheduled to open for another six months. Everything about the place was functional – the generators, the reservoirs, the compressors – the only thing missing was the liquid to pump.

But that would soon be rectified.

A member of Schmidt's team, the one they called Matthew, had earned an engineering degree from Stanford before he'd entered the military. His background was all the training they needed to complete this task, especially since everything had been planned out weeks in advance. All they had to do was follow simple step-by-step instructions, then get to the tunnel in Mecca, where the final phase would be completed.

But that would be the fun part. First they needed to finish their work here.

Matthew went into the control room and checked the gauges. As he did, the tanker trucks pulled through the front gate and drove to the rear of the facility, where they began pumping their flammable cargo into a system that was designed for water. The chemical itself, contained in cylindrical tanks that held 8,500 gallons each, was a petroleum-based product comparable to jet fuel, although it had been modified in several crucial ways. To curtail the effects of static electricity, they added dinonylnaphthylsulfonic acid, hoping to eliminate sparking and premature combustion. Corrosion inhibitors, a common ingredient in military fuel, were introduced in small concentrations to prevent damage to the piping system and possible seepage underground. And antioxidants were added to minimize gumming.

Using the video monitors in the security office, Schmidt watched truck after truck empty their tanks into the system, double-checking all the numbers on a small sheet of paper. From his aviation experience, he knew that larger commercial jets, such as Boeing 767s, carried approximately 21,000 gallons of fuel on take-off. That meant five trucks equalled two planes, the amount that brought down the Twin Towers in a giant ball of flames.

And thanks to one of their contacts, they had more trucks than that.

Looking through a telephoto lens, the Arab smiled.

He was paid top dollar to document everything, and so far no one suspected a thing.

He had followed Fred Nasir to Taif Air Base, snapping dozens of pictures along the way. Candid shots that his boss would love. Nasir talking to the American soldiers. Nasir visiting Al-Gaim. Nasir driving into Mecca. And, finally, entering the tunnel near the mosque.

His job was so easy it felt like stealing.

That sentiment continued at the water facility. At first, he wasn't quite sure what to expect, worried that the isolation in the middle of the Meccan desert would pose a problem. But as it turned out, it was easier than expected. He covered himself with a tan blanket, matching the colour of the surrounding terrain, and used a special lens that compensated for the darkness.

He snapped pictures of Schmidt and his crew.

All the fuel trucks as they rolled through the front gate.

Everything he needed.

More importantly, everything his boss required.

*

Shari Shasmeen was obedient for an entire day. For her, it was a personal record.

She knew she had promised Omar Abdul-Khaliq that she would stay away from the tunnel for the rest of the hajj, but the longer she sat in her hotel room, the more antsy she got. In her mind, her seclusion didn't make any sense. Why did it matter that two million people were going to be filling the streets of the old city? Her work was underground, far from prying eyes. If anything, she felt safer being in the tunnel than walking around Mecca, always worried that she was going to do or say something that would reveal her identity as a non-practising Muslim.

On the other hand, she wasn't looking forward to being back in the tunnel with the lead guard. He had creeped her out from the very beginning. Something about the way he looked at her. The way he touched her hand when he tried to take her keys.

It made her uneasy.

Of course, she had handled guys like him before. Mostly in bars, right after last call when dozens of stray men roamed around looking for something to hump. She figured if she could handle them, she could handle him. Just to be safe, she carried a small phial of pepper spray that Hennessy had purchased at a Meccan bazaar and given to her in case more violence occurred. The irony was that she was more afraid of the guard than anyone who was threatening the site.

Her hotel was a few miles from the tunnel, much too far for her to walk by herself since the mutaween were out in full force, looking for Muslims who were celebrating the hajj in an inappropriate fashion. Thankfully, Hennessy had offered to drive her to the site and stay with her while she worked. Shari took him up on the former but refused the latter, realizing that their car would be trapped there all day once the pilgrims descended on the mosque. Her decision was made easier when she realized that the new guards, the men she wanted to avoid, were nowhere to be found.

Normally Shari would have been angry about that. The guards were supposed to be there twenty-four hours a day, making sure everything was safe. Protecting her invaluable site.

But on this night, she took their absence as a blessing.

It meant she got to work alone.

She said goodbye to her friend, then descended to the bottom of the tunnel, boards creaking as she walked. Her shadow danced on the floor every time she passed one of the bulbs that hung from above. They stayed lit around the clock, so she didn't have to flip any switches or turn on any generators. In fact, the site looked the same both night and day. Same lights. Same temperature. Same everything. That was one of the advantages of working underground. A constant she took comfort in. Outside, she always worried about the wind and the weather, which could threaten her discoveries and wreak havoc on her schedule.

But inside, the environment was controlled. Perfect for the precision of her work.

Unfortunately, all of that was about to disappear.

In a few hours, she would be surrounded by chaos.

40

Taif Air Base
Taif, Saudi Arabia

The flight was a long one, crossing China, India, and several other countries before touching down at Taif Air Base, only forty-one miles east of Mecca. Time zones worked in their favour, so they arrived in Saudi Arabia only a few hours on the clock after they had left South Korea.

It was still 1 January. It was still before noon.

In their minds, they still had time to make a difference.

While in the air, Payne and Jones called Colonel Harrington and briefed him on Trevor Schmidt, the bloody cave, and a possible terrorist attack at the Great Mosque. They had kept him out of the loop long enough and realized Harrington's involvement was necessary if they had any chance of stopping Schmidt.

At first, Harrington was sceptical. His top people had assured him that Schmidt was dead, proven by DNA results and the large amount of blood, but as he listened to the details of Yong-Su's testimony, he

269

realized he was wrong. Schmidt had deceived them all.

Everyone except Payne and Jones.

The revelation changed Harrington's perspective on their involvement. Until then, he had given them minimal information, forcing them to figure things out on their own, his way of testing them under fire while protecting the integrity of his original black op. He had given them access to the cave but refused to reveal its true purpose or whom Schmidt had taken there to torture. He allowed Payne and Jones to talk to Dr Sheldon but had instructed him to keep his mouth shut about his real agenda. In Harrington's mind, he wanted to force Payne and Jones to use their own contacts, their own unique style, to uncover a nugget or two about Schmidt. Maybe colour in some of the grey areas of Schmidt's operation that had bothered Harrington from the very beginning. But he *never* expected them to contribute like this.

A jeep met the plane on the runway, picking up Payne, Jones, and Kia. They were taken to the same meeting room that Trevor Schmidt had sat in when a bomb ripped through Al-Hada Hospital and killed most of his men. It was the incident that had set things in motion, the event that had fuelled his rage. Now they were there to stop him.

Wearing desert camouflage and a stern expression, Colonel Harrington greeted them at the door and showed them to a conference table that was filled with other personnel from Taif. He offered no words of apology – colonels *don't* apologize to subordinates – but his gratitude told Payne everything he needed to know. They had earned the colonel's respect.

'Gentlemen,' said Harrington as he started the meeting, 'we're currently waiting on word from Washington, but time is of the essence, so we need to begin.'

As he spoke, he glanced around the room, making eye contact with each person, letting them know the gravity of the situation and how vital their role was to stop it. 'In the past, we've received hundreds of reports of possible terrorist attacks, but to my recollection we've never received one like this. According to our sources, a team of American soldiers is planning an assault on Meccan soil. These men are highly trained and highly motivated to carry out such a mission. As of now, we *don't* have a definitive time frame. However, if their goal is maximum devastation, our best guess is it's going to be carried out today.'

That was news to Payne. 'Based on what?'

Harrington pointed to an older man, who wore a civilian shirt and tie, not a military uniform like the other Taif personnel in the room. The man had white hair and dark skin, and was possibly of Middle Eastern descent, although he spoke with no accent except when he used Arabic terms, which rolled off his tongue with the fluidity of a native speaker.

'Right now, we are in the middle of Dhul al-Hijjah, the most sacred month of the Islamic calendar.

Translated into English it means Lord of the Pilgrimage. It is the time when Muslims converge on Mecca to complete the hajj, one of the five pillars of Islamic faith. It is a journey that all Muslims are expected to make during their lifetime.'

He tapped a few keys on the laptop in front of him, and a graphic listing the Islamic months was transmitted to a large video screen on the far wall. Everyone turned to get a better view.

'Unlike the Gregorian calendar, the one we use in America, the Islamic calendar is lunar. It is roughly eleven days shorter than our calendar, meaning Islamic holidays are celebrated eleven days earlier than the previous year – at least according to *our* calendar. This year Dhul al-Hijjah started on 23 December.'

Payne instantly recognized the date. It was the day that Schmidt faked his own death.

It corresponded with the beginning of the hajj season.

'You might be wondering, why is this date important? The answer is quite simple. The hajj is very structured. Pilgrims must perform specific tasks on specific days, or else they do not meet their sacred obligation. That means on any given day, at any given time, we know exactly where the majority of pilgrims will be.'

'How many are we talking about?' Jones asked.

'According to the Ministry of Hajj, which just released official data, there are nearly 2.4 million pilgrims in Mecca this year, nearly 1.7 million from countries other than Saudi Arabia.'

Click. A new graphic explained the pilgrimage, day by day.

'The hajj itself doesn't begin until the eighth day of the month, when all pilgrims walk from Mecca to the village of Mina, a journey of five kilometres, where they spend the night in 44,000 fire-resistant tents that the Saudi government has assembled. All of the tents are white, but signs are colour-coded by nationality so pilgrims can stay with their own. For prayer and safety.'

'Define safety,' Payne said.

'The Saudis would love you to believe that the hajj is a safe journey, but that's misinformation. The truth is, several people die in Tent City every hajj. In the past, the biggest concern was always fire. Blazes swept through every year until they put up fire-resistant tents. Now the biggest issue is disease. All those people coming from all those countries and assembling in one spot? The numbers are mind-boggling. On average, there are more than fifty people sleeping in each tent.'

Click. A picture of Tent City filled the screen. White tents in straight rows stretched as far as the eye could see. Like snow-covered peaks in the desert sand.

'From here, the hajj continues forward. But pilgrims will come back to Tent City on their return trip to Mecca.'

Click. The next photo showed a massive plain that surrounded a granite hill.

'Day two begins before dawn. They journey to the Plain of Arafat, where they ask Allah for forgiveness for all their sins. In the background you can see Mount Arafat. It is where Muhammad delivered his farewell sermon in AD632. Muslims also believe that Adam and Eve were reunited on this hill 200 years after their separation, punishment for their disobedience.'

'You mean *the* Adam and Eve?' Payne asked.

'One and the same. Most people find this surprising, but Muslims and Christians have many of the same core beliefs – including the *same* god. The confusing part is each group calls their figures a different name. Christians say God. Muslims say Allah. But it's the same deity. In fact, if you go through the Qur'an, you'll see several of the same names, albeit with different spellings, that appear in the Old Testament. Adam, Eve, Abraham, Ishmael, Hagar, and so on.'

Harrington cleared his throat. 'Professor, please get back on point.'

'Yes, sir.' He clicked on the next photo. It showed a long stone wall that was surrounded by pilgrims, all of them dressed in white. 'Today is the third day of the hajj. Pilgrims will perform *ramy al-jamarāt*, or the Stoning of the Devil, after the noontime prayer. They are required to throw pebbles, which they collected last night at Muzdalifah, at three stone walls that represent the temptations of Satan. Until recently, they threw pebbles at large pillars called *jamarat,* but the crowds have grown so large in recent years that they decided to build long walls to spread the people out instead of having them crowd around the pillars. In the past, hundreds have been trampled and killed.'

Next photo. It showed a slaughterhouse in Mina, filled with lambs, cows, camels, and goats.

'After the stoning, pilgrims are expected to slaughter their best animal, called *udhiya.* This represents the sacrifice that Abraham was willing to make when God commanded him to sacrifice his son Ishmael. In the past, pilgrims did the slaying themselves or directly oversaw the process. But now they are able to buy a sacrifice voucher that ensures an animal will be killed in their name. Today more than 400,000 animals will be slain.'

Click. A map of the hajj path filled the screen. It pointed out all the locations he had described. An arrow showed the traffic flow as it left Mecca, went to Mina and to the Plain of Arafat, then returned to Mina again. The final arrow pointed back towards Mecca.

'The ritualistic slaughter marks the beginning of Eid ul-Adha, the Festival of the Sacrifice. It is celebrated throughout the Islamic world, even by Muslims not in Mecca. Male pilgrims mark this occasion by shaving their heads, which represents the cleansing of their sins through the hajj.'

Click. A photo of the Kaaba and the Black Stone.

'Later today, pilgrims will start their journey back to the Masjid al-Haram, or the Sacred Mosque, to complete a ritual called the Tawaf az-Ziyarah. Using the Black Stone as a marker, they must walk around the Kaaba seven times in an anti-clockwise motion, which signifies the unity of all Muslims to worship one god. With each rotation they will try to get closer and closer to the stone itself. The truly blessed will get to touch it or even kiss it.'

Click. An overhead view of the Great Mosque.

'From there, pilgrims will honour Hagar's search for water by walking back and forth between the two hills of Safa and Marwah. These hills are actually contained *inside* the mosque, a building so large it can hold nearly one million people.'

'Did you say *million*?' an officer asked.

The speaker nodded. 'Not to mention the other million or so who will be standing outside the mosque, waiting to get inside.'

'And this is happening today?'

He nodded again. 'More than two million Muslims in one city block, all of them with the same goal. To get as close to the Black Stone as possible.'

41

The Pentagon
Arlington, Virginia

The White House was notified of the situation, but they passed the buck to the Pentagon, claiming they were more equipped to handle this type of crisis. Whether or not that was the case, the Pentagon was given an hour to sort through the political hotbed and reach a decision.

On the surface, it seemed like an easy choice. Rogue US soldiers were planning an assault in Saudi Arabia, where 15,000 Americans were participating in the hajj. What was there to even think about? They knew that a small explosion, if positioned in the right place in the Great Mosque, would kill far more people than 9/11, and the resulting panic would create a human stampede, the likes of which mankind had never seen. Injuries and fatalities would be so substantial that military experts couldn't even agree on a projection.

And that was with a *small* explosive.

If Schmidt had access to a larger device, the devastation would easily exceed Hiroshima, where an estimated 45,000 people died from the initial blast.

This should have been a no-brainer. Something needed to be done.

However, the longer their discussion continued, the cloudier the issues became.

Mecca was a restricted city, one where the US wouldn't be granted access no matter how convincing their argument was. That meant the only way to get troops inside the city was by force – something they wouldn't risk, since Saudi Arabia, the world's biggest oil exporter, was one country they couldn't afford to piss off – or through stealth, which might have been possible if they were given enough time. But in their opinion, it wasn't the type of operation that could be arranged in a few hours.

From a political standpoint, a failed mission would be far worse than no mission at all.

Religion complicated things even further. If word ever leaked that they had violated Islam's most sacred city on one of its holiest holidays, the US would feel the wrath of every Islamic nation for years to come. Homeland Security would have to come up with a threat level that was more severe than red, because every terrorist in the world would be gunning for revenge.

Sure, the Pentagon realized they might – and the key word was *might* – save thousands of lives in Saudi Arabia, but how many Americans would be killed in the future because the US had invaded Mecca? How many cities would be bombed? How many schools?

It was a compelling argument.

However, in the end, their decision hinged on one main factor. If the Pentagon knew with absolute certainty that Trevor Schmidt was planning an attack that day, they would have given their stamp of approval for a pre-emptive assault. But based on their current intel and all the negative ramifications if they were wrong, they simply weren't willing to risk involvement.

The verdict did not surprise Colonel Harrington. From the moment Trevor Schmidt disappeared, Harrington sensed the potential for a world-class shitstorm. Of course, he never imagined it would elevate so quickly. If so, he would have been more forthright with Payne and Jones from the beginning. Who knows? Maybe that would have made a difference. Maybe they would have figured things out sooner. Maybe this whole situation would have been averted.

Unfortunately, men in his position were often placed in no-win situations, asked to keep secrets for the good of the country, secrets that sometimes conflicted with other promises that were just as important. At some point they were forced to choose between the two, and when they did, it was rarely a simple choice. They had to ponder all the consequences before they made their decision, always weighing the good and the bad, the long term and the short term.

But this time, with millions of lives on the line, none of that was necessary.

Harrington knew he had to come clean ASAP if they wanted to stop Schmidt.

The conference room was cleared of everyone except Harrington, Payne, and Jones. They sat at the far end of the long table, talking softly so no one in the hall could hear.

'I just got word from Washington,' Harrington said. 'We've been told to do nothing.'

Payne didn't flinch. 'No shock there. That's what we expected.'

'Do you agree with it?'

'We wouldn't have flown in from Korea if we did.'

'So, you were willing to go to Mecca?'

Payne nodded. 'I'm *still* willing to go to Mecca.'

Jones agreed. 'I hear it's lovely this time of year.'

'In that case,' Harrington said, 'there are some things you need to know about Schmidt. Things I should've told you long ago but wasn't allowed. Hell, I'm still not allowed. But if we're going to prevent this tragedy, you need to know everything.'

He paused, trying to figure out where to begin.

'In early November, French authorities nailed a terrorist named Abdul Al-Amin, a member of the Soldiers of Allah. They busted him on a weapons charge, nothing too major, but for some reason he started talking. He gave up names, places, exact dates of future attacks. The type of intel that can make a difference. Obviously, we were sceptical at first – I mean, this seemed a little *too* easy – but every time we heard something through the grapevine, we were able to verify it. Small things, big things, everything checked out.'

Payne nodded. He had heard the same story from Nick Dial.

'We knew every country in the world wanted to get their hands on Abdul's bosses, men who were responsible for hundreds of deaths around the globe, not to mention millions of dollars in damages and manpower. But how could we let that happen? We were the nation they had targeted the most. No way in hell were we going to let some third-rate country snatch these guys before we could.'

He paused, taking a moment to calm down. 'We got word that Hakeem Salaam and all of his top advisers were meeting in Kuwait. If true, it was a once-in-a-decade opportunity, because none of us really knew what Salaam looked like, and he was the key to that organization. Thankfully, we had recent pictures of his lieutenants, so we figured if we tracked them, they would lead us right to Salaam.'

'Did Schmidt lead the mission?' Jones asked.

Harrington nodded. 'Went off like clockwork. We nabbed Salaam and two of his top men. Picked them *clean*. Took them out through the Persian Gulf and straight to Jeju.'

'Why there?' Payne wondered.

'Why not? We figured no one would ever look for three Arabs in Korea, and as far as we were concerned, that was the key. No one could know we grabbed these guys. Not Homeland. Not the CIA. No one. That edict came straight from my bosses. We were the ones who caught these assholes, so we were going to milk them before anyone else got the chance.'

'Is that where Sheldon comes in?'

Harrington shook his head. 'I know you have a problem with Dr Sheldon. He told me about your outburst in the cave. But believe me, the guy knows his field. That's why I chose him to re-create the crime scene. I figured he could shed some light on certain things.'

'Such as?'

'What *really* happened in there,' Harrington said bluntly. 'At first, the interrogations were going well. Schmidt gave me regular updates, most of which paid off. We busted smaller cells, stopped some arms deals, that kind of thing. But nothing major. No grandiose schemes, like we thought we were going to get.'

'Why not?' Jones wondered.

'Because Salaam wasn't talking. According to Schmidt, no matter what he did, no matter how hard he tried, he couldn't get Salaam to talk about anything important. And as you know, that doesn't happen in the real world. This ain't the fuckin' movies. If we want you to talk, we'll get you to talk. You guys should know that.'

He paused for a moment, trying to decide how much he should tell them.

'Ultimately, Schmidt got desperate and went way too far. He handcuffed Salaam to one of his advisers

282

– someone who'd been spilling his guts from the very beginning – and shot the bastard in the head. Just killed the guy in cold blood. After that, Schmidt threw them in a cell and left them there for several days. One alive, one dead, but still chained together.'

'Jesus,' Payne whispered, stunned that it had gone that far. 'Did he tell you this himself?'

Harrington shook his head. 'We found out about it later. Schmidt was required to keep a video log, describing all the techniques he used and the results he achieved. When we arrived in Jeju, we found some of his files, a whole lot of blood, and three dead Arabs in a back cell.'

'Including Salaam?'

'At first, that's what we thought,' he said cryptically. 'Remember, we had no idea what Salaam looked like. We had a rough description – age, nationality, and so on – but we couldn't identify him on site. All we knew is that he was meeting with his top advisers in Kuwait, and we snagged everyone in the room. So we assumed we had him.'

'And?'

'After we hauled the bodies out of the cave, we ran preliminary tests – ballistics, DNA, etc. – and came to a disheartening conclusion: the dead guy *wasn't* Hakeem Salaam.'

'How do you know?'

'Because we got a positive ID. And let me tell you, we fucked up bad on this one. Not only was the guy not a terrorist, he was a Saudi official who worked for the Ministry of the Interior.'

Payne winced, realizing that Schmidt would have known whom they grabbed very early in the interrogation process – if he didn't know from the very beginning. That meant he had spent several days torturing a government official, learning inside information about a multitude of topics. In Saudi Arabia, the Ministry of the Interior was responsible for public safety on many different levels, including the police, fire services, passports, and civil defence. In addition, it handled security for all major sites, such as Muhammad's tomb in Medina and, more importantly, the Great Mosque in Mecca.

'Obviously,' Harrington admitted, 'there's no way of knowing what Schmidt learned. But according to Dr Sheldon, we have a pretty good idea of how he's going to use it.'

42

Dr Ernie Sheldon appeared on the video screen in the Taif conference room, the same screen that had illustrated the days of the hajj. He was somewhere in a secure facility, no longer hiding behind the mask he wore in the cave. Both literally and figuratively. Harrington had finally given him permission to talk about his work.

'During the past several years,' Sheldon said, 'we've been conducting human-based experiments in compounds around the world. Ways to extract information and methods to prevent the same. Some people think our biggest concern is how to get secrets from the enemy. Sometimes it's more important to protect your own.'

He smiled, crinkles appearing in the corners of his eyes.

'For the sake of clarity, I'll keep the science to a bare minimum. No need to confuse you with a bunch of complex formulas when all you need are the basics. Thirty years ago the Chinese developed a procedure where they isolated a specific emotion in a test subject and elevated it through chemicals and verbal reinforcement.'

Payne spoke into the camera. 'You mean brain-washing.'

'Not *actual* brainwashing. They weren't able to take a peasant girl and turn her into a crazed assassin. However, they were able to take most subjects with a predisposed opinion – let's say a hatred of peas – and raise that hatred to an unhealthy level. If, for instance, the subject ever saw a pea again, she'd be willing to kill someone to get it away from her.'

Jones whispered, 'I feel the same way about broccoli.'

'From humble beginnings comes cutting-edge science,' Sheldon pronounced. 'During the past three decades, the scientific community has built upon these experiments, step by step, finally reaching a point where we can corral that undisciplined rage and focus it on a precise task. Different countries have different names for it, but we like to call it induction.'

'Induction?' Payne asked. 'Can you give us an example? One that *doesn't* involve peas.'

Sheldon smiled again. 'Of course I can. In fact, why don't we talk specifics? Let's discuss the reason we're all here.'

Payne glanced at Jones, neither of them liking where this was going.

'If ever there was a candidate for induction, it was Trevor Schmidt. He was filled with so much anger and guilt from the terrorist attack that killed his squad, not to mention his missed opportunity to stop it.'

Payne turned towards Harrington. 'What opportunity?'

Harrington answered, 'The day of the bombing, Schmidt had gathered his squad's families and driven them to the hospital himself. On their way inside they passed a number of Muslims who were praying. This is Saudi Arabia, after all, so that was pretty damn common. What *wasn't* common was the time of day. This wasn't one of their normal prayer sessions. These men were praying on their own, asking for courage to complete their mission.'

Jones understood. 'He walked right past the bombers.'

'Exactly,' Harrington said. '99.9 per cent of the population would've missed the significance of the prayer, but Schmidt blamed himself for not being in the 0.1 per cent. He felt it was his job to spot things like that. His duty.'

'From that point on,' Sheldon said, 'he was an emotional wreck. He hit the bottle. He turned to drugs. He got into several fights. He was on the verge of being kicked out of the military.'

Harrington agreed. 'Schmidt had just been arrested for another assault, and the military police were sick of dealing with his shit. So I contacted Dr Sheldon. I knew he specialized in behaviour modification, and in my mind, that was a much better alternative than prison.'

'Better for whom?' Payne asked.

'Better for *Schmidt*. You know damn well that he

loved the military, and it was pretty obvious to everyone involved that we needed to do something drastic or he was going to piss that all away. I figured this programme would give him a fighting chance.'

Payne wasn't sure if Harrington believed that, but this wasn't the time or the place to argue with the man. There were more important things to worry about.

Sheldon continued. 'As I mentioned, Trevor was filled with anger and guilt, yet was missing a productive outlet for either. The same could be said about the rest of his crew. These men were elite soldiers, trained to do amazing things, but their emotions were getting in the way of their performance. My programme, a combination of pharmaceuticals and subliminal suggestions, helped redirect their rage. It gave them a specific focus.'

Payne asked, 'Which was?'

'Islamic terrorists.' Sheldon smiled, proud of his work. 'Keep in mind, I didn't plant their hatred. It was already in there, imprinted in their brains from the moment the bomb went off at the hospital. I simply focused it. I gave it direction.'

Harrington chimed in. 'And the results were amazing. From the moment they left the programme, they were perfect soldiers. I'd give them a mission and they'd get it done. No questions asked. And all that other nonsense – the drinking, fighting, and drugs – stopped immediately.'

Jones cracked, 'Maybe that's because they were brainwashed.'

'Not *brainwashed*,' Sheldon argued. 'They were –' -

'Doc,' Payne interrupted, 'it's just semantics. It doesn't matter what you call it. The point is we have to stop it. As far as I can tell, you've created the perfect storm. Men who have elite skills, capable of doing some truly horrific things, yet no conscience to counteract it. I realize that wasn't your plan in the beginning, but that's the reality of the situation. Therefore, if you don't mind, I need to ask you a simple question: is there an off button?'

'Excuse me?'

'Let me rephrase. If I find Schmidt and talk to him, one on one, is there some way for me to get through to him? Some tactic that you'd recommend?'

'That's a difficult question.'

'But I *need* an easy answer. Can I convince him to stop?'

Sheldon frowned, a look of defeat on his face. 'Honestly? The odds are pretty slim. If Trevor truly believes that attacking Mecca is the best way to kill terrorists, then that's what he's going to do.'

'Even though Americans might be killed?'

'But that's the thing. He won't view them as Americans. He'll view them as Muslims. And in his mind, that's more important.'

When the video conference ended, Payne and Jones focused on the task at hand. They didn't have days or weeks to plan the mission. They had hours. And some of that time had to be spent on the road. Taif was an hour away from Mecca. Throw in the checkpoints and the foot traffic from the hajj, and they had no time to waste. They needed to start their journey immediately.

Thankfully, Harrington was one step ahead of them. His staff had arranged transportation, weapons, intel, and everything else they required, including four soldiers who were willing to risk their lives to stop this tragedy.

The biggest problem, as they saw it, was figuring out how Schmidt and his crew would attack Mecca, since thousands of Saudi security guards were positioned along the hajj route. Not only on the ground, but also in the air. Dozens of armed helicopters monitored the pilgrims' progress, literally herding them through bottlenecks that occurred in certain stretches along the way. In addition, a unit of elite soldiers was assigned to protect the Great Mosque at all times, a duty that took on added importance after 20 November 1979, when armed Islamic fundamentalists seized control of the site, ending in nearly 300 deaths and 700 injuries.

Eventually, Payne and Jones approached things from a different angle. Instead of planning a counterassault, one where they had to guess where Schmidt was and what he was going to do, they opted to plan an assault of their own, asking themselves how they would attack the mosque if that was their given task. With enough time, they would have set up shop close to the site, giving them somewhere to hoard weapons and a chance to survey the immediate area. Jones studied a map of the old city, the district that surrounded the mosque, and realized most of the homes had recently been demolished, making way for commercial projects that weren't listed on his map.

However, as it turned out, the old map provided them with a lucky break – the type that was needed on hastily planned missions like this one. When Harrington's staff searched property records for recent developments, one name jumped out at them: Omar Abdul-Khaliq. Not only did he own a large chunk of land down the street from the mosque, but he was also rumoured to have close financial ties with the Soldiers of Allah.

In fact, according to US intelligence, he was their biggest supporter.

43

The planning had been easier than expected. With enough time and money, he knew anyone could be bought and anything could be accomplished. Yet as Hakeem Salaam watched the hajj proceedings on Saudi television, he still fretted over the details.

Like a coach who was watching the big game from afar.

In some ways, this was like every other terrorist attack he had orchestrated in the past ten years. He handled the preparations, Omar Abdul-Khaliq provided the money, and his dedicated soldiers carried out the missions, often sacrificing their lives to better his cause. Normally their target was the United States, the country he blamed for most of the world's problems. The morning of an attack he would get on his knees and pray to Allah, asking for His blessing as they carried out their duty. Hoping for the negligence of all Americans, whether it was the police, the citizens, or the military — anyone who could disrupt his precise plans.

But today was different. Today was unlike any other mission he had ever planned.

Today he was praying for the Americans. Counting on their skills as murderers.

Realizing the more damage they did, the easier it would be to unite Islam.

The concept had come to Salaam shortly after watching the events of 9/11. He went to the desert to meditate and realized the best way to connect all Muslims was with a common enemy. The obvious choice was the one he hated the most. If he could somehow lure them into committing an unspeakable act in Islam's most sacred city, he knew he could sway his people to stand as one. The infighting that occurred among Sunnis, Shiites, and all other Islamic groups would suddenly disappear, replaced by a unified hatred of the United States.

But how to get them to cooperate?

And how to prove they were responsible?

Those were the issues he had to solve if he was going to make this work.

In his mind, the best way to accomplish the first task was through inside involvement, a technique with a proven track record. Ali Mohamed, the Al Qaeda operative who was charged with bombing US embassies in Kenya and Tanzania, was an Egyptian soldier who became a US citizen in the mid-1980s after marrying an American woman from California. From there, he joined the US Army, where he eventually became a drill instructor at Fort Bragg. Later he was hired to teach courses on Arabic culture at the John F. Kennedy Special Warfare Center, a school that trained personnel for army Special Operations forces. Meanwhile, he was also training terrorists on the side, including some of the men who were responsible for the 1993 World Trade Center bombing.

How foolish could the Americans be?

Salaam knew many men like Mohamed – Islamic operatives who were *still* inside the system they were trying to defeat. Any of them would be honoured to help. At the same time, he realized that none of these men could be directly involved in the attack on Mecca. Otherwise the news media would spotlight their involvement, claiming Muslims were just as responsible as the United States. In his mind, that was something he couldn't afford.

His message had to be pure. Unambiguous.

Sure, he could use Islamic operatives to feed him information; they had been doing that for years. But the attack itself needed to be committed by an American.

Someone who couldn't be confused as a foreigner. Someone the US couldn't deny. That was the only way this was going to work.

But the question was, who?

The answer was fed to him by one of his sources in the Middle East, an Arab who worked with the US Military Training Mission (USMTM) in Riyadh. He had heard rumours about a new programme where Americans were being hypnotized to fight terrorists, a concept that sounded like science fiction until he received clarification from one of his contacts at Fort Huachuca, who verified that *induced* soldiers were already in the field and producing amazing results. Behind the scenes, they'd even been given a nickname. These soldiers, who fought like Rambo and were pinpointing Islamic terrorists, were jokingly called 'Islambos'.

Immediately, Salaam realized that these were the type of men he could exploit. If, in fact, these soldiers were subliminally trained to attack a specific group, it wouldn't be difficult to convince them that their biggest threat was in Mecca – especially since that was accurate. For years, Islamic groups had used the sanctity of the holy city as a backdrop for their recruiting process. The most dedicated pilgrims flocked to the Great Mosque year after year, their way of purifying their spirit and staying close to Muhammad's righteous path. Events such as the hajj were used to locate potential members, men who were willing to give up their lives in the name of Allah. Salaam figured if the right people whispered this information in the right ears, word would eventually spread to these special soldiers and they would take care of the rest.

An Arab who worked as a snitch for the US military aided Salaam along the way, feeding the Americans false information whenever he was asked. At the same time, he gathered intel from his real sources and sold it to Salaam for top dollar.

In the world of terrorism, the best information could always be bought.

Six months after Salaam launched his plan, an American soldier named Morrison, a Special Forces operative who used to run missions out of Taif before most of his squad was killed in a terrorist attack, was spotted surveying the Great Mosque. A background check revealed the names of his entire unit, a group led by Trevor Schmidt. Deeper research showed that Schmidt was born in Ohio, trained as a MANIAC, and was a certified war hero. Not a hint of Middle Eastern blood in his family tree. Or in any other members of his crew.

To Salaam, these men would be the perfect scapegoats.

Now all he had to do was make sure they succeeded.

The guards had been gone all night. When they returned, they carried an assortment of tools.

Shari Shasmeen heard them as they clanked down the tunnel, metal banging on metal, their voices echoing in the darkness. They were speaking in Arabic, chattering on and on about timetables, delivery points, and all the money they were going to make for this job. None of it made much sense to her until she saw them coming her way.

As she focused on their pickaxes and crowbars, dread filled her heart.

They were coming to rob the site.

The click of their key as it turned in the lock felt like a death sentence. The guards were highly trained and accustomed to violence. Her only weapon was the small canister of pepper spray she clutched in her hand. They blocked the only way out.

At that point, she realized she didn't have a choice; she had to hide. So she crouched in the back shadows, hoping they didn't spot her, praying they just dropped their tools and went outside for additional supplies. If so, she could slip into the maintenance shaft that branched from the main tunnel near the bottom of the front incline. Then she could wait in silence until they returned through the metal gate and locked the door. If she was lucky, it would give her enough time to sprint up the ramp and call for help.

Then again, whom could she call?

The mutaween were just as likely to arrest her for being in public without a chaperone. Her colleagues were several blocks away, back at the hotel, and less accustomed to violence than she was. She knew she could always call Omar Abdul-Khaliq, but he had hired these guards to begin with. The one who had told her to get away for a couple of days while these men protected the site. Either that was a tremendous error on his part, or this was all his doing.

Shari wasn't sure which.

Of course, that was something she could debate later. *If* she escaped.

The odds of that diminished when they entered the chamber and locked the gate. There were four of them, and they weren't going anywhere. The lead guard ordered his men to get started while he set up some piece of equipment she couldn't see, since her view was obstructed by her position on the floor.

The biggest of the guards walked over first, putting his hand on the rocks, trying to decide where he should strike for the maximum amount of damage. He found a spot along the front edge and raised the pickaxe above his head.

In her mind, it was now or never.

She leaped from her crouch and sprayed the pepper spray directly into his eyes. He let out a loud yelp as he dropped the pickaxe to the floor. Before anyone could react, she grabbed its wooden handle and swung it at the next guard, a vicious blow that sunk into the left side of his waist and stuck there like a lawn dart. He twisted to the ground in a writhing heap of agony, generating so much force that it pulled the weapon from her grasp.

Suddenly she was unarmed and trapped.

Now it was just a matter of time.

Enraged, the lead guard charged forward, a combination of power and brutality. She raised her hands and tried to defend herself, but he was too strong – like a bull bursting through the tiny red cape and finding the matador behind. But instead of gouging her with horns, he swung his right elbow, smashing it into the bridge of her nose with so much fury that she was knocked unconscious on impact.

44

On this day alone, more than 400,000 animals were slain in Mecca to celebrate Eid ul-Adha, the Festival of the Sacrifice, commemorating Abraham's readiness to sacrifice his son Ishmael. After the ritualistic slaughter, Muslims distributed some of the meat to family and friends, but most of it was donated to the poor, symbolizing their willingness to give up something of value.

Charity was one of the five pillars of Islam, so generosity was expected.

Thousands of refrigerated trucks were driven into the city to pick up the animals, a variety of lambs, cows, camels, and goats. But not all of these trucks were alike. Two were designed with a different purpose in mind: dropping off was more important than picking up.

Payne and Jones sat in the back of one of these trucks, hidden behind a fake panel and several cardboard boxes that were filled with perishable food items and large bags of ice. It wasn't the best camouflage in the world, but it was the best that Colonel Harrington could come up with at short notice.

Two bulbs lit their secret compartment, giving them time to study maps, memorize the dossiers of Schmidt's crew, and formulate a plan of attack. Four other soldiers were joining them – two in the back of another truck and the two drivers, both Arab-Americans with perfectly forged paperwork. Without it, none of them would be getting into Mecca.

Wrapped in a blanket, Jones tried to stay warm in the frigid climate. Thankfully, the *ihram* stage of the hajj was over, meaning they didn't have to wear the traditional garments, consisting of two white unhemmed sheets and sandals, to blend in. Not only would it have been tough to conceal a weapon, but he blanched at the thought of going into a battle without underwear.

'You know,' he said, 'we might be the first people in history to get frostbite in the desert.'

As a Pittsburgh native, Payne shrugged off the cold. 'Pussy.'

'Wait! I'm sneaking into a forbidden city to save two million people and I'm a *pussy*?'

He nodded. 'Bet it feels good to finally admit it, huh?'

Jones laughed. 'Asshole.'

'Okay. Now that we have both sides covered, let's get down to business.'

Payne held up an aerial view of the Great Mosque that was taken from a spy satellite less than two weeks before. He pointed to a stretch of land to the west of one of the main gates. 'This is Omar Abdul-Khaliq's property. From the air, it looks like a large construction site. However, upon closer inspection, it appears to be missing something important.'

'What's that?'

'Construction.'

Jones grabbed the picture and took a closer look. He spotted giant piles of dirt and rock and several pieces of heavy equipment, but there was no foundation being laid. No building going up. 'Could be something, could be nothing. We won't know until we get there.'

'Obviously, the connection between Schmidt and Omar is pretty thin. We can link Omar to Salaam through a money trail, and Salaam to Schmidt through his advisers at the cave. To be honest, I'm not sure if one has anything to do with the other. Actually, I'm more interested in the official from the Ministry of the Interior. What was he doing in Kuwait with Salaam's men? And why would Schmidt torture him?'

Jones took a guess. 'Could be any number of things. Everything from security at the mosque to police response times. Not to mention parts of the city's infrastructure that could be useful: roads, water, power, telecommunications. If Schmidt grabbed the right guy, he'd have access to everything we don't, including security codes and building schematics.'

Payne swore under his breath. They were already facing long odds – a battle against the clock and a highly trained unit who had worked together for years. Now it was even worse. Not only did his opponents have months to organize their mission, but they also had access to inside information. Somehow it didn't seem fair.

Of course, despite all that, despite all the things that were stacked against them, Payne and Jones had one crucial thing that Schmidt and his crew didn't.

The element of surprise.

Her nose had been shattered, filling her mouth with the taste of blood. The room was spinning.

Shari tried to stand but couldn't get her legs to work. Everything was wobbly. Her body. Her brain. Her memory. Like waking up in an early-morning fog without actually falling asleep. She blinked a few times, trying to clear her vision. Trying to focus on something that would allow her to remember what had happened. The ground. The ceiling. The throbbing in her head. But nothing worked. There was a giant void.

Squinting in the darkness, she could barely make out shapes except for a series of vertical lines in the murky distance. They were thick and sturdy, a mixture of shadow and light, black and white, alternating one after another. She stared at them, trying to understand their purpose. Trying to figure out what they were. None of it made any sense.

How long had she been unconscious?

How had she got there?

Why couldn't she breathe through her nose?

Confusion reigned for ten minutes before details started to emerge.

The first thing Shari noticed was the cord. She felt it wrapped around her ankles, bound so tightly that she couldn't separate her legs. Her hands were tied as well, pulled behind her back and attached to a metal loop that had been driven into the hard ground. No matter how hard she pulled or twisted, she couldn't get it to budge.

Next, as her eyes adjusted to the gloom, her vision started to return. She focused on the vertical lines and realized what they were: a giant iron gate backlit by a series of dim bulbs that provided the only light in her cell.

Wait. That gate looked familiar. She had seen it before.

Suddenly, memories came flooding back to her. She was in the tunnel, tied up in the back room, where she had been attacked by the guards.

The site!

Oh my God, they were there to rob the site!

Panicked, she tried to swing her legs around, tried to contort her body so she could see if the relic was still inside. Unfortunately, as she struggled to get a better view, she kicked up a swirl of dust that filled her lungs. Coughing was instantaneous. Blood and mucus sprayed from her nose as she gasped for breath. Pain erupted in her head, throbbing in unison with her racing heart.

Tears streamed down her face, clouding her vision once again.

Alone. In agony. In the darkness. Barely able to breathe.

She didn't think it could get any worse.

But she was wrong.

Trevor Schmidt and his crew slipped into the tunnel, barely making a sound. All of them had packs slung over their shoulders and weapons in their hands. For big men, they ran silently. Years of training taught them how to move with stealth. The skill would serve them well as they strived to complete their mission.

From this point forwards, noise would be kept to a minimum. Hand signals would be used when possible. Their watches were synchronized to the millisecond, freeing them of the need to speak. Some of their actions would be based on time, not verbal authorization. They would do what they were supposed to do whether the others were ready or not.

It was the advantage of a multipronged attack.

Even if someone was killed or captured, the survivors could still make a difference.

Schmidt led the way, creeping down the ramp at a steady pace. They followed him in single file, always keeping space between themselves in case there was an alarm or a mine or anything they hadn't prepared for. The odds were against it – their source had been quite versed on the infrastructure of Mecca – yet they expected the unexpected. Ready for anything.

Well, almost anything.

When they hit the bottom of the ramp, Schmidt sent one of his men to inspect the back tunnel while the other two worked on the maintenance shaft that branched in the opposite direction. The soldier clicked on a flashlight and disappeared into the darkness, only to return a minute later, confusion etched on his face.

'What?' Schmidt whispered.

'You *have* to see this.'

'What is it?'

'I have no fuckin' idea. That's why you have to see it.'

Intrigued, Schmidt signalled for the others to keep working while he investigated the rear tunnel. The passageway had been carved with precision, lit with the same bulbs that lined the initial entry ramp but protected by a giant iron gate that had been anchored in the ceiling and floor. It prevented them from going any farther. Why it was there, he wasn't sure. But as far as he was concerned, it didn't really matter. They would be heading in the opposite direction.

'You wanted me to see this?' he asked.

The soldier shook his head. 'I wanted you to see *this.*'

He stuck his flashlight between the bars and shined it into the back room. Shards of broken bulbs littered the floor, intermixed with large chunks of stone and rubble. He tilted the beam upwards, revealing a man-made altar that had recently been chiselled to its core.

All that remained was a large hole, several cubic feet of empty space where something had been stored.

Hoping to get a better view, Schmidt turned on his light, too. 'What is it?'

'I'm guessing a tomb.'

'A tomb? Why do you say that?'

Instead of answering, he swung his beam to the rear corner of the room, where Shari Shasmeen lay motionless on the ground. Her eyes were closed. Her arms and legs were tied. Blood covered her face and clothes. She looked like a corpse.

Schmidt tilted his head to get a better view. 'Is she dead?'

'Can't tell from here. If you want, I can shoot her to make sure.'

He glanced at his watch. They had more important things to worry about.

'Why bother? If she's not dead now, she will be soon.'

45

They parked their trucks in an alley, several blocks south of the Great Mosque.

It was as close as traffic would allow.

Mecca was a multi-ethnic city, filled with people of all colours and nationalities. Still, to blend in, Payne and Jones had to dress the part. They wore white Saudi *thobes* (full-length cotton gowns that nearly touched the ground when they walked) and white skullcaps. The Arab-American soldiers added some variety. One donned a red-and-white *ghutra* (head-dress), held firm by a black *igal* (ropelike cord); the other covered his thobe with a light brown *bisht* (cloak). The remaining two wore beige *taqiyah* caps (brimless and accented with white-thread embroidery) and thobes of the same colour.

Ankle holsters, held in place by compression straps, were worn on both legs.

Extra ammo was stored in utility belts, concealed by their thobes.

Wireless transmitting devices were discreetly tucked in their ears.

All other equipment was varied, depending on preference. Payne was partial to blades. He wore one on each forearm, tucked in black leather sheaths.

Meanwhile, Jones carried a small set of tools, just in case he had to deactivate a bomb or pick a lock.

Walking briskly but never running, the men moved in pairs, weaving through the crowds of tourists that filled the sidewalks and ancient streets. The pilgrims would be entering the city from the east on the aptly named Pedestrian Road, trickling in initially before finally arriving en masse, a sea of white surging through the desert like a flood, monitored by thousands of guards and dozens of helicopters. Payne knew Schmidt would be somewhere else, probably concealed close to the mosque, patiently waiting for his prey to come to him.

Unless, of course, he had already planted an explosive device, one with a timer or a remote detonator, and was currently far from Mecca. If that was the case, then they were screwed because they didn't have the time, manpower, or authority to conduct a search. Their only hope was spotting Schmidt and taking him out before he started his assault.

Jones said, 'Omar's place should be up ahead.'

Payne nodded as he scanned his surroundings, searching for trouble. People. Windows. Rooftops. Hoping to spot something that seemed out of place. The city itself was not as he expected. He had travelled extensively in the Middle East and usually felt as if he had stepped through a time portal, leaping back to another era. Ancient buildings. Ancient streets. Ancient everything. But here, there seemed to be an equal mix of new and old.

Ancient traditions, yet contemporary comfort.

Ironically, the closer they got to the mosque, located in the centre of the old city, the more modern the infrastructure appeared. Building projects were popping up all over, areas fenced off for demolition and new construction. Dumper trucks and bull-dozers, cranes and scaffolding, rocks and sand. This *closed* city was definitely open for business – especially to American corporations. In one block, there were signs for Hilton Towers, Sheraton Hotel, and McDonald's.

'Where would you like us?' asked the Arab soldier in the middle pair, who were labelled team two. Payne and Jones were team one. The final duo was team three. The two Arab-Americans, who could speak Arabic, were split up in case their language skills were needed.

Payne heard the question in his earpiece. 'Team two, stay on the street. Team three, continue forwards to the mosque plaza. But stay close.'

Jones nodded towards Omar Abdul-Khaliq's prop-erty. It looked virtually unchanged from the satellite photo they had studied in the truck, a picture taken two weeks ago. Piles of stone and dirt filled one corner of the lot. Construction materials, protected by a chain-link fence, were stacked in the back near a small shed made of plywood. Payne stepped off the pavement and studied the terrain. Tread marks could be seen in the arid ground. They were recent.

'What do you think?' Payne asked.

'I think you were right. They're not building anything.'

'Then what's with the rocks?' They were fractured and covered in dirt, like they had just been pulled from the ground. 'They had to come from some-where.'

Jones agreed. Property this close to the mosque wouldn't be used as a dumping ground. It was too valuable as commercial space. However, as far as he could see, there was no excavation on the lot. Curious, he walked towards the chain link and spotted dozens of footprints heading into and out of the shack. 'I might have something.'

Payne scanned the street for witnesses. No one was paying attention. 'You're clear.'

Jones pulled a gun from his ankle holster and slipped through the unlocked gate, cautiously approaching the shed, which looked more like a long outhouse than a construction office. Yet for some reason, thick power cables ran through the right wall, the type of cords that were used for large industrial projects, not small shacks. The door was made of plywood and rested on iron hinges. Nudging it open with his free hand, Jones peeked inside.

As he stared at the interior, his eyes widened, stunned by what he saw.

'What is it?' Payne demanded.

'It's a tunnel. A big-ass tunnel . . . We're going to need more men.'

Payne hustled across the lot, not pulling his gun until he reached the door. He glanced inside before he spoke. 'We have a possible location. All eyes required. Team two, follow us in. Team three, guard the yard. Prepare to join us on my command.'

Jones waited, anxious. 'Ready?'

Payne nodded. 'I'll take the lead.'

The duo stepped inside, weapons raised, steadily moving forward as their eyes adjusted to the gloom. More than fifty feet in, they hit a branch in the tunnel. Lights were strung in both directions. Boards lined the floors. They waited there until team two arrived. Payne signalled for them to go to the right while he and Jones went to the left.

No words were spoken as they parted ways.

Payne led the way down the corridor. It looked similar to the main shaft, yet somehow newer. Like the ground had been burrowed in recent weeks. Possibly the source of all the dirt and stones in the vacant lot. If so, someone had gone to a lot of trouble to dig with such precision.

But why? What the hell was this place?

The mystery deepened when they reached the iron gate. Not only was it locked, but the bulbs that had lit their path suddenly stopped. Darkness filled the chamber in front of them. Intrigued, Jones reached under his thobe and pulled out a small torch. With a flick of the switch, he was staring at broken glass. And chunks of rubble. And something that looked like . . .

'Is that a body?' he asked, trying to get a better view. 'Jon, I think that's a body.'

Payne nodded as he stared through the bars. The beam barely reached the rear wall, but he could make out the shape of a woman, lying in the fetal position, her hands tied to her legs. He took the light from Jones and shined it along the gate's frame. No alarms or sensors. No booby traps. Nothing prevented them from getting inside. 'Pick it.'

Jones grinned. 'With pleasure.'

He removed a small toolkit and went to work. This was one of his biggest talents – in the past, he'd picked locks underwater and blindfolded – and he loved showing off his skills. Thirty seconds later, he pushed open the gate with a soft screech.

Payne went first, torch in one hand, weapon in the other. Glass crunched under every step. Moving closer, he shined the light on the woman's face and noticed two things.

One, she was covered in blood.

Two, she was still alive.

46

When Payne first approached, Shari started struggling, worried that he was one of the guards who had assaulted her or the men who talked about shooting her. But once they explained they were American soldiers who were there to help, she started to relax.

No tears. No messy, emotional scene. This woman was a fighter.

Payne cut the cords off her hands and legs and eased her to her feet. She was unsteady for several seconds, leaning against him as she filled them in on everything. The tunnel. The robbery of her site. And her boss: Omar Abdul-Khaliq.

'Is he in Mecca?' Jones wondered.

'I don't know where he is. I've never met the man. We do everything by phone. The last time we talked was two days ago, when he hired new guards to protect this place. There was a murder and —'

Payne interrupted her. 'A murder?'

She nodded. 'A delivery guy dropped off a package and was killed on his way out.'

'What kind of package?'

'An envelope for Omar. He asked me to keep it on me at all times. He seemed pretty worried about it.'

'Do you still have it?'

'I should.' She reached through the flap of her abaya and pulled out a hajj belt (an oversized pouch for pilgrims) filled with money, keys, and her travel papers. She handed the envelope to Payne. 'It's still sealed. He told me not to open it.'

'And when did –' Payne stopped in mid-sentence as a voice chirped in his ear. Team two was sending him a message. He raised his index finger, signalling her to wait.

'Team one, we found another tunnel. Repeat, another tunnel. Permission to access?'

He glanced at Jones, who heard the same transmission. 'Go check it out.'

Jones nodded and ran off.

Payne responded. 'Team two, permission denied. Repeat, *denied*. Team one will be joining you for entry. Talk us to a rendezvous.'

Voices chattered in his earpiece as he returned his attention to Shari. She was bloodied and battered but quite resilient. 'How long have you been working down here?'

'Probably a few days too long.'

Payne smiled, impressed by her toughness. 'Considering what's happened, I'm sure you'd like to get out of here. But before you leave, I'd like to ask you a small favour. Would you mind giving me a tour?'

'A tour?'

He nodded as they walked towards the gate. 'I'm

searching for an old friend who might've passed through here. The more I know about this place, the better.'

'One friend or several?'

'Why do you ask?'

'Because I heard people working in the tunnel. One of them spotted me and wanted to make sure I was dead, but the other said I'd be dead soon enough.'

Payne nodded. It sure sounded like them. 'How long ago?'

Shari thought for a moment. 'Less than an hour. They were doing something on the other end of the tunnel. Near the maintenance shaft.'

'Maintenance for what?'

'That complex up the road. They had to build their own water facility in the middle of the desert just to handle the water demand. Their pipes run past here, and our tunnel connects with theirs.'

'You mean the mosque?'

She shook her head. 'Abraj Al Bait Towers. It's being built next to the mosque. When they're done, it's going to be the biggest building in the world.'

'And it's across from the mosque?'

She nodded. 'Which seems sacrilegious to some people. Especially considering the owner.'

'Who's the owner?'

'The Bin Laden Group.'

Payne winced. It wasn't a name he was expecting. 'As in Osama bin Laden?'

'It's his family's business. His father, Mohammed, started the company himself.'

Despite their infamous surname, the bin Ladens shared a close relationship with the Saudi royal family, thanks to the construction work they did at the royal palace in Jeddah. King Abdul Aziz was so impressed with their craftsmanship that he gave them exclusive rights to all religious construction in Mecca and Medina, Saudi Arabia's two holiest cities, and even asked them to renovate the Great Mosque itself. Since that time, the bin Ladens had expanded their empire, building tunnels, dams, and thousands of miles of Saudi roads while branching into several diverse areas. They included power, chemicals, manufacturing, telecom, and real estate.

However, their latest development would be their most significant yet.

Once completed, the Abraj Al Bait Towers would be the largest building in the world. Not the tallest – its main tower would reach 1,591 feet, which would be 80 feet shorter than the Taipei Financial Centre in Taiwan – yet the biggest in overall mass, a combined floor space of 16 million square feet. The complex would consist of seven interconnected buildings, including a five-star hotel, a business conference centre, a prayer hall for 3,800 people, a four-storey mall built to resemble an outdoor Arab market, two heliports, a thousand-car parking garage, a self-contained transportation system, and several residential towers. More than 65,000 people would be able to stay there at one time.

The estimated cost was $1.5 billion.

Nevertheless, economic analysts expected the project to be a financial bonanza, capitalizing on the millions of Muslims who visited the Great Mosque throughout the year. Visitors from around the world would be able to look out of their hotel windows and stare down at the Kaaba, the holiest shrine in Islam. They would be able to hear the muezzin's call to prayer while in the air-conditioned comfort of their rooms. They would be able to walk across the street, day or night, and kiss the Black Stone. It would be a pilgrim's dream come true.

Unless, of course, Trevor Schmidt got to it first.

Payne met Jones near the entrance to the maintenance shaft. A large sealed door, which looked like it belonged in a submarine, had been wedged open before their arrival. Shari guessed it was the noise she'd heard in the tunnel, because the hatch was normally locked.

'Where's it go?' Jones asked.

'To the perfect target,' Payne answered. He explained what was being built, and more importantly, who was building it. 'Osama was shunned by his family a long time ago, but that won't make a difference to Schmidt. He'll remember all the family members who were killed in the hospital bombing and focus on the bin Laden name. In one attack, he can avenge his unit's death and 9/11, kill thousands of Muslims, and destroy their most sacred site.'

'Makes sense to me.'

'The only question is how.'

Jones glanced at Shari. 'Have you been inside the complex?'

'No. It's nowhere near done. They won't be finished for two more years.'

'So it'll be empty except for the builders?'

'It should be empty, *period*. Today's a religious holiday. No one will be working.'

'Any security? Cameras? Alarms?'

'I have no idea,' she admitted. 'I've spent all my time down here, not outside. Other than the maintenance tunnel, my knowledge about the Towers is strictly based on rumours. The bin Ladens are notorious for keeping their designs under wraps. Apart from the architects and a few government officials, no one has access to their plans.'

Back in 1979, the bin Ladens had been working on a number of religious projects throughout Mecca, exercising the exclusive rights that had been granted to them by the royal family. Because of this special relationship, bin Laden trucks were able to come and go without being inspected, a fact that was taken advantage of by Islamic rebels, who used the trucks – without the bin Ladens' knowledge – to smuggle hundreds of weapons into the city, including those that were used during the insurrection that ended with the seizure of the Great Mosque.

Ironically, since the bin Ladens were in charge of citywide renovations, including those at the mosque, they were the *only* ones who possessed maps of Mecca's underground tunnel system. That meant even though bin Laden trucks were used in the insurrection, the Saudi police had to turn to the bin Ladens for their assistance.

Jones asked, 'Which government officials would be notified about their designs?'

'The Ministry of the Interior.'

'Sonofabitch,' he muttered. 'It figures.'

'What?' she asked, confused.

Payne explained. 'The guy we're after tortured one of their officials. We weren't sure why, but now it makes sense. He wanted to know about the Towers.'

47

The entry route was exactly as they had been told. Follow the pipes directly into the sub-basement. Take the stairs to access ground level. From there, all seven towers were accessible via ramps and exterior construction elevators. Security would be virtually non-existent, since most of the guards would be outside, patrolling the plaza, stopping people from entering the work zone. They wouldn't be inside, worried about terrorists.

During the past six months, Schmidt had studied the building plans and surveyed Mecca on three different trips. However, until he was standing inside, staring at the tons of concrete and steel that surrounded him, he never fully grasped how big the complex was.

To build the Abraj Al Bait Towers, a large hole had been dug until they hit bedrock, which was less than 100 feet deep in Mecca because its layer was close to the surface. In some projects, such as the Petronas Towers in Kuala Lumpur, workers had to dig 394 feet underground to lay the foundation, a massive undertaking that cost millions of dollars. Next, footings were anchored in the hole to distribute the weight, much like a pyramid, before concrete was poured over the top, creating the bottom floor. Large cranes inserted vertical support beams and horizontal steel girders, which held the building together, forming a giant frame. Finally, a curtain wall, made of concrete and glass, was attached to the outside, providing water and wind resistance while improving the overall aesthetics of the project.

From there, work was done on the interior. Three thousand miles of electrical wires. Twenty-eight thousand miles of plumbing. Heating and cooling systems. Wood, marble, stone, glass. All of it laid in stages over several years, pieces slowly coming together until the complex was finally finished.

Construction had begun in 2004 and wouldn't be finished until 2009.

But as far as Schmidt was concerned, everything he needed was already in place.

The tunnel was narrow, lined in concrete and filled with massive pipes that seemed to go on for ever. With nowhere to hide and no way to spread out, they jogged single file, their footsteps multiplying with every echo. Fluorescent lights, covered in metal screens and bolted to the ceiling, lit their path, but the truth was they were heading into darkness.

No advanced recon. No knowledge of the building. Like a black hole of information.

Payne led the way, followed by Jones, then the other two teams. Their pace never slowed from the moment they entered the hatch until they approached the tunnel's end. It opened into a wide expanse, cluttered with equipment, raw materials, and the skeletal foundation of the buildings. The men scattered quickly, searching for architectural plans, schematics, or maps – anything to help them navigate the maze that surrounded them.

Three minutes passed before something was found. It was a simple pamphlet, written in Arabic and English, detailing the future amenities of the Towers, including a full-colour illustration of the complex upon completion. There were seven buildings in total, all of them facing the Great Mosque. Five were laid out in a giant horseshoe, while the space between was filled with a multistoreyed mall. The remaining two towers jutted away from the curve in the U – one tower on each side, yet still connected through a series of walkways and bridges.

The showcased building was the one in the centre. Simply called the Hotel Tower, it was nearly 1,600 feet tall, trimmed in gold, and topped with a crescent moon, an important symbol in the Islamic faith. It was nearly twice the height of the others, whose names and sizes were listed.

1. Hotel Tower 485 m, 1,591 ft.
2. Hajar 260 m, 853 ft.
3. Zamzam 260 m, 853 ft.
4. Qiblah 240 m, 787 ft.
5. Sarah 240 m, 787 ft.

6. Marwah 240 m, 787 ft.
7. Safa 240 m, 787 ft.

With the exception of the Hotel Tower, each of the names had its roots in Islam. Hajar and Sarah were women in the Qur'an. Zamzam was the famous well inside the Great Mosque. Qiblah was the direction of prayer in Mecca. Marwah and Safa were the hills that pilgrims travelled between seven times.

According to the pamphlet, each of the buildings was being treated as a separate project. All of them were interconnected, but they would be finished at different times. Two of the residential towers would be completed this year; the hotel would take until the end of the decade.

Payne considered this while he planned their next move. Meanwhile, his men gathered around him like a quarterback in the huddle, waiting for him to call the play.

'There are six of us and six exterior buildings,' he said. 'We don't know where they'll be or what they're doing. For all we know, they're spread throughout the complex. The best way to cover that much ground is by splitting up. Radio frequently. Concentrate on structural areas, places where an explosive will do the most damage. We don't have time to go room to room. Just follow your gut and we may get lucky.'

He pointed to a man, then pointed to a building,

each assigned the number in the pamphlet. 'You, four. You, five. You, six. You, seven. DJ and I will take the two towers closest to the hotel. If you see anything, let us know. We'll reassign manpower as needed.'

The soldiers dispersed, moving in pairs. Even-numbered buildings were on the left; odd numbers were on the right. The men would travel together until they were forced to split up.

Payne and Jones were the last to leave. They lingered in the sub-basement for an extra minute, looking for something to improve their odds, hoping to find a better map, one with floor plans or mechanical drawings. Anything to point out the weaknesses that Schmidt might have spotted when he did his research.

As it turned out, their biggest break wasn't an object. It was a sound. A simple sound. Nothing more than a drip of liquid falling on concrete. Like a droplet of rain hitting the pavement. Jones heard it as he searched for paperwork. On most occasions it would have blended into the outside world and he would have ignored it. But in this case, his senses were in overdrive. Adrenaline was flowing, and everything around him was part of a much bigger puzzle.

A sound could be a footstep. A sound could mean his death.

Drip. Somewhere to his left.

Drip. Back near the maintenance shaft.

Drip. What was that smell?

Suddenly his curiosity was doubled. Not only was

there a noise, but there was an odour. A familiar scent that reminded him of his time in the military. Back when he was flying planes and helicopters. Killing time in hangars. Waiting for his next mission to begin.

He took a few steps forward, searching the ceiling and floor for moisture. Finally he saw it. A small puddle underneath the massive water pipe they had followed from the hatch. Curious, he crouched and inspected the liquid. It was clear like water but had a strong chemical smell. He put his nose closer and took a whiff.

'Jon,' he called over his shoulder. 'Come over here.'

Payne spotted him in a catcher's stance, examining a puddle on the ground. He couldn't imagine what his friend was doing. 'Please tell me you didn't take a piss.'

Jones ignored him. 'I think it's fuel.'

'What do you mean?'

'I think this pipe is leaking fuel.'

'But that's a water pipe.'

He nodded. 'I know it is. But I'm telling you, this isn't water.'

Dubious, Payne leaned closer and breathed in the fumes. An acrid stench filled his nostrils, burning the back of his throat and making him gag.

'Told you it isn't water.'

Payne coughed a few times, trying to catch his breath. 'What the hell is that?'

But Jones didn't answer. Instead, he took a few steps down the maintenance shaft, trying to figure out what was going on. He glanced back into the sub-basement, following the plumbing, then back into the shaft again, the pieces still not fitting together. 'Where do those pipes go?'

'To some private facility in the desert. Shari said the towers were so big they had to pump in their own water.'

'But that's *not* water.'

'I know it's not water. I'm still choking.' He paused for a second as all the nasty possibilities started to sink in. 'Wait. What do you think it is?'

'Aviation fuel.'

48

Shari Shasmeen felt lucky to be alive. She had been brutally beaten and left to die, yet she had somehow managed to survive. Unfortunately, there was no time for elation.

This was a time for escape.

She was standing in a tunnel that was less than half a mile from ground zero. Payne and Jones had refused to tell her what was going on, but she could sense that it was something big. American troops weren't going to sneak into Mecca in the middle of hajj season without a reason. Throw in the look on Payne's face when she mentioned the bin Laden name, and she was bright enough to put the pieces of the puzzle together.

She needed to get as far away as possible.

The only question was how.

Her face was caked with blood. Her abaya was stained and torn. And she had no chaperone on a day when the mutaween were out in full force, looking for even the slightest infraction of Sharia law. If she waited another hour, she knew pilgrims would fill the streets and she could blend in with the massive crowd, thereby aiding her escape. But even with a minor concussion, she realized that was a foolish plan. It was the equivalent of turning down a parachute because the crashing plane might land safely in the minefield up ahead.

For all she knew, the crowd might be attacked. Or blown up. Or start to stampede.

No, it was better to get out now while she still had the chance.

While she still had control.

Shari rummaged through the tunnel, looking for anything that could aid her cause. The first thing she noticed was a large water jug that they had filled every morning during the dig. It was made of thick plastic and held several gallons of liquid. It hadn't been cleaned or refilled during the last few days while her team was banned from the site, but at this point she would have been willing to drink from an aquarium. She was dehydrated, and her tongue tasted like sand.

Putting her mouth under the spout, she released the valve and let the water pour into her throat. Each gulp seemed to invigorate her, as if it was an antidote to a poison that had sapped her strength. Next, she splashed some water on her face and tried to scrub off the dried blood. Not exactly a trip to the spa for a facial, but she wasn't getting ready for a wedding. All she was hoping to do was avoid detection. The plainer she looked, the easier it would be to blend in.

Shari glanced around the tunnel one last time, realizing it was probably the final time she would ever be in there. She focused her attention on the chamber where she had been tied up, studying the altar that had protected the artefact for several centuries, searching the stones for inscriptions or clues that might have historical significance. If she only had a camera, she could document everything on film, images that wouldn't fade from her memory, pictures that she could share with her colleagues back at the hotel.

'Wait,' she mumbled to herself. Suddenly it dawned on her that she still didn't know how long she had been unconscious. For all she knew, her colleagues were worried about her and might be coming to find her. If that was the case, they would be heading towards the mosque. Towards the impending danger.

In an instant, the site was no longer her priority.

The safety of her friends was.

Shari hiked up the fabric of her abaya and hustled towards the tunnel entrance. The sudden physical exertion coupled with the burst of adrenaline caused her head to throb. Her nose, which had been shattered by the lead guard, was clogged with blood and mucus, forcing her to breathe through her mouth even though it was covered by cloth. Ironically, this was the first time in her life that she was thankful for the Islamic dress code, because it allowed her to hide from the mutaween. By pulling the veil that covered her shoulder-length black hair across her face, she was able to conceal most of her injuries.

And that was crucial if she wanted to avoid detection.

As she approached the tunnel entrance, she shielded her eyes from the intense glare of the afternoon sun and waited several seconds for her vision to adjust to the brightness. Standing there, it dawned on her that everything had started to go to hell in that very spot. That was where Fred Nasir's body had been dumped, where she had met the guards who had attacked her, where they had loaded the corpse into the van, and later the artefact that they had stolen from her site. Now she was standing there, pondering what to do next.

God, she hoped that wasn't a bad omen.

Wasting no more time, she pushed the door open and walked into the hot desert air, which contrasted sharply with the coolness of the underground lair where she had been held prisoner. Construction materials shielded her exit, allowing her to scope out the landscape before she chose the safest path to her hotel. The Great Mosque was to her right, the opposite direction that she wanted to travel. Unfortunately, most of the foot traffic was heading towards the holy shrine. But these weren't pilgrims who would be arriving from the desert to the east. These were mostly well-wishers, Muslims who weren't going through the rituals of hajj but were there to watch the spectacle.

Shari eyed the crowd from afar, patiently waiting behind the chain-link fence until she spotted a group of women who were heading against the flow of traffic. Amazingly, she could deduce which country most of the women were from simply by looking at their clothes. Egyptian women preferred *galabiyeh*, ankle-length skirts, while Moroccan women opted for *kaftans*. Iranians typically wore long dresses known as *libas* and white cloaks called *chadors*. And *burqas*, all-encompassing outfits that covered every inch of a woman's body including her face and eyes, were common in the strictest regions of the Islamic world.

On the other hand, some Westerners (North Americans and Europeans) showed up in jeans and long-sleeved shirts, clothes that met the basic requirements of decency yet were frowned upon by some parts of traditional Muslim society.

Because of this, Shari decided it was in her best interests to avoid her fellow Americans. They would scrutinize her the closest, and would be the ones most likely to ask her questions about her background and why her abaya was stained and torn. And heaven forbid if they noticed the blood on her face or her broken nose. They would probably start screaming for help, which was the last thing in the world that she wanted.

In this case help would be bad.

It was liable to get her killed.

49

When designing a skyscraper, water pressure was a significant problem that had to be overcome. Large pumps in the basement usually serviced the lower floors. However, it was impractical to pump water directly to a penthouse, several hundred feet in the air. Most buildings were equipped with mechanical floors, every ten floors or so, which were filled with everything from air-conditioning units to ventilation systems. This is where intermediate pumps were stored, used to push water from one stage to the next until the liquid reached its highest destination.

Unfortunately, this was an inefficient system in the tallest of buildings, always relying on the pump below to send water to the pump above. One mechanical failure and the water stopped. This was a huge concern in emergency situations, when sprinkler systems could not afford to fail because ground-based fire equipment was incapable of shooting water above certain heights.

To remedy this situation, tanks were often installed on the upper floors, where water was stored in case it was needed. Sometimes the tanks were small, placed on every mechanical floor in the building. Sometimes they were large, scattered throughout different parts of the system, based on estimated demand. And occasionally, in really big projects such as the Abraj Al Bait Towers, the designers opted for something different.

In the mechanical penthouse, on top of every tower in the seven-building complex, sat a water tank with a capacity of 40,000 gallons. Engineers designed these tanks with a dual purpose in mind. First and foremost, they could supply water to the 65,000 guests who would fill the towers and all the extra people who used the mall, convention centre, and prayer halls. Second, the tanks served as tuned mass dampers, absorbing vibrations from high winds and possible earthquakes – not to mention from the 2.4 million people that strolled through the Meccan desert during the hajj season – which helped to protect the structural integrity of the building's core.

Ironically, the tanks were installed to keep the towers standing, but they were the very things that might bring them down.

Trevor Schmidt smiled as he placed the charge along the base of the water tank.

It was the perfect choice for the perfect mission.

C-4, an abbreviation for Composition 4, was a military-grade plastic explosive, one that was preferred by the US Special Forces because its velocity of detonation was ideal for metalwork. Not only was it malleable, allowing it to be moulded into specific shapes or wedged into the tiniest of spaces, but it was also highly stable. It could be shot, dropped, kicked, or thrown into a fire, but it wasn't going to explode without a detonator. For the past few hours, Schmidt had carried five pounds of it in a shoulder bag and never worried about it blowing up prematurely.

Of course, there were other reasons why he'd selected C-4 for this particular job.

Personal reasons.

Due to its precision, C-4 was frequently used by terrorists, including the bombing of the USS *Cole*, a guided-missile destroyer refuelling in Yemen, and the destruction of the Khobar Towers, a US military housing development in Saudi Arabia where nineteen servicemen were killed. Both of those were horrible tragedies that deserved to be avenged, but in Schmidt's mind, they paled in comparison to the incident at Al-Hada Hospital, where C-4 was used to detonate a fuel truck parked outside the private wing where his men were staying.

That was the attack that had ignited his rage.

He thought back to that painful day as he prepared the detonator. For him, it was a simple procedure, one he had done so many times in the past that it was second nature. Like brushing his teeth or tying his shoe. There were no nerves or trepidation. His hands simply did what they were trained to do.

Much like Schmidt himself.

Payne sent the transmission as he and Jones charged up the stairs. 'All teams, check in for priority update. Repeat, *priority* update.'

His men responded in turn, waiting to receive the information.

'Jet fuel has been found in the plumbing. Repeat, inside the plumbing. Focus your search on mechanical floors. Tanks and pumps are prime targets. Sweep for explosives.'

There was a three-second delay before one of his men spoke. 'Are floor numbers known?'

'Negative,' Payne answered. 'Floor numbers are *unknown*. But follow pipes when possible. Listen for machinery. Anything to suggest activity.'

Jones added, 'Maps might be posted in stairs or elevators. Check there before entry.'

Payne nodded. It was a good suggestion. 'Good luck.'

The man they called Luke was positioned high above the central plaza, giving him a bird's-eye view of the entire complex. Up there, he felt like God sitting on his golden throne, deciding who lived and who died.

Staring through his sniper's scope, he made his decision.

Death would come swiftly.

With the ball of his finger, he eased the trigger back, careful not to jerk his rifle. The bullet was discharged at 3,000 feet per second and slammed into the base of the target's skull, entering the cerebellum and instantly stopping his motor skills. Pink mist erupted in the lobby as one of Payne's soldiers fell to the floor.

Luke flicked his wrist, ejecting the spent casing before he chambered a new round.

The Arab-American never heard the shot. One moment his partner was jogging in front of him, the next he was falling in a violent burst of blood.

Stunned by the development, he reacted the way most people would: he rushed to his friend's side, hoping he could help. Unfortunately, it was a choice that ended his life.

The second shot arrived eight seconds later. Same pinpoint accuracy, same maximum devastation. It punctured his red-and-white head-dress, entered his skin and skull, then exited the other side, taking chunks of brain with it.

Two dead men in one messy pile.

Payne spotted them across the lobby and shoved Jones behind a thick stone pillar that shielded them from a frontal assault. They peeked around the corner, soaking in the details of the scene, trying to understand what had happened.

'Sniper,' guessed Jones, who was familiar with their techniques because he had trained as one before the MANIACs. He scanned the terrain, searching for possible positioning. 'Somewhere high, but not too high. Range is too tough to gauge.'

Payne listened as he swore under his breath, blaming himself for their deaths.

'Maybe in the hotel. Probably near an exit point.'

'What?' Payne asked, trying to focus on what was said. 'Which exit?'

Jones pointed towards the tower above them. Of all the buildings, it had the least amount of work done. Nothing more than a steel and concrete skeleton rising 500 feet into the sky. Not even a third of its intended height. 'Up there somewhere.'

Payne glanced up. Most of the building was hidden from view, blocked by a large overhang that would eventually support the atrium in the mall. Right now there was no glass, just an empty space that opened to the heavens above. 'How'd he get there?'

'Construction elevator. No way he walked it. Snipers need to control their breathing to get a precise shot. That doesn't happen if you're out of breath.'

'So he's just sitting up there, waiting to pick us off?'

'Probably.'

'Which means he *isn't* placing a charge.'

'Probably not.'

'Then we have to leave him,' Payne said with regret. 'At this point it's all about the maths. Bombs can kill a lot more people than the sniper, so we have to focus on the bombs.'

Jones nodded in agreement. 'Where do you want me?'

'Take building three. I'll warn the men, then slip around back to building two.'

Jones turned to leave, then suddenly stopped. 'Hey, Jon.'

'Yeah?'

'If you find Schmidt, don't focus on the past. Don't hesitate.'

Payne shook his head. 'Don't worry. I won't.'

50

They surged towards Mecca like a dust storm sweeping in from the desert. It started with a slow trickle, a few hundred people who left Tent City right after their required duties, closely followed by a flood of 2.4 million pilgrims, all of them looking to fulfil their hajj obligations.

Payne saw them in the distance on Pedestrian Road, the main route from Mount Arafat, as he rode up the construction elevator attached to the eastern end of Hajar (building two). The crowd's movement was like a ticking clock, for he knew Schmidt would coordinate his attack with their arrival. Thankfully, they were still a mile away, which gave Payne twenty minutes to find the explosives and render them useless.

Floors whizzed by as the open-air elevator continued to rise. One hand on the remote control and one hand on his gun, Payne slowed his ascent as he approached the top floor, more than 800 feet above the plaza. Before exiting, he scanned the rooftop, focusing on the corners, making sure that he wasn't walking into an ambush.

'Checking roof two,' he whispered.

Every few minutes his earpiece would buzz with

the latest update from his squad. So far, no luck in any of the towers. No sightings. No discoveries. No explosives. Nothing but two dead soldiers and nothing to show for it.

Time was running out.

Payne took a deep breath and sprinted across the beige roof, trying to reach the mechanical penthouse as quickly as possible. Although this building was currently the tallest one in Mecca, he was surrounded by eight tower cranes that could easily conceal a sniper. Sliding to a stop behind a stack of decorative stones, he turned back and stared at the closest mast, which rose 200 feet above him and had a working arm capable of lifting twenty tons. Thankfully, no one was up there, but it was the type of machine that could lift a massive water tank and move it into place.

'Going in,' he whispered.

The access door was thick and unlocked. He turned the handle and eased it open six inches, just enough space to glance inside. A set of metal stairs descended into shadows. The only light was the sun, peeking over his shoulder. Time was precious, so he didn't hesitate. He slipped through the gap and closed the door. He was instantly swallowed by darkness.

Instincts told him he had nothing to fear, that Schmidt and his men wouldn't be sitting in the dark, waiting to strike. Manpower was too valuable. So Payne slid his hand along the wall until he found a switch. One flick of his finger and the room filled with fluorescent light.

Gun in hand, he eased down the stairs, step by step, scanning his path for booby traps. From there, he shifted his focus to the room itself. Equipment and supplies were scattered along the perimeter wall, nothing that posed a threat or seemed out of place. Then, and only then, did he turn his attention inward, focusing on the object that dominated the centre of the room.

The water tank was the size of a small bus. Supported by steel cables attached to the building's frame, it appeared to hover in space. Payne was familiar with the basic principles of tuned mass dampers – skyscrapers sometimes swayed several feet in the wind, and TMDs were designed to counteract that, acting like a pendulum – but he had never seen one like this.

If Schmidt had filled one of these with jet fuel, an explosion would be catastrophic. Not only from the force of the blast, but also the lingering effects of the burning fuel, which would pour over the roof like a waterfall of fire, dousing millions of pilgrims, literally melting them in the streets. The prolonged heat would be so intense that the steel columns in the tower would start to melt and buckle. Couple that with the added sway from the disabled TMD and a pancake effect would occur. One floor would fall upon the next, which would fall upon the next, until the whole building collapsed in a pile of rubble. Just like the World Trade Center.

The impact and the debris and the panic and the

fire would turn the Great Mosque into a war zone. No one would be safe. No one would be protected. Chaos would run rampant in the city.

It would be the worst man-made disaster in history.

Payne tried to block those thoughts from his mind as he searched the room for explosives. It didn't take long to find one. Made out of C-4, it was moulded to the northern side of the tank and armed with a timed detonator. At first glance it appeared to be a simple design, one he could disarm by separating the explosive from the device, but Payne knew things weren't always as they seemed, especially in the world of munitions.

Who knew what kind of trigger was concealed?

Just to be safe, he decided to get a second opinion.

'Device located. I repeat, device located in building two.'

There was a slight delay before Jones's voice filled his earpiece. 'Location?'

'Attached to a water tank in the mechanical penthouse.'

A crackle of updates filled his ear as the remaining soldiers scrambled to check the penthouse tanks in their assigned buildings. Once things calmed down, Jones spoke again.

'Type of device?'

'C-4. Armed with a timed detonator.'

'How much time?'

Payne stared at the mechanism. 'Good question. The timer is covered in the housing.'

'Any triggers?'

'You tell me.'

Jones paused. 'Sorry, I can't see any from here.'

'No shit. I meant, what should I be looking for?'

'You're in the penthouse, right? Don't worry about mercury switches or tilt detonators. There's too much sway up there to risk it.'

'What would you use?'

'A hidden tripwire. I'd attach it to the water tank from the back of the casing. That way, if someone removed the device, it would detonate.'

Payne looked closer and spotted everything that Jones had described. A thin green wire dangled out of the device, affixed to the tank with some kind of epoxy. 'Okay. I found one.'

'You did? Then you owe me lunch because I just saved your ass.'

'Not a problem. Tell me what to do and the falafel are on me.'

'Do you have any tools? A screwdriver? Anything like that?'

Payne smiled. He reached up his sleeve and pulled a blade from its sheath. 'I have a knife.'

'Of course you do,' Jones said with a laugh, well aware of Payne's fascination with knives. 'With one hand, hold the wire steady against the casing. Do *not* let it pull away.'

'Okay.'

'With your other hand, use the knife to pry the wire off the tank.'

'That's it?'

'But *don't* cut the wire.'

'I won't.'

'Or let it pull away from the casing.'

'You already said that.'

'I know, but I *really* want to get a falafel.'

Payne smiled, thankful for the tension breaker. 'Is there anything else?'

'Nope, that's everything. Just do what I said and you'll be fine.'

He nodded, taking a deep breath. 'In that case, get back to work. I need to get this done and you need to search your tower.'

51

Several minutes passed before Shari spotted what she was looking for. A large cluster of women, all of them Caucasian and dressed conservatively, were walking against the flow of traffic that was headed towards the mosque. They paused for a moment to take a group photo, and as they did, Shari left the vacant lot and slipped in behind them, blending in like she belonged.

The women continued forwards, strolling at a slow pace that was mostly due to the direction they were headed. At times Shari felt like they were going the wrong way down a one-way road. And unlike some parts of the world where men would be chivalrous and allow the women to pass unimpeded, that was not the case in Saudi Arabia, a male-dominant country where men were leaders and women were not. Of course, Shari wasn't raised in this culture so it was just a matter of time before she got frustrated and decided to speed things along.

Glancing down a side street, Shari noticed a bank of three payphones. They were painted bright red and trimmed with frosted glass. Arabic lettering decorated the front, right next to the universal symbol for a phone – a drawing of one – just in case people were too stupid to know what a phone booth was. The middle phone was being used by an Indonesian woman while four of her female friends were standing on the pavement behind her.

At her current pace, Shari knew that it would take several hours to get back to her hotel, far too long to warn her colleagues. At this point she had to do what she could to keep her team as far away from the mosque as possible. That meant giving them a call.

Casually, as if she were home in Florida, Shari broke away from the group of women and walked over to the payphone. She reached under her abaya and dug her hand into her hajj belt, grabbing the appropriate coins. A telephone book, stored in a plastic binder that protected it from inclement weather, hung from a thick cord underneath a metal shelf. Shari was about to open it when she realized it wasn't necessary. She dug through her belt once again, this time pulling out her room key. The name of the hotel and its telephone number were stamped on the plastic key chain. A few seconds later she was being connected to one of their rooms.

'Hello,' Hennessy answered.

'Drew, it's Shari.'

'Where are you?' he asked, concerned. 'You've been gone all night.'

'Don't worry. I'm fine. I've been dealing with some issues at the site.'

'What kind of issues?'

'Bad ones, I'm afraid.'

She glanced over her shoulder, making sure that no one was watching or listening. The Indonesian woman standing next to her spoke rapidly in a language that Shari couldn't understand. The rest of the women chatted among themselves, paying no attention. Still, Shari wasn't about to reveal anything over a phone line. Especially not the truth. Instead she opted to make up a lie, one that would get her team to safety. At this point that was all she cared about.

She would tell them the truth later, once they were safely out of Saudi Arabia.

'We've been asked to leave the site,' she lied. 'The authorities found out about the incident, and we've been ordered to leave immediately.'

'But –'

'Listen,' she said, cutting him off, 'this isn't something that should be discussed over the phone. Just listen to me and do what I say, okay?'

'Of course.'

'Gather up the team, pack our stuff, and get out of Mecca as soon as possible. Do not come near the site or the mosque. This whole area is being sealed off as we speak.' She paused for a moment, thinking things through. 'I know you probably have lots of questions, but you have to trust me on this one. Get out of town immediately. I can fill you in at a later date.'

'Wait,' he said. 'You're not coming with us?'

She shook her head, realizing that her battered face was bound to cause problems at every security check-point in the Middle East. Questions that would put her team at risk since they were non-Muslims travelling with fake paperwork. 'I can't. I have to stay behind and deal with the political mess. But don't worry, I'll be fine. I promise.'

'Are you sure? Because –'

'Trust me, I'll be fine.'

Shari hung up the phone but didn't feel fine. Far from it. She was injured in a foreign country and the man who had arranged her employment, Omar Abdul-Khaliq, had hired thugs to steal her work and eliminate her in the process. As things stood, she had no job, no allies, and no transportation in the middle of a forbidden city. And to make matters worse, some kind of terrorist attack was about to take place at the Great Mosque.

All things considered, she'd had a pretty shitty day.

Of course Shari's luck started to change when she noticed the camera. It was sitting on the metal shelf in the centre phone booth, the one the Indonesian woman had been using a moment before. Shari glanced up the street, searching for any of the women, but they had vanished into the stream of people that surged up the main road towards the Kaaba.

Tentatively, Shari picked up the camera case and opened it. A brand-new digital camera, equipped with all the latest features and a fully charged battery, sat inside. The memory card was nearly empty, meaning there was enough space for several minutes of video or several hundred pictures.

She knew it was reckless and bound to get her caught or killed, but the temptation was far too great to resist. Underneath her veil, a sly smile emerged as Shari made her decision. She would return to the site to film what remained of the document chamber before she left Mecca for ever.

52

Payne held the knife like a surgeon – confident, yet with the utmost care.

His left hand secured the green wire against the casing while his right hand guided the blade, sliding the tip along the edge of the water tank until he felt residue from the epoxy. He knew different formulas produced different strengths. Some were weaker than modelling glue; others were used in aerospace construction. Obviously, he was hoping for the former.

With a hint of pressure, he inched his knife into the resin, trying to prise the wire loose. It quivered slightly, moving with his effort as he slowly broke the bond that held it secure.

First a chip. Then a crack. Then a huge sigh of relief as the wire popped free from the tank but stayed imbedded in the detonator. Just like Jones had promised.

Shit. I owe him a falafel.

Payne smiled at the thought, realizing it was a debt he'd gladly pay if he managed to get out of the city alive. Unfortunately, he wasn't ready yet. Not even close. The tripwire was one thing; the bomb itself was another. Not only did he have to disarm the timer mechanism, he also had to figure out what to do with the C-4 so it wasn't used by someone else. Whether that be Schmidt. Or the Saudis. Or some terrorist group who operated out of the area.

Which meant he had to do more than disarm the bomb.

He had to take the damn thing with him.

Jones finished his search of building three but came up empty. Literally.

The mechanical penthouse *did* have a water tank, just like Payne had described in building two, but there was no liquid inside. The massive tank was bone dry, not a drop of water or jet fuel to be found. When he tapped on its side, it sounded like a hollow drum.

'Three is clear,' he announced.

Jones hustled back across the roof and into the construction elevator. Due to the death of his soldiers, there were still two more towers to inspect. Building five (Sarah) sat to his west, in the back corner of the complex. Strategically, it would be the least likely target, since it posed the smallest threat. On the other hand, building seven (Safa) was right up front, overlooking the main road that would soon be filled with pilgrims. In his mind, that made it a probable target – until he stared down at it from the elevator and saw that the top floor was still being built. There was no water tank or mechanical penthouse. There wasn't even a roof. That meant unless

Schmidt found some other weakness on the lower floors, the odds were against its attack.

To Jones, the building that seemed most vulnerable was building six (Marwah). It was closest to the Great Mosque, sitting just north of Payne's tower, and its construction seemed to be the farthest along. He saw windows. And stonework. And painting. All the little details that get taken care of after the big stuff was finished. Including the installation of pipes and water tanks.

'Building six, what's your status?'

There was a slight delay. 'The elevator is broken, so I'm hoofing it to the penthouse.'

'Current location?'

'Floor nine.'

'*Nine*? What's the hold-up?'

'There's scaffolding everywhere, and I keep tripping on my goddamn dress.'

Payne heard the transmission and nearly burst out laughing; the only thing that prevented it was the severity of the situation. 'If Nancy needs my help, I'm available.'

Jones smiled, glad that Payne was still alive. 'Is two clear?'

'Two is *finally* clear.'

'Glad to hear it.'

Payne continued. 'I spotted a walkway that connects my building with six. I can get to the penthouse before he can.'

'Where do you want him?'

'Send him to one of the remaining towers. Which-ever is closest to the mosque.'

'Sending him to seven.'

'Where are you headed?'

'I'm going to . . .' Jones stopped, breaking off his response in mid-thought. Several seconds passed before he spoke again. 'I think I see the sniper.'

The soldiers known as Matthew and Mark were getting frustrated. According to their watches, they should have been heading towards their rendezvous point, not dicking around with the detonator in building six. The explosive had been placed, and fuel was in the tank. Just like it should be. Unfortunately, when Mark tried to set the timer on the device, it wouldn't start. Either it was defective or broken or its battery was lacking juice.

Whatever the case, the damn thing didn't work.

At this point, they didn't have many options. The other device was set to go off in less than twenty minutes, and when it did, they didn't want to be anywhere near the complex.

The clock was ticking and the pressure was building.

They couldn't afford any more delays.

Spotting the sniper was nothing more than a lucky break. Jones was in the construction elevator in building three, studying the layout of the complex while he spoke to Payne, when he saw a flash of movement in building one. The Hotel Tower would eventually be twice as tall as the others; however, right now it was just a partial shell, a third of its eventual height.

Jones slowed the elevator for a better look and confirmed his initial sighting. There was a man with a rifle positioned near the north-eastern corner. He was gathering his things, getting ready to leave. Maybe to find a better spot. More likely to evacuate the site. Whichever the case, Jones knew this was his best chance to stop him.

Payne had mentioned a walkway between two and six, and Jones knew the same thing existed between one and three. In fact, all of the buildings were interconnected with a series of bridges and corridors. Two connected with four and six. Three connected with five and seven. And one connected with two and three.

Seven buildings, but no need to walk through the lobby to move between towers.

At least that's how it would be when the complex was done. Right now, the only thing connecting one and three was a series of long steel beams separated by the width of a car. No floor. No ceiling. No windows. Just a lot of open air and 500 feet to fall if he took a misstep or a strong gust of wind decided to knock him off. If so, he would land in the central plaza, creating a much bigger mess than the two soldiers who were killed by the sniper.

Screw it, he thought. *This guy is mine.*

Jones exited the elevator and walked to the edge of the steel frame. In his mind, the key to staying calm was getting things over with before he had a chance to get nervous, so he pulled his thobe above his knees – not wanting to trip – took a deep breath, and stepped on to the narrow beam. It felt solid underneath his feet, like walking on a kerb.

Step after careful step, he moved at a steady speed. Never looking down. Always focusing on a point five feet in front of him. Make it there, then move to the next. Nothing but small segments. Never large. It was the best way to avoid being overwhelmed.

The entire trip took thirty seconds. By the end, his heart was pounding and his left hand was quivering from all the adrenaline. He flexed the hand a few times, took a deep breath, then continued forward. Refusing to look back at what he had conquered.

More concerned with the perils that waited around the corner.

Payne crept along the outer wall of the mechanical penthouse. Voices could be heard within. Shouting of some kind. He couldn't make out the words – the wind was whistling, and someone was giving him an update on building seven – but it was definitely an argument.

Something to be taken advantage of.

With gun in hand, he opened the metal hatch and slipped inside. Angry words were being exchanged.

Two men shouting about their responsibilities. One man said they *must* finish the job; the other disagreed. The detonator was broken and couldn't be fixed in the next fifteen minutes. They didn't have the tools or the extra parts.

It was music to Payne's ears.

He crouched on the stairs, listening to what was being said, hoping to get as much intel as he could. Neither of the voices belonged to Schmidt – that was too much to hope for – but this was half his squad. Two of the men responsible for the violence in the cave. The murders in the village. The plot to blow up Mecca.

He'd listen for as long as possible before he made his move.

And when he did, they'd pay for their transgressions.

53

When Jones arrived in the north-eastern corner, the sniper was no longer there. He had packed his things and abandoned his position less than a minute before.

Unfortunately, that was the problem with snipers. They were slippery bastards.

Jones cursed under his breath and scanned the area for exit points. At this height, elevators were the main option. As far as he could tell, one had been built on each side of the Hotel Tower. The front shaft was clearly visible from the plaza, something the shooter would want to avoid. His goal would be to eliminate exposure time. Less exposure meant fewer witnesses.

The other three were all hidden from the main street, the closest being on the eastern face of the tower. It was partially concealed by building two and less than thirty seconds away. Jones took a chance and sprinted as fast as he could, darting through the equipment and supplies that cluttered the massive space. The squeaking of cables greeted his arrival as the platform dipped below floor level. With no time to waste, Jones squeezed through the bars of the metal tube and jumped into the open shaft, plummeting several feet before landing on the top of the elevator.

Until then, the sniper had been oblivious to Jones's pursuit. More concerned with the targets below than with anyone lurking above. Now, suddenly, he was staring face-to-face with a black superhero. At least that's what Jones looked like as he stood on the plummeting steel cage, his white thobe fluttering in the breeze like he was in midflight.

The sniper screamed one word – 'FUCK!' – before Jones pulled his trigger.

The mutaween were feared throughout Saudi Arabia, where they were empowered to enforce Sharia, a system of strict religious laws based on the Qur'an.

Unlike normal police, the mutaween were given discretionary power to enter homes, interrogate suspects, and punish violators on the spot. Sometimes these punishments were as simple as a warning; at other times they were much more severe. According to Sharia law, the penalty for adultery was death by stoning. If neither of the participants was married, they got off easy: a hundred lashes in a public flogging. Thieves were typically imprisoned for a first-time offence (if the stolen item was inexpensive), but repeat offenders were punished with the amputation of hands or feet. Then again, a more vital body part was cut off if a man or a woman was seen performing a same-sex sexual act. And anyone who was caught campaigning for gay rights was beheaded in a public ceremony.

However, on such an important religious holiday,

the mutaween weren't searching for grievous offences such as these as they patrolled the streets around the Great Mosque. They were more concerned with the mundane violations that seemed to increase when Mecca was flooded with Westerners. Dress-code infractions. Consumption of alcohol. Possession of un-Islamic items such as American movies or CDs.

The last thing they were expecting was the sound of gunfire.

And it came from the Abraj Al Bait Towers Complex.

Covered in blood, Payne left the mechanical penthouse carrying two bags, one over each shoulder. Gun still in hand, he walked to the northern edge of the roof and peered over the thick wall that separated him from an 800-foot fall.

This was an opportunity he couldn't pass up.

The Great Mosque stretched before him, a series of arches and columns built from grey stones found in the local hills. Several towers, trimmed in green and topped with golden spires shaped like crescent moons, rose towards the heavens, casting shadows on the pilgrims who stood in line outside the main gates, patiently waiting to get inside, where they could fulfil their hajj duties. Shifting his focus to the centre of the open courtyard, Payne spotted the Kaaba, draped in black cloth, the holy cube that was honoured by all Muslims. From this height, he couldn't see the Black Stone, the focus of so much attention during the past few days, but he knew it was down there, set in the eastern corner of the shrine.

Thanks to him, it was temporarily safe from peril.

'Six is clear,' he said as he hustled over to the construction elevator that was supposed to be broken – at least according to his men. In actuality, Schmidt's crew had turned off the controls so it remained at the penthouse while they went about their work. A smart move on their part, but one that would benefit Payne. With a flick of a switch, it was operational again, and he was able to ride it all the way to the plaza.

Trevor Schmidt sensed trouble when the rendezvous point was empty. His men were always punctual – trained to be on time, every time – especially in situations like this. The clock was ticking and their escape depended on a precise schedule.

He glanced at his watch. The bombs would be going off in less than ten minutes.

They needed to get to the tunnel soon.

Scanning the plaza, Schmidt saw the two dead guards that Luke had gunned down. They were dressed in Arab clothes and lay in puddles of blood that matched the colour of the towel on one of the guys' heads. Schmidt smiled at the image. According to his source, patrols weren't expected inside the complex, but he always planned for contingencies. That's why he put his best sniper in the Hotel Tower.

He protected the unit while they went about their business.

'Luke, what's your status?'

Thinking back, Schmidt realized he hadn't heard from Luke since he had reported the shootings. Not uncommon for a sniper, who was more concerned with finding his next target than giving updates. Still, it was slightly unsettling when combined with his tardiness.

The same thing applied to the others. He hadn't heard from them in several minutes.

'Matthew? Mark? What's your status?'

No answer. Not a single word.

Last Schmidt had heard, Mark was having trouble with his detonator. He had called for Matthew, the engineer, who was in the control room, making sure that the jet fuel was pumped to the proper tanks in the proper amount, to come to the roof and help him with some rewiring. Once the levels were adjusted, Matthew had plenty of time to help. He had reported his movement – so Luke wouldn't shoot him – then had scurried to building six.

But that was a while ago.

Since that time, there had been silence. No updates. No complaints. Nothing.

All along, Schmidt had assumed that meant no problems. Now he wasn't so sure. Maybe there were more guards floating around that he wasn't aware of. Maybe someone was trapped in one of the towers. Or maybe, just maybe, his transmitter was broken.

That had happened once before, on a mission several years ago, but he never knew about it until a soldier was sent to find him. It was so embarrassing, to be pulled out of the field like that, but what could he do?

'Hello?' he muttered, hoping to avoid a similar incident. 'Can anyone hear me?'

A voice startled him from behind. 'I can hear you.'

54

Trevor Schmidt turned around, slowly, unsure if he was imagining things. He was in the middle of Mecca, a forbidden city in Saudi Arabia, on a secret mission, yet the voice he heard was out of his past. Like taking a remote control and rewinding five years from his life. Back before he had his own squad. Back when he was in the MANIACs, still learning from the best.

For the past several months, he'd been having trouble with his long-term memory. Nothing that affected his day-to-day efficiency, but disturbing none-theless. Pieces of things – incidents from his child-hood, lectures from his parents, even advice from his former commander – were no longer there. He tried to pull them up, tried to use them to shape his deci-sions, but they simply weren't available. Like files that could no longer be accessed.

Like someone had messed with his circuitry.

Of course, he had never been an emotional guy; emotions simply weren't his thing. In his mind, he always considered himself pragmatic, someone who focused on results rather than policies or repercus-sions. Leave that shit to Congress, he liked to say.

Just give me a gun and a target, and I'll take care of the rest.

Yet, for some reason, that viewpoint had grown stronger in recent weeks. Suddenly everything was black or white. Right or wrong. Good or evil. *Us* versus *them*.

Grey no longer existed in his world.

Somehow it had been erased.

Schmidt blinked a few times, just to make sure he wasn't seeing things. Years had passed since he'd seen his former mentor. Now Captain Payne was standing in front of him, wearing a white robe that was streaked with blood. He held a gun in his hand. Two bags sat by his feet.

'It's been a long time,' Payne said.

Schmidt nodded, still trying to decide if this was real or imagined. Worried that his conscience was fucking with him right before the bombs went off.

'You don't write. You don't call.'

Was this guilt? A manifestation of guilt?

'Schmidt!' Payne barked, just like he used to. 'I'm not worthy of a response?'

'Sir?'

'What's with that weak-ass *sir*? Say it like you mean it.'

'Sir, yes, sir.'

'Better. Much better.'

Schmidt stared at him, confused. 'What are you doing here?'

'I came to find you. I came to bring you home.'

'But –'

'But nothing. I heard you were in trouble and I came to get you. Case closed.'

Schmidt fiddled with the gun he held in his hand. It was pointed at the ground, completely non-threatening. Every once in a while he tapped it on his hip, absentmindedly, like he had forgotten it was even there. 'I thought you were retired.'

'I am. But all that changed when I heard about you. I came to get you out.'

'*We* came to get you out,' said Jones, who emerged on the other side of the plaza. Far enough from Payne that they had Schmidt hemmed in, just in case their words didn't work. They figured, with the bombs under control, it was worth a shot. 'We flew all night to get here.'

'DJ?' he said, even more confused. 'I don't understand. How did you know where I was?'

'The Pentagon figured it out,' Payne fibbed. 'They said something about evidence you left in South Korea. One thing led to another and they asked us to extract you. Just like old times.'

'They know I'm here?'

'Hell, yeah,' Jones said. 'And they applaud your initiative. Killing all these Arabs is a stroke of genius in their minds. Unfortunately, some politician found out about it, and the shit hit the fan. You know how it goes. If they sent a team of soldiers to help you out and they got caught? Think of the ramifications. That's why they asked us to help. Total deniability.'

Schmidt shook his head. 'But I don't need help. Everything's under control.'

Payne disagreed. 'No, it's not. There's a problem. A *big* problem.'

'Sir?'

'After you went dark,' Payne lied, 'the CIA received some terrible news. An Islamic group got their hands on some nukes, and we think they have them in Mecca. Probably somewhere near the mosque. Our guess is they're participating in the hajj, cleansing all their sins, in hopes of striking soon.'

'Then what's the problem? Let's wipe those fuckers out.'

'We wish,' Jones said. 'But that's not the problem. The problem is the wind.'

'The wind?'

Payne nodded. 'This time of year the wind blows to the east, right across the friggin' desert. If we launch an assault and the nukes go off, guess what happens?'

Schmidt paused, trying to figure it out. 'Shit.'

'Shit is right,' Jones said. 'The radioactivity will blow right across the peninsula. Within hours, it will blanket Taif Air Base, Al-Gaim, and Al-Hada Hospital. We're talking hundreds of dead Americans, all of them loyal soldiers. Hell, we probably know half of them.'

'Fuck!' Schmidt screamed, still tapping his gun on his hip. Much harder than before. Like the constant pounding was helping him think. 'Then we gotta hurry, because I already planted the charges. They're set to blow any minute.'

'Relax, man, relax.' Payne's voice was calm, not showing any stress. 'Were there two?'

'Yeah, in the eastern towers.'

'Then I got you covered.' He pointed towards the bags at his feet. 'We found the explosives before we found you.'

'On the tanks? You found them on the tanks?'

Payne nodded, confident. 'Someone taught you how to do this shit. And it sure wasn't DJ.'

'Screw you,' Jones teased, trying to keep things light. He figured the more banter there was, the less time Schmidt would have to think. 'I taught Trevor plenty of things. I took him to his first strip club.'

Schmidt frowned. 'No, you didn't.'

'Well, I would have. And *that's* what's important.'

Payne cut him off. 'If you don't mind, can we talk about it later? Right now we need to get out of here. The sooner the better.'

'Back through the tunnel?' Jones asked.

'Yeah. We need to keep off the streets as much as possible. Especially with all the pilgrims arriving. I already sent Trevor's crew ahead.' Payne turned towards Schmidt. 'Unless you have a better plan.'

'You talked to my guys?'

'Someone had to,' Payne lied. He remembered the troubles Schmidt had been having when he had first spotted him, repeatedly calling to his men, asking for their positions. 'They said they tried but

367

couldn't get through to you. Is your earpiece working?'

Schmidt shrugged. 'Apparently not. I haven't heard a damn thing in fifteen minutes.'

Jones laughed. 'Talk about déjà vu. Remember that time in Asia when we had to go looking for your ass? You couldn't hear a thing all night, but you stayed in the bushes for six hours even though the mission should've taken five minutes.'

Embarrassed, Schmidt nodded. 'I was *just* thinking of that.'

'The next day we bought him a case of Q-tips to clean out his ears and a Dumbo watch to help tell the time.'

'His trunk pointed to the hour,' Schmidt recalled. 'At six o'clock it looked like his dick.'

Payne smiled at the memory, glad to see the old Trevor was still in there.

During the past several hours, Payne had had his doubts, worried that he was going to find some kind of lobotomized zombie he would be forced to put down because nothing human remained. In fact, if Payne had stumbled across him earlier when the clock was still ticking, when he had no time to waste, he would have done just that. No regrets. No remorse. Anything to save the lives of all those people Schmidt wanted to harm.

But now, how could he do that?

The threat was over, and Schmidt trusted them enough to follow them back to their truck. From there, they'd sneak across the border and return to Taif, where he'd let Colonel Harrington deal with him. Whether that was prison, psychotherapy, or a combination of the two, Payne figured it was better than putting a bullet into an old friend.

Sure, he realized Schmidt wouldn't see the light of day for a very long time, if ever. And the truth was he didn't deserve to – not after all the pain and suffering he had caused.

However, in his heart, Payne figured his best choice was bringing Schmidt home alive.

Unfortunately, he never got the chance.

55

The bullet was fired over Payne's shoulder. It whizzed past his ear and struck Schmidt in the throat. One second he was laughing about the past, the next he was taking his last breath.

Blood gushed from his carotid artery, leaking through his pale fingers as he frantically clutched his neck. No words were spoken, no last-second good-byes. He simply dropped his gun and slumped to the ground as a puddle of red formed around him.

Payne spun and saw two Arab men, both of them armed, wearing dark uniforms that prominently displayed the emblem of Saudi Arabia. The patch had a green palm tree underscored by two crossing scimitars, a curved sword popular in the Middle East. A second insignia, beige and encircled with Arabic script, was sewn on their chest. Payne didn't need a translator to read their badges. He knew all about these men and their barbaric ways.

They were mutaween.

'Drop your weapons!' one screamed in Arabic.

When no one moved, the other repeated the command in English. 'Drop your weapons!'

'Don't shoot,' Payne said, keeping his voice as calm as possible. In stressful situations, he knew that people had the tendency to match the volume and the venom of those around them. If he screamed, their adrenaline would flow and they would get more aggressive. But if he stayed composed, they would subconsciously relax, possibly letting their guard down.

Payne smiled. 'It's about time you got here. We weren't sure how long you'd be.'

'Put down your weapon!'

'Relax. We're the ones who called you. We've been waiting for you to show.'

The lead officer did not bite. 'Drop your weapon or you will be shot like your friend.'

'My friend?' Payne repeated. 'Why would we be pointing our guns at a friend? He was the person we were sent to stop.'

'Put *down* your weapon.'

Multiple scenarios floated through Payne's head. He knew he could follow orders and turn himself in, which would probably result in the death penalty – maybe before they even left the complex, since the mutaween were known for their swift justice. He could start a shoot-out, an iffy proposition since his gun was at his side and his opponent, a proven marksman, was aimed and ready to fire. He could delay as much as possible, hoping the other two members of his squad heard him talking and were moving into position. Then again, that wasn't something he could count on – especially not from a soldier who was tripping in his dress less than twenty minutes before. Hell, for all Payne knew, the mutaween had hit the complex with force and had already disarmed his men. There could be twenty of them running around, securing all exits.

Payne glanced at Jones, who stood several feet away. He stared back at him, waiting for Payne to make a move. Whatever Payne did, he would follow. No questions asked. Over the years, they had developed a special bond that was hard to explain, one that was forged in stressful situations like this, where life and death hung in the balance. They'd reached a point where they could finish each other's sentences, a trait that was often seen in identical twins – although one look at them proved they had different parents – and guess each other's thoughts.

That's one of the reasons why they were able to convince Schmidt to come with them so peacefully. Payne started piling on the bullshit, and Jones immediately broke out his shovel. Throw in the fact that Schmidt had a long history with them, trusting them implicitly from all their missions together, and they were able to persuade him in record time.

Unfortunately, the current situation wasn't quite so easy. Payne knew he wouldn't be able to convince the mutaween of anything. They were too hardcore, as evidenced by their warning shot to Schmidt's throat. Too protective of their sacred city. As soon as they figured out that Payne and Jones were non-Muslims, they were going to open fire. No questions asked.

Still, Payne knew if he could buy some time, if he

could pile on enough bullshit to get an extra minute, he had an idea that just might work. It was going to take a grand gesture on his part and some even bigger cojones, but it was the best he could come up with on such short notice. Then again, it followed the creed he had been taught many years ago when he was training for the Special Forces, one he adhered to during his stint with the MANIACs.

A good plan violently executed *now* is better than a great plan later.

And if there was one thing Payne was good at, it was violence.

'Listen to me,' he said. 'I am a United States soldier who was invited by your government to track the man you just killed. He came to Mecca to damage the Great Mosque and kill thousands of pilgrims in the hajj. We called for backup several minutes ago. Are you them?'

'Put down your weapon!'

'Look,' he said, as he turned his gun backwards and lowered it to the ground. 'I am putting my weapon down. Just answer my question. Are you my backup?'

'Your partner, too! Tell him to drop his weapon.'

Payne nodded at Jones, who followed Payne's instructions. 'We are not here to hurt anyone. We are here to help. Your government should have told you.'

'Told us what?'

'We are here to save the Great Mosque.'

The officer shook his head. 'We know nothing of your tale.'

'Then you *need* to call it in. For your sake and ours. We have permission to be here.'

'What does it hurt?' Jones added. 'Call it in.'

The mutaween whispered to each other in Arabic, discussing what they should do. Currently, they were in a position of power. Both of them were armed and far enough away from the suspects, who willingly surrendered their weapons, that they couldn't be attacked without firing several deadly shots. Besides, if what the Americans were saying was accurate – that they did have authorization to be in Mecca – then harming them would result in the mutaweens' dismissal. Or even worse. Their bosses did not take kindly to incompetence.

Finally, the officer spoke. 'You,' he said, pointing at Jones, 'move closer to your friend.'

Jones raised his hands in surrender and took several steps towards Payne.

'Stop right there.'

He nodded and stopped about five feet away.

The officer returned his attention to Payne. 'Who is your contact?'

'His name and number are programmed into my phone.' Payne pointed towards the bag that sat near his right foot. 'May I reach inside and get it?'

More whispering in Arabic. Then an answer in English. 'Slowly.'

'Understood.'

Payne bent at his waist and inched his hand inside the bag. He fumbled around for a bit, his hand hidden from sight. An action that spooked the mutaween.

'What are you doing? Let me see your hand.'

'Relax,' he said. 'I already gave you my gun. My partner gave you his gun. I am simply accessing my phone. It is password-protected. I cannot read the screen without the code.'

'Let me see the phone. Let me see your hand!'

'Don't worry. I'm almost done. Just a couple more buttons.'

'He's almost done,' echoed Jones, who appeared borderline serene despite everything that was going on. 'He's just getting the name of our contact.'

'Let me see your –'

'There!' Payne blurted. 'The phone has been accessed. Now you can make the call yourself. He will tell you everything you need to know.'

'What is his name?'

'His name is Jabaal. He works for your government. Just talk to him and he will tell you everything. You will see.'

The officers whispered again, discussing who should make the call.

'Should I toss you the phone?' Payne asked, reaching towards his bag.

'Stop!' the officer shouted. 'Leave it alone. Back up ten steps and leave the bag there.'

'Fine,' Payne grunted. 'We'll both back up. Ten giant steps.'

Jones looked at him in understanding. 'We're backing up.'

'Giant steps,' Payne mumbled. 'Ten *giant* steps.'

One.

They kept their hands in the air. The perfect prisoners.

Two.

The mutaween moved closer, never taking their eyes off Payne or Jones.

Three.

Each step was huge. Getting as far away as possible.

Four.

More words in Arabic. Discussing their situation.

Five.

Payne scanned the plaza, searching for additional guards.

Six.

The officer reached the bag and tapped it with his foot.

Seven.

Jones glanced at Payne, ready to move.

Eight.

Still aiming his gun, the officer dropped to his knees.

Nine.

Confused, he opened the bag and glanced inside.

Ten.

Payne and Jones grinned, covering their ears.

The timer, which Payne had set a moment before,

sent a burst of electricity to the primer, which triggered the main explosive. The C-4 erupted with a vengeance, shredding the mutaween like they'd been struck by the sword of God, spraying chunks of bone and blood across the open courtyard and knocking Payne and Jones backwards on to the hard ground.

If they had been any closer, they would have been in the kill zone.

But their giant steps backwards had saved their lives.

Several seconds passed before Payne was able to shake off the blast. When he did, he crawled over to Jones, who was rubbing his eyes, trying to refocus. 'Are you okay?'

He nodded, even though he wasn't sure. 'What about you?'

'Honestly, I'm better than them.'

56

Less than an hour had passed since Shari had left the tunnel, but to her it felt like a lifetime ago. Maybe because her life had flashed before her eyes several times during the past day, or maybe because she felt threatened and her adrenaline was flowing at an all-time high. Whatever the reason, she viewed everything around her with a heightened awareness.

She had always been an observant person – it was a job requirement as an archaeologist – yet her brain shifted into overdrive as she roamed the streets of Mecca. Scanning the crowd for the mutaween, trying not to be noticed by anyone. Blending in with one group after another as she made her way towards the site. One mistake, no matter how small, could lead to her capture.

And her capture would lead to her death.

Shari arrived at the vacant lot without incident. Slipping into the wooden shed that masked the tunnel entrance, she glanced outside, making sure that no one had followed her. When the coast was clear, she turned her attention to documenting the site.

Armed with a digital camera, she started taking pictures as she walked down the long ramp. Tiny bursts of light filled the confined space as she took multiple shots of the passageway – the wooden planks on the floor, the support beams that held up the roof, the bulbs that lit her way. When she reached the bottom, she turned towards the massive security gate that had been installed to protect the site. In truth, it had probably saved her life because it had prevented Trevor Schmidt and his men from reaching her when she was chained and defenceless. Without it, there's no telling what they would have done to her, although the terms *bullet* and *brain* leaped to mind.

As she continued forwards, Shari switched the camera to video mode, filming the archway where the ancient door had been removed before slipping into the back chamber. Chunks of broken stone were scattered across the floor, remnants of the large altar that had protected the relic for centuries. A wave of emotion swept through her as she surveyed the scene – an equal mix of anger, guilt, relief, and disappointment.

Anger for what was done to her.

Guilt for trusting Abdul-Khaliq.

Relief for surviving the attack.

Disappointment for her missed opportunity.

She had worked so long and hard for a chance to examine the artefact, only to have it snatched away from her at the last possible moment. The mere thought of it made her nauseous, as did her surroundings. She was standing in a room where she had nearly died, making home movies of her biggest failure. The more she filmed, the more she realized this wasn't such a good idea. There were no clues, no hidden messages carved in stone that would lead her to the treasure. Only reminders of things that she would rather forget. The fear. The violence. The betrayal. Worst of all, she was risking her life to be there. And for what?

Taking a deep breath, she glanced around the room one last time, then turned off the camera.

It was time to go home.

Shari's plan hit a roadblock when she heard the footsteps. They were faint, like a burglar sneaking through the night, but she was so attuned to her surroundings that she noticed them.

Unfortunately, she had just locked the security gate and was standing halfway between the back room and the front entrance. Proverbial no-man's land. Stuck between the safety of retreat and the uncertainty of advancement. She lingered for a moment, trying to pinpoint their source, but the echo in the tunnel and the pounding of her heart concealed their location.

Were they on the ramp or in the maintenance shaft?

Which way were they headed?

The acoustics made it impossible to tell.

If not for the noise, she would have unlocked the security gate and slipped behind it, but the clanking of keys, the squeaking of hinges, and the clang of the latch were too risky to attempt. Thinking quickly, she realized the safest thing for her to do was to hide, and since she was wearing a black abaya, she knew darkness was her biggest ally. Covering her hand with her sleeve, she reached up and unscrewed the hot lightbulb that hung above her. She hurried to the next one and repeated the process. Suddenly the entire section of tunnel was cloaked in darkness and she was virtually invisible.

With her back to the gate, she crouched on the floor and waited. Not making a sound. Barely breathing. Straining to hear the footsteps in the tunnel. Praying that they headed up the ramp and on to the busy street.

But it wasn't to be.

One minute they were charging forward; the next they had stopped.

Shari cursed to herself when she heard a soft click and saw the steady beam of light. Someone had turned on a torch and was headed her way.

The beam got brighter and brighter as the footsteps got closer and closer.

How did they know she was back there?

She wanted to run, but there was nowhere to go. Wanted to scream, but what good would it do? No one would hear her except the people coming her way, and they were her biggest threat.

Things did not look good.

They were heading towards the ramp when they noticed the lights going off in the tunnel, one bulb after another. The leader stopped and signalled to his partner, who nodded his head in agreement. This was something they should investigate.

With weapons drawn, they crept along the corridor, searching for threats of any kind. The leader turned on his torch and lifted it high above his head, a trick he had learned years ago. When confronted in the dark, assailants often aimed for the light source, hoping for a fatal shot to the head or chest. This tactic lessened the risk.

Thirty seconds passed before they spotted her. She was crouching in the corner, trying not to be seen, completely covered by a black abaya.

'Shari?' he asked.

She flinched at the mention of her name, not sure if it was good or bad.

'Shari, it's Jonathon Payne. We met earlier.'

'Jon?'

He moved closer, making sure it wasn't a trap before he rushed to her side. 'What are you doing here?'

'I came back to photograph the site, and I heard someone coming. So I . . .'

Payne nodded as he helped her to her feet. 'Well, it's time to leave. This area isn't safe.'

'I know,' she said. 'I already warned my team. I told them to leave without me.'

Jones glanced at her and smiled, admiring her loyalty. 'Not a problem. You can come with us. We're going to get falafels.'

'Falafels?' she asked, unaware of the wager between Payne and Jones.

'Yep. And the best part is that Jon is buying.'

57

Tuesday, 2 January
Taif, Saudi Arabia

Payne and Jones were battered and bruised, but they reported to Colonel Harrington's office as soon as the Taif medical staff cleared them for duty. Each had sustained minor injuries, compliments of the bomb blast, but nothing a few days of rest couldn't cure.

Unfortunately, they realized a vacation would have to wait.

Harrington sat behind a large desk, staring at his computer screen, anxiously jotting notes on a legal pad. Every time he opened a new computer file, he flipped a page and started again. His concentration was so intense he didn't notice Payne standing in the doorway.

'Colonel, you wanted to see us?'

Harrington glanced up. 'Gentlemen, please have a seat. I'll be right with you.'

Payne walked in first, followed by Jones. Both moved slower than normal, still feeling the effects of the previous day – one that had spanned several time zones and resulted in multiple bruises. Adrenaline had carried them through their mission, but now that they were back on base, the only thing that kept them going was their thirst for answers. And a lot of coffee.

'First of all,' Harrington said as he finished writing, 'let me thank you again. I know we talked briefly when you arrived last night, yet somehow I feel the need to repeat myself. Thanks to you, a major crisis was averted, and I just wanted to express my appreciation.'

Payne and Jones said nothing, realizing that Harrington wasn't finished.

'That being said, there are still a number of loose ends that need to be dealt with, some of them more puzzling than others.' He turned the pages of his notebook and focused on the first item. A single name was written: *Shari Shasmeen*. 'What can you tell me about the girl?'

'Not much,' Payne admitted. 'We found her tied up and beaten pretty badly in a back room. She was in charge of some archaeological dig and gave us a tour of the maintenance tunnel before our assault. Other than that, we didn't have much time to chat.'

'Yet you brought her back with you?'

Payne nodded. 'After the blast, we slipped past the Saudi guards by going out the same tunnel. When we got back to the entrance, she was still in there documenting the site. Plus, it was tough for her to leave without a chaperone because of all the mutaween running around.'

Jones added, 'We figured she needed a way out, and we needed more information about Abdul-Khaliq. It seemed like a match made in heaven.'

'On the trip home, did she tell you anything about the envelope?'

'Not really,' Payne said. 'She slept the whole way back. Why? What was inside?'

'Two things,' Harrington answered, glancing at his notepad. 'One of them is confusing, the other we're still trying to decipher. While you two were getting your beauty sleep, my team spent the night trying to connect the dots. In fact, that's what I was working on when you walked in.'

'Go on.'

Harrington grabbed a manila folder that sat on the corner of his desk. Inside, there was a single document. He took it out and handed it to Payne. 'Don't worry. It's not the original. We sent that out for testing.'

The sheet was folded in two. It was written in English and had a simple logo on the front, a similar design on the back. Payne opened it and scanned the listings. He saw everything from nachos to hamburgers to chicken fingers. 'What the hell is this?'

'It's a take-out menu from the restaurant at Al-Gaim. We found it inside the envelope.'

'Someone sent her a menu? That doesn't make sense.'

'Like I said, it's confusing.'

Payne handed it to Jones, who stared at the menu

386

with great interest. He studied everything, paying particular attention to the interior text.

'Do you see something?' Payne asked.

Jones nodded, smiling. 'The club sandwich looks good.'

Payne ignored the comment, knowing that he would continue.

'Actually,' Jones said, 'the menu doesn't bother me. It's what it *represents* that bothers me.'

'Meaning?'

'Whoever sent the envelope knew about Schmidt long before we did.'

'How so?' Harrington demanded.

'Two years ago, when Schmidt's unit was killed at the hospital, where were you housing their families?'

'Al-Gaim.'

'And when Schmidt attacked the towers, what was his access point?'

'The tunnel,' Payne answered.

'Obviously that's *not* a coincidence. Whoever sent the package knew about Schmidt, knew about his motivation, and knew where he was going to attack several days in advance. Of course, that triggers a floodgate of questions that I'd rather not think about until I know what else was inside the package. That might put things in a proper context.'

Nodding in agreement, Harrington grabbed another manila folder. This time he handed it to Jones. 'We found this taped inside the menu.'

Jones opened the folder and stared at the image. It was a picture of an SD card, a computer storage device that was slightly bigger than a postage stamp yet capable of holding gigabytes of information. Some held more data than a DVD. 'What's on it?'

'We're still trying to figure that out,' Harrington admitted. 'All of the files are encrypted, including one substantial video file that we've been working on all night. Once we crack the code, we should know a whole lot more. I'm expecting to hear something soon.'

'In the meantime,' Payne suggested, 'would you mind if we talked to Shari? Since we bailed her out, I'm sure she'd be willing to open up. Who knows what she might know?'

Harrington smiled. 'I think that's a great idea. In fact, I've already set it up. She's waiting for you down the hall.'

Shari Shasmeen paced back and forth in the interview room. Her nose was covered in white tape; her eyes were black and swollen. She looked like a prizefighter the morning after a bad loss.

When Payne opened the door, she stopped and broke into a huge grin. The stress that had been evident a moment before was replaced with instant relief. 'Thank God, it's you.'

Payne smiled at her comment. 'God's a little formal. You can call me Jon.'

Jones followed him into the room, closing the door. 'And I'm DJ.'

She gave each of them a hug. 'It's great to see you both. It really is.'

Payne pulled out the chair that faced the video camera mounted on the ceiling and helped her to sit down. 'Are you okay? You seem upset.'

'What can I say? It's been a rough couple of days.' She took a deep breath, trying to relax. 'I guess I shouldn't complain. Things could've been a lot worse. I mean, I could be dead. But –'

'But what?'

'But I was *this* close to making a major discovery. *This* close to fulfilling a dream. And right before I could grasp it, it was taken away.'

'You mean the site?'

She nodded, an aggrieved look in her eyes.

'You know,' Payne said, 'we still don't know much about your time in Mecca. What you were looking for, how you were recruited, and so on. If you don't mind, we'd love to ask you some questions about your work.'

'Of course. Whatever you need.'

'Let's start with the basics. Who hired you for the dig?'

'His name is Omar Abdul-Khaliq, a wealthy Saudi with a vast network of connections. A few months ago, he contacted me by phone and asked if I'd be interested in running a team in Arabia. He'd heard about my research and felt I'd be the perfect person for the job. Clearly, it was flattering – especially when he told me that the dig would be in Mecca. Until then, I never thought I'd have a chance to work there.'

Jones asked, 'Because of your religion?'

'And my sex. Mecca doesn't look kindly on either.'

'But he got you inside?'

'Me and the others. All of us were Americans. None of us were Muslims. He said he was looking for the strongest team possible and felt we would work well together. So he got us the appropriate paperwork and snuck us into the city.'

'And you weren't hassled?'

'Not once. I'm not sure how Omar pulled it off, but we were never bothered at the site. At least not until recently. Obviously, things changed drastically over the past few days.'

58

Payne was known for his ability to read people. And in this case, he had nothing but positive feelings about Shari Shasmeen. She might have worked for Omar Abdul-Khaliq, but she sure as hell wasn't helping him. At least not knowingly.

'When did things start to go bad?' he asked.

'About a week ago, I called Omar to update him on our progress. When I told him that we were getting ready to verify the site, he was thrilled with the news. At that time he was out of the country but said as soon as he returned he was going to stop by for the big unveiling.'

'Did he ever make it?' Jones wondered.

She shook her head. 'A few days later he called to let me know that he'd been delayed. However, he was so confident that he'd make it to Mecca in the next day or two that he was going to have a package delivered to the site. He hinted that it was very important but wouldn't tell me what was inside.'

'When did it show up?' Payne asked.

'On Saturday afternoon.'

Payne nodded. That meant whoever sent it knew about the attack at least two days before it happened. 'And what can you tell me about the delivery guy?'

She closed her eyes and tried to remember. 'Middle-aged. Tan complexion. Probably Middle Eastern. But no trace of an accent. I'm guessing American.'

Jones glanced at Payne. 'What's with all the Americans?'

'I was wondering the same thing.' He paused for a moment, trying to figure out the significance, before he returned his attention to Shari. 'What happened next?'

'He gave me the envelope and left.'

'No conversations. No clues about who he was or where he was going.'

She shook her head. 'We found him about an hour later. Someone had slit his throat and dumped his body by the exit. There was blood *everywhere*. After that, I did the only thing I could. I called Omar and told him what had happened.'

Payne nodded. 'How did he react?'

'He was calm. No hint of panic. He said he'd take care of it. Less than an hour later, a team of guards showed up and removed the body.'

'Were they Americans?' Jones asked.

'No,' she said. 'They were Arabs.'

She gave them a basic description of the guards and explained how Omar had ordered her to leave the tunnel until the hajj was over. He had said the Arabs would protect the site while she explored the city or stayed in the safety of her hotel room, which was a few miles away.

'Yet we found you in the tunnel,' Payne commented.

'What can I say? I'm stubborn. I stopped by to get some work done late Sunday night, and the place was empty. No guards in sight. They didn't show up until Monday morning. And when they arrived, they were carrying tools.'

'And that's when they attacked you?'

She shook her head. 'That's when *I* attacked *them*. After that, everything's fuzzy.'

Harrington watched the interview from an adjacent room. Much like Payne, he believed everything that Shari said. Her answers were straightforward. She never stammered or avoided a topic. She constantly looked her questioners in the eyes.

In some ways, he was disappointed. Things would have been much simpler if she had partnered with Abdul-Khaliq. In that case he could have put the screws on her, getting as much information as possible before he sent her to military intelligence, who would have treated her even worse. Before they were done, she would have confessed to everything, including Abraham Lincoln's assassination.

Unfortunately, as things currently stood, it was his ass on the line. Not hers.

From the moment he notified the Pentagon about a possible attack, he knew his career was going to be put under a microscope. Committees were currently forming, all of them designed to look into his recent operations – including the black ops run by Trevor Schmidt. All things considered, Payne and Jones had done a remarkable job cleaning up his mess in Mecca. However, they didn't have the time or the resources to be perfect. By now, the Saudis were sorting through all the evidence at the Towers and had recovered the bodies, which meant they were one step closer to figuring out their true identities: non-Muslim American soldiers.

No matter how Harrington tried to spin it, he knew that he was screwed. American troops plus explosives plus the Great Mosque equalled an international crisis. Not nearly as bad as if the attack had succeeded, but bad enough that he would probably be relieved of his duties.

At this point, the only thing that could save him was a miracle.

Or help from an unexpected source.

After the interview with Shari, Payne and Jones were summoned to the conference room, where Harrington was waiting for them. A day before, photos of the Great Mosque had filled the large video screen while an expert lectured on the events of the hajj. Today, there was a single image – a freeze-frame of a Middle Eastern man sitting in a dilapidated warehouse.

'Gentlemen,' Harrington said, 'Christmas just came early.'

'Crap!' Jones joked as he took a seat. 'I didn't get you anything.'

'Actually, you did. You got me the best gift in the world. You brought me the disk.'

'The disk?' Payne asked.

'The SD card from the take-out menu. My tech boys finally cracked the encryption. It took all night, but it was worth their effort. That thing was filled with all kinds of information. Building designs for the Towers. Escape routes from Mecca. American contacts in Riyadh and Taif. The type of intel that would've been hard to explain if the Saudis had recovered it.'

Payne rubbed his eyes. 'I don't get it. Why would someone send that to the tunnel?'

Harrington grinned. 'If you'd like, I can sit here and explain it to you. Or if you'd prefer, you can hear it straight from the Arab's mouth.'

'Which Arab is that?'

He pointed towards the screen. 'Earlier today I mentioned there was a large video file on the SD card that we were trying to crack. Turns out it was a video message. One I think you'll enjoy.'

Harrington hit *play*, and the video sprang to life.

Filmed with a webcam in poor lighting, the man's face dominated the screen. He had dark skin and a five-o'clock shadow. His lips were dry and cracked. When he spoke, he whispered in serious tones, as if everything he said was a matter of life and death.

His English was fluent, yet tinged with a slight Arabic accent.

'My name is Raheem Al-Jahani, and I am twenty-six years old. I was born in Medina, not far from the final resting place of the Prophet Muhammad, *sallallahu alayhi wasallam*. For the past four years, I have been an active member of the Soldiers of Allah, an organization that strives to make the world a better place for all Muslims. Until recently, I was proud to call myself a Soldier. But that pride exists no more.'

During the next few minutes, Al-Jahani explained how he was recruited out of college, where he'd earned a computer degree and slowly proved his worth to the Soldiers by running a terrorist cell in London that was responsible for several bombings. Eventually he moved higher and higher in the network until he was contacted by one of Hakeem Salaam's top advisers, who asked him if he'd be interested in working on a mission that would utilize his technical expertise. Al-Jahani was honoured, especially when he discovered the project had been planned by Salaam, a man who rarely showed his face and trusted no one.

To protect the sanctity of the mission, Al-Jahani was transported to a secret location, where he was housed in seclusion for months. No phone. No Internet. No access to the outside world. He was given a brand-new computer, pre-installed with some of the best encryption software available, and several pieces of hardware. Every few days a guard would drop off food and an envelope filled with the materials for his next assignment.

In the beginning, the information was mostly American. Names of soldiers. Locations of contacts. Ways to manipulate them. To Al-Jahani, the prospects were thrilling because he longed to launch an assault against the country he hated the most. Unfortunately, as his work continued, the focus of the mission began to shift. Before long he started to see Arab documents. Maps of Mecca. Permits for digging. Diagrams of the Towers Complex.

None of it seemed to fit.

Several weeks passed before Al-Jahani pieced everything together. Hakeem Salaam, a hero to all Soldiers, wasn't attacking the United States. Instead, he was helping them stage an attack of their own – one that threatened the Kaaba, the most sacred landmark in all of Islam, and the millions of pilgrims who honoured it – by providing them with information through his vast network of Arab contacts, some of whom had worked with the Americans for years but, in actuality, were supporters of Salaam. The ultimate goal was to unite Islam against a common enemy, but millions of martyrs would die in the process.

The realization made Al-Jahani nauseous.

At that point he realized he had two options. He could stop working for Salaam, which would result in his swift execution, or he could try to sabotage the mission. Obviously the latter seemed the more promising of the two. The only question was, how?

He had no connection to the outside world. No way to communicate the threat to anyone.

All he could do was sit and wait, praying that an opportunity would present itself.

His big break finally arrived in late December, when he was ordered to take all the data he had been working on – the blueprint for the terrorist attack – and store it on an SD card that would be delivered to a team of Americans who were working in the tunnel. To Salaam, they were the perfect people to frame. Non-Muslims. Fake paperwork. Access to the Towers. Once Saudi officials were tipped off, they would find the SD card filled with all the damning evidence, and accuse the Americans of aiding the terrorists.

On the surface, it seemed like a good plan – another way to link the United States to the attack, thereby demonizing them as the butchers of Islam.

However, Al-Jahani viewed it differently. This was his chance to reveal the truth.

'As you have figured out,' he explained, 'my computer is equipped with a webcam. No one thought to remove it, since I have no connection to transmit a video feed. Yet this camera has many functions. I am using it to record this message. Earlier today, when the guards came in to give me my final assignment – to encrypt all the data for delivery – I filmed the entire conversation. It will be included on the disk.'

He glanced over his shoulder, afraid that someone might be listening.

'As the guards left, I heard them talking about a pickup they would be making at a tunnel in Mecca and a delivery to Jeddah. I do not know what this means. It could be nothing. It could be everything.'

He paused again, searching for words.

'For all I know, this message might never be seen or heard. Either way, I am confident that it will survive longer than I will. After today, they have no reason to keep me alive.'

He took a deep breath, realization in his eyes.

'In my heart, I know what they are doing is wrong. My only hope is they will be stopped.'

59

Shari Shasmeen sat in the lounge for more than an hour, staying as close to the interview room as possible in case Payne or Jones had any more questions. To her, the furniture looked like it had been donated by Goodwill. Mismatched chairs, a badly scratched card table, a coffee-pot that was older than Juan Valdez. She tried to get comfortable on the lumpy couch, but it felt like it had been stuffed with straw.

'I'm guessing you've never been in the military,' said Kia Choi as she entered the room. 'Otherwise you'd be used to our opulent accommodations.'

Shari smiled. 'I've spent the past few months in a tunnel, and it was nicer than this.'

Kia reached out her hand in introduction. 'I'm Kia, by the way.'

'I'm Shari.'

'Actually,' Kia admitted, 'I knew that already. I work with Jon, and he told me all about you when he returned from Mecca. How are you feeling?'

She touched the tape on her broken nose. 'About as good as I look.'

'Can I get you something? Some aspirin or –'

'Thanks, but no thanks. I'm tough. I can take it.'

Kia smiled. 'Do you mind if I sit down?'

'Of course not. I'd welcome the company. It's been a while since I've talked with another woman. All of my co-workers were men, so our conversations were somewhat limited.'

'In that case, I'm kind of hesitant to ask you my next question.'

'Why's that?'

'I wanted to ask you about your job.'

Shari laughed. 'Don't worry. It's fine. I'm happy to talk about it. What did you want to know?'

'Well, as I mentioned, Jon told me about finding you in the tunnel. Unfortunately, he didn't have enough time to tell me about the site. So I was wondering –'

'What we were looking for.'

Kia nodded. 'Is that too personal?'

'A few days ago, I probably would've played stupid and said, "What site?" But as things stand, I guess there's no harm in talking about it now.'

'Just so you know,' Kia said, 'I work as a translator for the military, and Arabic is one of the languages I speak. So I'm not a total novice when it comes to Islam. I know some of the basics about its history and culture.'

'What do you know about Muhammad?'

'I know Muhammad is revered as the Prophet. Muslims believe he received the word of God, and his revelations form the pages of the Qur'an.'

'I'm impressed. That's more than most non-Muslims know.'

Kia smiled. 'Unfortunately, that's where my knowledge ends.'

'That's okay. I can pick up the story from there. Even though Muhammad died in AD632, the first copy of the Qur'an wasn't written until AD650. It was compiled by Uthman ibn Affan, the third caliph of Islam, based on all the transcripts and teachings he could find.'

'Eighteen years *after* Muhammad died?'

Shari nodded. 'Some scholars, myself included, have always wondered what might have been omitted in that span. Languages were evolving, politics were changing, and Muhammad's original followers were dying off. There's no telling what could have been lost during that time. Furthermore, many people believe the oldest surviving Qur'an was written in the eighth century, approximately one hundred years after the Uthman version. Suddenly we're talking about a wide chasm in history that could've altered Muhammad's initial message.'

'So what did you find?'

'As I mentioned, the Uthman version was compiled from transcripts of Muhammad's direct recitations, recorded by his companions on anything they could get hold of. Bark, bones, whatever was available. Uthman formed a committee that sorted through all of these messages, eventually agreeing on the text of the first Qur'an. For years I have been searching for one of these copies, thinking it was the purest version available. But I was wrong. I neglected to consider the transcripts themselves.'

'The transcripts?'

'The bark, the bones, the loose parchments of text. In actuality, *they* contain the original message from Muhammad, the literal word of God. All this time I was looking for the first Qur'an and neglected to search for its source.'

'And *that's* what you found?'

Shari nodded. 'I think we did. Unfortunately, before I had a chance to find out for sure, the site was violated and everything was stolen.'

The discussion stopped when Payne and Jones walked into the lounge and closed the door.

'Shari,' Payne said as he took a seat next to the couch, 'I have some photos that I'd like you to look at. Please tell me if you recognize anyone.'

He handed her a folder filled with pictures from Al-Jahani's webcam. Harrington's staff had decrypted the files and altered the brightness so the photographs were much clearer.

The instant she glanced at the first image, her face went pale. It was a reaction she couldn't fake, a combination of fear and hatred.

'Oh my God! That's the guard. The one who attacked me!'

She flipped to the next photo and nodded. And the one after that. She recognized them all.

'These are the guards. The ones from the tunnel.'

Payne smiled. 'We had a hunch they were.'

'Wait. Does this mean you caught them?'

'Not yet, but we're working on it. We're running down some leads.'

'Then where did you get these photos?'

'Actually, we got them from you. They were inside your package.'

'What do you mean?' she asked, confused. 'I had pictures of the guards?'

Payne told her a simplified version of the story about the SD card, not wanting to overwhelm her with all the details. When he was done, he shifted her focus back to the photographs. 'I know you've been through a lot, and I know the last thing you want to do is stare at the guys who attacked you. But if you could, I'd like you to take a closer look at them. Maybe their faces will jog your memory. Something from the tunnel or something they said. At this point, any information would be helpful. Sometimes the smallest things mean the most.'

'Sure,' Shari said. 'Whatever you need.'

She took out the first picture and studied the face of the main guard. She stared at his eyes and mouth, trying to remember anything she could about the man who had knocked her unconscious. 'He talked on his phone a lot. The first day he arrived he made, like, twenty calls.'

'Did you hear anything?' Jones asked.

'To be honest, the guy spooked me from the very

beginning, so I stayed away from him as much as I could. I spent half the day avoiding him.'

'This was when? On Saturday?'

She nodded. 'Omar called them to remove the body.'

'What were they driving?' Kia wondered.

Payne looked at her and smiled. It was a good question.

Shari tried to remember. 'It was a red van. Kind of new-looking. They backed it all the way to the tunnel entrance so they wouldn't have to carry the body very far.'

'That's good. Real good. Try the next picture.'

Shari handed the first photo to Kia, who looked at it more closely while Shari took the next one out of the stack. 'This guy searched the body. He frisked him for his wallet and keys.'

'Did he find anything?' Jones asked.

'Keys. He found his keys. After that, he ran off to move the guy's car.'

Shari handed the photo to Kia, then moved on to the next one.

'This guy,' she said as she stared at his face, 'helped move the body. He pulled out a big carpet from the back –'

'Jon,' Kia said, interrupting Shari, 'where were these pictures taken?'

'What?' he asked.

'These photos. Where were they taken? Were they taken in Jeddah?'

405

Payne glanced at Jones, perplexed. Al-Jahani had mentioned the city during his video testimony, but neither of them had brought it up during this conversation. 'Why do you ask?'

'Because of this photo,' Kia said. She pointed over the shoulder of the second guard and tapped the background. 'All these crates. They say Jeddah.'

Payne leaned forwards, hoping to see, but all he saw was a bunch of lines and squiggles.

'*You* won't be able to read it,' Kia stressed. 'It's written in Arabic. But I'm telling you it says Jeddah.'

Shari took the photo from Kia and held it up to the light. She stared at it for several seconds before her lips curled into a huge grin. 'Actually, it says a lot more than Jeddah. It's stamped with the name of a business.'

'Which business?' Payne demanded.

Her grin grew wider. 'One I know quite well. It's owned by Omar Abdul-Khaliq.'

60

Jeddah Seaport
Jeddah, Saudi Arabia

With a population of more than three million people, Jeddah is the second-largest city in Saudi Arabia. According to legend, it was named after the Arabic word *jaddah*, which means grandmother, because the mythical tomb of Eve, the matriarch of all civilization, was there until 1928, when the Saudi government, fearing the perversion of Islam, had it destroyed.

Nowadays, Jeddah is the commercial centre of Saudi Arabia, anchored by a sprawling seaport that sits on the Red Sea and handles the majority of the country's shipping. Barges, tankers, and ships of all sizes fill the blue water, but on this day the US military was more concerned with the buildings that surrounded the harbour.

While flying to Jeddah, Payne and Jones studied satellite images of the terrain, focusing on four warehouses owned and operated by Omar Abdul-Khaliq. An advanced team that was already in the city on another mission had located the suspects from the photographs and secured the immediate area while they waited for Payne and Jones to arrive. Their chopper landed on one of the port's helipads, less than a mile from the site, where a young soldier met them and briefed them en route.

'The suspects are in warehouse 29,' he said, pointing to a detailed map. 'Multiple points of entry. Minimal security. Right now they're loading cargo into a shipping vault.'

'Cargo?' Payne asked, hoping it was the artefact from Mecca.

'Can't tell what it is, sir. It's boxed up in a large crate. Must be important, though.'

'Why do you say that?'

'The old guy keeps yelling at them.'

'What old guy?'

'Sorry, sir. I should've mentioned him. There are five men in total. Four suspects and some old guy who's bossing them around. We've been calling him the Sheik.'

'The Sheik?'

'Yes, sir. Because he looks like a sheik.'

'Creative name,' Jones said sarcastically.

'Thank you, sir.'

Payne glanced at Jones. 'Would Omar be dumb enough to be here himself?'

Jones shrugged. 'According to Shari, the cargo would be invaluable to the Islamic world. So who knows? If Omar wanted to see it or doesn't trust the guards, he might've made the trip.'

'Seems kind of stupid to me. Why would he risk it?'

'Hey,' Jones said, 'the same could be said about us. We're supposed to be retired.'

'Good point.' Payne smiled as he refocused on the soldier. 'Do your men understand the parameters of this assault?'

'Yes, sir. The suspects are wanted for questioning. Non-lethal force unless necessary.'

'Be extra careful with the Sheik. We want him alive.'

'Understood, sir. I'll stress it to my men.'

Payne nodded. 'What do you have for transport?'

The soldier pointed at the map. 'Our boat is waiting in the harbour. On my signal, he'll make his approach along this channel and stop at this dock. If all goes smoothly, we'll load the boat in five minutes. After that, we're off to international waters.'

'Can you handle some extra weight?'

'Why, sir? Are you thinking of joining us?'

Payne shook his head. 'I was referring to the cargo. We want to take that as well.'

The assault started with a flash-bang, a non-lethal grenade that was commonly used in hostage retrieval. No shrapnel. No toxic gas. Just a flash of light that was so bright it activated all of the photosensitive cells in the suspects' retinas, blinding them for several seconds. Couple that with a blast that was so deafening it disrupted the fluid in their inner ears, and they had no chance to fight back. One moment they were standing; the next they were falling to the ground in agony.

Temporarily blind and completely disorientated.

Soldiers breached the warehouse from multiple angles, swarming the suspects before they had a chance to recover. Within seconds they were bound and gagged and ready for transport. Payne and Jones studied their faces, making sure they had everyone in their grasp. Four guards in total, including the one who had assaulted Shari.

'Let me break his nose,' said Jones, who was only half joking.

Payne shook his head, realizing that the guards would be roughed up worse than that once Harrington's men started interrogating them. Early in his career, Payne had asked one of his commanders what would happen to a prisoner that they had just captured, and his response was one that always stuck with him.

He's gonna be beaten until he starts leaking answers.

For some reason, that expression seemed to fit.

Next, Payne turned his attention to the old guy. As luck would have it, it was Omar Abdul-Khaliq. He did not look very happy.

Like the soldiers had mentioned, he looked like a stereotypical sheik – though not nearly as dignified, since he was hog-tied on the floor. Payne wanted to ask him why he was there. Why he was dumb enough to give up the sanctuary of his oil business, which made him off limits to some American politicians, to supervise the shipment of an artefact that had been stolen during a terrorist attack.

It was one thing to send your goons. It was quite another to be there yourself.

Now the door was wide open. They had caught him red-handed and could question him about anything they wanted, for as long as they wanted, and they wouldn't have to worry about lawyers breathing down their necks. And if Payne guessed right, the process would go on indefinitely.

In the vernacular of the US military, it was called a *ghost detainee*.

Abdul-Khaliq would enter their system and simply disappear.

61

Wednesday, 3 January
US Department of State
Washington, DC

The US Department of State, better known as the State Department, has its headquarters at the Harry S. Truman Building, a few blocks from the White House. Yet due to recent developments, there was a lot more distance between the two entities than a few city streets. The President had been fully briefed on the events in Saudi Arabia, but his staff felt it wasn't in his best interests to get directly involved with the political nightmare that was starting to brew.

He needed to insulate the Oval Office. He needed to stay clean.

Therefore, he passed the responsibility on to James Henderson, the Secretary of State, who was the highest-ranking cabinet member and the President's main adviser on foreign affairs. When he wasn't advising the President on matters of policy, Henderson's primary function was to negotiate with foreign governments on issues that included protection of American citizens travelling abroad, international crime, and support of US agencies working overseas, particularly the Department of Defense.

In other words, Henderson was the perfect choice to handle the Meccan mess, which was what they were calling it in Washington, DC.

But before he could pacify the Saudis, he had to chat with Payne and Jones.

Wearing a navy-blue suit and tie, Henderson took his seat in the video-conference room and waited for the secured video link to be established. Two monitors sat on the table in front of him, as did a tiny video camera that would transmit his image to Taif Air Base.

Despite his buttoned-down appearance, Henderson was known for his easygoing nature and calm demeanour, traits that often served him well during negotiations. No matter how tense the situation, he rarely lost his cool.

It was a skill that would be tested in the coming weeks.

'We're ready, sir,' said the video technician.

Henderson nodded and both screens clicked on, each displaying a face that he recognized from their personnel files. Jones was on the left, and Payne was on the right. In some ways it felt like they were sitting across from him at his conference table in the Truman Building, not several thousand miles away in the desert.

'Gentlemen,' he said, 'thank you for taking the time to speak with me. As you know, a lot has happened in the past week, and my job as Secretary of State is to smooth the diplomatic waters before any permanent damage is done. Earlier today I spoke with Dr Hassan al-Madi, my counterpart at the Saudi Ministry of Foreign Affairs, and, for lack of a better term, he was *pissed off*. And to tell you the truth I can't blame him. If these events had taken place in Washington or New York, we'd be readying our troops for military action.'

Payne and Jones stared at Henderson on the video screen, waiting for the tough questions that were sure to follow.

'That being said, I'd be remiss if I didn't congratulate you on a job well done. I've read all the reports, so I know what you did for our country. Without your contributions, we'd be way beyond diplomacy. We'd be dealing with the largest loss of life in the history of the world.'

Jones nodded. 'Thank you, sir. Jon and I are always happy to be heroes . . . Oops! Did I say *heroes*? I meant to say we're happy to help.'

Harrison smiled. 'I'm glad to hear it. Because as luck would have it, I need your help on one additional matter, something that wasn't fully addressed in your debriefing with the Pentagon.'

'Oh?' Payne asked, knowing exactly where this was going. 'What might that be?'

'The item that was seized in Jeddah.'

'Item? What item?' Payne turned towards Jones. 'Do you remember an item?'

'I remember an Arab. You know, that bearded terrorist guy that we captured while we were saving the planet from mass destruction. Are Arabs considered *items*?'

Payne shook his head. 'I don't think so. Technically, if you can't store it in an overhead locker on a plane, then it's not an item. And the last time I checked, pilots don't like Arabs on planes.'

'Gentlemen,' Henderson interrupted, 'allow me to be more specific. I'm referring to the archaeological artefact that was unearthed by Shari Shasmeen, stolen by Abdul-Khaliq in Mecca, and seized by you during your raid in Jeddah. Does that ring any bells?'

Jones shrugged. 'Here's the thing, sir. We used a bunch of flash-bangs in Jeddah, and those suckers tend to throw off a person's circuitry. My ears are still ringing. I'm still seeing spots. And my memory comes and goes like that.' He snapped his fingers for effect. 'Wait, what was the question again?'

'Speaking of questions,' Payne said while keeping a straight face, 'may I ask you a question?'

Henderson nodded. 'You may.'

'If memory happens to improve and I'm somehow able to remember the item you were talking about, what would you do with it?'

'Honestly, that remains to be seen. At this point in time, we still need to verify that the contents are authentic. But if they are, we could use them to our political advantage. It might go a long way towards re-establishing trust with the Arab world.'

'So,' Jones asked, 'you wouldn't just dump it in a crate and bury it in some nondescript warehouse like they did with the Ark of the Covenant at the end of *Raiders of the Lost Ark?*'

Henderson frowned. 'Is that a serious question?'

'I don't know. Does that warehouse actually exist?'

Payne tried not to laugh. 'I'll tell you what, sir. Give us a night to sleep on it. Who knows? With a little rest, our memories might start to improve.'

Located in Küsendorf, Switzerland, on the southern slopes of the Lepontine Alps, the Ulster Archives were originally built by Austrian philanthropist Conrad Ulster in the 1930s and rebuilt by his grandson, Petr Ulster, less than a year ago, after fire damaged several floors in the wood-framed chalet. The well-guarded facility housed some of the rarest artefacts in the world, and its main purpose was to foster the concept of sharing when it came to historical research, something of a rarity in the academic world.

Shari Shasmeen wasn't sure what to expect when she arrived at the front gate. All she knew was that Payne had made all of the arrangements – including her flight to Switzerland – and the Archives staff were looking forward to her arrival. Considering what she had gone through during the past few days, it sounded like the type of getaway she needed.

Of course, Payne never told her the real reason for her visit.

Armed guards led Shari into the main lobby, where she was greeted by Petr Ulster, a round man in his early forties with a thick brown beard that covered his multiple chins. He was known for a youthful enthusiasm that lit up any room he entered.

'It is so wonderful to make your acquaintance,' he said with a faint Swiss accent. He emphasized his feelings by giving her a kiss on both cheeks. 'Jonathon has told me so many wonderful things about you.'

Shari smiled. 'That's nice to hear. I owe him a lot. He and DJ saved my life.'

'Mine, too! They saved it last year during the big fire. I won't bore you with the details right now. But I'll tell you all about it later when I give you the grand tour. In the meantime, I'm sure you probably want to see the artefact. Don't worry, it arrived safe and sound about an hour ago.'

'Artefact? What artefact?'

Ulster studied her face and realized she wasn't kidding. 'You mean you don't know? That is *so* like Jonathon. Always surprising people with his generosity.'

'What artefact?' she asked again.

A familiar voice answered from behind. 'Our artefact.'

Shari whirled around and saw Drew Hennessy. He was standing next to Ape and Milton Wheeler. Each of them was grinning from ear to ear.

'Oh my God!' She rushed forward and gave them

a group hug, completely stunned by their presence. 'What are you guys doing here?'

'We came to see you,' Ape said.

'And the artefact,' Hennessy added.

'Wait a second. The artefact is *here*? How in the world did it get here?'

Ulster laughed in delight. He loved participating in a good surprise almost as much as he enjoyed history. 'Actually, I'll let Jonathon explain that to you some other time. Meanwhile, if it's all right with you, let's head back to the document vault. I have something that you're probably dying to see.'

Epilogue

Tuesday, 9 January
US Army Base Kwajalein
Republic of the Marshall Islands

A week had passed since Payne and Jones had wrapped up their mission in Jeddah. Afterwards, they spent several days in Taif, tying up loose ends and dealing with the political mess that their unauthorized trip to Mecca had caused. Harrington was the lightning rod in the whole ordeal, taking the blame for Schmidt and the massacre on Jeju but being congratulated off the record for saving the Great Mosque and capturing several terrorists who could be linked to the Soldiers of Allah.

Payne wasn't privy to what Abdul-Khaliq and his men had revealed during their first few days of questioning, but Harrington hinted that Hakeem Salaam would soon be in their grasp.

As for the Saudi government, they were furious when they first learned the identity of Schmidt's crew. They demanded an explanation from the United States, wanting to know why Special Forces soldiers had threatened their most sacred city. Obviously, the

Secretary of State responded in the only way he could: he lied. Henderson claimed that Schmidt and his men were Muslims and had been sent to Mecca to rescue the lives of some American archaeologists who were being threatened by terrorists. While they were there, they stumbled across a bigger plot and eventually saved the day.

The Saudis didn't believe it for a minute, but were willing to overlook everything when the State Department sweetened the deal. They mentioned the stone crypt that they had recently found, which was filled with dozens of documents that were written by Muhammad's closest companions. Transcripts of Muhammad's revelations. If the Saudis were interested, the US would be happy to let them examine it as a token of goodwill. The Saudis were so excited about the possibilities that they were willing to overlook the fact that a woman, Shari Shasmeen, was in charge of the research team and they'd have to travel to Switzerland to examine it.

Eventually, when Payne and Jones were permitted to leave Taif, they decided to take the long way home. Instead of flying west towards Pittsburgh, where it was cold and snowy, they flew east, towards the Pacific, where it was warm and sandy. Besides, Kia Choi had told them they were free to visit anytime, and they wanted to take her up on the offer before she forgot.

The plane landed on a familiar runway and eased to a stop near one of the main hangars. The temperature was in the low eighties but felt cooler due to the tropical breeze that blew across the Kwajalein atoll. Jones glanced out the tiny window and admired the sapphire sky.

'Wow, would you look at that sun! I can't wait to work on my tan.'

'Yeah,' Payne joked. 'You've been looking kind of Caucasian.'

Jones smiled as he grabbed his bags and headed for the open hatch. Taking one step outside, he suddenly stopped in his tracks. A beautiful island woman, wearing a coconut bikini and a hula skirt, stood at the bottom of the plane stairs. A flower lei swayed in her hands as she moved to the rhythm of a Don Ho song that played over the hangar's loud-speakers.

'Welcome to the Marshall Islands,' she announced.

Jones stared at her, then glanced back at Payne, who was struggling to hold in his laughter. He'd been dying to tease Jones about the kissing incident with Kia for several days, and now he had managed to do it in style.

'You know what?' Jones said. 'Screw you and screw Kia. That's *not* funny.'

'You're right,' he said with a laugh. 'It's hilarious.'

'Ha, ha. I get it. Make fun of the pale black guy.' He dropped his bags and glanced into the cockpit, where even the pilot was laughing. 'Driver, I've had enough. Take me home.'

Which made Payne laugh even louder.

'Fine,' Jones said. 'Be that way. But I'm telling you, I'm marching down there and slipping her the tongue.'

'You better not,' said Kia, who had snuck up the stairs behind him. 'She'll charge me extra.'

'She's a hooker?'

Kia laughed and gave him a hug. 'She's not a hooker, but she *is* single.'

'In that case, we can stay.' Jones turned towards the cockpit and shouted. 'Bellman, change of plans! Please get my bags. I'm going downstairs to make a friend.'

Payne waved him off, glad he was being such a good sport.

'Wow,' said Kia, who had set everything up at Payne's request. 'That worked well.'

He nodded in agreement. 'Perfect. Simply perfect. No way you can top it.'

'You don't think?' she flirted.

Payne smiled at the possibilities. 'Honestly, I can't wait to find out.'

Author's Note

Even though *Sword of God* is a work of fiction, most of the locations in my novel are quite real. Al-Gaim is a military housing compound in Taif, Saudi Arabia. Lava tubes stretch for miles underneath Jeju, South Korea. And the Abraj Al Bait Towers are being built across the street from the Great Mosque in Mecca.

(Payne and Jones showed me the blueprints. They look amazing!)

When I first started researching this book, I quickly realized an important fact: I can't read Arabic or Korean. That meant I was forced to rely on translated documents to provide several details in my story. Normally this wouldn't be a problem, but there was one major issue that kept popping up over and over. Translators tend to disagree on the spelling of proper nouns. I swear, to this day I still don't know the official name of Jeju. Some call it Jeju-do. Others use Jejudo. Then there is Jeju Island. And Cheju-do. And Cheju. And, well, you get my point. After a while, I realized that I needed to choose one spelling for every location – even if many linguists disagreed with my choice – and stick with it throughout.

Then again, I guess that's what writing is. A series of choices.

That being said, I think the riskiest choice I made was the concept of a terrorist attack in the holy city of Mecca. My goal was to entertain, not to offend. If I crossed any lines, I sincerely apologize. As I mentioned during my story, there are a number of similarities between Islam and Christianity. That might seem strange, considering the clear cultural differences between Saudi Arabia and the United States, but if you take the time to examine the sacred texts of the two religions, you will find many shared beliefs.

Obviously, it would be great to live in a world where everyone got along.

Until that day, stories about terrorism will continue to be written.